# The Woman
## in the
# Picture

Katharine McMahon studied English and Drama at Bristol University. She has worked as a teacher in schools and universities, as a Royal Literary Fund Fellow supporting student writing, and has run national training courses. She is involved with local theatre and lives in north London.

www.katharinemcmahon.com

Also by Katharine McMahon:

*Season of Light*
*The Crimson Rooms*
*The Rose of Sebastopol*
*The Alchemist's Daughter*
*A Way Through the Woods*
*Footsteps*
*Confinement*
*After Mary*

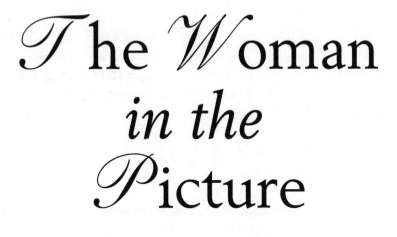

# The Woman in the Picture

KATHARINE MCMAHON

Weidenfeld & Nicolson
LONDON

First published in Great Britain in 2014
by Weidenfeld & Nicolson
An imprint of the Orion Publishing Group Ltd
Orion House, 5 Upper St Martin's Lane
London WC2H 9EA

An Hachette UK company

1 3 5 7 9 10 8 6 4 2

ISBN 978 0 297 86603 9 (hardback)
ISBN 978 0 297 86604 6 (export trade paperback)

Typeset by Input Data Services Ltd,
Bridgwater, Somerset

Printed and bound in Great Britain by
Clays Ltd, St Ives plc

The Orion Publishing Group's policy is to use papers that
are natural, renewable and recyclable products and
made from wood grown in sustainable forests. The logging
and manufacturing processes are expected to conform to
the environmental regulations of the country of origin.

www.orionbooks.co.uk

For Wendy and Pete, Mo and Mike, with thanks

# Chapter One

On the afternoon of the day my grandmother died, I dealt with the case of a burnt letter. Blown into the foyer of Great Marlborough Street Magistrates' Court on a gust of drizzly wind, I was confronted by the usual smell of cigarettes and wet wool. A scattering of defendants, hunched in damp clothes, eyed each other surreptitiously or peered through the glass panel in a courtroom door.

My client, Miss Gertrude Wright, was weeping on a bench under a noticeboard but as I headed towards her across the muddy terrazzo floor I was obstructed by a man wearing an aged suit and with a military polish to his shoes.

'You Miss Gifford?' he demanded.

'I am.'

'I come to tell you, don't you be letting my girl down.' His index finger jabbed to within inches of my nose and he had the strut of a lady's man with his pale gold hair and staring eyes of forget-me-not blue.

'You must be Mr Wright,' I said.

'Yeah. And I was expecting a proper lawyer. A gentleman. Then Trudy goes and tells me she's got some woman.'

'I shall do my best for your daughter, Mr Wright.' A worm of antagonism twitched in my breast but I had learned not to be so easily provoked. After all, I had met his type time and again both in the dock and on the bench: cocky, misogynistic and self-righteous.

'Yeah, you do your best, little lady. And I might as well tell you here and now, we ain't got no money to pay . . .'

'I shall be representing your daughter pro bono, Mr Wright, as I expect she has told you. It will cost you nothing.'

'What are you doing it for then?' If anything, he was even more suspicious.

'My firm has a policy of taking on worthy causes such as your daughter's if we think that otherwise there could be a miscarriage of justice.' I was hardly going to confide in Wright why it was that the burning of the letter had particularly captured my sympathy. His daughter, with her pathetically bandaged fingers, had given a near incoherent explanation, 'It burnt so fast. I changed my mind but it was too late . . .'

A curled notice above Miss Wright's head advertised Christmas closing times. Her damaged hand was still in a sling – I'd hinted to her that visible signs of injury could do no harm. I sat beside her, touched her free elbow and said softly, 'Bear up, Miss Wright. It will all be over in a few minutes.' From somewhere she had borrowed a dark brown suit with a long jacket that obscured her youthful figure, and her round-chinned face, unbecomingly framed by a hat trimmed with a pom-pom over each ear, was blotchy. Her penitent tears might help our case; it was the father who could be our undoing.

'You are aware, I'm sure, Mr Wright,' I said, 'that you must not say anything in court unless the magistrates invite you to do so.'

His response was a sudden grin, a wink and a dimple. 'Oh, I can behave very well when pressed.'

The usher called the case of Gertrude Wright and the father made an elaborate play of holding back the swing doors of the courtroom for me; as I passed him I caught a whiff of tobacco and alcohol. While his daughter was escorted into the dock he planted himself in the front row of the public benches, arms folded, legs wide, his gaze fixed on me. Behind him sat a woman dressed in a matching hat and coat in puce, a colour my mother couldn't abide. ('*Nobody* can wear puce well,' she said. 'Or orange.')

Chin high, I took my place in the lawyers' benches. I couldn't help it; I still felt a surge of adrenalin and pride each time I defended a client. This was my arena, this courtroom with its scratched oak surfaces and seats upholstered in tired green leather. The ticking of the institutional clock, the rustle of papers, the scratch of a nib and male murmuring were the background noises against which I was used to pitching my woman's voice. Three years ago

2

my greatest challenge would have been to apply for an extension in licensing hours; now I had my own portfolio of clients and had grown successful at pitting my wits against even the most intransigent police prosecutor. And I had a reputation here – the chair of the bench raised a sardonic eyebrow when he saw me, and the woman on his left, who was sporting a rather dashing buckle in her hat, had a sisterly gleam in her eye.

'Miss Gertrude Wright,' intoned the clerk, 'you are charged that on 20 January 1926, being employed by Mrs Jane Derbyshire as a housemaid, you did feloniously steal a letter with the intent to deprive its rightful owner of the whole benefit of this chattel, namely the opportunity to read and respond to said letter. Do you plead guilty or not guilty?'

Gertrude clung to the front of the dock, fixated by the sight of the woman in puce who was taking notes in a very small, black leather-bound book – Mrs Derbyshire, presumably. I stood up. 'Your worships, before my client makes her plea, might I be allowed to address you?'

The chairman sighed theatrically. 'Miss Gifford, why is it that whenever I see that you are the lawyer acting in defence, my heart sinks to my boots?'

Acknowledging his quip with a swift smile, I said calmly, 'I wish to make an objection to the indictment. I want to show you that technically no crime was committed. The point is, the letter concerned Miss Wright herself and was asking for a character reference.'

'This surely aggravates the offence.'

The regard of the woman magistrate was warm and intrigued. 'My client was in such great fear of her mistress, Mrs Derbyshire,' I continued. 'She dared not tell her that she had applied for a new position. When a letter arrived postmarked Ealing, Miss Wright lost her nerve. Her intention had been merely to hide the letter, but as she found herself alone in the kitchen she, very foolishly, threw it into the stove thinking that she would rather lose the chance of a new job than risk the letter reaching Mrs Derbyshire.'

All eyes swivelled from the heavily powdered face of Mrs Derbyshire, who gave the chairman an aggrieved stare, as from one well-heeled householder to another, to the defendant who obligingly cradled her injured hand and made a fruitless attempt to suppress her sobs.

'The moment Gertrude Wright closed the lid of the stove she recognised her own folly and attempted to pull the letter out again,' I continued. 'As you can see, she is still recovering from severe burns to her fingers and thumb and it was because of her injuries that the whole incident came to light. That afternoon, when serving tea, she fumbled with the teapot and the reason for her clumsiness was exposed. Her mistress, Mrs Derbyshire, felt she had no option but to report the matter to the police and discharge her without pay from the position she'd held for the last five years – at fifteen shillings a week.' I added this last detail for the benefit of the lady magistrate, who I thought was bound to disapprove of so miserly a wage.

'Miss Gifford, I wonder if you might come to the point?' said the chairman. 'Is this your way of informing us that your client is going to prove not guilty? Ah, I see the cavalry's arrived.' The courtroom door had wheezed open and I guessed, without glancing round, that Daniel Breen, senior partner in my law firm, was now behind me. The bench threw him comradely smiles over my shoulder and there were the distinctive sounds of him flipping down his seat and unscrewing the lid of his pen.

'I am going to be very frank with your worships,' I lowered my voice confidingly, 'and say I will not take this case to trial, even though we have an excellent defence. My client, as you can tell from her demeanour in court, has already suffered fear and remorse and agonies enough, and you have heard that Mrs Derbyshire has meted out her own punishment.' Only by the slightest inclination of the head did I direct their attention to the puce costume on my left.

'Then what *are* you saying, Miss Gifford? It's nearly four o'clock and we've not yet heard the facts. You've told us you won't take this to trial so is your client pleading . . .?'

'I'm asking you to take the unusual step of quashing the indictment, your worships.' (An audible *tsk* of incredulity from the puce lady.) 'It is a sheer waste of court time and if the case is heard and Miss Wright receives even so much as a discharge, she will lose any vestige of her excellent character.'

4

'Presumably we have only your word for said good character, Miss Gifford.'

'Is my word not good enough, your worship?' As I was thirty-two years old, my smile was wry rather than flirtatious. 'And she obviously comes from a close-knit family – you'll note that her father has taken the time to lend Miss Wright his support today.' The bench glanced at Wright who was leaning forward, hands planted on knees, blue eyes guileless. I moved on swiftly. 'Hasn't she been punished sufficiently already? No job, no reference, no pay, a scarred hand – and all for a letter that was for the benefit only of herself. It was so easily done, that moment of impulse, so irreversible. She simply didn't think . . .'

The chairman seemed a little discomfited by my vehemence. He was not to know that I had done the same myself, received a letter, consigned it to the flames unread, sought to rescue it, failed. The finality of what I'd done, the disbelief that paper could be consumed so quickly, the frantic staring into the fire, willing it to be restored had been relived by me time after time. Even now, eighteen months later, I yearned for that letter. So I understood Trudy and her helpless tears. She couldn't comprehend how such a small action should have such awful consequences; how a page of writing, once reduced to ashes, could become so much more significant than its contents had perhaps deserved.

The police prosecutor, on being asked whether he wished to comment, raised his eyes to the ceiling. 'It would be a most un-usual step, your worships, to quash . . .'

With a scraping back of chairs the bench retired. Behind me Breen had risen to his feet. As usual, his trim figure was engulfed in his trademark oversized coat, his appearance carefully honed for maximum effect in court. His wild hair was greying but his skin was smooth and clean-shaven. He was leaning against the seat back with folded arms and furrowed brow, as if mildly di-verted by what he'd just witnessed.

'It was good of you to find the time, sir,' I said.

'I had a trial go short. And I wanted to see how you were getting on. As I told you earlier, you've a fifty per cent chance of success but you might be lucky with this particular bench. The lady winger has a lot of sense.' He made a note in the margin of a document. 'What's in your diary for tomorrow?'

'I'm seeing Lady Petit at three.'

'So you are. Of course. I was wondering if you'd meet me for a spot of lunch beforehand? Talk a few things over.'

I was surprised. For three years Daniel Breen had been my boss, mentor, guide and critic. In the face of the incredulity, even the ridicule of his peers in the legal world, he had taken me on as a clerk, nurtured my career, pooh-poohed my self-doubt, berated me for my failings, laughed at my mishaps and (more rarely) rejoiced with me in my triumphs but he had never, in all that time, invited me to any social function beyond the Christmas party during which our secretary, Miss Drake, covered her typewriter and the four of us who comprised the staff of Breen & Balcombe sipped sherry and nibbled cheese biscuits.

'There's no need to look like that, Miss Gifford,' he added, glancing up and sweeping his papers into his briefcase. 'Like everyone else I have to eat. If you have other plans or you can't stand the idea of sitting across a table ...'

'Thank you sir.'

'Outside Bow Street, then. One o'clock.' He departed, pausing to nod encouragingly at Trudy Wright, scowl at Mrs Derbyshire and exchange a word or two with the usher. Odd that he hadn't even stayed to hear the outcome of the case. When I approached the dock, Trudy was pressed into a corner and the cuff of her coat was wet with tears. Her father was tapping a tobacco tin on his knee, head lowered, still glowering at me. Mrs Derbyshire averted her eyes.

At a quarter past four the magistrates were back. The lady winger, I thought, was suppressing a smile.

'Miss Gifford, we've listened carefully to what you have said and are inclined to agree with you. We abhor the idea that our servants should indulge in any kind of dishonesty but in this case, since by taking the letter your client was punishing only herself—' dramatic pause interrupted by a sob from Trudy '—we have decided to advise the police prosecutor that the case should be dismissed.'

'I'm grateful, your worships.'

Trudy cast herself down with her arm over her eyes. Mrs Derbyshire snapped shut her notebook and clutched her arms tightly beneath her breast. She could barely bring herself to stand when the bench rose, and after they'd gone approached me and hissed in a low, vehement voice, 'Unnatural woman.' I said nothing, only packed my briefcase, awaiting the next onslaught and noting that the shoulders of her coat were powdered with dandruff.

'I pity you that you should have to stoop so low, presumably for want of a husband,' she went on and directed her glinting eye at the naked third finger of my left hand. With one last furious glare at Trudy, she click-clacked from the court in a gust of violet perfume.

Even a year ago I might have risen to the bait and followed her. Defiant words rushed to my tongue but I bit them back. Wright was standing very close and had heard every word. He too would resent my success, I thought, even though it benefited his daughter. I judged him to be a man who preferred to think the world was against him and to find himself indebted to a woman only proved his point.

Trudy clung to my hand. 'Is it over then, Miss Gifford? Have I heard the last of it? Will she come after me again?'

In reassuring her, I found myself promising to visit her prospective employer and explain the circumstances of the missing letter in the hope that she might still offer Gertrude employment. Before I'd finished speaking, Wright was steering his daughter towards the door, his arm flung protectively round her shoulders. Tensing at his touch, she darted me a backwards, apologetic look.

## Chapter Two

The flat I shared with Meredith and her eight-year-old son, Edmund, my dead brother's child, was on the garret floor of a house in Pimlico. When I arrived home at six, I found her wrapped in scarf and mittens, sitting cross-legged on a cushion before the undersized gas fire we'd installed at crippling expense the previous winter. It was dark outside and our living room, draped with fabrics gleaned by jackdaw Meredith from market stalls and the oddments bin at Selfridges, looked very snug. From the walls gleamed more jewel colours: canvases daubed with striking figures blocked out with ever more confident brush-strokes – Meredith again. There was even one of me, though I was unrecognisable, being merely the silhouette of a woman at a window, her long limbs dark slashes of paint and her head averted in a most disturbing attitude of wistfulness and solitude. One corner of the room was dedicated to work in progress, so that there was a heady aroma of oil paints, turpentine and gas. Perhaps we had survived asphyxiation only because, being in the roof and with three ill-fitting sash windows, the room was aswirl with draughts.

Edmund, who'd been perched in his mother's lap while she listened to him read aloud, scrambled to his feet to hug me and I picked him up so that he clung on and buried his face in my neck.

'You smell of buses,' he said, throwing back his head and scrutinising me.

'And you smell of school and small boy,' I retorted, kissing him again. He had inherited his father's thatch of light brown hair and full lower lip but his nature was altogether more impish and sensitive and he had his mother's wide-open, appraising eyes.

He settled back with his book while Meredith pointed to a note on the table written in my mother's florid hand. *Your grandmother is dying. Come at once. You're needed.*

'Oh Lord,' I said, 'when did that arrive?'

'About an hour ago. She sent the neighbour's boy. I gave him sixpence.'

Dropping into the only armchair I pulled off my hat, which had become a dead weight on my brow. 'Don't go dashing out again,' said Meredith while her son, thumb in mouth, gazed at me pensively. 'You look all in. Go tomorrow or leave it until the weekend – you know how your mother exaggerates things, it won't be that urgent. Or I could call in sometime later in the week.'

I should love to have sprawled there and done nothing but watch them. The wind rattled the windows, my head ached and I was still a little shaken by the animosity that had followed the Wright case. Besides, there was a hint of challenge in Meredith's tone: us or them. She was a little dishevelled, with her cropped hair spiked up like an elf's, a sure sign that she'd had a bad day. Yet I knew I would have to go out again. My grandmother had been bedbound for months; uncomplaining, feeble, sometimes fighting for breath. A similarly melodramatic missive arrived most weeks and thus far, when I reached the bedside, the patient had always been peacefully asleep or supping tea. The notes, I realised, were my mother's way of keeping me at her beck and call, but how could I take the risk?

I prepared what we called a Bohemian supper which we ate huddled round the fire. Edmund had a boiled egg with Marmite soldiers and Meredith and I sardines while I told them about my afternoon in court and explained to Edmund what Gertrude Wright had done and the potential gravity of the offence of theft from an employer.

'Edmund will grow up such a moral child, thanks to his Aunty Evelyn,' said Meredith. 'He will know all about retribution for bad behaviour. And he will be an expert on crime, especially how to avoid conviction.'

'Needless to say the alleged victim wasn't best pleased.'

'Who was the alleged victim?' asked Edmund.

'The horrible woman who'd employed Gertrude Wright. She was very cross with me. In fact, she said she pitied me because I don't have a husband.'

'People in court are always getting cross with you,' he said. 'Don't you mind?'

'Of course I mind. I hate it. But it's my job to take sides so there are always bound to be losers.'

'Good old Evie,' said Meredith caustically, and the tension between us tightened. Having lived in such close proximity for eighteen months we were so used to each other that I felt every nuance of her swiftly changing moods. 'And now you'll trek out to Ealing on this girl's behalf and wrestle with the new employer whose ill-timed letter caused all the fuss in the first place. Really, I do applaud you.'

'And this from a woman who has spent her morning performing smallpox vaccinations in a clinic in Spitalfields.'

'Not by choice,' she snapped. 'I only do it because no one will give me any other work. Whereas you seem compelled to martyr yourself.'

Edmund, who was gnawing the skin off an apple, glanced at her nervously.

Meredith and I shared a room so small that there was space only for a chair between our beds and Edmund slept in a near cupboard on a mattress beneath our clothes rail. We were adept at stepping round each other so that while Meredith put Edmund to bed I boiled a kettle and washed up. Afterwards I packed an overnight case and again put on my hat and coat.

'I knew you'd go,' called Meredith who was now stretched beside her son reading the latest chapter from *The Wind in the Willows*. 'You can't help yourself. They have only to squeak and you go running.'

'You're right.' I crawled along the mattress to kiss Edmund who put his arms around my neck and hugged me tightly, that wonderful, tough, small-boy's grip. 'And the only gain will be that my conscience is appeased about them all for the next twenty-four hours or so. I shall stay the night and be home again tomorrow evening so you can go to your class.'

She followed me out on to the staircase where Edmund couldn't hear. 'Yes, you've arranged it all very well, haven't you? As usual you're able to do just as you please.'

'On the contrary, I don't want to go at all. You know that.'

'Then stay here. It will be yet another false alarm, a ruse to get you to Maida Vale. The fact is, I need you here – have you thought of that?'

This rare admission of weakness arrested me. Her head was to one side and she was half smiling, as if amused by her own bad temper, but there was a tremor in her voice and I felt a further pang.

'I've been on my own since lunchtime,' she said. 'It's driving me mad, all this inactivity. Especially now you're so busy. You keep telling me that you want to share in Edmund's upbring- ing but it will never be equal between us when you are able to dash off whenever you like. And there's something very par- ticular I wanted to discuss with you concerning Edmund's education.'

'Tell me.'

'Oh, so now you'll stay because it's about him?'

'Meredith, you're being unfair.'

'Maybe I am. Or I'm just being lonely. And I feel wasted, that's what. I'm not able to get involved in anything properly.'

'But your painting is going so well.'

'It's so darn cold here, my fingers won't work.' She was laughing now at her own litany of complaints. 'But off you go, I know you must, don't mind me.'

'I do mind you. I'd really much rather stay. We'll talk tomorrow.'

'I have my art class tomorrow.'

'The next evening then.'

'Whenever you can spare a moment.' She grudgingly accepted my kiss on her prominent cheekbone. 'You know what this is really about? I'm jealous, of course. I want to be told that too.'

'What do you want to be told?'

'That another woman pities me.'

'Honestly, Meredith, it didn't feel—'

'No, but you see she said it because she knew you were power- ful. Pettiness was the only weapon she had. I should know. Look how I've behaved since you came in.'

I left her there at the top of the stairs, her diminutive figure swathed in woollens, the tip of her nose reddened with cold and her fingers fluttering in a gesture of farewell.

# Chapter Three

The further the omnibus took me towards Maida Vale, the more I wished I was at home in the flat, bent over my files under the lamp with its drunkenly asymmetric pottery stand glazed by Meredith. I loved evenings accompanied by the little scrape of her brush, the biting of her bottom lip, the sense of purposeful companionship as I prepared my files for the following day, and Edmund asleep in the next room, the quirky little pivot upon which our lives were balanced.

Meredith and I, after a shaky and mistrustful start, had become close friends though she kept me on my mettle. I'd not known either of her existence or Edmund's until six years after my brother's death, when the pair had turned up on the doorstep of my family home in Maida Vale. Small wonder, perhaps, after years of grieving for Jamie, that we had been suspicious and even unkind to her when she had claimed to be the mother of his child. Edmund had been conceived in desperate circumstances weeks before my brother's death, while he had been recovering from an arm injury and Meredith was his nurse. Providing mother and child with a home was the very least we could do to make reparation for my brother's recklessness and our initial hostility.

Through my life with Meredith and Edmund I had found unexpected delight and her reproaches stung because I knew they were well founded. While my life was full, hers was often solitary because, as an unmarried mother and a Canadian, she was condemned to be even more of an outsider than I was. Her own set, the art crowd with whom she sometimes went to clubs and parties, tended to be somewhat flighty and self-absorbed while I, a recently qualified lawyer at Breen & Balcombe, had an ever-expanding set of clients and above all the comradeship of Daniel

Breen and my legal women friends such as Carrie Morrison, fellow pioneers and encroachers on the hitherto wholly male domain of the law.

By the time I reached Clivedon Hall Gardens in Maida Vale, drizzle was hazing the street lamps and as usual the ground floor of my family house was in complete darkness. I rang the bell and turned the key in the latch, a combination bound to irritate the maids but the alternative, which was to surprise everyone by *bursting in*, as Mother put it, was unthinkable. Inside there were glimmers of light beneath the drawing-room door and from an upstairs landing, otherwise all was gloomier than the street beyond and the miasma of the house clung to me like ageing cobwebs.

My childhood home was a place that never failed to cast a dark shadow on my soul. Time was frozen there, despite a recent succession of female lodgers. While the world outside surged on-wards – unrest in the coal industry, shorter skirts and hair, a return to the gold standard, the unnerving clamour of fascism in Italy – here in Clivedon Hall Gardens the past hung in tattered banners from the stairwell. There had once been joy: Mother pirouetting in her pre-war gauzy party frocks; my brother Jamie squealing with delight and fear as he straddled the banister rail and landed with a spine-wrenching thud against the knob at the bottom; myself as a schoolgirl, hurling down my satchel at the end of the day and proclaiming to Min, 'I'm absolutely *starving* . . .' as she ushered me downstairs for bread and jam. And more recently Meredith had darted up and down the stairs in her pastel frocks and dainty shoes with her heart-warming, other-worldly little boy, son of James, at her heels. They had brought tempestuous emotion, tears and laughter, music, fun. And it was to this house that I had returned suddenly, violently in love with a man called Nicholas Thorne. But those were all memories now and all that remained were six women who could not or would not change.

A light flicked on and Min, one of a pair of elderly maids, came creaking up the back stairs wearing a pastel blue cable-knit cardigan buttoned at the neck, and no overall since it was evening.

'Oh, it's you,' she said. 'I might have saved myself the bother.'

I embraced her as Meredith had taught me to do – unthinkable, before her arrival, that one of us Gifford ladies would have hugged a servant – and smelt sparse hair in need of a wash. 'I had a message saying Grandmother was ill. I thought I'd better come,' I said.

'She's not a good colour,' said Min and I had the first premonition that this time Grandmother might really be failing.

'Has the doctor been?' I asked. Mother, who counted every penny, would only send for him in dire circumstances.

'Indeed he has and he's left her a drop of medicine but we could tell from his face he didn't think she would last the night.'

'Good heavens, Min, is it that bad? I had no idea.'

I threw open the parlour door in case Mother was there but it was occupied only by four stuffed birds in glass cases inherited from my paternal grandparents, and the latest lodger, a woman in her early sixties with thin plaits coiled round her head, who had taught needlecraft at a girls' school and infuriated my mother and aunt by doing virtually nothing.

'I'm retired,' she explained. 'I tell myself, haven't I given enough?'

Actually, I suspected that the poor thing had no cash to spare for knitting wool or embroidery silks, and that sooner or later she would default on the rent.

She gave me a spiritless wave. 'Your mother will be glad to see you. We never hear the last of how you're always too busy to come home.'

I took the stairs two at a time. Grandmother's room was in the front of the house on the first floor, next to Mother's. Her thespian roots were evident in the framed photograph of herself as a soft-haired Ophelia, the Indian shawls draped over the bed rail and the hardened Leichner make-up on the dressing table. Everything usually smelt of eau de cologne and toffee bonbons but today there was no mistaking a new odour; the air had gone sour. I heard the rasping breath of a very sick woman and could immediately see, as Min had suggested, that she was a very bad colour indeed. Grandmother habitually wore glasses thick as bottle-bases over her near-blind eyes which now, unobscured, bulged in her face like a baby bird's and her fingers plucked at the quilt until my Aunt Prudence, who was in attendance and couldn't bear disorder of any kind, lifted her hands one by one and crossed them over her chest as if she were already dead. They immediately fluttered apart.

Mother was seated by the fire with a copy of the *Essays of Elia*, a book which she purported to find comforting, though I believed she chose reading material rather as she approached the rest of life – as a source of self-persecution. She was dressed as always in funereal colours, a mauve frock and long black cardigan. Prudence wore beige, apart from a string of yellowish pearls at her throat. 'Ah,' she said, catching sight of me, as if I were the answer to a question.

Mother only turned away her face and pressed her lips together to hold back a sob.

'How is she?' I asked.

'Very poorly,' said Prudence, who had three degrees of sickness in her vocabulary: *off colour, not too good* and *very poorly*, the latter invariably prefacing a fatality.

Considering how used we had all been to mortality less than a decade before, it was strange that I had never actually witnessed a death. My brother Jamie had died in France and my father's death had been abrupt, while I was at Cambridge. I took Grandmother's hand, thinking that I must grip it tight and haul her back from the abyss, and kissed her forehead.

'Don't do that,' Mother snapped.

'Why ever not?'

She had no answer. Of course she didn't. The inhabitants of Clivedon Hall Gardens were governed by rules: most *don'ts*, some *musts*. Had not the war proved that this reliance on absolutes was unquestionably right? For example, when Jamie had put himself beyond the Gifford jurisdiction to fight overseas, he had conceived a child out of wedlock and got himself killed. And look at me, Evelyn, unmarried and unmarriageable, dealing in sordid court cases and living in a cramped little flat with the irrepressible Meredith.

Now it seemed that Grandmother was almost free of regulation too. To break the appalling atmosphere of attentiveness to death, I plumped down on the bed, causing her to bounce on the mattress and her eyelids to flutter. 'It's Evelyn, Grandmother,' I said loudly, in her ear.

Perhaps there was the faintest of smiles.

'She can't hear you,' said Mother.

'I'm not so sure.' Prudence fixed her stern gaze on Grandmother, as if challenging her to come clean, and for once I found her uncompromising presence a comfort. If Grandmother were to die, Prudence would know what to do.

I stroked the wispy hair from Grandmother's forehead and looked about me at the souvenirs of her glory days: the feather boa, the little velvet slippers trimmed with gold braid, the strings of beads that used to click on her chest. Where was she now, as her breath ground in her throat?

'If you like,' I offered, 'I'll take care of her for a while. You must both be in need of a rest.'

'Oh you wouldn't know what to do,' said Mother, who never missed an opportunity to reproach me for being a professional rather than a proper woman, or for my decision to leave home. But Prudence gave my shoulder a squeeze with her fierce, embroiderer's fingers and left the room. Mother looked decidedly nonplussed at this defection. 'What if she passes away the minute I'm gone?' Her forlorn logic was stifling; to every solution there was a snag. 'I really wondered if you'd bother to come,' she added.

'Of course I'd come.'

'You're always so busy.'

'Mother, please. Not now.' I stretched my legs and closed my eyes, still with Grandmother's hand in mine.

'I don't know what will become of us all once she's gone,' Mother whispered.

'Hush, she might hear you.' I stroked Grandmother's hand. 'I'm going to read to her.'

'That might be nice, Evelyn, she loved to hear you read. And Jamie. Do you remember how he would fire quotes at her to see if she could remember the next line?'

'And then he'd throw in something really obscure, like *Cymbeline*.'

'But he couldn't catch her out, even then.' Thus, fleetingly, we were reconciled as my brother lingered, a dog-eared copy of *The Complete Works* open on his knobbly knees as he hunted through pages wafer thin and soft as muslin. He was always attempting to roll his rs: *Rrrrage! Blow! You catarrrracts and hurrricanoes* ... To my secret satisfaction I could do it and he couldn't. 'It's inherited, Jamie,' Grandmother had told him as he practised in front of her dressing-table mirror, spraying it with spittle, 'something to do with the structure of the mouth. If you can't do it, you can't.'

At last Mother did go, with a whispered, 'Whatever you do, don't touch anything,' and I began reading, as I always used to, from the *Oxford Book of English Verse* – Matthew Arnold, Keats, Emily Brontë, the ones Grandmother loved.

> Yea, as my swift days near their goal,
> 'Tis all that I implore:
> In life and death a chainless soul,
> With courage to endure.

And how you endured, Grandmother, I thought, through all those years of darkness when your sight failed you, confined to a sofa here in Clivedon Hall Gardens, recalling during those interminable afternoons the exhilarating days of stage and politics. What had remained was her astonishing recollection of words, and the ghostly timbre of her actress's voice so that sometimes when I read to her she would lean forward, extend her hand and take over from memory ...

> Children dear, was it yesterday
> We heard the sweet bells over the bay?
> In the caverns where we lay ...

I shivered again, as when she'd first recited 'The Foresaken Merman' to me, at the evocation of damp, salt caves and the hoarse wind.

But now she gave no sign that she heard the poems, and I wished I might have some last connection with her and that my words were not floating about in the room but were touching the profound part of her that loved wonderful language.

> I met a lady in the meads,
> Full beautiful – a faery's child;

Her hair was long, her foot was light,
And her eyes were wild.

I cleared the ash from the dying fire and shook more coal from the scuttle. Though the noise was shocking in the quiet room, Grandmother didn't stir. As I warmed my hands I remembered Trudy Wright and the burnt letter. It was in my old bedroom, above this, at a hearth surrounded by blue and white tiles patterned in fruit and flowers, that I had immolated my own letter from Nicholas Thorne before giving myself a chance to read it. I never did find out, therefore, whether it was a love letter or a litany of reproachful explanation and self-justification. I had been too horrified by what had happened, by how complicit he had been in a fatal miscarriage of justice, by the weakness of his words: *You know it will destroy me, if it comes out . . .*

Caressing Grandmother's cheek with my fingertip I wondered what she had known of love. Grandfather had died young because, according to Mother, he had overworked himself as a schoolteacher. She described how he had donned overcoat, hat and briefcase in the morning, even though his walk to work was a few yards from schoolhouse to schoolroom, because he was punctilious in all he did. In the photograph beside Grandmother's bed he looked far older than his mid-thirties, posed uncomfortably on a hard chair with hair carefully combed back from his deep forehead, owlish glasses and the merest twitch of a surprisingly mischievous smile as if he were party to a joke and the photographer wasn't.

'So, Grandmother,' I said. 'I wonder what you would have made of my day in court.' I moistened her lips, as instructed by Mother, and dabbed her temples with rose water but she gave no response. After the next inhalation there was a longer pause so that I held my own breath and wondered if her lungs had the strength to draw another.

'Do you remember when Edmund first came here from Canada, Grandmother, and was so forlorn and homesick? The rest of us were unsure what to do but you never hesitated. You just loved him and made him welcome. I used to find him in here by the fire with all the old albums spread out on the hearthrug, or playing with your button box, matching them up by colour or size. Look, here it is.' I shook the old chocolate box so that the buttons chattered close to her ear and opened it so that its smell of cardboard, the merest hint of strawberry fondant filling and the perfume of all the clothes from which those buttons had been snipped or fallen, might cover the appalling smell of her dying. She gasped and was still.

I shouted, 'Mother! Come quickly, Mother,' rang the bell beside the bed and again seized the little clenched hand. The silence went on until at long last there came another long, rattling exhalation. Footsteps pounded up the stairs, first Mother, then Prudence, then the maids. Even the lodger hovered in the doorway.

Grandmother didn't breathe again. Her spirit had slipped between the green velvet curtains and away into the night. And the room, in the wake of its passing, was full of cheap and tawdry theatrical souvenirs, a corpse with the fine bones of some ancient bird and a cluster of shocked women.

'There,' I said. 'There.' And for once overcoming the dread I had of embracing her lest she hold on too tightly, I reached out to my mother so that we stood in each other's arms.

Prudence, who as my late father's sister was not a blood relative to Grandmother, watched us before moving forward to kneel before the bed; an oddly biblical figure despite her hand-knitted sky-blue cardigan and black skirt.

'We should say a prayer, of course,' she said.

*Chapter Four*

We drew the sheet over her face, quenched the fire, turned off the lights and drank cocoa together in the chill parlour. We didn't say much, even though the lodger had crept away to bed. Our throats were tight with remembrance and perhaps, had we said more, we might have choked. This new death had opened the half-shut portals of Jamie's so that the much more violent grief I had felt for him came flooding back. In the days following the news of his death – I had blithely answered the door myself – we had staggered through these silent rooms as if our blood had turned to lead.

I could not cry, being too practised at holding myself in check, and Prudence would not, as a matter of principle, show strong emotion in public, but Mother collected a seepage of tears on the back of her hand. Afterwards I took her upstairs to bed and helped her undress. Just this once Evelyn, I thought, being patient couldn't hurt you. But it did. I hated the soft fabrics of her blouse and chemise, her defeated shoulders as they disappeared under the voluminous folds of her nightgown, the limp fall of her hair. It was her passivity that so repelled me; that alternative way of being that sucked the life from me yet was, in its way, so very demanding.

When she climbed into bed I pressed a handkerchief into her hand so that she might dry the tears. 'I did my best for her,' she kept saying. 'She was never happy here, I know that, but we had no choice. There was no money to set her up on her own after your father died. She'd have needed a live-in maid. Where would I have found one?'

Her parting words as I kissed her forehead and prepared to creep away were, 'And now, Evelyn, we can make arrangements for you to come home. There'll be plenty of room for you and the boy. And *her*. It would be a sin to keep on that flat of yours when there's so much space here.'

I lay sleepless in my old bed, missing the youthful stirrings of Meredith and her son in the little rooms in Pimlico, hurtled back to the years immediately post-war when we four women and our two maids had retired to bed each night in our separate rooms, straining to hear just *one* sound from the street, a cat even, a drunkard, that might break the burden of silence.

The next morning I got up at six and dressed for work as usual, not knowing how else to manage a first day of mourning.

Aunt Prudence, who already wore a black silk mourning blouse – pre-war pintucks in the bodice and a high collar with a narrow lace trim – was at the breakfast table. Min's eyes were red as she brought the toast but Prudence seemed as normal, her hair pulled back from her forehead so fiercely that her brows were drawn up in their habitual expression of surprised displeasure.

'You need not worry about us,' she said, before I'd had time to speak. 'We will manage the arrangements perfectly well without you. You will have to take a morning's leave to attend the funeral. Far better that you proceed as normal until then. I shall explain this to your mother when she gets up.'

I had the distinct impression that she had planned these instructions in order to forestall argument and I was so grateful for her thoughtfulness that tears started to my eyes. Duty, after all, was her watchword and it must have gone somewhat against the grain for her to acknowledge that in my complicated, modern life there might actually be a conflict. We ate in near silence, accustomed to the scrape of each other's knives on toast, the unfortunate sounds of crunching and masticating. Before I left the room I stood behind her chair, looking down at the well-regulated waves of her iron-grey hair, and wondered if I ought to kiss her. But she was unyielding as ever, and the lodger was sidling in apologetically from the hall so I thought better of it.

When I arrived at the offices of Breen & Balcombe another redoubtable female, our secretary Miss Drake, who wore her winter dress of dark blue with minute polka dots, was tidying herself before the mirror in the narrow hall.

'I should like a word with Mr Breen,' I said.

'He's at Uxbridge this morning. He told me not to expect him until mid-afternoon.'

'My grandmother died last night,' I said, because I felt desolate that life was apparently to go on as normal.

She rammed in a grip and adjusted the back of her hair, cut straight across the nape of her neck, with a cupping movement of both hands. Miss Drake, who was even-featured and had a good figure, could have been a handsome woman had there been more light in her face. I knew nothing about her because she chose never to engage me in personal conversation of any kind. *Vaulting ambition, which o'er leaps itself*, might have been her opinion of my career in the law, had she shared Grandmother's knowledge of Shakespeare.

'Are you sad?' she asked abruptly.

'Yes, of course I am sad.'

'As one would expect you to be.' Pause. 'No doubt you will want time off to attend the funeral. Please put the request in writing.'

Her words snuffed out any temptation I might have had to confide further. It was cold in my basement office until I'd lit the gas fire but over the years that unlovely space had become such a symbol of my liberty that I wouldn't have exchanged it even had a better room been offered, which it certainly hadn't. Work is the thing, I told myself, at a time like this. Aside from the unexpected lunch appointment with Breen, my only engagement that day was with the socialite and art gallery owner, Lady Petit, who had telephoned to ask for a meeting, specifically with me, to discuss an *intimate* legal matter.

'I told her we have two very experienced partners in the firm,' Miss Drake had informed me frostily, 'but she insisted on "Miss Gifford".'

Meanwhile I was soothed by the dipping of my pen in the inkwell, the unravelling of a knotty codicil to a will, the occasional jangle of the telephone on the floor above.

Punctually at one I arrived at Bow Street where Breen was waiting outside the magistrates' court, neat in his winter overcoat and trilby, which he doffed when he saw me, thereby unsettling the wiry hair which sprang up around a premature bald patch. We set off at pace for John Smith Square and a restaurant with starched tablecloths adorned with silver-plated vases of spring flowers. Breen, who had reserved a table for two in a little alcove, studied me as if I were a favoured but puzzling client.

'You don't look at all yourself, Miss Gifford. I thought this would be a treat. Whatever's the matter?'

'Grandmother died last night.'

Despite his bluster I knew him to be a very kind man but as he pressed my hand I had the distinct impression that he was a little discomposed and was making some kind of rapid mental adjustment. 'I'm sorry.' He flung himself back in his chair and twiddled his thumbs. 'You probably didn't know this, but I'd heard of your grandmother before I met you.'

'Had you, sir?'

'Actresses' Franchise League. Clara Fielding. Anyone interested in suffrage knew all about her. She gave women confidence, taught them the art of public speaking.'

'I didn't realise . . .'

'Well, why would you? I thought it best to keep quiet the fact that I'd heard you were related or the next thing you'd be thinking I only took you on because of your illustrious grandmother.' His gaze, lingering on my face, was both teasing and tender and I found I had to grope for a handkerchief and wipe my eyes. In his company that day I felt as fragile as glass. 'Shall we order wine?' he asked. 'Toast your grandmother?'

'Sir, perhaps you've forgotten I'm meeting Lady Petit this afternoon.'

'Then alcohol's just what you need. The woman will be a monster if she's anything like her husband. He's one of my least favourite politicians – regards himself as a radical golden boy when he's really a right-wing hatchet man. Plenty of time to get over one glass, don't you think? Make the most of it. There'll be precious little opportunity for self-indulgence in the weeks ahead.'

With a belligerent glint in his eye he ordered a half-bottle of white burgundy. The other diners were male save for one young woman whose winsome features were framed by a swansdown collar and pert powder-blue hat and who was all softness and rosiness compared to my angular self in high-necked blouse and grey suit. Breen chose steak, I, grilled chicken, and a flurry of waiters appeared to unfold our napkins and adjust the cutlery while we sat like patients tucked up in newly made beds.

Breen wanted to know the outcome of the Wright case. 'You did well, Miss Gifford. In less skilled hands that girl might even have landed in prison.'

'Thank heavens she didn't. The Derbyshire woman beat her regularly for five years.'

'Yet you chose not to mention that to the bench.'

'I didn't want to confuse the matter or imply that Miss Wright was seeking any form of revenge.'

'Very wise.' He examined a fork as if contemptuous of its embellished handle. The soup, when it arrived, was dull and salty, scattered with squares of toasted white bread.

'And did you notice the father?' I asked. 'Poor girl – caught between one bully and another. I told her I'd do my best to help her find work.'

'And who will pay for your time?' But he was twinkling at me as we discussed Breen & Balcombe, which was apparently thriving such that we could expect higher profits this year. 'Even you, Miss Gifford, have begun to make money instead of causing me to fritter it away on appeals and the like – though you have acquired my own unfortunate habit of working for nothing where we think we can do some good.' Cocking his head to one side like an attentive blackbird he tore off his napkin. 'You're still trying to work out why I invited you here. Of course you are.'

Next he launched into a tirade about the likelihood of a general strike. In his limited spare time Breen served as a councillor for the Labour Party and was therefore deeply engaged in the debate. And yes, he was keen that Breen & Balcombe should be prepared for the turmoil ahead. 'I fear a bloodbath. Neither the government nor the unions have the wit to settle their differences.'

'Or the will, perhaps.'

'Or the will. The Tory government is culpable because it has no real intention of addressing the fundamental issue, which is the absurdity of the nation's fuel being in the grip of a few mine owners who care for nothing but profit. And the unions, it seems to me, are divided about what they're fighting for. Some of them want to bring down the whole system – government, establishment, capitalism, all of it. Others think they're simply defending the right of miners not to have their wages cut. There'll be a terrible clash, and nobody will know how to sort things out.'

'So what role do you envisage for Breen & Balcombe?'

'All kinds of people will find themselves on the wrong side of the law. Remember those communist activists who were arrested and charged with sedition last year? Joynson-Hicks, our beloved home secretary, is a bigot and I don't trust him to have a proportionate response to anything. So we have to ensure that justice is done.'

'All by ourselves?'

'I can't rely on Wolfe. I never know whose side he's on. But you, Miss Gifford?'

'I shall of course try to be on the side of what's right. I shall—'

'My view is that the mine owners, the industrialists and the government can take care of themselves. It's our duty, therefore, to keep an eye out for the workers.'

'Our *duty*? Do you mean my professional duty?'

He flashed me an appreciative smile. 'You are reproaching me, Miss Gifford. Of course, it is not my place to tell you your duty, moral, personal or indeed professional. You're quite right – I shouldn't let politics get in the way of justice. My goodness, you have no idea how crushing the expression in your eyes is sometimes. No wonder you succeeded in having that poor little maid's case dismissed yesterday.'

I refused pudding, thinking that the discomfort of the occasion had gone on quite long enough. 'If you're sure you've had sufficient to eat, I could walk with you across the park to the bus stop,' suggested Breen.

It struck a little blow to my heart to see him scrutinise the bill, reach into his wallet and proffer a ten-shilling note; he was never quite able to hide the fact that in former days money had been in short supply. The day was cold and blustery but fortunately I was wearing a thick overcoat and a hat that pulled well over my ears.

26

'I was hoping the sun would be out,' said Breen as he performed a skipping manoeuvre to get himself on the kerb side of the pavement, case tucked under his arm, hat pressed low on his brow.

The park was crowded with orange-trumpeted daffodils. Ducks and geese squawked on the lake, beating out territory for the new nesting season. London parks always disturbed me with their paradoxical promise of freedom when, in reality, few parts of the city were as well regulated.

'During the war,' Breen remarked, 'I used to regard the parks as no-go areas. No pleasure, I told myself, until the fighting is done.' And then drawing himself up, he added, 'You know I was a conchie? I've often wondered how sympathetic you feel about that, given what happened to your brother.'

'I understand, of course I do. Sometimes, since the war, I've thought it was the only sane course of action. But Jamie was younger than you and rather conventional. My father was keen for him to join up straight away.' It was dawning on me that this conversation contained more personal disclosure than I'd ever heard from Breen's lips and that it was his way of consoling me – of letting me know that he, too, had been faced with bitter emotional crises.

'I wasn't one of those fellows who refused absolutely to lift a finger – not that I didn't admire them for going the whole way – so I drove ambulances. I thought I should help to clear up the mess at least. Now I believe I was wrong even to go that far. We scraped men off the battlefield and then, if they recovered, shipped them back for another stint of slaughter.'

'You might easily have been killed yourself. My brother was full of admiration for the ambulance drivers.'

'Point was I reached the stage when it simply didn't matter. I certainly shouldn't have minded if I'd been gunned down, so long as a thorough job was made of it.'

'I'm glad you survived, Mr Breen. Nobody else would have taken me on.'

'They would in the end. Despite how it might appear sometimes, not everyone in the profession is a complete fool.' When I unravelled this remark later, I decided it was a compliment. 'Well, here you are. And here comes your bus,' he said. 'Remember what

I said about Lady Petit. Treat her with extreme caution.' And then he wrong-footed me again because I thought he'd forgotten about Grandmother. 'Are you feeling a little better now?'

'Thank you, sir. Yes, I feel a bit better.'

'We must do this again sometime. What do you think?'

*Chapter Five*

On the omnibus journey I sat on the left side of the upper deck, slightly heartened because Breen, of all people, had tried so hard to cheer me up. In his early forties, he was a confirmed bachelor and I knew little of his private life except that he liked walking in the Highlands and lived alone in Battersea where he was a local councillor. He was always in a hurry, always on to the next case, and was so intolerant of so many things – the death penalty, weak tea, British fascists, women who wore drooping feathers in their hats – that to be in his favour was to feel the heat of the sun on one's face. I had seen the stoniest magistrate melt under Breen's sudden smile or one of his shamelessly ingratiating asides – 'You sir, with all your experience, I can rely on to understand the law in this case . . .' – because to be singled out for praise by Breen was to join a rarefied company indeed, one that included Keir Hardie, digestive biscuits and wild, empty places.

As for me, he had early on earned my unwavering loyalty and devotion, not least because I owed him everything. It was Breen who had lifted me from a mire of grief and joblessness and given me work, purpose and hope. When I qualified he had been the only lawyer in London who would risk taking on as their clerk a young woman with wayward hair, an air of desperation and an urgent desire to exercise her newly trained legal muscles. His imperfections – he was somewhat tight-fisted, vain, unpredictable and irascible – only made a glimmer of approval from him all the more exciting. And he had been so unexpectedly kind about Grandmother, revealing her in quite a different light. Typical Breen, to have provided me with a fresh angle on her.

\*

The house at 5 Cottingham Grove, Kensington was four storeys high and painted white, inhabited by one Lady Petit, owner, according to the racket on the other side of the door, of a suspicious dog. A maid answered, her fingers hooked into the collar of a taut little canine, her cap pinned at a rakish angle above staring green eyes. The hallway through which we passed was vast and stylish and I recognised the effortless elegance of a home where both taste and money had been lavishly expended. The smell was sultry, that of perfumed flowers and even incense, and I was shown into a room decorated in a feast of bright colours and, or so it seemed to me – the product of austere Maida Vale – a glut of paintings, sculptures and ornaments.

Poised on a peacock-blue sofa sat a woman in a dress the colour of old gold. Her glossy chestnut hair was cut in an angular bob so that two long points met under her chin, and her face was dominated by a pair of huge, almond-shaped eyes. With nervous fingers she caressed the tousled head of a young child who was curled under the crook of her arm. The greyhound sat at her feet as if made of china, thereby disassociating itself from the creature that had barked so frenziedly a few minutes earlier. A nursemaid hovered nearby.

'Miss Gifford.' Lady Petit extended her hand so that for an absurd moment I thought I should kiss rather than shake it. 'Forgive me for not rising but I don't want to disturb Annice. Take a good long look at her.'

The little girl, whom I estimated must be about three years of age, had her mother's dark hair and wore a pair of loose trousers and a matching blouse. When I smiled she tucked her head down and wouldn't meet my eye.

Lady Petit, on the other hand, appeared to be focusing on a point behind my forehead. 'I'm a friend of Lady Curren's,' she added. 'You no doubt remember her.'

Thus, abruptly, did she gain my full attention. Of course I remembered Lady Curren – she and I had once clashed over the cruel practices of the children's home of which she was proud to be a board member.

'She described you in great detail,' said Lady Petit, in a voice which contrived to suggest immeasurable depths of character as it broke slightly on certain vowels and leaned on unexpected syllables, 'very accurately, up to a point, but she said you were strong-featured and there I think she understated the matter. You have an unforgettable face.'

I was neither in the mood nor the habit of being the subject of such scrutiny. She put her hand to her mouth and gave a little gasp of dismay. 'Ah, you disapprove of me. You think I'm being too personal. Trust me to get it all wrong. But can't you see yourself in that picture above the mantel? It's a Dupas. See those brows. They're just like yours.'

The woman in the picture had a long white neck, prominent brows that winged upwards then slanted down over wide-set, pondering eyes and a rather sweet red mouth.

'Please, Miss Gifford, do take a seat,' said Lady Petit. 'I have ordered tea to be brought and then we can have a proper, private conversation.' Drawing Annice closer she covered her head with kisses. 'Run along now, sweetheart. Mama will come up and see you very soon.' She kissed the child's cheeks and stroked her hair from her wide, smooth forehead as if they were to be parted for a month rather than half an hour.

The armchair I'd chosen was decorated in dashes of purple and green. To my right were long windows overlooking a still-wintry garden. While the teacups were set out Lady Petit fondled the silky head of her dog but the instant we were alone she seized the tea strainer and began speaking at a great rate. 'It's the fact that you argued with Lady Curren that made me send for you. She's part of my mother's set but I can't stand her. Well, one evening we met her in the Crush Bar at the Garden, *Parsifal*, and I've never seen anyone so hopping mad. She said that in her view you had done a great disservice to the suffrage movement and to all women who aspired to enter the professions by behaving stridently and unprofessionally. How I wished I'd been there! Anyway, I stored up the memory of you for a rainy day.'

I sipped tea from a cup of astonishing beauty – orange-rimmed with stripes of pale yellow, white and grey – and attempted to gather my wits. In that room there were so many conflicting de-signs in rich colours that wherever I looked I had to work out where a swirl or triangle or limb began and ended.

'The matter I'm going to discuss with you is delicate ... and some people are so funny about sexual matters,' continued Lady Petit. Despite the bravado of her words, her too thin frame was trembling beneath the sheer fabric of her dress. 'My husband is taking me to court because he claims that he is not the father of my child. *Our* child, I should say. If he wins he will disinherit her and divorce me.' Flinging her arms around the greyhound she cried into its neck. 'Oh God, how could he be so cruel?'

I waited until she'd calmed down and was gazing at me expectantly from drowned eyes. 'And yet he is definitely Annice's father?'

'Of course he is. There's no one else, if that's what you're wondering.'

'Then upon ...?'

She took a cigarette from the sliver of a silver box on the table and gripped the holder between quivering fingers as she employed a lighter the size of a cricket ball. 'He will say our marriage was never consummated.'

With sinking heart I remembered Breen's warning and saw the quagmire into which Lady Petit was dragging me. Pouting her red lips she puffed a perfect smoke ring. 'I'll say it was – but not in the usual way. You know?'

She could probably tell that really I didn't know, could only imagine what she was talking about. 'My husband, as you'll be aware, is a prominent member of parliament.' She flicked her hand towards the photograph of a moustachioed man with a fine head of fair hair parted across a deep forehead – not unlike Annice's. 'He's just been appointed to the Cabinet Coal Committee though Lord knows why. He's never dirtied his hands in his life or been *North*, as far as I can tell. You'd think he'd back down, wouldn't you, just to avoid the publicity. But I know Timmo, he doesn't care two hoots what anyone else thinks.'

After this outburst, she lay back, hands resting on either side so that ash dropped on to the fabric of the sofa.

'You say your husband wants a divorce.' I said. 'What if you were to win this case? Would you really wish to stay married in those circumstances?'

The moon-grey eyes opened, spilling tears. 'Of course! For Annice. I think a child should know its father, don't you?'

Well yes, as a matter of fact I did because I knew how Edmund suffered for want of one. Although, being so young, he was unaware of the stigma of his mother's unmarried status, he was all too conscious of a vacuum none of us could fill. His most treasured possessions were a photograph of his father, chisel-jawed in army uniform, and his signet ring, which was kept in cotton wool in a little leather box.

Was Lady Petit prescient, that she had touched so unerringly on another nerve? 'You saw her, my darling girl,' she continued, 'and Timmo is her father, that's the thing, so he must take responsibility for her. You see—'

I held up my hand. 'Before we go any further, I need to clarify my position. And I want to be sure that I'm the right person to help you. First, although Breen and Balcombe does occasionally deal with family cases, we are by no means specialists and it might—'

'You're not going to refuse me?' she said, with that odd little break on *refuse*.

'There are firms that specialise in family work. In fact, a friend of mine, Miss Morrison, who qualified at the same time, handles very little else and has developed a far greater expertise in the area. And you may think that at this stage matters of intimacy are easier to discuss with me than with a male colleague.' She gave a raw laugh and shook her head vigorously so that the points of her hair swung out. 'But when your case comes to court you will find yourself in a brutal environment. We would probably have to instruct a male barrister.'

A look of stubborn abstraction came into her eyes. 'How amazing; I'd anticipated that you would fall at my feet with gratitude when I offered you this case. Now I understand exactly what it was in you that riled Lady Curren. Well, I've listened to what you've said and I still want you.'

I ought to have consulted with Breen before I agreed. The trouble was, I was fairly sure he'd advise me against taking on the case – he'd always steered clear of divorce suits and yesterday in the restaurant he'd warned me about Timothy Petit. But little Annice, with her stern, unchildish face, had taken her nursemaid's hand so gravely as she left the room that I had been touched both by her obedience and by her trust. Her seriousness reminded me of Edmund, during his first days at Clivedon Hall Gardens, when his future seemed so unsure. I would therefore protect her, if I could, from being caught up in a damaging wrangle between her parents. Besides, she, like every child, had a right to know who she was.

'Very well then, Lady Petit, I shall write to you tomorrow with our terms and arrange a further appointment at our offices.'

Lady Petit rushed across to kiss me on both cheeks. 'Marvellous, marvellous woman! I knew you'd do it. You won't regret this, I promise you. Oh, thank heavens, now I'll be able to sleep at night. And so will Annice.'

# Chapter Six

We put a notice of Grandmother's death in *The Times* and Mother and I spent an evening writing to shadowy relatives with abbreviated names such as Aunt Glad (sister-in-law's niece), Beat (the niece's daughter) and Madge (a cousin), most of whom lived in Surrey and were therefore, my mother said hopefully, too far away to come to the funeral in uncertain weather.

'What about her friends from the theatre?' I asked. 'Should we write to some of them?'

'We won't be able to keep them away,' Mother said nervously. 'I only hope there won't be any silliness.'

'Silliness?'

'You know what these people are like.'

'Which people?'

'Theatre people – they're so false. I'm glad to say Mother never really fitted in with them, though she liked to think she did.'

'Why do you say that?'

'She was so ladylike. You can always see through a proper actress's veneer to something common beneath.'

When I knocked on Breen's door and asked for a morning's absence for the funeral he told me that I could take the entire day.

'That seems excessive' I protested. 'I don't want any special favours, sir.'

'No special favours. Do you think I have no heart?' His chair made little movements, side to side and he tapped the top of his pen on the blotter. 'I wonder what your grandmother would have said about this,' he indicated the booklet before him, 'Samuel Report. At last. I presume you knew it was out today. It's on the state of the mining industry. I'll pass it on to you later if you're interested.'

'Thank you.'

'No need to look so wary. I found it fascinating reading. It suggests reforms but also recommends a pay cut for the miners. Bound to be a strike now.'

'And did you know Lady Petit's husband now has a place on the Cabinet Coal Committee?' I said, heart in mouth.

'Of course, you met her yesterday. Tell me all.' That did the trick. Having heard the details of the Petit case any vestiges of sympathy for my bereaved state were forgotten, at least temporarily. 'You shouldn't touch the case with a bargepole,' he said. 'We'll send her details of firms who might be persuaded to represent her, heaven help them.'

'I'm afraid I've already agreed to take her on,' I replied, quaking. 'She did seem very distressed.'

He stared at me in utter incredulity. 'I don't care how distressed she was. I'm not interested in rich people and their nasty squabbles. It will be poisonous. They'll drag each other through one court after another and stop at nothing in their determination to destroy each other. I know these types.'

'Surely rich people deserve to be as well represented as the poor?'

'So they shall be, but not by us. There'll be a queue of brilliant lawyers willing to represent this woman and good luck to them. Petit is a ruthless beast intent on running the country into a showdown with the unions. If he's contesting paternity it will be bloody. It's not our kind of case at all.'

'But what about the child? He's using her. The little girl will have no father if he wins.'

'Ah, so that's it. That's how she's got to you, through the child.'

'Is that so wrong?'

'Oh, it's not wrong, Miss Gifford. It can never be wrong to champion the cause of an innocent child as long as your desire to do so isn't clouding your better judgement. But is this really a battle worth fighting, have you asked yourself that? If Petit's set on disowning the little girl wouldn't she be better off without him?'

'He shouldn't be allowed to disown her just because he's taken it into his head he doesn't want her.'

'But if he treats her coldly, if she grows up knowing that he's a reluctant father . . .?'

'At least she'll still have a father. That's the point.'

Our gaze had snagged and to my surprise the usual combative spark died from his eye. 'It's absolutely typical that a type like Lady Petit should get her own way. You women.' He waved me out of the room. 'Write to her then. Arrange an appointment; ask her to bring any papers you think might be relevant to the case.'

As I was shutting the door he called: 'And I thought, perhaps one evening next week after the funeral, you might like a decent meal. I expect it will be grim, funerals usually are – rain, and such. What do you think? Nothing ostentatious.' He was pushed far back in his chair, diary in hand.

'I should like that very much, sir.'

It seemed, then, that I was to be let off very lightly indeed for taking on Lady Petit. Offering a quick prayer of thanks to Grandmother, I sat down and drafted a letter, before he could change his mind.

The hearse was an old-fashioned horse and carriage, which delighted Edmund although the expense made Mother's eyes water. She and I, followed by Meredith in her poignantly low-brimmed hat, hand in hand with Edmund, processed into the church after the coffin, which was decorated with a single spray of narcissi and accompanied on the organ by an ambitious rendition of *Jesu, Joy of Man's Desiring*. My first impression was of the frigid temperature, more bitterly cold even than outside, then of the surprising number of faces swivelled round to watch; a veritable crowd in fact, a few of whom such as Mrs Gillespie I knew from the parish, others complete strangers. The majority were female; some wore veils, others were heavily made-up or had time-worn faces framed by elaborate hats, their chins resting in the too-wide collars of borrowed blacks. 'He Who Would Valiant Be' was sung so lustily that the organist struggled to keep up and the pallid vicar looked apologetic as he began a bowdlerised account of Grandmother's life, as fed to him by Mother: *Married to a teacher . . . devoted mother*

*... bore her disability with great fortitude*. No mention was made either of Grandmother's distinguished acting career – Nora in *A Doll's House*, Grace Harkaway in *London Assurance*, Desdemona – or of her political adventures, and there were discontented mutterings in the pews behind us.

Nevertheless, I was brought up sharply against what we'd lost. Prudence had compiled a list of Grandmother's favourite hymns and they all carried the same ardent message: be stalwart and loving on this difficult journey through life. She had been an enthusiast, an egger-on, an encourager. 'In the theatre,' she had told me, 'I became used to disappointments but they were always worth it for the excitement of a first night.'

When we were very small, Jamie and I had sometimes been left with Grandmother in her Clapham apartment while Mother went shopping, and we were allowed to sit in on the elocution lessons which had been her chief source of income throughout her widowhood. Her main room had been set out like a salon with the furniture pushed back so that a pupil might have scope to enunciate, and there were stacks of books containing suitable poems and voice exercises. The thick blue velvet curtains could be swept aside and looped up in summer or closed to form a cosy backdrop when the afternoons drew in and the fire was lit.

Each pupil was treated as if they were incomparably gifted, escorted to a particular spot on the carpet and given Grandmother's undivided attention while they recited such gems as 'The Lady of Shalott'.

Up Grandmother would jump after a minute or two and make a gentle adjustment to the pupil's shoulders or hip, raise their chin or stroke the tension out of clenched fingers. '*She left the web, she left the loom, She made three paces through the room*,' she murmured, defining the Lady's cramped cell with the flat of her outstretched hand so that we were all transported to that shocking moment when life itself was cast aside for the sake of a direct glance at a man.

Under cover of the opening chords of *Jerusalem* Mother whispered, 'Surely they won't *all* want to come back to the house. However shall we manage?' In the dining room of Clivedon Hall Gardens a cold collation awaited, each meagre plate of sandwiches labelled with a flag on a cocktail stick in Min's laborious print – *ham*, *cucumber*, *cheese*. There were a couple of dozen sausage rolls, cheese straws, a fruit cake and four bottles of sherry.

Prudence, who had seemed most uncharacteristically willing to please since Grandmother's death, came to the rescue. 'The maids and I won't attend the burial,' she said. 'We'll go back to the house and prepare more food instead.'

So those three missed the slow journey to the cemetery, the blast of icy wind across the tombstones, the tossing in of the first clod. I comforted myself by thinking that at least Grandmother's death had been timely and there was no nightmarish production-line quality to the London cemetery; no mashed-up foreign field, thigh-high in mud, no wooden cross, one among thousands, meticulously marked with name and number. The rituals we were performing made us pause to think of her small, near-blind self and to speculate, at least on my part, on the life she had led before I knew her; a life disparaged by Mother and admired by Breen. And I had the bizarre feeling that she was somewhere close by, watching from behind her pebble-lensed glasses, itching, as always, to play a more significant part.

Even in pre-war days I had never seen our house so crowded or inviting. Min and Rose had taken matters into their own hands by lighting fires in both downstairs hearths. Mourners pouring up the steps and into the hall dropped their coats into Edmund's outstretched arms so that he staggered under the weight and had to toil upstairs a dozen times, his face submerged in tickly collars and stiff cuffs. People leaned against the hall furniture, crammed into alcoves or ensconced themselves amid the stuffed birds in the drawing room. Within minutes the sherry had gone and the girls and I had raided Mother's spartan drinks cabinet, so I emptied my purse into the hand of one of the few men, a second cousin or such with burly shoulders and a ruddy face. Twenty minutes later he returned with a crate of stout and more sherry.

Edmund, released from cloakroom duties, moved from group to group showing off Grandmother's scrapbook, his eyes dark with pride and grief for his former ally, while Meredith propped herself by the hall stand, glanced at the front door whenever it opened, chain-smoked and introduced herself as *the dead grandson's woman*.

She was definitely up to something. Turned out with exquisite care, she was half a head shorter than most of the other adults, her complexion porcelain-fine and her eyelashes subtly painted. A silk scarf in midnight blue was draped about her throat, thereby transforming her mourning dress into something a little subversive, with gloves to match. After a while I lost sight of her as I passed around a plate of cheese straws. 'You have exactly your grandmother's hair, lovey,' said one mourner. 'You're the clever lawyer we've heard so much about.'

I offered the last cheese straw to Miss Lord, one of the friends Prudence had left behind in the country when she'd moved to Clivedon Hall Gardens, for reasons of economy, after the war. Miss Lord's mannish jacket obscured every vestige of feminine shape and a dead fox's glum face rested on her bosom.

'I remember you when you were a child, Miss Gifford, visiting your Aunt Prudence,' she told me. 'We always predicted you would have a difficult life.'

'I hope not too difficult.'

'Your aunt and I were the wrong generation. We had plenty of brains but no education yet neither of us wanted marriage. You, my dear young woman, must be the standard-bearer for us all.' She leaned closer so that I caught a distinct whiff of mothball and possibly – surely not – whisky. 'Don't get trapped by your mother. Give her a wide berth, is my advice to you. She'll be very needy, now that your grandmother's gone, and Prudence too.'

'Prudence? Where is Prudence going?'

'Worlds away, of course. Didn't you know? Ah, I can see I've jumped the gun and she hasn't got around to telling you yet. She and I are off to India. And afterwards, if funds allow, New Zealand.' There was more than a hint of malice in Miss Lord's beady eye as she licked crumbs of cheese pastry from her lips.

'I had no idea . . .'

'We planned the trip years ago. "I cannot leave while poor Clara is so poorly," she used to say. "My sister-in-law couldn't possibly cope." But now we'll be off as soon as we can. We've waited so long, you see.'

It had never occurred to me that Prudence might have plans, let alone a comrade with whom to share them. Prudence treated money with the same discipline she applied to everything else: a florin to the collection in church on a Sunday, one new blouse every other spring, a meticulous refusal to waste even half an inch of embroidery thread when sewing in her ends. Surely a trip to a far continent was a wild extravagance for one as spendthrift as she? While Miss Lord set off in pursuit of Min who had brought in a fresh plate of ham and mustard sandwiches, I tried to picture her and my Aunt Prudence, in their woollen combinations, in *India*. This was Meredith's doing: it was she who had goaded Prudence into leaving the confines of Clivedon Hall Gardens and introduced her to modern art and The Commonwealth Exhibition. My initial, selfish thought was that Prudence's defection would have awful consequences for Mother, and therefore me. If she left, so would her contribution to the household budget and Mother would be solely responsible for the management of servants, lodgers, finances, failing roof, all.

Meanwhile Mother, oblivious to her fate, couldn't quite conceal her love of a party. For the funeral she had unearthed a long, gathered, silk skirt, pre-war, and a flowing black cardigan, and she had not yet removed her hat, which was the size of a serving plate, because it made her look delicate and even original. Unaccustomed sherry had brought a glow to her cheeks.

'You see my mother was never destined to be an actress,' she informed a group comprised of Mrs Gillespie and other church friends, 'it was just that she came from a theatrical family. As soon as she met my father, she gave it up like a shot.'

'Ah, but there was always something so vivacious about her,' said Mrs Gillespie, whose mourning hat was newly decorated with a viciously pointed black quill. 'She could never resist music, could she? I remember you brought her to a Red Cross dance in the church hall, before your son ... How she danced! Such zest. My husband was so taken with her I could scarcely get him to partner me at all.'

'It is true that even to the end of her days she was very graceful,' said Mother. 'I only wish Evelyn had inherited her posture.'

The other guests fell into two distinct categories. First were those who colonised the parlour and were enthusiastically tipping back the new sherry, admiring everything from the photograph of my brother James in his uniform to the evil-eyed sea birds. They told me to sit down, do, and tell them all about myself. These were the Kingston relatives, Grandmother's paternal cousins and their offspring, who didn't seem to care that their skirts rode up above the knee or that their bunions bulged against the overstretched leather of their cheap shoes.

In the hall, an even more undesirable crowd clustered around Meredith: theatre people, political women from the Actresses' Franchise League, dressed in clothes that might have been lifted from a costume store – embossed satin, furs, stoles and hats so broad they outdid Mother's. They thought nothing of refreshing their lipstick in public, even at a funeral, and had loud, beautiful voices that reminded me of Lady Petit's. I was drawn to them, moth-like, to be told stories that painted a rather different picture of a Clara Melville – or Fielding, as they insisted on calling her – who had stormed through London on behalf of the Actresses' Franchise League and to whom I no doubt owed my pioneering spirit. She had been there right from the start, they said, at The Criterion, when they met to form the league. And she'd appeared in the revolutionary play *Votes for Women* and dedicated much of her time, for no financial reward, to coaching other women in public speaking.

Mother was plucking at my sleeve, urging me to come away and speak to Aunt Gladys, and for the next half-hour I was occupied by a flurry of departures. But later a woman with faded auburn hair called Peggy Spencer cornered me in the hall. She smelt of musty fabric and had greenish eyes which fixed on my face and sparkled as she spoke.

'And are you worth it?' she asked in a deeply resonant voice.

'Worth it?'

'The sacrifice she made. Your mother was nothing much, I always thought. But *you* . . .'

'I don't understand.'

'I was one of the few who knew the whole story. Your grandmother and I went back many years. My first break was as a maid in *London Assurance* to her Grace Harkaway. The great Patrick Rusbridger – you must have heard of him, marvellous character actor – was playing the lead. Clara always looked ridiculously small on stage but the part suited her. It was the last thing she did because after that she fell pregnant, you know, with your mother.' The speculative look in her eye was that of a terrier let loose in a rabbit hutch. 'Daft soul, she was. Headlong in love. I remember her frock at the altar was very artful because the wardrobe mistress at the Haymarket had created it for her. And that was that, the end of her career in theatre, at least until the Franchise League.'

There was a beat, such as I'd noticed happen before the great crises of my life, between momentous news and the blow that follows; a stillness of the heart. 'What do you mean? What are you suggesting? That she and Patrick Rusbridger ... that he was the father ...?'

'Oh come, Evelyn, surely you must have suspected.'

The doorbell had rung and in came a slight young man, bearded and inappropriately dressed in a light-coloured suit.

Meredith rushed up. 'Angus, you came,' and she kissed him full on the lips.

When Angus took my hand I smelt nicotine, something else, something sweet and forbidden, and turpentine. Meredith, avoiding my eye, told one of the actresses in a voice so clear and arresting that the room went silent, 'He and I are going to Sanary-sur-Mer for the late spring and summer. It's the light. We artists must have light. And we shall take Edmund, for sure.'

# Chapter Seven

After the guests had gone Meredith went home to put Edmund to bed, Prudence retired with a migraine and Mother sat with the lodger in the drawing room while the maids and I rearranged furniture and washed glasses in the scullery. It was bleak down there, lit by a single bulb, the stone floor always damp, mildew in the whitewashed walls and the past peeking out in the form of the mangle which James used to work sometimes on washdays, turning the wooden handle so energetically that he sprayed us all with suds.

The girls insisted I put on an apron and silently replaced my tea towel whenever they noticed it was sodden. They were still wearing their best black skirts and cardigans and their fine hair, not quite recovered from the crush of their hats, was set in soft ripples. Above us the old house was silent and had it not been for their familiar, undemanding company, I might have been tempted to smash the glasses or rest my head on that old, unforgiving iron mangle and weep. Surely Meredith wouldn't be so cruel as to leave without even discussing it with me first? Surely she would not separate me from Edmund? Did she not know how far he, that earnest, affectionate little boy with his slow Canadian twang, had healed me by filling a little of the gaping hole left by my brother's death?

If I felt compelled, by the defection of Prudence and Meredith, to return to this house, there would not even be ghosts for company, only the furniture that had loomed so large when we were children that we had played hide-and-seek among its legs and sailed away among its cushions. As I climbed the narrow staircase to the hall, I glimpsed the maids' little sitting room with its popping gas fire and gate-legged table at which James and I used to play snakes and ladders. Mother must have been on the lookout because she hurried towards me, hand outstretched in that way she had of intimating that if she was not supported by some other person, she might fall. I avoided her by reaching for my coat.

Had she but known it, her unbridled neediness, which had perhaps developed as a riposte to her own mother's independence when a young widow, and which had served her in good stead while my father was alive, was a trait guaranteed to irritate and repel me. I had not realised, until safely installed in a room of my own at Girton, how it would feel to be without family ties. The course had been demanding, my tutors dictatorial and college rules petty, but at least nobody commented minutely on every garment I wore, awaited me at breakfast or sought my opinion on every last purchase of curtain material or notepaper. Nobody expected me to talk or walk with them, even though they had nothing to say and nowhere to go. I was not required to fritter away an afternoon in the same room as women who had nothing to do but kill the long hours until dinner.

Oh, the relief of that moment when the porter had first unlocked the door of my college room and I had breathed in the unfamiliar aroma of institutional bed linen, taking in the fact that I was by myself in a large, complicated building in a strange city: I, Evelyn Gifford.

And so Mother's efforts to pin me down distressed me beyond measure. I wanted to cry out, For God's sake, leave me be, but I could not because she was my mother and Clivedon Hall Gardens forbade such honesty.

'Aren't you staying?' she moaned. 'I thought you'd be bound to stay tonight.'

'I need to talk to Meredith.'

'You must come back soon and help me sort through Mother's things.'

'There's surely no hurry.'

'Oh, but it's so dreadful to think of them all left lying about.'

She wore her habitual half-pleading, half-petulant expression as she anticipated the next obstacle. Well, good Lord, Mother, I thought, I'm not even sure who you are any more. According to Peggy Spencer, you're not at all what you think. Thank goodness

I bit my tongue; the front door closed behind me and I leaned on the railings, inhaling the damp night air. This was hardly the time to consider family history. Instead I must decide how best to tackle Meredith.

By the time I reached Pimlico she had poured herself a whisky and was tucked up in the easy chair with her hands over her ears, deep in a copy of *Vogue* she could ill afford. I looked in on Edmund who was fast asleep, burrowed under the quilt, a telltale sign of distress because when he was happy he flung his arms wide and snored softly. With a toss of the head Meredith refused my offer of scrambled eggs. Nevertheless, I melted butter in a pan, impaled a slice of bread on the end of a fork and toasted it against the gas flame. Occasionally she shifted irritably in her chair and I sensed that actually she was very hungry.

'Are you going to tell me about Angus Strangeways?' I asked at last, attempting to keep my voice neutral.

'What do you want to know?'

'Why didn't you tell me that you and Edmund are going away with him? It was very unkind to let me hear news like that as if by accident. If you wanted to hurt me, you have succeeded.'

She said nothing.

'Is it really going to happen?' I asked.

'You mean the South of France? Of course. You know I always do what I say. I cannot stand another disappointing summer in this country.'

The eggs had caught on the base of the saucepan and though I boiled water and scoured vigorously it would not come clean. When I returned to the living room my first task was to write a reference for Trudy Wright and in the purposeful action of unscrewing the pen top I thought of the office and Daniel Breen and was a little comforted.

It was cold by the window where the wind-rattled panes strained against the wads of paper we'd used to seal them up. Tomorrow I had arranged to trek over to Ealing for an interview with Mrs Fitzgerald, author of the fateful letter concerning Trudy Wright and her quest for employment. I cursed my own wretched conscience. I did not want to go to Ealing and plead that Trudy be taken on as a maid despite her lack of references. I did not want to dismantle my grandmother's room. I did not want to be sitting here with Meredith in such a foul mood.

'What will you do with the flat when I'm gone?' she asked too brightly, at last.

'I haven't thought. Try to keep it going on my own, I suppose.'

'I don't expect you'll mind what happens to it, since you're never here.'

'Of course I'll mind. Good God, Meredith, do you think I'm made of stone? You know that I've been very happy, living here with you and Edmund. You, on the other hand, are unhappy. I do know that. I wish you weren't, but try as I might I can't seem to make things better for you. I want to do the right thing and yet I only succeed in annoying you. I cannot help who I am. I cannot help having a needy mother in another household who depends on my support. For all our sakes I have to work.'

'This is not about you. Why do you think you're the cause of everything? It's about *me*. I meant what I said the other day. I shall lie down and die if I have to put up with things as they are any longer. I want a new life. I want to *be* someone. Surely you don't begrudge me that? I used to know who I was, when I was hoping to be a nun, even when I was nursing in the war. You know who you are.'

'What about Edmund's education? You can't just take him away from school.'

'That's the whole point. I didn't tell you because it was the night your grandmother was dying and you had to dash out. You know we'd discussed that there might be a scholarship or bursary at your brother's former school for the children of old boys who'd been killed? Well, there is and I went to the school to enter Edmund's name for the entrance exam. The secretary remembered James. She had drawn up the list of the war dead, you see, for a memorial and knew the names by heart. Then she said, "But I wasn't aware that James Gifford had married. I had heard . . ." She went quiet for a bit and said, "Excuse me asking, my dear, but now I remember there was talk of a child, but this is surely not the one you're thinking of sending here?"'

'They mustn't have understood,' I said. 'My father was an old boy too. Surely they should show some loyalty? I'll go and talk to them.'

'Why bother? Do you really want Edmund to be educated in such a place? The reason they won't admit him is the very same reason why your father chose the school for his precious James in the first place: because it's an exclusive bastion of the British establishment.' Her cheeks burned with rage and my heart went out to her in her fiery loyalty to her son. 'And you expect me to go on living in this rotten little country?'

'Why didn't you wait until I could come with you? I would do anything to spare you that type of pain.'

'Because you never have any time.'

Her fingers gripping the whisky tumbler were as small as a child's. Kneeling beside her, I put out my hand for the glass and after a moment she passed it to me and tugged my hair as a sign of penitence. 'Look how pathetic I have become. I used to have such heart. Before the war, even during it at first, it was as if I was riding on this wave of purpose, of love, even. Now I grub about, looking for ways to make Edmund's life possible, and my own, because it turns out that we are not vital after all, he and I, but insignificant and tainted.'

'Not to me. Never to me.'

'I know. But every time I reach for some way to extend myself or use my talents, I am knocked back. I think to myself, well then, I'll get political and join the Labour Party. Surely they will be sympathetic. Instead I find they are just as hostile to women as everyone else and won't so much as discuss the issue of birth control. Even my paintings cannot be done properly here. I'm forever peering through the gloom of some badly lit room and I don't want to paint greyness. I want my eyes to be open wide. I want light to flood into my life.'

'Then tell me about this Angus.'

When she laughed, her face lost its tension and instead filled with mischief. 'Oh, Angus! He's just a bit of a drifter who says he's in love with me. The thing is, we're both using each other so it's all right. And he has a kind of aunt who owns an apartment in Sanary so it will be very cheap.'

'Is that the only reason you're going with him?'

'You mean, do I love him? Of course I don't. Angus understands that I feel pretty indifferent but he seems happy enough with the little I give him. And don't look so worried. All I do is tease him and in return he flirts with me. I'm pretty sure he doesn't want a full-blown love affair any more than I do, at least not with me – or indeed any woman. So it's convenient for Angus too, because he's escaping a father who despairs of him. Angus is a rich man's son and incapable of earning money, but he likes the idea of being an artist.'

'You sound so cold.'

'Perhaps I do. Sometimes I frighten myself because I can't seem to love anyone.' She fell back in the chair and was herself again, truthful and reflective. 'I used to love God of course, when I wanted to become a nun, but now I wonder if that wasn't a substitute for a lack of human love . . . I was too cold and detached for proper love, so I went for an idea.'

'I don't think you're cold at all. You're not detached from Edmund.'

'Oh well, yes, of course I love my son. And there's you, by the way. I love you for sure, despite your infuriating determination to do the right thing, even at the cost of not doing the most beautiful or exciting thing.'

'That's not how I see myself at all,' I said, a little discomfited by so frank a declaration.

'You can't know how I have sat here on the sidelines of your life and so admired you and so wanted to be you, and at the same time thought: if only she would let go. If only she would allow that passion that is all curled up inside her, like a spring, to be loosed.'

'Good heavens, Meredith, I wasn't aware of revealing much curled-up passion.' How adroit she was at pulling the rug from under me.

'You couldn't have fought your way into a legal career without it. And when I first came to your house, when your brother had been dead for six years, the air in the rooms still quivered with expectation because you were all longing for him to walk in. You stared at Edmund as if he were a little spectre from the past. Your mother has never forgiven him, of course, for being her son's child rather than her son, but you – you couldn't keep your eyes off him.

49

I used to worry that your love would burn him up, but of course it didn't because you are far too measured for that, too much in control.'

'Is that why you're taking Edmund away, because you think I love him too much?'

'Don't be ridiculous. What I'm saying is *you* can love, really you can. Remember, I saw you once, when you were in love with the man called Nicholas. You were molten. And when it was over you were so broken you *gaped* with the loss of it. I would have given everything I possessed to have felt as deeply as you did in that moment, although I could see you were suffering. And since then, although you hardly speak of him, I know that you yearn for him still. I've seen you riffling through the post at your mother's house, or sitting at the window with your eyes all sorrowful, and I've thought: if only I could love like that.'

I drank the last of the whisky. The trouble with Meredith was that her artist's eyes saw far too much. No wonder I frustrated her, if all this time she had sensed my repressed desire for Nicholas – a desire that I would never properly admit, even to myself. Self-restraint, among Gifford women, had always been regarded as a virtue, but perhaps it was only a step away from self-delusion.

'Even your Aunt Prudence, even she can love better than I do. In her, duty and love collide and become something rather hard but unwavering, nonetheless,' Meredith said. 'But who knows what I might discover about myself if my hands were always warm and the sun shone all day? And then, Edmund will be safer among artists, people who don't care about all these rules. And to crown it all there's this unrest brewing in England. Everyone says that if there's a general strike, there's bound to be violence on the streets.'

'I hope that's an exaggeration.'

'If I stayed, I would want to fight like your grandmother. I would take Edmund by the hand and lead him out among the strikers and show him that this is what happens when all the power and all the wealth are in the hands of the uncaring few.'

'Then why don't you stay if you feel so strongly?'

'Because it's not my battle and since nobody wants me in England, nobody deserves my support. I feel peevish about it. So I'll extract us both and take us to a safe place where we won't get embroiled.' Her fingers played in my hair as she asked, much more gently. 'What will you do, then, dearest Evie, when we're gone?'

I lay on the hearthrug, propped my head on my hand and watched the flames. 'I'll stay in this flat if I can. I've decided that. I'll work. And I'll try to forge other friendships.'

'That's what I hope – as long as you don't quite forget about us. But perhaps it is fortuitous that I'm going away,' Meredith said. 'We can't go on bickering like this. And when I come back maybe you and I will live together again, or maybe not. Either way we should each pledge that we will allow the other to choose freely. And perhaps you really will come to France and visit us there. Can you imagine a blue, blue sea? And sunshine? Can't you visualise the colour of it already? Won't you come?'

# Chapter Eight

Mrs Fitzgerald, Trudy Wright's would-be employer, occupied a brick-built semi-detached villa in Ealing that was approached by a chequerboard path of black and white tiles, with undulating lead edging to the lawn and unpromising hydrangea bushes under the window.

The lady of the house was in the front drawing room, which was dimmed by thick net curtains – plain but clean, as Prudence might have described them – and furnished in undemonstrative shades of beige and pale blue. She was a woman of about forty with a large nose and earnest grey eyes. Her voice was so bright and girlish and her smile so ready that for a moment I allowed myself to hope.

'You say that Gertrude Wright has been involved in a criminal matter?' she said. 'How extraordinary. I thought her such a shy little girl when I interviewed her.'

'The point is, Mrs Fitzgerald, I wanted to explain in person why no reference will be forthcoming from her previous employer. I think, when you understand what's happened, you'll gladly take Trudy on.'

Mrs Fitzgerald seized the hat that had been resting on the arm of her chair. 'This sounds very complicated,' she said with a trilling laugh. 'Gertrude was a straightforward girl, I thought. That's what I liked about her. Not bright but hard-working was my verdict. But then it's always the way. I'm afraid my bridge club starts at . . .'

I explained about the burnt letter while Mrs Fitzgerald was pinning the hat into place, but I knew by then that I was wasting my time.

'My husband works in taxation,' she said, 'for the government. Everything must be above board.'

'She's done nothing wrong.'

She raised an eyebrow. 'But then, you see, there's no smoke without fire, as I used to tell the children when they were small. I'm so sorry; I forget who you said you were in your letter. Some sort of legal—'

'I'm a solicitor. I represented Trudy – Miss Wright – in court.'

'How wonderful, a woman lawyer.' Her eyes were now as hard as marbles. 'But how do you stand it, all these sordid little cases? Don't they keep you awake at night? I prefer to leave that kind of thing to the men. Old-fashioned of me, I know.' She consulted the minuscule face of a china clock. 'And now I'm afraid I really must dash.'

'You won't reconsider employing Gertrude then, perhaps on a trial basis? She said that she thought you were very kind when she met you—'

'Miss Gifford, we are discussing someone who would be living in my home. In this house we have always counted the servants as part of the family – I have never hesitated to call a doctor if one of them falls sick. And you tell me this girl is in the habit of burning letters? My goodness, she sounds like a Bolshevik. No, and I'm amazed you should ask. But then, I suppose you have to if you're being paid for this.'

'Actually I came here voluntarily because I was concerned for Trudy. The fact is she will now find it very difficult to get domestic work.'

'Exactly my point. And you are trying to fob her off on me. Excuse me, Mrs Webb will see you out.' She departed, too flustered to consider the risk of leaving me, the representative of a letter-burning felon, alone in her domain.

The Wrights' battered front door had been painted green so long ago that patches of maroon showed through. Since there was no knocker I used my knuckles. Nobody answered although I could hear a male voice shouting from within. After my second knock the door flew open and I was confronted by a young man with a mop of tangled hair, dark, angry eyes and a face ingrained with soot.

He shot past me, then turned back and demanded, 'Who are you? Are you from the welfare? Who sent you?'

'Nobody sent me. I'm Miss Gifford, Gertrude's solicitor.'

His rough, strong hand gripped my wrist. 'I'm Robbie, Trudy's brother. She told me about you getting her off in court. Thank Christ you're here!'

'Why? What has happened?'

'I've got to go,' he muttered, 'but make sure you get a look at ma's face. Promise me.'

Gertrude Wright had appeared, pale even to her lips, and with her unwashed hair scraped back. She stared at me, aghast. 'Miss Gifford.' She was thinner than I remembered, wearing a buttoned-up cardigan over a crumpled cotton dress, and her hands were swollen and wet. 'It's all right, Robbie,' she told the young man. 'I'll deal with this.'

'It's not bloody all right. I keep telling you – he's got to go.' His eyes pleaded with me to pay attention. 'Tell her what happened, Trudy. I'll be late.' And he darted off along the street.

No invitation to step inside was forthcoming from Gertrude, though the rain was falling steadily. 'I wondered if we might have a word,' I said.

'Is it about Mrs Fitzgerald? Did you go and see her?'

'I did, but she's not prepared to employ you, I'm afraid. However, I've written you this character reference. I could also write to Mrs Derbyshire and demand she pays you the money she owes.'

'For God's sake don't do that! It might upset her even more.'

A male voice yelled, 'Shut the bloody door for Christ's sake! There's a fucking draft. Who in Christ's name is it?'

'No one,' called Trudy sharply and she began to close the door.

Too late: the father appeared. At the sight of me he stood up straighter and ran his hand over his hair which had been cut very short and was textured like the pelt of a dog. 'I do beg your pardon,' he said, with mock refinement. The top buttons of his collarless shirt had been left undone, showing off his fleshy throat.

'Miss Gifford writ me a reference,' said Trudy.

'Well ain't that kind.'

'Not at all,' I said.

'A cup of tea?' he suggested, his blue gaze travelling insolently from my eyes to my breasts, stomach and thighs. 'We should offer the lady a cup of tea at least. Where are your manners, Trude?'

'The kettle's not boiled, Father.' She held the door half-shut while he loomed at her shoulder.

'You ask the lady in,' he insisted, still staring. Even more frightened, she nodded and I shook out my umbrella, propped it by the door and followed her through a chill parlour. Three assorted chairs were arranged around the empty hearth and a gate-legged table stood in the window adorned with a doily and a statuette of a shepherdess.

'It's warmer in the back,' Wright was at my shoulder, reeking of stale tobacco. 'Take her in, Trudy.'

Beyond the steep staircase was a back room. The house was so silent that it was a shock to find three little girls ranged around the table, aged between about five and ten. The two oldest were tearing a chain of dollies from a sheet of newspaper folded into a fan but the third rested her chin on her arm and gawped at me from an infected eye. The rest of the room ought to have been cheerful – I had encountered a dozen similar in my career thus far – with its sole armchair drawn up close to the range upon which a kettle simmered. On the head-high mantelpiece were arranged an oak-cased clock, a jug, a teapot and a couple of decorative plates. Wright offered me the chair and then, when I refused, sat in it himself, his fists clenched on the arms as if he were upon a throne. There was no sign of a mother.

'You'll be wondering why the kids ain't at school. Before you take us to court,' he winked conspiratorially, 'I'll hold up my hands and tell you: no shoes. The state wants them to go to school but it won't clothe them.'

Without shifting his gaze from my face he dipped his hand in his pocket, took out his tobacco tin and rolled a cigarette. Upstairs a bedspring creaked. 'Wife's sick,' he said, watching his daughter pour water from kettle to pot. 'I have to hold this family together single-handed. So tell me again, Miss, what you want.'

'I was concerned that Trudy might have difficulty getting another job and I wanted to help.'

'Oh, jolly good. Are you going to find us all work? Know anyone in the haulage business who'd like to take me on, a man with a ruined back?'

'I'm sorry to hear you're unwell.'

His gaze bored into me. 'Yes, well, some of us been through a war.'

'There might be assistance, if you need it. I could look into it for you.'

A strand of hair had fallen over Trudy's nose and tea slopped over the sides of the pot as she stirred the leaves. 'You mean from the corporation?' Wright said. 'That's for shirkers and wastrels. I've never asked anyone for help.' He favoured me with that charmer's smile of his. 'And I don't, as I recall, remember asking *you*.'

'Father,' Trudy protested, handing me a cup. 'Miss Gifford has been so kind to me. She got me off.'

'So she did. Trouble is, I don't expect kindness from strangers. I always think there's a catch. You'll have to excuse me.'

'Really, Miss Gifford, there's no need to worry about us,' said Trudy. 'Robbie, my older brother, he earns quite well. The one you just met. He's in the coal.'

'He'll be out on strike any moment now,' snapped the father. 'Like a lamb to the slaughter, and they'll not have him back. None of my kids do what I say, that's the trouble.' He grinned at me as if to ask: what is a poor fellow to do with such a wayward lot? 'I told Trudy, if you're going into service, keep your head down. But she weren't satisfied, got too big for her boots. See what happened?'

'She was being paid very little by Mrs Derbyshire.'

'Probably all she was worth, knowing my Trudy.' He winked at me again. 'Not the sharpest knife in the tray, eh, Trude?'

A door closed on the floor above and there were unsteady footsteps on the stairs. The children froze and Trudy glanced nervously first at her father, then me. 'Thanks for calling, Miss Gifford,' she said. 'It's very kind of you. I'll show you out, shall I?'

The father nodded. I put down my cup then adjusted my hat while Trudy held the door open, glancing up the stairs behind her.

'This way, Miss Gifford, please.' But a woman had appeared on the landing, shivering spasmodically and clutching a faded, too-large cotton dress about her body. Gripping the banister, she descended one step at a time. Her feet were naked and the hair falling across her eyes did not conceal the damage to her face; a cheek so battered that her distorted lip was drawn up, revealing broken teeth.

'You should be in bed, Mother,' said Trudy.

'Call of nature.' Mrs Wright grasped the door frame, sucking back saliva so it wouldn't drip through her stiff lip.

Behind us Wright sat with his knees apart, arms crossed, knuckles white on the chair arms. 'I'm Miss Gifford, Trudy's lawyer,' I told his wife. 'I represented her in court.'

It occurred to me that Wright must have wanted me to see his handiwork. He, after all, had insisted on me entering the house. He had seemed to resent my success in court, so perhaps this was his way of rendering me as powerless as the other women in the room.

Mrs Wright nodded and glanced towards Wright. Her mouth could scarcely form words. 'Trudy said you was a good woman.'

'Have you seen a doctor?'

She shook her head and again her eyes shifted to her husband. 'I'm quite all right, thank you. Only clumsy, as ever.'

'What happened? Can I help at all?'

'You can't help a woman who will go tumbling down the stairs, I suppose.' There was such a pleading softness in her brown eyes as she glanced at her silent children that I registered for the first time a mother's touches in that bleak little room: children's pictures pinned to the door, a cross-stitch pot holder for the kettle, a child-sized pink gingham pinafore hanging on the door.

Trudy pressed me onwards but I turned back and looked directly into the mother's bruised eyes. 'Are you sure I can't help?'

'No, no, I'm well cared for here by Trudy. Excuse me. Like I said, I was on my way through to the yard.'

I stepped outside and opened my umbrella. Trudy's face was closed up tight. 'You've been a great help Miss Gifford, really. But we're fine. Thank you. No need to trouble yourself with us any further.'

'What happened to your mother, Miss Wright?'

'I have no idea.'

'Did anyone call the police?'

'Please,' she had already half shut the door. 'I beg you, leave us alone.'

# Chapter Nine

The Wright family haunted me. Again and again Mrs Wright appeared at the top of the stairs, clasped the banister and spoke to me through shaking lips, or I remembered the boy Robbie and how his eyes had been full of rage and anxiety; the release of pent-up energy as he ran off down the street. And the silence within the back room, the little girls frozen under their father's stare, the infected eye with its yellow crust.

'I see a dozen women like Mrs Wright every day at the clinics,' said Meredith when I told her. 'You cannot help her unless she wants you to.'

'Then why did she show me her face?'

'Perhaps it was a first step. But Evie, not even you can save someone who denies she's being struck.'

She was right, of course. Breen & Balcombe rarely dealt with cases of wife beating because the outcome was always the same: the woman pulled out before the hearing. Breen, usually so determined to support the weak against an oppressor, hated such cases and the atmosphere at Breen & Balcombe was dismal when we agreed to take one on. Occasionally a woman would scuttle along the hall to his office in the wake of queenly Miss Drake, who always supplied such a victim with a pitying glance and three garibaldi biscuits rather than two, but as far as I knew not even Breen had ever persuaded a woman to give evidence against her husband in court.

Meanwhile I was dealing with a troubled marriage of an entirely different nature. On the day before Lady Petit's appointment at our office a missive arrived written on such luxuriant paper that each typed letter was embedded, as if on a cushion. So impressed was Miss Drake that she actually brought it down to me in person.

From a well-respected, not to say swanky firm of solicitors, Pearman & Washbourne, it read:

*Dear Miss Gifford,*

*Our client, Sir Timothy Petit, understands that you have been appointed the legal representative of his spouse, Lady Petit.*

*I am instructed by Sir Timothy, lest you be under any misapprehension, to inform you that these legal proceedings have been provoked entirely by his wife, who has forced his hand in the matter. He regards a public argument over the paternity of the child, Annice, as a last resort and in nobody's best interest.*

*Sir Timothy had no intention of taking this matter to court, indeed was disinclined to question his paternity of the child until the matter was raised by his wife following an argument, even though the circumstances in which the child was allegedly conceived had always seemed to him highly questionable. Once Lady Petit had informed Sir Timothy of the identity of the child's true father, he offered her the opportunity of a separation, which would have been a private agreement on exceedingly generous terms to herself and the child, but she would not hear of it, instead reversed the allegations she had made and accused Sir Timothy of deliberately and maliciously casting doubts on his paternity. Sir Timothy has several witnesses, including medical men of the highest professional standing to support his claim. Should he win the case, your client would of course be required to pay our costs in this matter and she could have no expectation of any form of financial assistance for herself or the child in the future.*

*My client also instructs me to inform you that there are circumstances relating to his wife's health which demand that this matter should be settled expeditiously and out of court if possible. During the four years of their marriage he has witnessed numerous fits of irrational behaviour that reveal a severe disturbance of mind. He has, indeed, spared no expense in seeking treatment for her. It is for her sake, therefore, as much as his own, and of course the child's, that he would prefer affairs to be settled out of court, between lawyers.*

*I look forward to meeting you at the earliest possible mutually convenient date,*
*Yours sincerely,*
*Ralph Pearman.*

The following morning Miss Drake received a telephone call from Lady Petit who said that as she was terribly busy and short-staffed would I meet her in her Maple Street gallery during her lunch break. Meredith, who had taken it upon herself to visit the gallery incognito and *do a recce*, as she put it, had told me that in order to understand a woman like Annabel Petit I really should familiarise myself with her world. It therefore suited me to see where she worked although I wondered, as I dashed off to Bow Street Magistrates' Court next morning, dragged down by the weight of papers generated by three criminal cases (shop theft of five handkerchiefs, attempted arson of a motor vehicle and the overzealous punishment of a young child), what *terribly busy* meant to the proprietor of an art gallery.

It was the beginning of April and a sappy perfume wafted above the paving stones and among the emerging green leaves. When I pushed open the glass door to the gallery there was no sign of Lady Petit but a sharp-eyed girl with glossy hair and beautiful legs was perched on a desk, staring into space, while a couple of ladies in furs and with the kind of willowy figures only the very rich achieve, were exclaiming over a print. The girl took my name, disappeared briefly through a door, then returned and slid sinuously into a chair behind the desk.

I had lived with Meredith long enough to feel at home with art, even in a gallery as dauntingly intimate as this. On Saturdays she, Edmund and I often visited public galleries and museums, or burrowed our way through market stalls, and under her tuition I had learned to handle pottery and discuss paintings almost as confidently as I dealt with legal documents. Nevertheless, this domain of Lady Petit's was an exclusive one. In a city where space was costly there were naked expanses of white-painted wall and the display cabinets and plinths were arranged sparsely about the floor. The Petit Gallery specialised in esoteric glassware. 'She has real taste,' had been Meredith's verdict. 'Whatever else she might be, she is not an amateur when it comes to buying art.' Pieces of unearthly loveliness winked in the electric light: medicine bottles, decanters, fragile drinking glasses with split stems by Lalique, a mirror with a gilt frame wrought by a Hungarian called Lajos Kozma. Though each object was labelled, as in a museum, none was priced.

Eventually the be-furred ladies headed towards the door and I imagined them tip-tapping across the pavement and entering some expensive restaurant, smaller and less overtly ostentatious than the one I'd visited with Breen, and ordering white wine so pale that it barely tinted the glass. Next I heard laughter as the door to an inner room opened and I saw Annabel Petit, who was wearing red, at a sartorial disadvantage because she was accompanied by a woman six inches taller whose understated dark grey costume was trimmed with a small white collar and a row of little white buttons from neck to dropped waist, and whose pale shining hair was scooped into a chignon which on any other woman would have been unfashionable but on her was supremely elegant.

'Miss Gifford,' cried Lady Petit, tripping towards me with the dog at her heels, 'you came.'

'I've been here a while.'

She introduced her friend as Kit Porter and me as, 'The marvellous Miss Gifford I've been telling you about, Kit.'

Kit was *gamine* (the word with which Aunt Prudence described women who lacked a bosom), with an unusually long white neck upon which the heavy knot of her hair rested almost like a burden. The fabric of her gown clung to the long lines of her body. 'Oh heavens,' she said, 'my first woman lawyer. Well, you don't look in the least like one but then Bella told me you didn't. She said you've got to see her, she's a marvel.' The enthusiasm of her words was belied by her strangely flat voice, as if she could not quite summon the energy to vary her tone.

'Kit's going to sit in,' said Annabel.

'Unless you're intending to say terribly private things,' put in Kit indifferently. The similarity between her narrow face and the greyhound's was uncanny; the dog apparently thought so too because it gazed up at her adoringly. Her cool eye had fallen on a writing set laid out on a desk and with a tapering white finger she touched the red leather case.

'Suetin. Absolutely *ideal*,' said Annabel, 'for someone's birthday. How about your brother, wouldn't he just love it?'

'Brilliant idea,' said Kit, 'but I thought some wonderful wine.' The uninterested voice, the casual brushing aside of Annabel's suggestion, seemed to me a little chilling.

'I don't have much time,' I said, though aware that this insistence on getting back to business placed me in a social position well beneath theirs. Lady Petit looked taken aback but ordered the assistant, Claire, to serve us coffee, and then told her to leave us absolutely in peace for at least an hour. A silver coffee pot appeared, gracefully curved beneath the spout, with three tiny cups and then at last we all settled in a back office, Lady Petit and Kit on one side of a catastrophically untidy desk, myself on the other and the dog obligingly coiled on a cushion in a wicker basket.

'First,' I said, 'you should read this letter from your husband's solicitor.'

While Lady Petit read Pearman's letter, I sipped tepid coffee and noticed that part of the room was incongruously equipped as a child's nursery. Picture books were piled on a shelf along with a doll's tea set, and there was a large photograph of a solemn Annice wearing a sunsuit and bonnet. Kit Porter picked up a glass bowl from the desk and turned it to study the design of grappling, naked wrestlers. Lady Petit, who had withdrawn a pair of wire-rimmed spectacles from her little bag, gripped the thick paper in both hands so that the edges creased, then, having passed it wordlessly to Kit, pressed her hands to her face.

'Pearman's right. It's all my fault,' she said in that broken voice of hers. 'I pushed Timmo too far. It's what I've done all my life. That's the reason I married him in the first place. I couldn't stop it happening.'

Kit, having swiftly read the letter, laid her upper arm along the back of her chair and examined her friend gravely. 'I thought it was more a case of Timmo making a play for *you*. He and my late husband were pals,' she told me with the flicker of a smile, 'so we are all terribly close.'

'You've probably seen from pictures of Timmo that he's very

beautiful,' said Annabel. 'At the end of the war he was in business with Father and just starting up in politics. All the girls thought him rather dazzling. When he proposed to me I was so shocked I didn't know what to say.'

Kit, who had been conducting an examination of her own beautiful fingers, now leaned forward and said, 'I would have thought you'd be the first to understand how terribly impulsive we girls can be, Miss Gifford. After all, you've had the most fascinating love life from what we've heard.'

There was a stunned silence while Kit pressed the back of her hand lightly to her mouth and observed my reaction from cat-like eyes. Of course I should have seen this coming. During our first meeting Annabel had talked of being in the same circle as Lady Curren who would have known all about my presumptuous affair with Nicholas Thorne. He had been engaged to one of their set, after all, and his defection to me must have created quite a stir.

'Lady Petit, in his letter Mr Pearman says that it was you who raised the whole question of Annice's paternity,' I said briskly, 'and that you told your husband the identity of the child's real father.'

'Yes, but it wasn't true,' she cried. 'Timmo knows that. I just wanted to get a reaction. For the last few months he's been so cold and hardly takes me anywhere.'

'Be honest, Bel, you never liked his political crowd,' put in Kit with a deep sigh, as if this was well-worn territory.

'That's not the point. It's just so obvious that Timmo would much rather I wasn't around. Well, I got fed up with it. You know when you're standing on the edge of a cliff and you lean over and there's a part of you thinking: how much further should I lean, and what would it feel like to fall? That's what it felt like when I told Timmo that he wasn't the father of Annice.'

'Tell Miss Gifford who you said *was* the father,' said Kit, holding up the bowl as if it were a chalice.

'Richie Leremer.' Lady Petit pronounced the name as if it was bound to be the answer to all my queries but it struck only a faint chord. 'You *must* have heard of Richie, he's a socialist, was even a member of parliament with the Labour Party for a brief spell. Timmo can't abide him. That's why I did it.'

'You did it because you knew it would ring true. You've always had a thing going with Leremer,' put in Kit.

'A thing?' Lady Petit sat quite still, her eyes full of fear and something indefinable, a kind of submerged longing. 'Well, yes, I suppose . . . Anyway, one night Timmo went out even though I had a blinding headache and I waited up for him until dawn, just sitting on a hard chair and drinking brandy to keep warm. When he came in we had this screaming row and at last I said, "You think I don't matter and that you can do anything you like but there's one part of me you can never reach." And I told him that Annice wasn't his child but Richie's.

'He looked as if he'd been stabbed and the next day he told me he was divorcing me. I was on my knees, clinging to his legs, telling him I was so, so sorry and hadn't meant it but he just waited until I let go. Since then he's scarcely spoken to me. And he won't see Annice though she keeps asking for him.'

'Lady Petit,' I said softly, 'did you ever have a relationship with Mr Leremer?'

'Before I was married.'

Kit threw back her head and grimaced at the ceiling. 'Oh, come on, Bel, you've been with him since then.'

'Of course I saw him when I came back from honeymoon but I didn't sleep with him.'

'So Leremer definitely isn't Annice's father,' I said.

'*Timmo* is her father, I keep telling you. She was conceived on the night of 24 June on the boat train when we were on our way back from honeymoon.'

Kit was now skimming the rim of the glass bowl with the tip of her index finger and a faint glow had infused her pale cheeks. 'Honestly, Bel, do you really want me to hear this again?'

'I can't hide anything from you. I need you,' and Lady Petit leaned across the desk, seized Kit's hand and peppered it with kisses. 'So much.'

Kit folded her arms, extended her long legs under the desk and with the toe of her elegant shoe stroked her friend's calf. 'Go on then, tell Miss Gifford all. You must.'

Lady Petit pressed her palms to her cheekbones and her forehead contorted with the pain of remembering. 'For my wedding

I had a gown by Jeanne Paquin and a honeymoon in Paris. Kit says it was rather flashy of Timmo to have chosen the Ritz but I didn't mind. All kinds of people were there: Laurencin, Bourdelle, Pompon, *everyone*.' She obviously did not expect me to have heard of these luminaries but actually Meredith and I had viewed Laurencin's plaintive *Portrait of a Woman*, with the slash of a black scarf about the subject's pale throat, like a wound.

She plunged on, 'The trouble was that at night we would go to some club or other and get horribly drunk and fall into bed and . . . nothing, because frankly neither of us was conscious. Next morning he'd be up and into the bathroom before I was awake. He'd bring me coffee, sweet as anything. And out we would go.

'During the day he seemed to be in love with me. We visited studios and he presented me practically with a blank cheque so I could buy my favourite pieces. Soon I had enough to stock this gallery a dozen times over. But at night . . .' In the charged silence the dog stirred uneasily in its bed and lay, sphinx-like, with its head on its paws. 'He said it was the war, and being in France, and memories. It was only on the way home on the train that we – you know – made love, although now he's saying we never did.'

'Lady Petit, I have to be clear. Is your husband going to claim that you and he have never made love at all?'

'That's exactly what he'll say. Because he didn't actually, you know . . . inside me. Anyway, a few weeks after that night on the train I realised I was carrying Annice. That's why we chose a name that had an English beginning and a French ending, because she'd been conceived halfway between the two countries.'

The atmosphere in that stuffy office, the smell of the women's perfume mingled with coffee grounds, the terrible intimacy of Lady Petit's disclosures and above all Kit Porter's aloof watchfulness made me long to escape. Closing my notebook I said, 'Lady Petit, I understand that you are telling me categorically that Annice is your husband's daughter. But are you sure you want to fight this? Shouldn't you consider a divorce if your husband no longer loves you?'

She sat bolt upright. 'I told you, I want Annice to have a father.'

'Miss Gifford has a point though,' Kit said soothingly. 'Why on earth you still want to stay married to Timmo is beyond me.'

'Don't talk like that. I hate it when you pretend to be so cynical, Kit. Ask Richie,' said Lady Petit suddenly. 'Ask him if he and I slept together. He'll tell you the truth.' Her complexion was deathly white as she woke the greyhound with her foot. He seemed resigned to having his sleep disturbed and obligingly put his paws on the chair and licked her cheek. 'In that horrible letter Pearman says I'm ill. I'm not. Or at least I don't want to be. For Annice's sake I am resolved to be strong. You've got to help me, Miss Gifford. I know you can.'

'Then my next step must be to write to Pearman and tell him that we want a reconciliation.'

'That's *exactly* what I want. I knew you'd understand. Thank you so much, Miss Gifford!' And she fell back against the chair, as if satisfied that she'd passed the entire burden of her life over to me.

Kit showed me out, manoeuvring expertly among the glass shelves and ignoring Claire who twirled a lock of short hair with her index finger and watched us keenly. But after she'd unfastened the door Kit placed her hand lightly on my arm. 'Bel is terribly sick, you know, whatever she says. We're all appalled that she wants to take this to court. It will destroy her. She cannot have a hope of winning, surely?'

When I didn't reply she observed. 'Nobody ever wins against Timmo.' Dipping her long neck, like a swan, she added, 'Nobody.'

As I walked away through the softness of the spring afternoon I reflected that Breen had been right and that this was a case for which I was totally ill-equipped. For a start, I had no idea if a child could be conceived as Lady Petit suggested. Thank goodness for Meredith, who would doubtless set me straight. But once again it was the child Annice who put fresh determination into my step. Her identity was being manipulated as if she were nothing more than a marital pawn. I began to relish the prospect of an interview with Richie Leremer and afterwards Pearman, he of the opulent notepaper.

But while crossing Fitzroy Square, I received such a shock that I stopped dead in my tracks and thought no more about Lady Petit and Annice because I recognised the height of the man who had just emerged from a little French restaurant on Fitzroy Street, the tilt of his head, the particular lift of his elbow as he manoeuvred his hat to a more comfortable angle. I almost cried out and started forward until I registered that his companion was a young woman with a pert little upturned face and that he was holding out her coat which had a silken lining; when she turned her back on him and shrugged it on I imagined the cool slither of the fabric along her arms. She glanced over her shoulder to smile at him again, reached up her gloved left hand and tucked it under his arm, and together they walked away, swept along by the April breeze. I'd scarcely seen his face, just caught the merest hint of his old smile and the fact that his moustache was gone but there could be no doubt that it was him, Nicholas Thorne.

I was aware of a brief flurry of traffic: a bicycle, a delivery cart, a green van with gold lettering. Nicholas and his companion turned a corner and disappeared – his head was inclined to catch something she said, just as he used to lean towards me. So he was back in London. But for how long? For a holiday? For good?

There had been a self-consciousness about his companion that suggested insecurity, a touch of flirtatiousness in her smile.

Well then, I told myself as I walked on at last, he's in London, Evelyn. And the truth is that he's not made the least effort to see you. But then why would he, given that you told him you couldn't forgive him and when he wrote to you didn't reply but instead burnt his letter? It was you who wanted it to end so why do you keep hankering after him?

Because, I thought, I'll never know what he said in that letter. I never gave him another chance and perhaps I was too harsh.

But he was complicit in a man's betrayal and death – isn't that enough?

He might have changed. I might have got it wrong . . .

Thus did I torment myself, over and over again. The city hurt me with its harsh paving stones and glass shopfronts, and the brief walk back to Arbery Street felt as if it was too difficult a journey to make. A bad judgement while crossing the Euston Road caused me to spring out of the way of a taxicab and afterwards I waited on the far side in the wind and fumes, my eyes stinging and my heart pounding as I struggled to adjust.

# Chapter Ten

In light of Meredith and Edmund's imminent departure, and especially since I still had not recovered from the shock of seeing Nicholas Thorne again, I did not relish the prospect of spending a Saturday afternoon with Mother, sorting through a dead woman's things. Nevertheless, we began purposefully by removing all the clothes from the wardrobe and drawers and piling them on the bed. Mother declared that Meredith should be the recipient, grateful or otherwise, of the best of these garments which were far too small for the rest of us. I guessed Meredith would love the pleated silk petticoats and tight-bodiced pre-war gowns, although they would have no place by the sea in France. The more intimate, darned or faded items we packed away in suitcases for the next church sale and, like all discarded garments, they immediately looked shabby and formless.

'I'm not sure Mrs Gillespie will want them,' Mother said doubtfully, 'even though the lace is so beautiful.'

The difficulty was that most of Grandmother's possessions had a story, which was why Edmund and, before him, Jamie and I, had been so drawn to her room. On the dressing table was an ancient, octagonal tin with an identical painting of a flaxen-haired girl on each face, in which she'd kept bonbons, bought clandestinely by Rose.

'Used to be for sugared biscuits, to sustain me between a matinée and an evening performance,' Grandmother told us. She had a gramophone which smelt divinely of teak oil and baize – 'A very dear pupil gave me that when he was made captain of a ship – said his promotion was all thanks to losing his lisp' – and folded away in a chest she kept a high-waisted dress of palest green muslin, its white stitching rotten. She claimed it had been her own grandmother's when she was a child. 'Do you know, Evie, I think it was this gown that inspired me to become an actress. She was on the stage you know, and she dressed me up in it sometimes. I could never get over how different I felt in someone else's clothes.'

There was even a hairpiece, made out of real hair the colour of my own and kept in a cigar box, which she had worn in *She Stoops to Conquer*. As a child I had viewed this last exhibit with horror and would not touch it because Grandmother said it was from the head of a dead person, or at the very least someone who'd been *reduced* to selling her own hair.

'That should definitely go in the rubbish box,' said Mother, then took it out again because it might be worth something.

There was very little jewellery but Mother gave me a silver brooch wrought in the shape of an edelweiss, and we chose a necklace for Meredith (garnet) and one for Prudence (jet). Mother chose a locket. 'Is there a photograph or picture inside?' I asked. 'Shouldn't there be?'

She inserted her thumbnail and flipped it open. 'Nothing.'

Edmund was to have the buttons and some of the books, though we decided to sort through them another day. Instead we set to work on the bottom of the wardrobe and after we'd burrowed through the slippers and little lace-up boots we came upon a writing box, which I lifted out and set on the floor between us. Amid all the shabby footwear and soft old clothes, the box was wonderfully solid and compact. A length of string had been tied round it on to which were secured a key and a label inscribed in Grandmother's large, laborious hand: *For Evelyn*.

'How very odd of her. That old thing will be of no use to you at all,' exclaimed Mother irritably. 'I used to play with it as a child. Post offices. It will just clutter up your room – totally impractical.'

But I remembered the writing box very well. Of all the many treasures in the room, it had been my favourite. At the centre of its polished walnut lid was a brass plaque engraved with Grandmother's maiden name, Clara Fielding, and it had further brass trim at the corners and around the lid. When I was a child she used to scrabble about for the key in a dressing-table drawer then show me how the box opened to become a sloping desk with a scarred leather surface. There were slots for pens, nibs and sealing wax and, at either end, squat ink bottles.

Best of all was a wooden partition which could be wrenched up to reveal two small drawers, each with an ivory handle the size of a grape pip.

'What are they for?' I had asked.

'Precious things,' she replied firmly, 'such as love letters.'

She always tucked something away in the box for me to discover: a square of chocolate, a green glass bead, a windmill charm for my bracelet with sails that actually turned. Now, when I unlocked the lid I took greedy inhalations of the smell: raw wood and Grandmother, the perfume of all her unmentionable years ... Because she had been nearly blind for so long and unable to write letters, the contents of the ink bottles had turned to powder and the stationery was yellowed at the edges.

Mother had lost interest and was moving about as if touring a stately home. 'Don't you think that this really is a beautiful room?'

My heart sank because I knew that the conversation I'd been fending off all afternoon was upon me. 'The ceiling is too high and Grandmother always found it rather draughty because of the bay,' I said discouragingly.

'But in the summer it's full of light. I often wish your father and I had chosen this room for ourselves. When you come back, Evie, I think you should have this room and new lace curtains and fresh wallpaper. What colour would you like?'

I locked the writing case, retied the string and said, as calmly as possible, 'I won't be coming back.'

'Of course you won't, not straight away. But when Meredith and Edmund have gone and Prudence is in India you'll *have* to.' She settled on the arm of an old chair, triumphant. 'There certainly won't be the money to keep up two places.'

'I'm going to stay on in the flat. We'll have to find some other financial solution.'

'Please don't use that word. It's not about a *solution*. It's about duty. I want you home, Evelyn, isn't that reason enough?'

'Meredith and Prudence will both be back in a few months.'

'That's where you're wrong. Prudence tells me that if she does come back – apparently nothing is certain – she will return to her cottage in Buckinghamshire.'

I clutched the writing box to my chest and leaned my cheek on its tarnished surface. Prudence had inherited a cottage on my paternal grandfather's estate. When the family money disappeared – largely due to my father's profligacy – she had come to live in Clivedon Hall Gardens and all these years had received a small income from renting out her own property. For Mother, the cottage was merely a reminder of the ways in which Father had failed – but I had very particular memories of the little house, and could not speak of it without wincing.

'Heaven knows why she'd want to go back to that wretched place,' added Mother. 'I thought she'd find it very parochial after living here in Maida Vale. But she's been camping out there all this week, you know, having it painted so she can let it out again while she and Miss Lord are in *India*.' She spoke this last word as if the country were a figment of Prudence's imagination. 'And you know Mother has left us nothing at all but this worthless stuff. There's no money, Evie. When Meredith and the boy come back they will be very welcome to live here too, so we'll be together and it will be so much cheaper.'

I'd let her continue long enough in this fantasy. 'Mother, you were never comfortable when Meredith and Edmund were living here.'

'What nonsense! He's my grandchild. Of course I'd like him to live here.' Her mouth was downturned, a preface to tears. 'You can't abandon me. I accept that you would have to work and come and go exactly as you pleased but at least you would be some kind of companion for me in the evenings. Can't you see how terribly lonely I am? Why are you being so hard-hearted?'

'Because this is your home, not mine, and I can't be myself here. This house is full of memories,' I was speaking as soothingly as possible, 'and I for one don't want to be constantly living among them. I want to be *free*. That's why I'm going to keep on the flat, even though I can scarcely afford to live there on my own.'

'Oh, how I abhor this modern obsession with freedom. It's just another word for selfishness. Don't you see? It's for the sake of your father and your brother that we must keep the house on. This was their home. Your father worked all his life to provide for us comfortably and now you're prepared to throw it all away.'

This was hardly the moment to point out that due to his drinking, bad management and lack of foresight, Father had left us very far from comfortable. 'Not throw it away,' I said. 'The house can be a source of income for you if we set it up as a proper lodging house, or sell it.'

Mother turned her face aside as if I had struck her. 'Are you asking me to live in some squalid little flat like yours? By myself? What about the girls? They've worked for us for more than thirty years. Am I to turn them on to the street?'

'Then don't sell. Let out the rooms as I've suggested. You could have four or five women here, gentlemen, even. It might be fun.'

'*Fun*. Do you call it fun, that I should be reduced to keeping a sordid boarding house because my own daughter cannot bear to live with me? This is my home. It means everything to me. Think of what I have lost here.'

It was that melancholy time in an early spring afternoon when the light dims with a suddenness that transforms day into night in the blink of an eye. The house was even quieter than usual with Prudence in her Buckinghamshire cottage and the girls in their basement sitting room. Mother and I stared at each other helplessly, each willing the other to change but unwilling to make any compromises ourselves. All in all, it was high time I left before anything too rash or irreversible was said.

That night in the Pimlico flat Edmund and I unpacked the writing box while Meredith was out at a gathering of artists. First we sniffed its scent of resin and brass, then we took everything out and laid it on the table. Edmund, of course, was fascinated by the nibs and sticks of sealing wax, the dried-up ink bottles and the hinged writing surface. Out fell a tissue-wrapped parcel of pale blue hand-knitted bootees for a very small baby – Jamie's, for sure – and beneath them, in his unmistakable copperplate scrawl but written large so that its recipient would be able to read it, a letter on thin, lined paper addressed to *Dear G'mother*. It had been penned on the night before he was due to cross the Channel for the first time, and dotted with cartoon sketches of life in camp.

*Can't say wish you were here*, Jamie had written, *not sure you'd like the facilities* (sketch of shower block and stick figures quaking under the shower heads). *Thank the Lord we will be off soon. All in fine fettle but missing you, G'mother, and all the others.*

'Well, Edmund,' I murmured into his hair, 'it's been a very long time since I read this letter.'

He held the cheap page in his neat little hands and peered closely in case there was any more of his father to be found hidden behind the words. At the bottom of the letter was a sketch of a bed with another stick figure reclining upon it, so tall that its feet dangled off the end. 'He could draw too, like Mommy and me.'

In each of the other compartments of the writing box Grandmother had left me *a little something*, as she would have put it: a note from Ellen Terry: *Thanks so much for the violets, Clara. Shall you be coming to see my Portia?* A carved cat an inch tall, presented to Grandmother for good luck on the first night of *Othello*; a fine lawn handkerchief embroidered in blue with the initials *GM*.

As for the secret drawers, they eluded me. Edmund, of course, was fascinated by the idea of them but though we twitched and tweaked and pulled, we could not find the catch.

'Perhaps I imagined the secret drawer,' I said, 'it's so many years since she first showed me it.'

'You wouldn't imagine anything like that,' he said, disappointed in me.

He took to bed with him both the button box and his father's letter, which he tucked under his pillow.

# *Chapter Eleven*

At about three o'clock on the day that Breen and I had arranged to meet for supper he sprang into my office and announced that he'd like to change the rendezvous because he was off to observe a rally outside Wandsworth Prison. 'It's in support of the group of communists wrongfully gaoled last year for seditious libel. You ought to come with me, Miss Gifford, see for yourself what's going on.'

'Perhaps ...'

'Excellent. Although I warn you, there may be trouble. You'll see history in the making. And it'll be a test of the law on public demonstrations. I've had Miss Drake call a cab.'

He clattered back upstairs and I heard him yell to Miss Drake that I was going with him and that neither of us would be back until the following day. When I passed along the hall a few minutes later her typewriter was still silent – she disliked surprises of any kind.

Once in the taxicab Breen threw himself back on the grimy cushions and opened a copy of *The Times*. Because he knew I couldn't read in a moving vehicle without feeling sick, he fed me snippets while I watched the passing traffic on the Charing Cross Road and marvelled at the speed with which I'd been whisked away from my work.

'Our demonstration is disapproved of, needless to say. Joynson-Hicks says it justifies the locking up of these communists in the first place – he calls them rabble-rousers. I'm glad we're here. We might be needed.'

I couldn't help goading him a little. 'Mr Breen, you've never asked me what I actually think of the imprisonment of these communists.'

He looked utterly astonished. 'Forgive me. I had assumed that you would be on their side, given that their arrest was an abuse of the law. You must be, surely?'

'I am on the side of freedom of speech, of course. I do not believe these people should be criminalised . . .'

'Well then.'

'But it seems to me there is a blurring of my role here. It's one thing to choose to go on a political march – I may or may not do so – it's another to be there in a semi-professional capacity.'

His eyebrows had shot up. 'You didn't have to come with me.'

'You didn't really give me a chance to think about it. But in future I should like to be clear whether I'm making a professional or personal decision.'

So interested was the cab driver in our conversation that he narrowly missed a bicyclist who swerved against the kerb, lost his balance and had to jump hastily off his machine. We were now crossing Wandsworth Common and had caught up with the rally's stragglers: men in shabby overcoats and a mix of flat caps or brimmed hats, women in overlong skirts.

'I thought you'd be interested in attending the demonstration,' Breen said.

'I am interested.'

'But apparently I've coerced you.'

'No, sir, you misunderstand me. I want to be here. I would just prefer to have been properly consulted rather than have my views and allegiances taken for granted.'

All around us men swarmed forward, home-knitted scarves or even blankets wrapped around their threadbare jackets. There had been several arrests, we were told angrily, because the police had tried to break up the rally and some protesters had fought back, but for the last hour or so they had been allowed to proceed peacefully. Their cotton banners, soggy in the drizzle, read: *No Batons. No force. Release the Prisoners. All we want is a voice.* Nearby, as if deliberately to contradict Breen's assertion that we were becoming a police state, there was a good-natured exchange between a policeman and a marcher who, it turned out, were distant cousins.

Breen ushered me to the inside of the pavement where we could make better headway than in the body of the march. Troubled by the sight of his hunched shoulders and how he'd pulled the brim of his hat forward, I said, 'I didn't mean to provoke an argument. It was just that you left me no time to think. And unlike you, I'm not used to being involved in politics.'

'If you don't want to be involved, don't stay. Please.' He turned to me abruptly so that we were suddenly face to face and I was taken aback to see a most uncharacteristic confusion in his eyes.

We were moved on and overtaken by the crowd. At one point Breen seized my arm so that we would not be separated and we surged forward in a throng reeking of cigarettes, beer and wet wool. Outside the prison gates Tom Mann, leader of the communist-led National Minority Movement, shouted into an inadequate megaphone, his voice drifting in and out of earshot. 'We call upon . . . release the prisoners . . . What crime have they committed? The workers need the power to make their wishes be respected by the capitalist . . . I urge you to join us . . .'

The men around me were hollow-eyed. Most Londoners were too thin and the winter had been sour and cold. How would they fare in a general strike, given that they had no spare flesh to lose? It felt voyeuristic to be there, amid such raw and defiant protest, when until this moment I had involved myself so little.

'Miss, Miss!'

The crowd parted to allow a young man through. His high cheekbones were white with cold and his bright eyes – of the same blue as his father's – were full of excitement. 'Miss. It *is* Miss Gifford, isn't it? You came to our house.'

'Ah, yes I did. Good afternoon, Mr Wright.'

'What are you doing here?'

'I'm probably here for the same reason as you.'

Robbie looked proud, as if he owned the demonstration. 'We've got a cracking turnout, don't you think?' Lowering his voice he added, 'Trudy says you saw my mother and the state she was in.'

'How is she?'

'Up and about, although still not able to go out. Did you report what you'd seen to the police?'

'I couldn't. She told me she'd fallen down the stairs.'

His eyes went hard and his face paled. 'I thought you'd help. I might have known.'

'That's hardly fair. You could have gone to the police yourself. Why rely on me?'

'She won't let me report him.' The anger left him abruptly. 'Tell me what to do, Miss Gifford. When I met you I felt such hope. I hate him, what he does, but every time I threaten to leave or tell her to leave, there's a terrible row. But I can't look after her all the time. Do you understand? I can't be there night and day to protect her.'

'Does she have relatives she could go to with the children?'

'Nowhere she can stay more than an hour or two. There's no room.'

'I can talk to your mother any time, if it would help, if she'd like to see me.'

He touched his cap and grinned as if I'd solved all his problems. 'You're a good woman, Miss Gifford,' he called as he darted away. 'I knew you were, the minute I saw you.'

Breen came forward, offered his arm again and told me that if I was still up for supper he knew an excellent pub in Clapham, so we set off together at a brisk, companionable pace, braced against the foul weather and the cold smoky air. It seemed that my acquaintance with the activist, Robbie Wright, had redeemed me. In the snug he made me take off my coat and gloves so that I might feel the warmth of the fire. 'Draw your stool closer and hold your hands to the blaze. For goodness' sake, your fingertips are blue.'

Taking both my hands in his he pressed the chill out of them and I was touched that a man who cared so much for the wider picture, for politics and the impending strike, should pay such attention to my cold hands. But I was also relieved when he retreated to the far side of the table and began urging me to tell him about Robbie Wright and his abused mother. The sudden physical proximity had been disturbing and I could no longer quite convince myself that Breen was motivated purely from a desire to educate me as a lawyer. There had been something, I thought in amazement, almost lover-like in his touch.

'Matrimonial matters are always a minefield,' he said, 'which is why I was so reluctant to let you take on Lady Petit. I have always tried to steer clear of domestic affairs.' His glance was shy. 'I expect you've heard that I was once badly burnt myself.'

'Nobody has told me the details.'

'It seems I have a bit of a weakness for complicated and beautiful women.' He gave a small, inward smile. 'The lady in question was the daughter of a colleague, and like so many others we became engaged too hastily in the second year of the war. She was not faithful while I was away, I knew that, but I was a fool and went ahead with our plans to marry. At the time I thought that I deserved no better treatment, and anyway, I was besotted. Now I think I was in a muddle because of the war and therefore behaved on all fronts like a whipped dog, crawling back to a woman who quite rightly treated me with contempt. We were to be married on one of my twenty-four-hour leaves and she simply didn't turn up – nobody from her family did – though I waited for an hour with my brother at my side and my parents in the pew behind. Next day, she wrote me a note telling me she just hadn't been sure. The truth was that she'd found someone else, far more glamorous. She lives in a great house now, in Richmond.'

'I'm sorry, sir.'

'Nonsense!' His mood immediately swung from reflective to bracing. 'You should be glad for me. Can you imagine what I'd have endured with such a woman if the marriage had gone ahead?'

'And I assume you've never been prepared to take that risk again.'

I regretted the remark immediately because, in the context of our relationship thus far, it seemed both audaciously personal and dangerously provocative. Here we were, ensconced before a blazing fire like a courting couple, and there could be no doubt that I was somewhat out of my depth. Breen, who had gone very still, quickly recovered himself, went to pay the bill then helped me on with my coat. We took a cab together and sat far apart until we reached my Pimlico flat and all the time I felt a mix of exhilaration and dread because while it was exciting to be singled out by Breen, it was also alarming because I had no idea where or how far I wished this friendship to go. Before I went inside we shook hands; a firm pressure through our leather gloves.

'Would you like to meet again?' he asked. 'I thought perhaps I could cook you supper at my house. Might that happen, in the spirit of friendship, or would you prefer not?'

I was curious, flattered and more than a little afraid of offending Breen by refusing him, of raising his expectations, of making a fool of myself. He was such a good man, and I recognised that the risk he was taking with our hitherto purely professional relationship was profound. He had also been a rock to me over the past few weeks, and I appreciated his support more than I could say.

'I should like that very much,' I said at last and was rewarded by a grin of relief and delight. At the front door I turned to wave goodbye and saw that he was still standing by the automobile, watching me.

# *Chapter Twelve*

A few days after my encounter with Robbie, I received a laborious, hand-delivered note from Trudy Wright, asking if we could meet *somewhere nobody would know* and please could I reply care of a neighbour's address. I suggested neutral territory, my favourite Lyons tea shop on Regent Street where I was friendly with a member of staff, Carole Mangan, who had recently been promoted.

Arriving deliberately early, I took my usual table under the clock. Carole's new-found seniority gave her permission to join me for a while, though the lower half of her body was turned away in case she was required to dash back to her duties. When I first met her she had been a lowly waitress but now, as a tribute to her status, she no longer wore the ungainly cap that used to slide over her eyes. She had important news, which she delivered sotto voce and with an eye on the manager's office: she had just become engaged to a man called Michael Craig.

'He's a police officer. I suddenly realised that a particular young man kept coming in and ordering tea and toast at odd times of the day. Then one evening he was waiting outside for me after work and he told me that I was the reason. We've been walking out together ever since and we plan to marry in the autumn.'

Although we could not embrace while she was at work, we did shake hands. 'They'll make me leave,' she said, 'and I'm bound to miss it terribly. I've not told them yet, by the way, because they go a bit funny, even if a girl just gets engaged. At first I thought Michael was quite scary, he seemed too quiet and he didn't smile much, but underneath ... And I do worry about him, especially if there's to be a general strike. They're being trained up to deal with riots and they have to be prepared to go anywhere in London if trouble flares. Michael hates it all, because he sides with the miners but he won't have a choice. Do you think there'll be a strike, Miss Gifford?'

'I do. Everyone I know thinks that the mine owners and the unions are spoiling for a fight.'

'Our manager has been buying in extra supplies of sugar and flour. It's milk and eggs that will be the problem.'

'Carole, I have a favour to ask. I was wondering whether you have any vacancies here? I'm meeting someone in a minute who was unfairly dismissed from her last job and is without references, except from me.'

She looked doubtful. 'We've got girls queuing up for work at the moment but I'll put in a word if you like.'

Trudy Wright was approaching the table, followed by her mother who was stooped like an old woman and wore a drooping black coat and a worn orange hat that concealed her face. Carole sprang to her feet and drew back a chair for Mrs Wright. With her long experience of serving tea, that time-honoured panacea to a broken heart, she probably took in every detail of Mrs Wright's shadowed face and trembling hands, which were clasping an over-large canvas bag. Another waitress came to take our order and Carole melted away to her high desk at the far corner of the room.

I ordered teacakes because I thought it unlikely that the Wrights would have eaten a square meal for days, though they were horrified by my extravagance. While we waited they told me that Robbie was completely geared up for the strike.

'Father's sure he'll lose his job,' said Trudy who was more confident than I'd ever seen her, 'and Robbie is the only breadwinner so that would be a disaster for us all. At the very least he'll miss out on pay.'

I thought it best not to mention the rally in Wandsworth. 'Are you surprised that your brother is prepared to strike?'

'Not at all. He's a bright lad, though a bit of a dreamer. He did really well at school and he reads any paper he can lay his hands on. Mother would have liked him to have had a better education, wouldn't you, Mother?' Trudy spoke louder, as we used to at the dinner table in Clivedon Hall Gardens when we had wished to draw Grandmother into our conversation. 'He could read from when he was three but then so many of us others came along that he couldn't stay in school. I had two more brothers who died.'

'I'm so sorry, Mrs Wright.'

'The boys did seem to be weaker,' she murmured from within the shadow of her hat, 'except for Robbie. And it were cold in that house. It were the flu or some such that took them. Robbie was my best hope. I always thought he could have worked in an office.'

'I don't know how Robbie would have managed in an office, he's a bit fiery,' Trudy said. 'He nearly got himself in trouble with the police last year, for fighting outside a pub. Just about got away with it. And thank God he kept his job delivering coal though it's one he hates.'

'His boss has a soft spot for Robbie,' put in Mrs Wright. 'Ever such a nice man, he seems.' She spoke as if terrified of raising her voice, and her too thin frame quivered like a cornered rabbit's.

'Didn't your husband once work in haulage?' I asked, attempting to reassure her with gentle questions.

'He done his back in. Says it was the war what wrecked it so he won't do nothing about having it seen to. Says he should be on a pension but he's not eligible. And he won't try for other work. Just sits there.'

When the tea came she raised her head to watch, fascinated, as the table was set and the first gush of liquid poured from the metal pot. Though Trudy was no great beauty her mother might perhaps have been described as such, if one overlooked the strangeness of her gaze. Her wide-open eyes, once fixed on an object, never blinked but stared so hard that the iris was fully exposed. And now that her face was unguarded by the hat's brim, I saw that there was a new bruise on her cheek, shaded from virulent red to black like a rotten plum.

'Good God,' I exclaimed.

'Robbie told us to come to you,' said Trudy, her rather heavy features knitted with concern. 'None of us knows what to do next. It's happening time after time. Go on, ma, show her.'

Mrs Wright set down her cup, placed her right hand flat on the table and with her left pushed back the side of her hat, and within it a lint dressing, so that the full extent of the bruise, from mid-cheek to hairline, was revealed. 'Next time he will kill me,' she said, wincing as the hat fell back into place. 'He kicked me in the stomach too, so that I was sick.'

'He doesn't really mean to hurt her so much,' said Trudy pleadingly, 'honest, Miss Gifford. He just hits out when he's drunk or bored. Doesn't know his own strength.'

Mrs Wright stared at her daughter, patiently absorbing her words, before reaching out and taking her hand. 'Poor Trude. It's hard being the oldest girl. She takes all the troubles of the family upon herself.'

'Tell me what happened, Mrs Wright,' I said.

'It were the day before yesterday when we was arguing about Robbie and the strike he wants to join. He got hold of my head and smacked it down on the corner of the table. When I fell to the floor I knew what was coming, I seen him draw back his foot. He never takes his boots off in the house.'

'And you never thought to go to the police?'

'What would the police do? The children say I should know better than to provoke him.' With the tip of her knife she speared a butter pat and watched it melt on a teacake but when she took a mouthful she flinched and after a moment gave up the struggle to eat.

'That's not what we think at all, Mother. I hate him for hitting you. It's just that if he's drunk you should leave him alone.' Trudy spread her own butter vehemently, but didn't take a bite. 'He's out of control.'

'Mrs Wright,' I said, 'what would you like to happen about your husband?'

She looked across the restaurant, through the hanging cloud of smoke, at the cane-back chairs pushed neatly underneath empty tables, the out-of-work men in their raincoats and plaid ties, the chinking of thick crockery. 'I want you to stop him hurting me. He'll kill me, for sure. The children need me, you see . . .'

'How long has he been beating you?'

'Since we was courting. He used to pinch my arm if he thought I was glancing at another boy. You know.'

'Ma was very beautiful when she was young,' said Trudy proudly.

'I was no great catch, let's be honest. My dad wanted rid of me.

I was in service like Trude, but it was different before the war, harder to find work if you wasn't that strong. And when I first knew him Ned was all set up in the transportation business so I thought he would give me a comfortable life. He always said he didn't mean it when he hit out at me. In those days I never realised he was a drinker. He kept it hid.'

'Drink is the problem,' agreed Trudy. 'If only he wouldn't drink.'

'He was roaring drunk on our wedding night. Had to be carried up to bed. I used to put it down to high spirits when we was young. Now I know he can't – or won't – stop hisself. Trudy's right, it's the little things that wind him up but I can never tell what kind of thing is going to aggravate him. You know – could be if the dinner's too hot or too cold, or I'm slow with the hot water for his wash, or if the tea's stewed, or the children's shoes are in holes. All those things might send him wild sometimes. Or he might just say never mind, Het, it'll all come good. Thing is, I don't know which it will be and that makes me nervous.'

'He hates it when she's nervous,' added Trudy.

'Does he hurt the children?'

A glance was exchanged between mother and daughter. 'Only Robbie, a couple of times, when he was small. Not now.'

'Has something changed lately, that you have come to talk to me?'

Mrs Wright had risked another mouthful of teacake and was chewing slowly. 'It were you,' she said. 'When Trude told me that you'd stood up for her in court against that Derbyshire woman I suddenly had a little bit of hope. I thought maybe if you'd helped her, you could help me. And then Robbie come home and said he'd met you at a rally so I thought, well, she must be a woman who knows her own mind. She'll be strong.'

I couldn't help being touched, but I was also a little afraid of the expectations I'd raised unwittingly. 'I'll have to be honest with you, Mrs Wright. It's very difficult to win these sorts of cases when a man beats his wife. Often the husband is found not guilty because he says his wife nagged him so much he had to do it. And because there's no other evidence, it's just his word against hers.'

'What about the bruises?' cried Trudy.

'They will be healed by the time we go to court.'

'Then what should we do?'

'Were there witnesses this time, when he struck you, Mrs Wright? Was Robbie actually there?'

'No, like I said, it was Robbie we was arguing about. I got the blame for Robbie sayin' he'll go on strike. Ned said I poisoned my son's mind.'

'It doesn't matter what you'd said or done, Mrs Wright,' I said sharply, 'no woman deserves to be struck, let alone as badly as you have been.' She nodded but I guessed she had heard similar advice before and that it made no sense to her.

Trudy pushed aside her plate and did up the top button of her coat. 'Maybe I should just keep a better eye on Dad. After all, I'm home much more now because I'm not working. It feels awful being here, behind his back. But look at her. She can't even eat.' She put her rough, girlish hand on her mother's emaciated wrist.

'Mrs Wright,' I said, 'if you wish your husband to be prosecuted you must go to the police and make a statement. I will come with you and we could even go now, if you like. Alternatively, you could sue him for divorce but that would be very costly and time-consuming and you might find it hard to prove the grounds of cruelty if there's no conviction against your husband.'

'In the end he'll kill me,' she said for the third time.

'Then we must take action.'

'The trouble is, Miss Gifford,' said Trudy, 'Mother is upset now because she's been laid up for a couple of days with the bang he gave her on the head. But when she feels better she'll soften again and you won't be able to get her to say anything bad against him.'

Carole brought over a plate of fairy cakes sprinkled with hundreds and thousands, and more hot water. Trudy ate nothing but her mother tucked into a soft sponge. I again offered to go to the police station that afternoon but Mrs Wright, having collected the crumbs with the tip of her index finger, said she would think about it further and, if she wanted to go ahead, she'd get Trudy to write to me again. Her eyes shone with gratitude and I suspected that her renewed sense of well-being, fuelled by tea and cake, would deter her from going to the police. As they left, Trudy linked her arm through her mother's and steered her among the tables. I felt a pang, not only for the hopelessness of Mrs Wright's situation, but also because I never took my own mother out to tea and, if I had, would never have dreamed of taking her arm.

# Chapter Thirteen

Meredith and Edmund were to leave the country by the middle of April, Prudence a week earlier. Although my aunt did not wish to be seen off from the dockside, she did send each of us, including Edmund, a note inviting us to a farewell high tea in Buckinghamshire to view the work that had been carried out. Every instinct told me to avoid that cottage of hers, especially now I had seen Nicholas Thorne again, and in the company of another woman. In my mind, that prosaic little dwelling was enshrined as a place of ecstasy and heartbreak, because it was there that I'd enticed him to make love to me. The memory of our last evening – Prudence's bedroom, the smell of sheets in need of airing, his hot, demanding body and the understanding that this, this was how lovemaking should be – was engraved on my soul. Yet it would have been churlish to refuse Prudence's request, so the four of us, in our Sunday best, duly set forth on the Metropolitan Line train to Amersham, laden with going away gifts for Prudence.

It was mid-April, a wildly blowing day of intense sunshine interspersed with threatening clouds. Mother, in a mood to punish us all, especially me, gave a martyred performance, looking eagerly out of the train window as if she was never, in a future doomed to solitude and penury, likely to see spring woodland again.

'Shall you come and visit us in France, Mrs Gifford?' asked Meredith mischievously. 'Evelyn has promised that she will. I should like to see you in a bathing suit. The sea in summer is as warm as milk. And Angus's mother's cousin is putting us up in her boarding house, so I'm sure there will be plenty of spare rooms.'

'I could never set foot in Fr . . . that country after . . . my boy . . . the soil that claimed my boy. And in any case I'm afraid there's no money for holidays at the moment. Evelyn may do as she pleases.'

'What about our leaving party? At least you'll come to that? You would meet Evelyn's legal ladies. And her boss, Mr Breen. They're all coming.'

'Mr Breen may not,' I said hastily. 'He is in Birmingham that day and might not arrive back in time.'

'You see, I don't travel alone at night,' said Mother, 'so I won't be able to come either.'

'But I tell you what,' I said impulsively, because she looked so very wan and because I had been chastened by the way that Trudy Wright had taken such care of her own abused mother, 'you and I should go out in the evening together sometime after everyone's gone. How about a play, as a tribute to Grandmother? I would see you home afterwards.'

'Oh, I don't expect you'll have time,' she said.

Having considered his grandmother unwaveringly for several minutes, Edmund crossed the carriage, tucked his arm through hers and rested his head against her shoulder. At least she did not shrug him off, although I felt again the jarring implications of what Peggy Spencer had said at the funeral. If Mother knew or even guessed at the truth – that she was perhaps the illegitimate daughter of an actor – her hostility towards Edmund and all that he represented was even more understandable. Her face was, as usual, shaded by an old-fashioned picture hat trimmed with a brooch of grey beads, and the wounded expression she habitually wore did nothing to enhance her soft features. I saw Grandmother in her, certainly, in those delicate cheekbones and the pert nose, but Mother's eyes were defensive and fearful rather than bright and enquiring. It had never occurred to me to question whether she resembled the schoolteacher in his owl glasses whose photo had been positioned all these years beside Grandmother's bed.

Perhaps aware of my scrutiny, she shifted, fumbled in her bag and produced a small bar of chocolate for Edmund. Together they peeled off the thin dark blue foil – he ate it according to Clivedon Hall Gardens rules, a minute nibble at a time – and I acknowledged that she might actually be trying to accommodate him at last, now that it was too late.

We waited nearly half an hour for a bus, which wound its way slowly through hedgerows hazy with green buds. It was the kind of journey that lodged in the memory even as it was being made: the toiling engine as we rounded yet another tight bend; the sitting next to Edmund who leaned against me as he huffed on the glass so that he could draw faces in the mist of his breath; Meredith across the aisle in her bright green hat and coat, her slender knees exposed and that faraway look in her eyes, as if she already had one foot on the train to France.

The bus stop was almost opposite Prudence's cottage and suddenly there it was, smaller and a little smarter than when I had last seen it, with the back door freshly painted pillar-box red and leaves just appearing on the gooseberry bushes. The upstairs window in Prudence's bedroom was wide open and for a moment my sense of how near I was in space yet how far in time from that hour with Nicholas was so intense that I faltered, gripped Edmund's hand and told him about another memory instead.

'Your daddy and I came to stay here when we were little,' I told him. 'We didn't really understand the country because we were city children so we got lost in the lanes. The hedges were so high we couldn't work out where we were.'

Edmund looked about in obedient wonder as I recalled the dust and the flies of that interminable walk; the escape from yet another expedition into the village with Prudence to hold mind-numbing conversations with women I didn't know about others I'd never met. But today, as she threw open her door to greet us, wearing her best peach silk blouse, I realised that she, like her cottage, had a new gloss. I avoided glancing towards the staircase but discovered that in the front parlour the windows had been given a fresh coat of paint and there was a different hearthrug. A metal travelling trunk waited by the door and the table, decorated with a jar of catkins, was laden with sandwiches, scones and a fruit cake. She even led Edmund into the kitchen and opened the meat safe to show him a mould containing strawberry jelly with evaporated milk beaten through it, his favourite pudding.

Tea was a festive affair, marred only by the occasional sighing remark from Mother. 'I am making the most of every last minute of having my family gathered around me,' she told us with a courageous smile.

'Of course I shall wish you to paint me pictures and send me a letter telling me all about France, Edmund, and in return I shall write to you about India,' said Prudence.

'Mommy's friend Angus can paint incredible pictures,' Edmund piped up. 'He loves the colour blue. All of his paintings are blue.'

'Not all, Edmund,' said Meredith, 'but he does love blocks of colour. He's on the fringes of the Bloomsbury crowd,' she explained to the rest of us. 'His influences are Augustus John and of course Duncan Grant. Oh, and Cézanne.'

'Well, perhaps he will have contact with other French painters in Sanary-sur-Mer,' said Prudence faintly. Even her new-found determination to be open-minded and travel to another continent could not quite withstand the mention of Bloomsbury.

Prudence regarded my gift to her, *A Passage to India*, with a mix of pleasure and suspicion. She turned it over several times and studied the flyleaf as if I had presented her with an incendiary device. 'I've heard that this book has very modern themes,' she said. 'But still, it's thoughtful of you, Evelyn.'

Mother presented her with a couple of brown paper parcels for her medicine chest. 'I should open them later,' she said, glancing pointedly at Edmund, 'but I did just wonder how you'd fare in India with your' (lowered voice) '*gastric* problems.'

Edmund had drawn Aunt Prudence a painstaking picture of the four family members she would be leaving behind: myself with a cloud of brown hair and a pile of books, his mother in bright green, brandishing a paintbrush, himself a squat figure with a grin and bristly hair, and his grandmother, very thin, in black.

Meredith's gift was, I suspected, the most welcome of all, being a hip flask. '. . . full of something very alcoholic which you're bound to need from time to time,' Meredith told her.

After tea Edmund and Meredith were sent to explore the garden and told that if they peeked through the trees they could view the great house, built in the eighteenth century and so grand that its porch was supported by two white columns. This was where Prudence and my father had spent their childhood, in the days of Gifford wealth. Mother was easily persuaded to rest on a sheltered bench in the sun while Prudence and I washed up in the scullery. She handed me a floral pinafore to protect my best pink and grey frock and as I wiped each porcelain teacup with the thoroughness she had taught me, I realised how much I would miss her. Though her rigidity infuriated me, she had been the household's rock since Father's death and it was thanks to her that I had been able to leave home in the first place.

'So you're looking forward to going away,' I said.

'Very much. My own life has been held in abeyance far too long.'

'You have been very good, Aunt Prudence, keeping Mother afloat all these years. I'm not sure I ever truly appreciated that until now.'

'I was very fond of your grandmother but your mother and I, as I'm sure you noticed, never saw eye to eye.' She rinsed the cut-glass milk jug and handed it to me. 'I tried to dissuade your father from marrying her, you know. When she found out – through him – she never forgave me.'

'I wasn't aware of that.'

'I thought your mother was a fluffy-headed little thing who would do him no good compared to the girls he could have had. She was the daughter of an actress, you see, and a complete un-known to us whereas in our circle everyone was acquainted with each other's family.' She avoided having to look at me by scrub-bing vigorously at the breadboard. Good gracious, I thought, and how would Prudence have regarded Mother had she know there was a whiff of scandal about her birth?

'I think it was the one remotely brave thing my brother did, marrying your mother. And now, for what it's worth, I believe that he was the weaker of the two, and that she is the one who could have done better. The right man might have enabled her to bloom. It's why I stuck by her; I felt I should make amends.'

'Didn't she have the kind of life she always wanted?'

'Possibly. But we had spoilt your father, just as you all spoilt your brother Jamie.' She stopped scrubbing and fixed me with her pale, hard eyes. 'Come now, Evelyn, you did, you know, more than a little.'

'I didn't spoil him, I simply loved him.'

'You adored him. And who can blame you? The pair of you were left too much to your own devices in that great house. You were very protective of him and it worried me because I'd seen the way

92

your father turned out. But then he and I were of a generation and class brought up to believe we were right, which is neither an attractive nor an effective state of being, as I've discovered since Meredith came.'

'You usually *are* right, I've found,' I told her. 'And I'm afraid we haven't always been very grateful for all you've done.'

She actually laughed. 'Well, this is my moment to take flight and discover fresh pastures. But you mustn't fall into the same trap as I did, and remain in thrall to your mother. She's a survivor.' She was silent a moment, swabbing the sink and draining board. 'You perhaps don't remember that you once visited me here with your brother when you were a little girl and that I sent you home early. You thought, I presume, that it was because you had been very naughty – you and your brother had disappeared for a day without my permission. In fact, I just couldn't stand the responsibility. I thought it would be easy to manage two small children but you, in particular, were so fierce that I saw myself in you. Equally, I knew that you, unlike me, would never be trammelled by duty or rules. Or at least, they wouldn't have the last word with you. That's why you frightened and enraged me. So I sent you away.' She untied her apron, shook it out and hung it on a hook as if to say: I've let this sentimental chat go quite far enough.

'I'll sit with your mother,' she said.

'Might I take a peek upstairs to see the new decoration?'

'There's only the same two cramped little rooms. They haven't changed much.'

'Nevertheless.'

She looked pleased and as I crept up the steep staircase I thought of how horrified she'd be if she knew the truth of what had happened between Nicholas and me in this cottage. Or per-haps not horrified after all. Perhaps she would have been relieved to know that I had lived a little. I caught a glimpse of myself in the round mirror at the top of the stairs, my hair smoothly drawn back in deference to Prudence's preference for tidy hair, my face very grave but rosier than usual, touched by sunshine and the pink of my dress.

In her bedroom Prudence had taken down the prints – surely she was not transporting *The Light of the World* to India? – and there was fresh wallpaper patterned with sprigs of honeysuckle. The room smelt of paint, of bed linen and the outdoors. I remembered the scent of the garden that evening with Nicholas, the July heat lingering in the walls of the house, on his skin.

In those days the quilt had been cotton patchwork, not rose-pink satin, with seams that made criss-cross indentations on naked flesh. He had stood by the window while I sat on the bed with my hand full of hairpins and my hair tumbling down my neck and shoulders. So beautiful he had been with his soft-collared shirt and boyish throat, that I thought I would have died at the least touch from him, the weight of his body on mine, the taste of his wondering, unstoppable kisses.

But even as I had pressed my mouth to his neck, I had known that it would be for the last time. I knew he loved me, but had lied to me. And so I had made love to him, with the evening soft on my skin, and afterwards seen his eyes drugged with passion in the few moments before I told him what I'd found out.

And yet, if I had my time again I would have done the same, for sure. I had no choice. Take him. Leave him. And when he wrote to me afterwards, burn the letter.

# Chapter Fourteen

Breen came to the door of his small, smart house near Battersea Park in a waistcoat of heathery tweed, his hair unnaturally tidy and a spark of nervous anticipation in his eye. He showed me into the front room, which was dominated by an upright piano with a score thickly annotated in pencil propped open on the music stand. I might have anticipated the oriental rugs, modern furniture, shelves of books about travel and the law, buff folders and closely typed papers – dog-eared and riddled with notes in Breen's familiar scrawl – relating to Battersea District Council and even the leather-bound volumes of poetry, but not the piano.

'It's still quite light,' he said. 'Perhaps you would like to take a look at the garden.'

There were touching signs, as we passed through the kitchen, of careful preparations for supper; cheeses were laid out on a marble slab and there was a casserole in the oven. It was typical of him to be equipped with the latest gas stove and even a refrigerator. The floor was of brown linoleum patterned to resemble tiles. This space, with its shelf holding a coffee canister and tea caddy, and its row of steel-handled drawers, should have been tranquil and domestic but it felt far too much an invasion of his privacy as we paused for a moment on either side of the kitchen table. His head was down but he was watching me from beneath his brow as if to test my reactions. He was a man whom I guessed to be self-conscious even when alone, and would probably prepare and eat his meals as if before a bench of three.

The garden had a border of herbs and a vigorously dug vegetable patch, and the air smelt of the coming night, of new grass and traffic fumes. We stood at a careful distance from each other on the lawn, talking intently about other people while I tried not to shiver in my too thin clothes. I'd not admitted to Meredith, when selecting an outfit from my limited wardrobe, that Breen and I would be dining alone. In the end I'd chosen a coral blouse with a long cream tie and I realised, with a tremor of excitement, that Breen was entirely conscious of how the evening breeze caught the silky ends of the ribbon. And in the transparency of that April twilight, as the light faded and lamps were lit in neighbouring rooms, he too was thrown into deeper relief and emerged not as a lawyer and politician but as a red-blooded male who saw every bit of me.

At first we talked intently about other people. 'You know Timothy Petit is one of the architects of the government's riposte to the General Strike.' Breen's tone was light and dispassionate. 'He now serves on the Supply and Transport Committee.'

'His wife was very disparaging about all that. She said he'd never been near a coal mine.'

'I've always thought of him as flashy, and hugely ambitious. For the last few months he's been running round the country setting up local committees. He's said to have attended about a hundred different meetings so that, in the event of a strike, each district will be able to manage its own base for essential supplies.'

'He must be a glutton for punishment.'

'This crisis could make or break a man like Petit. If the government comes out on top it will be because he and his cohorts have kept the country going.'

'Don't you think the timing of this paternity suit is very odd? It must be quite a distraction.'

'He'll perhaps be hoping the press won't notice, with everything else that's going on. Or they'll be on his side. Have you written back to his solicitor?'

'I have. I said we wished the case to be dropped because Lady Petit had lied in a moment of passion and that Petit definitely is Annice's father. But they're having none of it. They say if she won't accept a divorce on his terms and admit Leremer is the father, they are determined to go to court.'

'I know Richard Leremer slightly,' said Breen. 'He came to speak in Battersea before the last election and he is certainly a rival who would be particularly irksome to Petit; a socialist heart-throb with the looks of a film star and, if one is prepared to overlook rumours of a torrid love life, one who appears to have firmly egalitarian principles. If Annabel Petit indeed chose Leremer to father her child she would be the object of considerable envy within a certain group of political ladies.'

'Do you think we women are so susceptible that our heads are turned by mere good looks?'

Breen had used the teasing tones of one who considered himself to be well out of Leremer's league when it came to attracting women, and yet his breathing was unsteady and his posture determinedly over-casual.

As for me, I too was light-headed and in a way, I welcomed this heightened state of being. Everyone else was moving on, after all – Meredith, Edmund and Prudence. Did I wish to be left behind like my mother? And I was aware of an absurd and unworthy need to prove to Nicholas, who had attended so alluringly to that adoring other girl outside the restaurant on Fitzroy Street, that I too was not without alternatives.

We ate supper at an oak table in a dining room decorated in old-fashioned flock paper. The ink drawings of game birds against a background of lowering Scottish mountains were by Breen's father, he told me, as we sipped red wine from heavy cut glasses. This house was remarkably calm and uncomplicated compared to conditions in the Pimlico flat, where every inch of floor space was filled with Meredith's complex packing arrangements: clothes to go, clothes to stay, clothes to be washed or mended. Here order was punctuated only by friendly suburban noises from nearby gardens: a child's call, a sleepy blackbird, the motor of an automobile being cranked up. With every mouthful we took, each time we sipped from a glass, we seemed to inch a little closer, part of the evening's slow dance. His features were soft in the evening light, his smile disconcertingly shy.

'Promise that you will come to our party if you can,' I said. 'I'd like you to meet Meredith.'

'I'll do my best. Though I'm not good at parties and I'm out of town that day – I might not be back in time.'

To spare him – he clearly didn't want to come – I said hastily, 'Mother won't be there, though. She's furious with me because I won't go and live with her.'

'I could never live with my parents again,' he said, 'fond as I am of them.'

'Do you have that choice?'

He laid down his fork, pressed his fingertips together and spoke in that considered way I'd grown so used to at work. 'Mother has never stopped fretting that I, a bachelor, should be living alone. Every time we meet she compares my fate – unfavourably – to my brother's, who has three children and a very dear wife. She thinks a man's destiny is to be looked after by a woman.'

'Whereas I'm afraid my mother has never shed the belief that a woman should be protected by a man or, failing that, a dutiful daughter.'

'How will you deal with her disappointment?'

'Well I certainly don't want to be protected by a man.'

'I understand that but don't, whatever you do, confuse protection with being cherished.'

His voice was so soft that it was as if he had caressed me and I shied away. 'Mother has the choice, although a rather dismal one, of a smaller house or lodgers.'

'That sounds clear enough.'

'It *is* clear until I am in her company and she scrambles my brain by treating my career as an aberrant excuse not to spend my life with her.'

Our words skimmed the surface like pebbles on thin ice. Fading light filtered through the dozen or so panes in the French windows. Colours were subtly intensified; the ruby wine, the white of his shirt cuffs, my own pale hands. He was watching me closely, like one who cannot tear his gaze from a beloved face. In the silver cruet set, highly polished and heavy-bottomed, my distorted reflection stretched and shrank. He reached across the table, his palm turned upwards, and after a moment's hesitation I gave him my hand. Time stretched agonisingly as we sat there on the brink. I knew now, without a shadow of doubt, that he had fallen in love with me, all of me, not just my mind or my pioneering spirit. He was no longer simply amused or distracted by me. He desired me.

I felt it in the trembling of his hand, the flush on his cheek, the concentration of his gaze.

The implications of that realisation, an almost terrified acknowledgement that everything was bound to change, held me breathless. For one moment more we sat with our hands linked, but intact, our separate selves, while his quiet house gently intruded itself upon me. This might be my future – the unknown rooms upstairs, the chunter of the refrigerator in the kitchen, this polished oak table. A clock was ticking elsewhere. To break the tension, and because I could not bear, at that point, to allow things to go any further, I said, 'Would you play the piano for me, before I go?'

He acknowledged the shift in mood with a little grunt and released my hand in order to spread his fingers and show me a distorted knuckle. 'The war did a bit of damage, makes me clumsy on the trills.'

His hands were familiar and benign – I had watched them so often writing or gesticulating.

'Play for me anyway,' I murmured.

With great delicacy he rose and waited for me to precede him from the room. I knew, by the way he pressed himself back so I could pass without touching that the message – no further, not now – had been received. I stood at his parlour window while he switched on a light above the piano, squeezed and flexed his fingers, played a couple of scales and then began a Chopin nocturne. The room was scented with books and outside the street was lamplit, an orange blaze in the darkness. At first his shoulders were a little stiff, but gradually his head dropped and he became absorbed in the music. He had already taken such care of me that evening and now the notes were tenderly, carefully pressed from the keys like an offering. I liked watching the shape of his head, the clean angles of shoulder and elbow, his nimble fingers.

And then the music carried me away and inevitably, in that heightened emotional state, I was transported to my second meeting with Nicholas when he and I had listened to music together; a lunchtime concert, sunlight falling through coloured glass, the realisation that he had been watching me. It had been the start of everything, including his betrayal. *You probably won't believe this,* he had said, *but I have been hoping to run into you these past couple of days . . .* He had carried my briefcase and walked so swiftly that even with my long stride I could scarcely keep up. The sun had been hot on our backs and I didn't know, was too stupid and inexperienced to realise that I was already falling hopelessly, pitifully in love.

After he'd finished, Daniel rested his hands in his lap but did not look at me.

'I'm amazed,' I said. 'I never thought . . .'

'Did you suppose I had no life beyond work and politics?'

'It never occurred to me that you could play the piano like this.'

'Did you like it?'

'I did, yes, though I confess to having no ear.'

'I'll help you learn to understand music if you like.'

Though the station was barely quarter of a mile away he insisted on accompanying me there. Blossom was ghostly in the lamplight and we passed bay windows where the curtains had been left undrawn. In one room a family sat around a card table, in another a woman was reading a book, her rigidly set hair illuminated from above by a standard lamp.

As we neared the corner of the street I said, 'Thank you, Daniel. For everything.'

He stood still, his brow creased, eyes focused on some far-off point, as he did in court when he was gathering his thoughts. 'You spoke my name.'

I laughed. 'I did.'

But he was not smiling. His face was white and stunned. 'I have never heard you say my name.'

'Well, there it is. Daniel.'

'I love you,' he said, the words spilling from him like a blessing.

There was still a paving stone's distance between us. As a figure rattled past on a bicycle Daniel took a step closer until our hands were joined and he kissed my cheek. Closing my eyes I felt the slight pressure of his lips on my mouth. I wanted both more and less as he kissed my mouth reverently, drew back his head to smile – that suddenly altered smile, fragile and sweet – then kissed me again. His eyes were vulnerable and dazed. I wanted him to be taller, more definite in his kisses, a different man. I wanted to feel more than curiosity.

Afterwards he drew a long breath. 'I must ask – I'd decided to keep quiet but now this has happened I find I can't – I *have* to ask. Did you know that Nicholas Thorne is back in the country? Wolfe bumped into him last week at the Royal Courts of Justice.'

'Oh yes,' I said after barely a pause, 'I knew. I happened to catch sight of him the other day near Fitzroy Square.'

'What a relief. You've seen him. You see, I thought you might have other scruples, to do with what happened with Thorne. Please don't, on my account.'

I recognised his attempt to contain the past, to reassure me. Instead, had he but known it, the spectre of Thorne arose clearer still as he and I walked on, saying not a word until we reached the station. 'Did you buy a return ticket?' he asked, reaching in his pocket for change. When I nodded he took my hand, wished me a safe journey and waited until I reached the steps.

Before I moved out of sight I turned to wave and saw that he was willing me to look back. The image of his still, neat figure and those eyes, dimmed with longing, branded itself upon my mind. Five minutes later when I was inside the carriage and could sit down, I gripped the handle of my bag with both hands, shut my eyes and thought: My God, Evelyn, is this what you want? And what next? What on earth are you going to say if he asks you to *marry* him?

# *Chapter Fifteen*

On the same day that Aunt Prudence embarked on her great adventure to India, Breen & Balcombe's junior partner Theo Wolfe and I took a taxicab to Eccleston Square to meet Richard Leremer at the Labour Party headquarters.

Over the past couple of years Wolfe and I had developed an almost sibling-like relationship in which he treated me in public as a troublesome younger sister and I berated him, privately to Meredith, for his well-honed ability to avoid difficult work. But we held for each other a rather grudging respect and I had come to rely upon his legal cunning and his ability to keep himself – and the rest of us – out of trouble. At Breen & Balcombe he and I often helped each other out – I took on the tedious spadework of his cases and in return he offered me priceless information, as in the Petit case, about the various parties and their less public personae. He could also, when his interest was sufficiently engaged, bestir himself to offer fresh approaches or unexpected insights.

'Just as well I'm with you,' he said slyly when we were closeted together in the cab. 'Leremer's a notorious womaniser and we wouldn't want you succumbing to his charms, Miss Gifford. Level-headed you might be, but could you withstand an advance from the Lothario of the Labour Party?'

A chronic asthma sufferer, Wolfe had been absent from work for over a week due to a cold which had inevitably settled on his chest. He was somewhat overweight for a man in his early thirties and dressed with obsessive care. Today his socks and handkerchief were of matching canary yellow and his patent-leather shoes gleamed. Despite being laid low, he had made enquiries about the Petits amid his nebulous but far-reaching network of acquaintances, who corroborated the contents of Pearman's letter.

'Lady Petit is known among her set to be barking mad,' he said, peering through the dirty window at the chaotic forecourt of Victoria Station. 'She's capable of the most outlandish behaviour. Once, during a party, she threw herself down on a lion-skin rug, rolled herself up in it and said she'd rather be dead like the beast than talk politics any longer. She's been carried home on numerous occasions – both she and Petit are heavy drinkers but he's better able to contain himself under the influence.'

'What about the paternity of Annice? Are people gossiping about that too?'

''Fraid they are. Seems to be common knowledge that Leremer is the father.'

The headquarters not only of the Labour Party but of the General Council of the Trades Union Congress, 33 Eccleston Square, was in a state of utter confusion as we stood in the front hall waiting to be noticed. The latest news was that the mine owners, in a move said by trade union leaders to be purely provocative, had pinned notices at the pitheads stating that employment on existing terms would cease on 30 April, the day the government subsidy for coal was due to end. After that date most of the miners, apart from the ones who had been made redundant, were to be employed on different, less favourable contracts. In other words, as far as the mine owners were concerned, there was nothing further to be negotiated. Certainly there was no prospect of the industry being reorganised on terms more favourable to the miners, as had been suggested by the authors of the Samuel Commission's Report.

A keen-eyed girl at last directed us to Richard Leremer's office on the first floor and as we passed open doors we were assaulted by a blast of sound – the pounding of typewriters operated by women in knitted suits and the intent conversation of men who'd loosened their collars in the heat of argument. Leremer, in charge of communication, was speaking into a telephone but waved us towards a couple of tatty chairs.

Wolfe was right. Leremer was notably handsome: broad-shouldered and chisel-jawed with thickly lashed, toffee-brown eyes. He spoke with a pronounced Derbyshire accent, had a thatch of nut-brown hair, but bore no other resemblance that I could see to the child Annice.

At first he was warm in his welcome when I introduced myself as a lawyer. 'Very pleased to hear that, Miss Gifford. There aren't enough of you professional women about.' He was less civil to Wolfe who was rheumy-eyed and had wound a blue and yellow striped scarf three times about his neck. Pale Wolfe, with his rounded stomach and camphor-soaked handkerchief could not have provided more of a contrast to Leremer whose strong throat was exposed by a half-open collar and whose waistcoat was undone, as if he found clothes too confining.

In my introductory letter I had explained that I needed to interview Leremer on a personal matter but it was a while before his attention could be fully diverted from the hubbub in the building. Once he understood the nature of the Petit case his manner grew markedly brisk. 'We are in the midst of a national crisis. I cannot be expected to turn my mind to a sordid domestic squabble.'

I glanced at Wolfe for moral support but he was casting an eye over an upside-down document on Leremer's desk. 'We are asking only that you give evidence on behalf of Lady Petit when the case comes to trial next month,' I told Leremer. 'As I said, she is sure that her husband is Annice's father but Petit will argue that he could not have fathered the child and that the only other candidate is you. Lady Petit actually named you in the heat of the moment, during an argument.'

'Hold on,' said Leremer. 'Let's sort this out. What do you mean Petit says he could not have fathered the child? Why not? Is he saying he's infertile?'

'He'll claim, I think, that the marriage was not consummated, at least at the time of Annice's conception.'

With a crack of laughter Leremer swung back in the chair, clasped his hands round his knee and laughed again. 'Bel told me he was a hopeless . . . My God, I'd love to let that one loose in the press. The way he's swaggering about at present, organising all these supply committees, makes me rage. He'll be after a peerage following this strike, I'd put money on it.'

'Didn't Lady Petit tell you then, that the marriage was unconsummated?' asked Wolfe, adjusting the knot of his silken tie.

'She said, as I recall, that he'd turned out to be a useless lover and that isn't the same thing at all, is it?' He cocked an eyebrow at me and my stomach lurched.

'At any rate,' I said, 'we would like you to confirm in court that you are not Annice's father.'

Leremer ran his fingers through his hair so that it stood up in a youthful brush. 'Of course I'm not the father. But I definitely don't want to get mixed up with the Petits again. I have nothing to do with Annabel Petit any more.'

'But at the time, four years ago, in the months after she was married . . . the end of June or the beginning of July 1922—'

'For God's sake! Must we rake all this up? It's extraordinarily painful. Perhaps you don't realise that Bel and I were practically engaged at one time.'

'I apologise for raising something so personal, but the fact is your evidence will be vital to her case.'

'Will it indeed? So he's going for her, the bastard. Oh, apologies, Miss Gifford. But then she treated me very badly so perhaps I should say it's no more than she deserves.'

'Could you tell us what happened?'

He glanced from his watch to the cascade of papers on his desk, but there was an energy and sense of self-righteousness about him that ensured for the next few minutes at least he would give us his full attention. 'Bel was part of a very fast set of which I was on the fringe at first. She and her best friend Mrs Porter, wife of the automobile millionaire, were a famous pair; *the dark and the fair*, was how they always introduced themselves. Glamorous. Bold. They could drink every man in sight under the table. My head was somewhat turned since I was fresh from working as a journalist in Derbyshire where we tend to behave rather differently.' His eyes were candid as he studied my face and I estimated that he must be very young, in his mid-twenties probably, and therefore could only have been involved in the tail end of the war, if at all.

'So you had an affair with Annabel,' I said.

'You've seen her, what she's like. She's so beautiful. I thought her completely out of my league. I couldn't believe it when she fell for me. For a month or two, yes, we were lovers. Oh yes, I should say that was how long.' He was lost for a moment in a disturbingly sexual haze of recollection.

Wolfe reached for his pocket watch and polished its case against his lapel. 'In the fullest sense of the word?'

'Of course. God. She was so nervy. Dangerous. Expensive. She ran rings around me. Fascinated, I was, but sometimes terrified. Her behaviour was so extravagant and unpredictable.'

'Could you give us an example.'

'She was an acrobat. Her body could do anything on the dance floor – and elsewhere, as a matter of fact.' He looked at me sideways and I willed myself not to go hot at the graphic image I had of waiflike Annabel in Leremer's ambitious arms. 'And her clothes were wild. She loved to show off by doing the splits and such, and then bang, she'd be too exhausted to move and I'd have to carry her out to a cab. She was such a little thing to hold – sometimes I thought I'd break her. But I really thought she loved me and I adored her. I would have taken her on, however difficult she was but then Petit, although he'd been in her set for years and never shown any particular interest, suddenly went for her. It was because he couldn't bear the thought of me having her, I'm sure of that. I'd arrive for a date only to find he'd already swept her away. I couldn't keep pace with him, and I had virtually nothing to spend compared to him. But he was terribly bad for her. She had that quality – sparkle, I'd call it – that Petit could quench in seconds. She'd be in a group holding court, brandishing a cocktail, absolutely brilliant as she mimicked some political grandee and Petit would approach her, cold as ice, lay a hand on her arm or drop a word in her ear, and she'd just go limp. They were married within weeks. I was in a terrible state over it. Heck knows what I'd have done with myself if it hadn't been for work.'

'And afterwards?' I prompted.

'You mean when she got back from honeymoon? Well, she started telephoning me again. Petit was neglecting her, she said. And her best friend, Kit Porter, was out of the frame because her husband had recently died. He was a nice chap – retiring, but with masses of money. He'd had a bout of influenza during the epidemic and never fully recovered. So Annabel used to telephone me instead of Kit if she wanted to go dancing or such.'

'Did you become lovers again?' I asked.

'We did not, Miss Gifford. Do credit me with some scruples.

She was married, for God's sake. And I was angry with her – and myself, because she had only to click her fingers and I found myself turning up again on her doorstep. And besides—'

When the telephone on his desk rang he snatched up the receiver, listened intently and yelled, 'I'm sick to the back teeth of Battersea! That blasted man. Our line is very clear, they must not cooperate with the comm—' He glanced at Wolfe. 'I'll call back in five minutes. Say nothing to the press until I've spoken to you again.'

'Saklatvala, I expect,' observed Wolfe. 'Now there's an interesting chap. I bet you wish he was safely back in India.'

Leremer, who was jotting something down on a memo pad, seemed not to hear.

'You were about to say, before the phone rang . . .' I prompted, '. . . you said Annabel was a married woman and besides . . .'

'Oh yes, besides, her pregnancy became obvious very soon. She's so slight, as you know. So I did see her occasionally, but as her friend and escort.'

'Would you come to court and give evidence about all this?'

'I'll think about it.' His mood had darkened. 'It's tough. These people, they pick you up and set you down, that's what they do. Bel's hurt me but now she needs me again I'm expected to come running.'

'Perhaps you would give what we have discussed some thought,' I said. 'Lady Petit is very distressed on behalf of Annice. Here is my card, should you care to get in touch.'

'Listen,' said Leremer as we reached the door, 'there's one reason alone that would persuade me to go to court and that has nothing to do with Annabel – I'm through with her – or the child, whom I've barely set eyes on. It's Petit. Have you ever met him? He's the worst kind of Tory. Blinkered and cruel. One of those rare types who emerged from the war much better off than when he went in; I'd guess there were all kinds of smart financial dealings going on that were just this side of legal. If Annabel was crazy before she met him, she became much crazier afterwards.'

Wolfe, who was watching the activity in the hallway below, asked as if in afterthought, 'Do you think Petit has been faithful to her?'

'I doubt it. The man doesn't know the meaning of words such as trust or faithfulness, or loyalty. But he'd be good at discretion, unlike her. She's never cared about what people think. Good for her, I say.' He gave me a lopsided grin and perhaps the suggestion of a wink as he again picked up the telephone receiver. No wonder he'd won Annabel Petit's heart – he contrived to give the impression of being both a cheeky kid and an important young man burdened with matters of national moment and as I left the room I couldn't help glancing at my reflection in a glass door: no-nonsense hat of a somewhat Wellingtonian shape, blouse tied at the neck with a narrow ribbon. Prim, I thought.

Such was the effect of Leremer.

In the taxi Wolfe favoured me with his opinion of left-wing politicians. 'You see the trouble with socialists is that they think they mean it when they utter words such as *just* and *equal* but the likes of Leremer don't live the ideal. He'll say he was brought up in some northern town or village but I'll bet you he went to a prestigious grammar school, served five minutes in some regiment – probably never even crossed the Channel – and then went up to Oxbridge where he will have rubbed shoulders with all kinds of political and social high-flyers. He'll certainly know nothing real about union men or what it's like down a pit.'

'The name you mentioned – Saklatvala.'

'Saklatvala is a communist. Indian. The Labour Party is not keen to embrace him on either count, even though he's the Independent Labour Party MP for North Battersea – our Daniel Breen's own member of parliament, in fact. The likes of Leremer are fatally in thrall to the establishment. They secretly want the world to look much as it already does only a shade pinker. Saklatvala has all kinds of uncomfortable ideas, such as liberating India from British rule and improving the working conditions of Indians in this country, so he's way too radical for the likes of Leremer. And like so many of his type, he can't resist the lure of the beautiful people whose world he professes to despise. Hence the affair with Annabel.'

'Would it make any difference if we could prove that Petit had been playing around too?'

'I am certainly happy to put myself at your disposal, Miss Gifford, by making a few enquiries as to what our Timmo gets up to when he's not preparing to take the unions apart. Just up my street. But he probably knows he couldn't get a divorce from Annabel on grounds of adultery, because they belong to a set of people who are misbehaving all the time. It's why he's gone for a paternity case. Lady P. played right into his hands by naming Leremer as the guilty party, even if it's not true.'

'I don't think you like Leremer very much, Mr Wolfe.'

He gave me a charmingly disingenuous smile. 'I merely make generalisations about his type. In my view they could do a great deal of damage, so-called conviction politicians driven above all by ambition.'

'Although he seems to have been genuinely in love with Annabel at one time.'

'Oh, we men are very susceptible, Miss Gifford. He will have been an easy victim. The thing is, we have to be so careful about where we tread when we don't understand the turf.' He stared at the passers-by on Great Portland Street, many of whom had opened black umbrellas. 'I worry sometimes that people – with the best of intentions or perhaps out of a desire for excitement or power or merely change – will want to flex their muscles a little, make a few ripples, and before they know it they've done untold harm. Created mayhem, like the strike, or at the very least broken a few hearts.'

His averted face was tucked up within hat, coat collar and scarf but I knew exactly what he was talking about. Though he said nothing more I sat transfixed because it was quite clear that he had noticed what was happening between Breen and me – although I had been so sure we'd given nothing away. In fact, since having supper together we had been painstakingly businesslike; only an additional formality might have indicated to Miss Drake or Wolfe that there was anything going on.

Indecision tormented me when I considered that Breen might propose. He certainly wasn't the type to prevaricate. Sometimes the prospect of being married to him felt invigorating and reassuring. I suspected that now, if he didn't take things further, I might feel disappointed. There was hardly a queue of other candidates, and compared to the type of men I'd recently been dealing with – Timmo Petit, Ned Wright, even the thrusting Richard Leremer – he was ideal. He loved me and in return I felt a kind of amazed affection and knew there was plenty more I might discover, if he were to allow me to draw closer. And he understood me better than almost anyone.

But I wasn't in love with him. I knew what being in love felt like and it wasn't this. I liked being with Breen, I enjoyed watching him and I loved the way he worked, his waywardness. But his kisses made me sad because I was so unmoved by them. I knew how it felt when my body was charged with passion – sleepless and wide open with desire; how it was to be absorbed in another being even when standing up in court, sitting at a family dinner or trying to sleep; to be greedy for one glimpse, one touch, one word; to be so alive to another's presence that the smallest detail – the shape of a finger, the exact curve of each eyelash – registered in my soul.

To be transfigured, vibrantly awake, sexual, needy, generous; that was being in love and perhaps, I told myself, as I alighted from the taxicab with the too-observant Wolfe, I owed it to Breen not to settle for anything less.

# Chapter Sixteen

For the first half-hour of Meredith's leaving party my friend Carole Mangan and her new fiancé, Michael Craig, were our only guests. Meredith was still dressing when they arrived and the three of us propped ourselves against the wall because the furniture had been pushed aside to make room for dancing. At first Craig seemed dourer even than Carole had suggested, monosyllabic and un-smiling. Edmund, however, who was prancing about in harlequin pyjamas, had none of my reservations and took him aside, subjecting him to a volley of questions about police procedure.

Carole, though a regular visitor, regarded our room with awe. We had new cushion covers made by Meredith in block-printed cotton patterned with yellow and pink flower heads and green leaves on an azure background. 'Oh these colours,' had been Prudence's pronouncement, 'they dazzle the eye. In my day, colours were so *dim*.' The candles we'd stuffed into empty bottles were as yet unlit so that by standing on tiptoe and pressing one's nose to the window one could see the glint of a lantern as a barge passed across our sliver of the Thames.

'By the way,' Carole said, 'I've had a word with our manager and persuaded him to give your Gertrude Wright an interview. I said she was a special case because she'd been recommended by you.'

'I hope she doesn't let you down.'

'It's only an interview.'

'I don't even know if she'll be pleased or not. Sometimes I wonder whether I've inherited too much of my Aunt Prudence's desire to put other people's lives in order.'

'Isn't that your job? When people can't manage to sort things out for themselves you do it for them.'

'What if they don't want to have things sorted?'

'I'm sure they always hope things will get better. It's just that they might have a rather different idea about what's best for them than you do.' She smiled diffidently, amazed as usual that I should seek her opinion.

There was hammering on the street door far below and Edmund went pounding down the stairs to let more people in. Meredith emerged, her eyes rimmed with kohl, her hair oiled to a slick cap and wearing a midnight-blue dress which had once belonged to Grandmother and was therefore some forty years out of date with its swishing skirt and tight bodice. Her art friends had loud voices and their clothes smelt of dust and turpentine. They had attached ribbons and sequins to old frocks – nobody had any money – and the women wore velvet bands in their hair. My own party frock was plain by comparison, with its gathered pale blue skirt and embroidered bodice. My arms were bare and the round neck revealed my throat and collarbones so that I felt altogether much more exposed than usual.

What effect would the dress have on Daniel Breen, I wondered, if he came? Meredith would realise the state of things at once if he looked at me as he had when bidding me farewell at the station. I was nervy and distracted as I watched her unwrap gifts which her friends said *must* accompany her to Sanary-sur-Mer, although her cases were already so full that we'd used canvas ties to hold the lids shut. There was no possibility of accommodating a three-volume edition of George Eliot's *Romola*, a large, hand-thrown pottery mug or four jars of plum chutney.

Carrie, one of my very legal lady friends, as Meredith had dubbed them, arrived next, accompanied by the formidable Ambrose whom she was to marry the following year. She was wearing an eye-catching black necklace and warned me that they were on their way to another do.

'We heard you were representing Annabel Petit,' she said with her usual bluntness.

'Indeed I am. Not without trepidation.'

'We're all amazed,' said Ambrose. 'We didn't think Breen & Balcombe would touch a case like that. You do realise what you're up against? Rumours abound. It's said her behaviour's driven her husband almost to the point of having her sectioned. If you win he'll hate her all the more, and if you lose she'll be publicly branded as the mother of an illegitimate child.'

'It's Annice, the little girl, who I care about most. She's the real reason I took the case on. She stands to lose not only her father but her name.'

The gramophone had been wound up and the party was getting into its stride. Despite his ghostly white skin, Angus Strangeways had proved strong enough to haul crates of beer up more than fifty steps. Red wine was sloshed into teacups and mixed with lemonade to create a froth and eke out the alcohol. Cigarettes were lit.

'Is a name so important?' Carrie asked.

Everyone was clapping in time as Edmund led his mother on to the cleared floor to partner him in the Shimmy. He approached dancing as he did most activities – with complete dedication; his steps were precise and he had a most endearing way of holding his partner's eye as if he'd been born with an instinct for gallantry. He and Meredith were so obviously a pair with their neat limbs and shining mops of hair, caught up in each other's rhythm. What would Jamie have thought, I wondered, if he could see Edmund now? James had been a much more self-conscious child, lacking his son's ability to lose himself like this in the moment.

'And who is the father?' demanded Carrie. 'What's your hunch? Everyone says it's not Petit.'

'Whatever happens, there'll be no happy ending,' I said. 'Even if we win, Annabel Petit will be faced with a loveless marriage.'

'Well then,' said Carrie, 'I'd say, first win the case, second, get her to divorce him anyway, but on her own terms.'

Edmund stood before me panting, eyes shining. 'Come and dance, Aunty Evelyn, *please*.'

He and I were well practised as dancing partners. I loved the swing of my skirts across my knees, the flicking of my hands and feet, the rhythmic jolt of my hips. Soon Michael Craig and Carole joined us and they must have danced together often because their hands clasped, feet tapped, hips swayed in jaunty syncopated time. Even Carrie kicked off her shoes and drew the stately Ambrose into the dance.

Meredith scooped up her skirts to free her ankles and knees

– she was wearing blue stockings secured with a garter halfway up her thigh – and danced with everyone except Angus, who leaned against the wall between the two windows, drinking and smoking until the scent of hashish wafted across the room. At one stage I made an effort to engage him in conversation and he peered at me blearily as if he had no idea who I was.

'Are you looking forward to the South of France, Mr Strangeways?'

'Mr Strangeways? Good Lord, is that my name? I'd forgotten; it's been so long since anyone called me that. And yes, travel is always good for the soul, don't you think?' His smile had great charm, transforming him into someone boyish and hopeful.

'I wish we'd had more of a chance to get to know each other, before you left.'

He nodded seriously, although I sensed he scarcely knew why an acquaintance between us should matter at all. But then he leaned towards me and whispered, 'Don't fret about that little boy. Merry told me you would miss him very much. I'll take great care, *great* care of him.' And he nodded gravely several times.

A few minutes after I'd left him, his eyes closed and he slid down the wall, his pipe-cleaner-thin legs a hazard to us dancers.

When Meredith and I partnered each other her bony forearms rested on my shoulders and she threw back her head so that the air from the open window cooled her neck. At this stage of drunkenness she became lonely and wild, always wanting something more. 'I made you dance,' she said, raising herself on tiptoe and approaching her hot, painted lips to my ear. 'You would not be dancing if I'd never come to England.'

'I know that. You've taught me so many good things.'

'Even so, it's not really me you care about losing when we go to France, it's Edmund.'

'You know that's not true.'

'Whereas I love you,' she said, 'far, far too much.'

'Nobody can love anyone too much, surely.' I was propping her up, my tone dry to tease her out of being so maudlin.

'Oh yes they can, you silly old bird, if it's not an equal love.' Her drunken eyelids fluttered and she flung her head so far back that all I could see of her face was the underside of her pointed chin.

We had been dancing so wildly that my hair came loose over my ear.

'You should let your hair down. I dare you,' she said.

'It's a mess. It needs washing. I should get it cut.'

'Never get it cut. You'd be like Samson. All your strength is in your hair. Didn't you know?'

I took the pins out of my hair and let her unravel and pull and tease it until it stood in a fuzz behind my shoulders and felt heavy and hot on my neck. I liked the way she made me conscious of my physical self – Carrie was watching and it felt rather daring to let her glimpse this other side of me; the still-young woman who could hold conversations about passion and had been made love to in a cottage bedroom. Afterwards Meredith went on dancing with a succession of friends – Philip and Cecil and Kathleen. One, John Nash, took me aside and said earnestly, 'She must paint in France. Don't allow her to stop painting. She gets distracted so easily. She's really good you know. Such an eye for colour.'

By now Angus Strangeways was asleep on the floor with his head on a cushion. Carole and Michael stepped over him as they left, hand in hand – a tactful departure in light of Craig's role as a police officer and Angus's consumption of illegal substances. It was time to capture Edmund and steer him to bed.

'I won't be able to sleep,' he insisted. 'It's too noisy and I'm too excited.'

'Of course you will. I wish I was all snug in my bed like you.' He was slight and childish in his silky pyjamas; his newly washed hair smelt of shampoo and almost at once his head lolled against my arm. I stroked his cheek and rested my face near his on the pillow. Lovely, lovely boy, I whispered. When I kissed his forehead, smooth and cool as an eggshell, he stirred, only to sink more deeply into sleep.

Returning to the party I was almost too late to catch Carrie and Ambrose as they headed for the door. 'See you on Wednesday for tea,' she called. 'Law Soc. Usual time. Actually we're sorry to go. Best party in years.' She cast a somewhat wistful glance back at the candlelit room.

I nodded, speechless, thinking that by the time I next saw her, Edmund would be gone. As I pressed myself into an alcove, I wished everyone else would leave too so that I could spend a last night alone with Meredith and her sleeping son in the bead of light that was our flat, this charmed place where I used to think we were so happy.

There was a gust of cooler air as the door to the stairs was opened and Daniel came in. Heart in mouth, I watched him negotiate his way through a cluster of women in their scanty dance frocks, searching for me among the crowd, a touch diffident but every bit himself – composed, expectant and with a couple of bottles of beer in the pockets of his overcoat. It was his red cravat that moved me most; that he had taken the trouble to dress for our party. I didn't hesitate any longer but manoeuvred my way through the dancers and reached for his hand.

'I was beginning to think you wouldn't make it.'

His eyes blazed with love. 'Yet, here I am.'

I took his coat and piled it with the others on my bed, showed him where Edmund lay sleeping in the next-door cubbyhole and introduced him to Meredith who was amid a group in the narrow kitchen, mixing rough cocktails of gin and lemonade.

'Ah, it's so good to see you again at last,' she cried, 'the famous Mr Breen. Evelyn talks about you all the time but we've scarcely met. Do you remember that time in court a couple of years ago?'

'Please call me Daniel,' he told her, a little diffident but meeting her eye warmly.

A combination of alcohol and hashish had made her eyes enormous as she clung to his hand. 'You are a very good man,' she informed him, 'you have done great things for Evie.'

'Evelyn has done great things for herself,' he retorted, laughing.

'We were arguing about the General Strike,' said Kathleen whose headband drooped low over her eyes as she leaned against the gas ring.

'I'm sure Daniel will tell us what to think.' Meredith lurched suddenly, tucked her hand under my arm, leaned her head on my shoulder and stared at Breen. 'Daniel's a lawyer.'

'Another lawyer. Gracious. Well, if there's a strike, whose side will *you* be on, Daniel?'

'I shall be on the side of the strikers,' I said, a little needled that they had not asked for my opinion.

'Me too,' said Kathleen.

'But the unions are hopeless,' said Meredith, 'which is one of the reasons I'm leaving this country. Why can't they get themselves organised?'

'Because the unions are divided between those who want to do too much – to overthrow the government – and those who want to do too little, i.e. not upset anyone,' said Daniel. 'The result is an impasse.'

'Whereas the government,' said Meredith, 'you know, people like Evelyn's Timothy Petit, has recruited an army of volunteers to keep the wheels turning. If the unions would only do the same I'd stay, really I would. But are we going to stand here all night being earnest, Mr Daniel Breen, or are you going to dance with me?'

As she led him away he threw aside his jacket and became utterly different to the Daniel I'd seen thus far, laughing, quick-footed, yes, a good dancer though perhaps a little too accurate in his movements. Later, when he partnered me, our eyes met and my pulse raced because I knew that something was going to happen that night. Annabel Petit's words were ringing in my ears: *You know when you're standing on the edge of a cliff and you lean over and there's a part of you thinking: how much further should I, could I, lean, and what would it feel like to fall?*

At midnight precisely the elderly gent who lived on the floor below banged on the ceiling and everyone trooped off to the Café Royal, leaving me in charge of Edmund. 'And now you have your Mr Breen to keep you company too,' Meredith whispered, 'so I'm sure you'll be just fine.'

They were gone, and in the silent flat Daniel and I self-consciously collected glasses until he wound up the gramophone and played the last record again – Bessie Smith's 'I Ain't Got Nobody'. 'Dance with me,' he said.

I kicked off my shoes and his arm came confidently round my waist. 'I didn't imagine you'd know how to dance,' I told him.

*And I'm sad and lonely* ... I was very hot, the familiar room felt too enclosed and it seemed to me that Daniel was suddenly a stranger. Either it was the lateness of the hour or the fact that Edmund and Meredith were leaving, but I felt desolate, detached. 'When did you learn to dance?' I asked.

'Everyone learned before the war. And my fiancée, Sally, sent me to dancing classes while I was on leave.'

'That heartless woman,' I said, and he pulled me closer.

*But since my daddy left me . . .*

'I'll leave if you want me to. Just say the word,' he whispered.

But I didn't say anything. Tomorrow, after they were gone, at least this would be something that was mine and had not been torn from me. So I tightened my arms about his neck and discovered that being kissed by Daniel for a second time was as decisive and interesting as all the other activities we had undertaken together. Yes, I could imagine desiring him, if not now, then soon. When I drew back my head for breath he pulled me closer and kissed me again, his hands firm on my back through the sheer fabric of my dress. The music stopped on a jolting, fading beat and we pulled away and stared at each other, his face naked with love as he gripped my hand.

'I love you,' he said. 'So much.'

My eyes were hot with tears. Raising my hand to his lips he kissed the knuckles. 'I've been preparing all kinds of eloquent speech for weeks, months, but now it's come to it I have nothing to say except that I have fallen in love with you.'

My head went down and I covered my eyes. I was crying and I couldn't understand myself. It was gratitude, and release, perhaps; pent-up tears for Grandmother, for the abrupt reappearance of Nicholas, for the imminent departure of Meredith and her son. Drawing me on to a heap of cushions Daniel held me curled against him as he stroked my hair and cheek and kissed me again and again. I leaned into him and blotted out the familiar room in all its disarray – bottles and dirty glasses, strewn cushions, overflowing ashtrays.

'The last thing I want is to make you unhappy, Evelyn. I've had so much time to prepare for this moment and you haven't. And I know how sad you must feel tonight. I should wait, I'm prepared to wait but the difficulty is I can't hide my feelings from you or anyone else. Wolfe . . .'

'Yes. Wolfe.' I mopped my tears with the handkerchief he offered and managed to laugh. It was so easy to be lying there with him, to feel his tentative fingers lifting the hair from my forehead.

'Perhaps in some ways, if I'm honest, it's been there from the first. I'm not a fool, I know how inconvenient, dangerous, this could be for our work. I've thought about it and fought it for that reason and I want you to know, I promise you, that whatever happens I will never let this affect us professionally. Evelyn, you do understand, don't you, that I'm asking you to marry me.'

Speechless, I could only catch hold of his hand and press it to my cheek.

'I'm not expecting an answer at once. Take as much time as you need. A year even, I wouldn't mind. And I'm telling you here and now that if you turn me down, it will make not a jot of difference at work.'

'I can't tell you . . . I feel so privileged—'

He laughed. '*Privileged*. You're not privileged. That's just the trouble, that's why I hesitated. I'm quite sure you think of me simply as Daniel Breen, stuffy partner in a law firm, to whom you have cause to be grateful because I dared to take on a woman articled clerk when no one else would have her. Whereas I,' his eyes were a lighter shade of grey and more vulnerable than I had ever seen them, 'I find it well nigh impossible not to think of you morning, noon and night.'

By now he had got hold of both my hands and was kissing them as if they were the most precious things he'd ever touched. 'So will you give the matter some thought?'

'I will. I will.'

'After all, it would be superbly helpful to your career,' he told me, much more light-heartedly. 'No other husband would countenance a legal wife whereas I'm more than happy to break new ground. Think of it, we'd be husband and wife, partners in a law firm. I for one see that as an extraordinarily stimulating prospect.'

I pressed my hand to the soft hair on the back of his head and kissed him until I felt his body go taut and demanding and his mouth open under mine. No need to think of an answer; just hold and be held. But it was gone two, Edmund was asleep in the next room, Meredith would be back at any minute. Eventually he got up, pulled me to my feet and sent me to fetch his coat.

'My dearest girl,' he said, rubbing my naked arms as I stood shivering in the doorway. 'Sleep. And don't worry about what I've said. Give it time. Allow yourself to get used to the idea. And try not to be too sad tomorrow when they leave.'

He spoke a little wistfully, I thought, as if he were struggling to disconnect the two events, his proposal and the fact that tomorrow I'd be alone. I stood at the top of the stairs listening to the boards creak as he reached each landing. When the front door closed I ran to the window and saw him emerge on to the street and wave up at me. Returning the gesture, I felt another start of joy that I had made him suddenly so carefree. But the euphoria quickly died as I undressed.

I lay for a couple of hours in a state of semi-consciousness, adrenalin and alcohol pumping through my veins, reliving again and again what had happened, until I woke fully to hear birds scrabbling in the roof and see our skylight grey with dawn. It was after four when I heard Meredith's footsteps on the stairs and her key in the latch. When she did not come to bed I crept out and found her perched on a hard chair, fully dressed, eye sockets smeared with make-up.

'Did you have a lovely time?' I whispered, then added, 'It was a good party, a good send-off – I hope you're pleased.'

'A party shouldn't be good. It should be tedious or marvellous, not good.'

I kept quiet.

'*Everyone* was there at the Royal,' she said. 'All the girls were talking about how they are going to join the police as a volunteer or drive a train if the strike happens. I wish I was staying in London if it meant I could be a train driver.' She was hard-eyed, calculating her barbs. I recognised this remorseless stage of drunkenness.

'Shall I make tea,' I asked, 'or are you coming to bed?'

'I'm not moving a muscle ever again. I feel all broken up, Evie. Can't you at least try to hold me together? I know I should take better care of Edmund. It's not right to tear him away from his school and family. And I saw you talking to Angus. You don't like him, do you?'

'Oh come on, Meredith. I've only met him twice and spoken to him for about five minutes in total. You can't expect me to have an opinion.'

'You're always making snap judgements. Don't hold back on my account.'

'All right. As a matter of fact I thought he was probably very well meaning but a bit of a drifter, like you said. But the point is Edmund has you, and that's all he needs, and I think you will love France and so will Edmund. You take wonderful care of him, he's a very happy little boy. Can't you tell?'

'He is, at the moment. But that's because he thinks that when we come back in September everything will be the same. Whereas I know *exactly* what will happen. Either there'll be some other inky legal woman, a Peggy or a Helen, because you say you can't afford to live here on your own. Or there'll be a man.' She watched me as I moved into the kitchen to make tea. 'There already is a man, isn't there?'

I gripped the handle of the kettle then placed it carefully on the hob. 'Yes . . . there's a man.'

'Daniel Breen, as I live and breathe. Of all people.' She sprang to her feet, her eyes ablaze. 'And you didn't think to tell me?'

'There was nothing to tell until tonight.'

'And? Evie, don't tell me he *proposed*. Oh my God, you're going to marry him.'

'I've not decided anything yet.'

'Well, well. First let me congratulate you – I suppose that's the done thing.' She clutched me in her thin arms then abruptly released me. 'Oh Evie, don't do it unless you're sure. Is it because we're leaving? Do you love him?'

She was maddening, interrogating me like this in the small hours. 'Oh for God's sake, what do you expect me to do?' I cried. 'After all, I've discovered that I'm terrified of being without you.'

We stared at each other – I wrapped in my old camel dressing gown, she in Grandmother's full-skirted frock, her complexion ashen in the grey light of dawn. 'Evie,' she said, appearing to soften, 'don't you think it would be better to deal with that first, rather than running away from it by marrying Breen? Think of the damage you could do. After all, you were surviving perfectly well before Edmund and I came along.'

I was too overwrought to decide whether she was being deliberately cruel. '*Surviving*. It was barely that. When you came to London it was as if you brought me back from the dead. And now I've come to regard Edmund almost as my son, and you as my sister. But now you are leaving, with that Angus who you clearly don't love, as if even to be with him would be better than living here with me. It's obvious that you don't think I matter much at all as far as you and Edmund are concerned.'

As I spoke I was shaking and a small, detached part of me realised that I was not used to displaying real anger, and hadn't recognised the heat in my throat and the hardening of my bones for what they were until now.

Meredith covered her face and shook her head. 'I'm sorry. I'm sorry. I didn't realise how strongly you'd feel.'

'And Daniel loves me. He has never let me down, ever. He would never do such a thing as to tell me at my grandmother's funeral that he was leaving me.'

'I'm sorry.' She held first my arm, then hugged me. Her hair smelt of cigarettes and of the musky oil she used to give it a shine. 'I'm so sorry.'

'Oh for heaven's sake,' I laughed shakily, 'we're such fools. Let's go to bed before we say anything else we might regret. After all, as you keep telling me, it's just for a few months.'

She gripped my hand. 'At least we've spoken out so we know where we are. We must take better care in future. But for God's sake promise me you won't do anything rash while we're away.'

Edmund was still sleeping peacefully and I lay down on my mattress in our room while Meredith undressed. Her eyes shone in the gloom as she lay down on her side, gazing across at me. Being Meredith, she had one more question to ask. 'But what about the tall one who made you so unhappy?'

'If you mean Nicholas Thorne, he's out of the frame. He's back from South Africa and he's with some other woman.'

'Ah, isn't it strange? I always thought he would be your man. Just shows you how wrong a girl can be.'

# Chapter Seventeen

I waved goodbye to Meredith and Edmund from the ticket barrier at Waterloo Station, grateful that the fashion was for hats with brims that came low over the eyes. This was a haunted place. I remembered the stench of wet overcoats, sweat and coal, a swarming mass of khaki, the hefting up of kitbags and the uttering of stupid words, 'See you in a couple of months . . .' 'Say goodbye to grandmother for me . . .' 'Did you remember to pack the scarf she knitted?' Each time we did it, our smiles became brighter and falser because we knew, we *knew*, that so far we had just been lucky.

And he knew, my brother, with his rough, young man's hair, and his eyes so unguarded, what horrors lay beyond that innocent London station, the ordinary train. He knew the stink and the mud and the cold, the boredom and the fear. He knew where it was going to end. He wanted me to leave, would rather I'd stayed at home, because I was too soft a reminder of the life from which he was being wrenched. So, a brisk handshake – our father was there, obscure in his overcoat – and 'Safe journey, let us know how you go on . . .' then for the last time Jamie held me in a hard embrace, his kitbag lumpen between our feet, his great coat so stiff that I couldn't feel his shape beneath, smelling as it did not of him but of journeys and still, despite Min's best efforts, of stagnant water, his cheek smooth because he never was old enough to grow a proper beard.

He walked away and much as I loved him, I lost him, simply couldn't make him out any more as he merged with so many others in the depths of the platform beyond the barrier. I didn't move, though everyone else was barging about. The train began its slow, wheezing shift away from the buffers. Father was talking but

I didn't hear what he said because I was thinking of Jamie perched on a hard bench in some dirty carriage, a sacrifice, a boy with a gun and a number. Nevertheless, I supposed that he would be glad that the parting was over, might even be sharing a joke.

I blamed myself, I still did. We had known by then what the odds were. We had known there was no point to any of it. But we never had the conversation Daniel Breen might have inspired that would have begun, 'What if you don't go back?'

The telegram came. He'd died, and that was that. We'd let it happen. And now here was Edmund, Jamie's son, with his brow crinkled in the confusion of sorrow and excitement he felt because he too was leaving. Fortunately he always wore his mother's somewhat eccentric choice of clothes with great nobility because he was dressed in a second-hand light green tweed suit, surely too cumbersome for travel or the seaside.

Meredith was brittle in her goodbyes. Her eyes were darkly shadowed and I wondered if she'd slept even for an hour. 'Of course I have our passports and the sandwiches. Stop checking up on me, Evie.' She pecked my cheek and was gone, tripping away in frivolous shoes tied with silken bows to where Angus Strangeways hovered with a portfolio under one arm and a misshapen suitcase under the other because the handle had broken. He smiled across, gave me the thumbs up and put a clumsy arm around Meredith.

I kissed the salt skin on Edmund's forehead. 'Off you go, boy.'

'I wish you were coming with us. Please come.' Clasping his arms about me he looked pleadingly into my face.

'I shall. You just try and stop me. But I'll wait until you've discovered all the best places to show me.'

It was asking too much of this child's imagination, surely, for him to visualise Aunty Evelyn, who was currently wearing her Saturday pullover of turquoise wool (a fine cable-knit by Prudence), and her black coat, shedding all this wintriness in a sunshiny place. But he punched the air suddenly and laughed as if all his problems were solved, and ran off to his mother's side. Next minute they were through the barrier and on to the platform, Edmund skipping and swinging his right arm round in a circle as he always did when he was excited.

*

I returned to the flat and swept the floor, packed the empty bottles into crates and washed up dirty cups and glasses. In our bedroom I shifted the piles of clothes Meredith had left behind so that they occupied as little space as possible. Next door, as I stripped Edmund's bed I felt a hint of warmth from his body and I savagely tore off the sheet. Now it was coming, I couldn't keep it at bay any longer and I sank on to the mattress and buried my face in the rough cotton so I wouldn't be heard in the flat below. Grief had lost none of its power to grind its way into my belly, to wind me so I was doubled over, shocked by my own stifled cries.

When I finally caught my breath I raised my head and saw that I was in Edmund's room still, and that his walls were decorated with his mother's bold, abstract paintings of the river and a few of his own which, unlike hers, were full of laborious detail and labelled: *Aunty Evelyn drying her hair* or *A boat I saw on Thursday*.

Work would surely steady me. Meredith usually colonised the table by the window with her art materials but that morning I had the luxury of spreading out my papers and books. I even lit the gas fire, an unheard-of extravagance, but with Prudence far away there was no one to suggest that donning an extra vest would be far cheaper. Finally, I allowed myself to be distracted by the sight of Grandmother's writing box, which had been pushed under a chair the night before for safekeeping. Its sturdiness and age comforted me, though unlocking it on my own was yet one more reminder that Edmund had gone. This time I was a little more dedicated in my search for the hidden drawer. After all, it couldn't be a sophisticated mechanism and sure enough, by patiently lifting and poking, I found the correct partition, pulled it up and saw a panel spring open.

The first drawer contained a bit of whimsy, a miniature mother-of-pearl needle book which I used to admire, hardly bigger than a postage stamp, with lint pages. In the second was a folded letter, tied with a scrap of ribbon.

It was in a stranger's hand, and dated Friday, 15 March, 1872.

*My dearest, my dear Clara,*
*Draw aside the curtain, darling, look down to the corner of the street and you will see that I am waiting for you.*

*News came to me only last night that you are to be married tomorrow. Why the rush, headlong? All you've told me about this schoolteacher of yours is that you find his attentions touching. Don't marry touching. Don't go ahead with it. Give me one last chance.*

*My darling, I am all burnt up 'til there is nothing left of me but one hot ember, one thought: Clara. A month ago when we met in that Baker Street hotel I had a speech prepared; one of the most despicable and self-deceptive of my career. I told you that in the end, after all those months of loving you, I had to choose my wife and children. I remember your precious face – small, downturned so I couldn't see your eyes, only your pale cheeks and the way you compressed your lips so you wouldn't cry.*

*You didn't plead. Such dignity, you showed. But if only you had put up a fight I might have realised my folly there and then. As it was, you were silent.*

*All day, since I heard of this precipitate wedding of yours, I have been storming about the house, thinking of you.*

*I love you. I love you. I love you.*

*It is quite simply this. I have been asleep and now I am awake. I have loved before but not with a love that consumes me in a swirling red heat. So I have booked a sleeper to Paris. Think. Tomorrow morning we will wake in the rue Saint Honoré in that same room, my precious love, where you and I lay, and I kissed your eyelids and your breast at that place I love most, and I wept because you brought me such joy. Do you remember the Parisian traffic outside, my lips on your skin, your sweet, soft kisses that transported me into God knows what heavenly place? My Clara. My true love. My witch. The sunlight moved across the ceiling and on to the hard bolster, which you loved, you said, because it was French. And when you left me for a moment, I rolled into the imprint of you, and I pressed my face into that bolster and smelt, faintly, your hair.*

*Without you I am a shadow man. You enchant me with your smile and that wicked twitch of your lip, the touch of your fingers like butterflies on my flesh, so tender and shy yet in the end, ah, Clara, bold. Your perfume, which is the essence of you, and all your secret places.*

126

*This time it will be for good. No more partings. There will*
*be a storm, of course, but now I can't even think of that, or my*
*career, or all those other distractions. I am waiting for you.*
*Bring only what you stand up in. I will provide all else.*
  *Darling Clara.*
  *Come to me . . .*
  *Patrick*

After that, of course, I couldn't sit still. Here was the proof that
Grandmother had had an affair with Rusbridger and that I was
not, therefore, the woman I'd always believed myself to be. The
blood in my veins was actually a much more potent mix and my
poor, repressed mother, who was so afraid of the world that she
rarely even glanced at it directly, was as illegitimate as her dangerous grandson. And the language of love, albeit overblown (I
noted the actorish flourish of *Ah, Clara*) was so sensual, so overwrought, that I felt again the blow of my solitude, and beyond
that a craving for something else altogether, even more shattering
to my peace of mind.

Having prowled the flat and reread the letter, I clapped on my
hat and went walking along the Embankment. There, the sight
of the river where Edmund and I used to watch the boats made
me wince. He especially loved the barges because the thought of
living on water with a real stove puffing out woodsmoke was his
idea of perfection. We had discussed at length what it would be
like to live in so contained a place, how we would manage the
basics of life, and how well we'd sleep with water lapping against
the sides.

Finally I went to the Tate Gallery and at last found a little
solace. The Pre-Raphaelites had been condemned by Meredith
for being too sentimental and leaving nothing to the imagination,
although she did admire their brushwork. Nevertheless I stood
before Arthur Hughes's *April Love* and sank my consciousness
into the blue of the young girl's gown, as she had taught me.

'Even an unsympathetic painting,' she had said, 'can sometimes
be like a soft stroke to the soul. You can see through it to the artist's intention; the great care he's taken with that fallen flower or
the hem of her skirt, as if perfecting the translucency of a petal or

a fold of cloth were the only thing that matters in all the world. And for a moment, while he painted it, while we study it, that's the truth. There is nothing more. And thus, we are elevated.'

'*Elevated?*' Edmund had repeated.

'Elevated,' Meredith had said firmly. 'Above everyday life.'

Studying the painting, that face turned aside, the eyes brimming with tears, the shy hand on the scarf, I again thought of Grandmother and her love letter. How she must have adored her Patrick – Rusbridger, presumably, as named by the actress at the funeral – to have kept the letter all these years. But instead of him, she'd chosen her schoolteacher, to give herself some respectability and security, and to be the father of her unborn child.

And I thought of last night's party and Breen's proposal, and tried to imagine how I'd be feeling now if I'd answered yes.

# Chapter Eighteen

That night I was to be elevated again, by Noël Coward's new play, *Hay Fever*, to which I had invited Mother as a distraction from that first night alone in the flat. I again wore my party dress but this time attached a low, tie collar upon which I pinned Grandmother's cameo. So this is what Daniel sees, I thought, peering into our round mirror with its spotted glass; a sad-eyed woman with an unfashionable mass of hair.

I then set off by omnibus to Maida Vale where Mother was waiting in the hall, dressed head to toe in black, fearful eyes peering out from beneath a favourite hat that was more than a decade out of date.

'Did they get off all right?' she asked when we were safely aboard a bus.

'I saw them on to the train.'

Silence. 'You'll be sorry to see them gone.'

'Yes. But then aren't you, Mother?'

'He's turned out to be a dear little boy,' she conceded.

'And isn't it high time you forgave Meredith?'

'*Forgave.* What an odd word. I have nothing to forgive her for.'

'Your son loved her,' I insisted. 'Shouldn't that be enough for you?'

This was too much. 'We have no idea what really went on between those two.'

'We have his last letter, Mother, in which he told us to look after her.'

'Nothing was as it seemed during the war,' she said. 'We'll never know what she really meant to him,' and she turned her face away as if this was the last word. I knew she'd be crying behind her veil and I felt a sudden wild exasperation because surely Patrick

Rusbridger's letter was proof that Mother, like Edmund, was the product of an illicit relationship. I suspected she had known this all along – it would explain her antipathy to Edmund, her rejection of the acting profession, her determination to keep Grandmother out of the public eye – but even if she hadn't, it was high time we all stopped hiding things from each other.

Perhaps that is what made me utter the words, 'Mother, I have something to tell you.' As the omnibus lurched around the corner of Charing Cross Road I sensed her readiness for some fresh blow. She'll be transformed, I thought, and could not help feeling a little childish excitement that I was at last about to say something that would make her happy. 'I've had an offer of marriage.'

A pause, almost stagy, and she gripped my arm. 'Oh, Evelyn. You *haven't*? Who from?'

'I don't want to tell you until I've made up my mind, in case it all falls through – I just didn't want to keep you in the dark. Do you understand? I think you'd like him – he's a lawyer – like Father was.'

Beneath the veil she did a rapid calculation. Yes, that would do. This news could be presented with due pride to the likes of Mrs Gillespie. 'Oh, but this is *extraordinary*. I had no idea.' She swept her hat off and she was really smiling for once and looked a decade younger. 'Of course in my day,' she said, laughing, 'permission was generally requested from the parents before a gentleman proposed but you're such a *modern* woman, Evelyn. But what is holding you back from giving this poor man an answer?'

'I'm not sure. There's been so much change in our lives of late. It's hard to be sure of anything. I just thought you'd like to know.'

'Of course you must be sure. It's such an important decision. Perhaps I could help you make up your mind, talk things over? But I can't help thinking you wouldn't have mentioned the matter if you hadn't already decided. Oh, don't look at me like that. I won't say another word, not until it's all definite.'

By the time we'd reached the Criterion she was a different woman – back straight, eyes alight with pride and expectation. The hat was still off and she stood in the foyer and looked about at the naked arms and throats of other women. 'I would never dream of wearing something cut so swoopingly low at the back were I her age,' she murmured. 'It's so unflattering to have so much skin on show.'

The Criterion, being largely underground, did not subject audiences in the upper circle to the humiliation of an outside staircase. Mother perched in her narrow seat, then leaned over the rail and watched attentively the arrival of the more privileged sections of the audience. Every minute she grew more expansive as she smiled benignly on those wishing to reach a seat deeper in the row, or held the programme at arm's length – she was far too vain to wear spectacles – so that she could read it with professional interest.

'In the old days when we used to come to the theatre your father always took a box and people used to dress so beautifully. We came to this very theatre – it was while James was a baby – on the gala night they held to mark its reopening. Every woman had jewels in her hair, furs, tiaras, wonderful gowns, feathered headdresses. I don't think that up-and-down shape that is so popular nowadays is at all flattering to most Englishwomen.'

When she'd removed her hat I'd seen that she had dressed her cloudy hair with the pearl-headed pins she used to wear for great occasions. 'I don't expect I shall like the play,' she whispered. 'It's said to be terribly modern. No plot. Never mind. I shall think *everything* is marvellous tonight.'

I had fixed on Coward as an uncontroversial choice; *Hay Fever* had been running for six months and was a smash hit but Mother was quite right, there was precious little plot and in any case every scene in which Marie Tempest appeared was greeted with prolonged applause, thereby breaking the flow entirely. Between scenes Mother reached for my hand and gave it a conspiratorial squeeze.

I, on the other hand, hardly listened to a word of the play because I was hot with my own rashness at telling her my news. For the first time in years I had won her approval but I had been far too precipitate. As far as she was concerned the engagement was a fait accompli and it seemed perverse to raise her hopes in this way and then dash them. What on earth had I been thinking?

To distract her in the interval I suggested we go down to the dress circle so that we might have a better view of the people in the stalls.

'Of course it's nothing like the kind of play Mother used to take me to see in the old days,' she told me in her new, confiding mood. 'Ibsen. Chekhov. The greats. Shakespeare. Now that's what I call theatre.'

It was astonishing how, now that she was allowing herself to be happy, a different mother emerged, the lovely girl – whimsical, shy, filled with a longing for a better life – who had captured Father's susceptible heart. She glided across the foyer and up the grand staircase with the assurance of one who truly belongs, which was ironic given that she had spent her married life disassociating herself from her own mother's theatrical background. Clara Fielding had played Kate here in *She Stoops to Conquer* and been present at the launch of the Actresses' Franchise League, and I imagined her whisking down these same stairs in her velvet slippers. Along the wall were photographs of the more famous actors who had graced the stage, each labelled with a little plaque: Charles Wyndham, Athene Seyler, Eva Moore and Patrick Rusbridger.

My sudden halt caused a jam on the staircase. 'Mother, look, do you recognise him?'

She peered at the name, then the photograph. In fact she remained there, quite still, just a moment too long.

'Not at all,' she snapped, then walked on.

Rusbridger had been photographed in his role as Hamlet, no less – in tunic, tights and a pageboy wig, holding the skull of Yorick; the same Patrick Rusbridger whose letter I had read that morning. He had an actor's face: prominent cheekbones, an arrestingly fixed stare and pronounced brows. Yet I knew him in the core of my being because something in his face, particularly in the shape of the nose and jaw, was reflected back at me each time I brushed my hair in the morning.

The throng on the stairs moved me on. In the dress circle the audience was more flamboyant and the ladies wore enough jewels to satisfy even Mother, who smiled brilliantly and spoke very fast, presumably in case I should ask her any more awkward questions. We stood at the brass rail and looked across at the boxes.

'That's where we used to sit, your father and I, with a crowd from the business and the legal world. Do you remember how, when you were a little girl, you always helped me dress for the theatre?'

I indeed remembered the sheen of her powdered upper back, the ruffles of oyster silk, the lovely hush of her pleated petticoats; also the thrill of seeing her happy at the prospect of being on show. Despite herself, she'd always had an actress's need to make an entrance. Rusbridger was her father, I was sure, whatever she chose to believe. In the flush of my new understanding I linked my arm through hers and as the five-minute bell rang we took a last look up at the fairy-tale chandelier and down at the gentlemen in tailcoats and the ladies in hip-skimming frocks, before heading back to our much humbler seats.

'Miss Gifford!'

He was above me on the red staircase, arm in arm with the same young woman as before, though this time she wore a diaphanous pink gown and a diamanté band in her hair. An older couple stood behind, the lady in a white fur stole. But these other people were out of focus for I saw only him, changed in some respects from the man I had loved two years ago, but so much the same; thinner-faced, tanned, eyes dark with shock but still Nicholas Thorne, as engraved on my soul.

I recovered perhaps an instant sooner than he. 'Mr Thorne.'

His friends bowed indifferently as he introduced them. 'Mr and Mrs Hatton, Miss Catherine Hatton.' This last was the lady on his arm, her rippling auburn hair framing those neat features and a flawless complexion. She shook my hand with unnecessary enthusiasm but I could tell she desired only to please Nicholas, was probably in love with him, and had therefore sensed how I had snagged his attention.

'I'm very surprised to see you, Mr Thorne,' I said, quite coolly, 'I thought you were in South Africa.'

'I've been back a month or so. It was high time. The prospect of the General Strike drew me. I'm doing some work for the Federation of British Industry.' He nodded to Hatton as if he were the FBI personified. 'I have gained some experience with mining and such in South Africa so I hope I can be useful.'

Already the ghost of the old feeling was upon me, of being out of my depth in his company, thanks to the worlds in which he moved so effortlessly and the connections he'd made. His gaze flickered again and again to my face.

'And you,' he was asking, 'how are you?'

'I'm well. Busy. I finally qualified in January.'

'Miss Gifford is a lawyer,' he told Catherine Hatton and I could see she liked me even less.

'How *fascinating*,' said her mother.

We all smiled a little more and then I drew Mother away. There was no question of taking another look at Rusbridger's photograph. Instead I swept her along so fast that by the time she was restored to her seat she was quite breathless.

'He seemed like a pleasant young man. You might have introduced me.'

'He's just a colleague, a barrister I once worked with on a case.'

'Is he engaged to that young lady?'

'I have no idea, Mother.'

She smiled to herself.

The second half of the play was entirely lost as I relived again and again first the encounter with Rusbridger in two dimensions, then Nicholas in three. I tested my feelings as I might have probed a fresh wound. He had been dressed for evening, every inch of him groomed. If he'd only returned to the country a month ago, how could he be on such intimate terms with that girl? The answer must be that he had become acquainted with her through business; already he was in the thick of things, re-establishing his networks.

And yet, though I cursed my weakness, I still found him utterly compelling. The particular mix of his figure, features, voice and posture moved me, body and soul, as none other. We had not shaken hands yet I had so wanted to touch him. His smile had been forced, his voice studiously indifferent but the connection was still there, that judder of recognition.

*I have gained some experience with mining and such*, he had said, as if the outcome of the General Strike now depended on him. The arrogance.

# Chapter Nineteen

In Pimlico, a hand-delivered note from Daniel awaited me.

*I couldn't keep away,* he'd written, *even though I knew you'd be at the theatre. Try not to be sad now that your nephew has gone. Remember I love you. That's all.*

I heated milk, almost relieved that Meredith and Edmund were gone so I could at least stride about or peer again at my incredulous face in the mirror above the mantel. There she was, the grandchild of Patrick Rusbridger – his jaw, his eyes. It seemed to me that this face, Evelyn Gifford's face, was not as it had been at the beginning of the evening. Now it was marked by tension and passion; Grandmother's illicit liaison, Breen's kisses of the previous night, my hasty words to Mother, his note, Thorne's return. Dear God! At that moment I would have torn off my face, Rusbridger's face, if only it might have calmed the frantic beating of my heart.

Eventually I went down to wash in the shared bathroom on the half-landing where a woodlouse edged dolefully along the skirting and the cistern clanked. But I was interrupted by a tumultuous knocking and ringing on our street door below, four stabs at the bell and then four more, and for a moment, as I ran down, I thought it might be Daniel or even – foolish, wild thought – Thorne, but it was a police officer, a Sergeant Woodward with whom I'd had dealings in the past.

'There's a Mrs Wright asking for you,' he said. 'We need to take a statement from her but she says she'll not speak another word unless you come.'

'Don't tell me she's under arrest.'

'Not she. I've come from Guy's 'orspital. Her son brought her in. They called us.'

'Is she all right?'

'She'll live. But neither she nor the son will talk to us. He keeps on saying, fetch Miss Gifford, she'll talk to Miss Gifford.'

'Did you tell them they don't need a lawyer to make a statement?'

''Course I did. Endlessly. I also said it could wait until morning but the boy insists his mother must speak now and you must be there.' He looked reprovingly at my towel and dressing gown. 'I'll be in the car.'

When we reached the hospital I was taken to an emergency ward where Mrs Wright was lying in a bed, the pale green blanket drawn tightly across her bony figure. A dim light shone over the iron headrest, revealing her bandaged jaw and bruised eye sockets. Her son Robbie sat beside her. He reminded me more than ever of my brother; the clear skin, the large hands held loosely in his lap.

He sprang up when he saw me. 'I found her in the kitchen and I ran for an ambulance. The others was asleep. Trudy come back later. She's at home, looking after the kids. There's no sign of my dad.'

'Presumably your father did this.'

'She says it's her fault. She always does. He asked her for money and she had none. He's been on at her since Tuesday because she'd hidden a bit of savings and bought some shoes for the younger ones so they could go to school. My wages don't come in 'til the end of the week so I couldn't help.'

Mrs Wright's eyelids fluttered open.

'Can you speak, Mrs Wright?' I murmured. 'Will you tell the police officer what happened?'

She nodded.

Woodward took long, creaking strides from the end of the bed and stood over her. 'Can you confirm it was your husband who did this?'

Another nod.

'What did he do?'

'He picked up a chair,' she said, barely audible, 'by the legs. And he brought it up under me face so he could break it over me head. But the back of the chair clipped me on the chin and flung me back. I banged me head on the edge of the table. Should've seen it coming.'

'Seen what coming, Mrs Wright?'

'It were brewing all week. I knew he were mad. His mates took him out for a few beers. He was in a right rage.'

Woodward nodded. 'That's all we need. I do apologise for bringing you over here, Miss Gifford, in the dead of night, but if she wouldn't say anything . . .'

Mrs Wright seemed to have fallen asleep. A nurse ushered us along a ward which had an orderly atmosphere that I found troubling after the recent, glamorous jostling of the theatre.

Out in the corridor Robbie Wright stopped dead and said, 'I'll kill him.' Then, 'I hate myself for not stopping it.'

My heart was wrung by his boyish anger and self-recrimination. 'What could you have done, Robbie? As you said at the rally, you can't keep guard over her night and day.'

'I fought him once and he knocked me over. And she won't have it, if I shout at him.'

'It's your father who's to blame, not you.'

'You've seen what she's like. She trusts you. I'm going to make her talk to you again. She'll do what you say.'

'The police will deal with your father now.'

'She wouldn't speak until you came.' He was watching me fervently and I was stricken with a wave of affection and fearfulness, because of his trust in me.

'There's nothing much I can do except try and persuade her to give evidence in court. If need be, I can be a witness to her injuries and to what she has just said but the police statement will do the same job. If your father is convicted, I can help her deal with what the future might hold. You'll need a court order to keep him from the house.'

He wrung my hand and then, most unexpectedly, darted his head forward and kissed my knuckle. 'I'm sorry. I shouldn't have done that. You don't know how much . . . you can't imagine what it means that you are here. When she asked for you the police said we couldn't get you out at dead of night. But I knew you would come. I knew when I met you that you would change everything.'

# Chapter Twenty

Although I had no official function in the first hearing of Edward Wright, held the next day, Monday 26 April, at Lavender Hill Magistrates' Court, I went anyway, determined to keep a close eye on proceedings. On disembarking from the omnibus I was caught by a strong gust of wind that blew my scarf across the pavement and nearly lifted off my hat. I was lacking sleep following the events of the weekend and felt thin-skinned and dishevelled.

By contrast, despite spending the night in a police cell, Wright was clean-shaven, wore a collar and tie and altogether seemed in much better shape. His daughter Trudy, who assiduously avoided my eye, and a plump woman wearing an unbecoming cloche observed from the public gallery. When he caught sight of me, Wright subjected me to one of his expressionless stares. I looked away.

He also showed no emotion when the charge was read but stood as if on military parade, staring at a spot a couple of inches above the magistrate's head as the clerk intoned, 'That on the night of Saturday 24 April you did make an unprovoked assault upon your wife, thereby causing her actual bodily harm, namely a suspected hairline fracture of her jaw and a contusion on the back of her head. Do you have a legal representative, Mr Wright?'

'What d'you mean?'

'A lawyer. Do you have anyone to speak for you?'

'Don't need no one, I didn't do nothing.'

'These are serious charges. I must warn you that the magistrates may even consider committing your case to a higher court for sentence or trial.'

'Like I said, I can speak for meself.'

The police prosecutor, an old adversary of mine, was grey-haired and dusty-fleshed, the type who would regard such domestic cases – which either collapsed before trial or resulted in an acquittal – as a waste of court time. Already he'd downgraded Mrs Wright's injuries by charging her husband with actual, rather than grievous, bodily harm. The bench of three men, after a whispered conference, decided they had sufficient sentencing powers to hear the case in this lower court.

'Mr Wright, do you plead guilty or not guilty?'

'*Not* guilty.'

'How many witnesses do you intend to call to your trial, Mr Wright?'

'My daughter Gertrude and my sister, Kathleen.' I glanced, surprised, at Trudy but she dipped her face, hiding from me.

'Were these women witnesses to the incident?'

'They were not.'

'Then why will you call them?'

'To vouch for my good character. And I've written to my sergeant, the one I served under in the war.'

'Good character, I'm afraid, doesn't apply in this case, Mr Wright. The issue is factual: did you deliberately hit your wife, or didn't you? Good character will only be relevant when it comes to sentencing.'

Wright did not protest but his face reddened and I knew he'd clock this up as another institutional injustice against his innocent self.

'And for the prosecution, how many witnesses?' asked the clerk.

'Just the injured party, Mrs Wright, and her son, Robbie. Statements will be read from the policeman who attended the scene and from a doctor at the hospital.'

'I presume the son was a witness to the assault.'

'Only to the injuries, sir.'

The trial, which it was estimated would take one and a half hours, was fixed for the following week. There was some discussion between the clerk and the prosecutor about whether the strike, were it to go ahead, would affect the everyday running of the court but it was thought not. 'The wheels of justice will doubtless grind on,' said the clerk. 'None of the officers of this court will, I believe, be called out.'

'And the bench, I presume, won't be on strike?' said the police prosecutor wryly.

Guffaws of laughter from the bench at the very thought, since they were paid nothing anyway.

'Which brings us to the question of bail.'

'As is usual in this type of case, your worships,' said the police prosecutor, 'bail should not be granted. I'm relying on the evidence of the injured party, Mrs Wright, who lives in the marital home where she has the care of several children under ten. It is highly likely that were Mr Wright to be released, he would put pressure on her not to come to court.'

'I'd do no such thing,' exclaimed Wright.

'Is there a surety?'

'Mr Wright can offer a surety of twenty pounds from his sister, Mrs Kathleen Norris, who is sitting in the public benches. She will also accommodate him until the trial.'

Mrs Norris glanced apprehensively at her brother in the dock.

'Twenty pounds is a considerable sum of money for Mrs Norris, who is a widow. She has a lump sum thanks to her late husband's life insurance.'

Bail was granted on the basis of the surety and on Wright's being bound over to appear at his trial. As he left the court, his stare was again directed at me, and this time I forced myself to outface him, though at great cost to my equilibrium. By the time the next case was called he would already be collecting his possessions from the police cell and then swaggering away from the court.

In the lobby, I caught up with Trudy. 'I have some good news, Miss Wright. The manager at Lyons in Regent Street has offered to interview you with regard to a permanent position.'

She looked at the floor. 'Why would he do that? I haven't applied.'

'I was able to put in a word for you because I know one of the supervisors.'

She bit her lip then burst out suddenly, 'I bet you hate me now, don't you, Miss Gifford, for saying I'd stand up for him.'

'I don't hate you. I was just a little surprised, given what you'd said when we met that day in the café.'

'He asked would I speak up for him, and given he's my own father, I didn't know how to refuse him. Oh God, do you know what, Miss Gifford, I wish I'd never clapped eyes on you. I swear everything's got worse since you came on the scene. Robbie's more cocky and pa just sits in his chair watching ma like he's ready to pounce. God knows what would happen if he knew we'd met you in that café.'

'Trudy, he nearly killed her. We can't allow that to happen again.'

'*We.* No, I'm sorry, Miss Gifford, it's got nothing to do with you. We took your advice in Lyons and look at us . . .' Now that she was defiant I could connect her with the abused maidservant who had at last plucked up the courage to apply for another position.

'Your brother Robbie sent for me in the middle of the night because he was so worried about your mother,' I reminded her.

'Robbie don't know nothing about it. He's never there, for a start. He's a troublemaker. It's just like him to stick his oar in.' She moved away.

'What about the interview for Lyons? Shall I . . .?'

'I s'pose you told them all about me and how I was a thief but that was all because my dad was violent. Is that why you arranged to meet me there, to show me off? One of your charity cases.'

Seizing her aunt's arm, she led her away and when I followed, Trudy turned on me again. 'You don't understand, nothing can make it better. I've realised that now. Ma won't come to court next week and he'll be more furious with her than ever.'


When I arrived back at the office in the late morning, Trudy Wright's words were still ringing in my ears. I was used to being blamed when clients were found guilty or punished more harshly than they'd expected, but her sudden animosity had wrong-footed me. I had regarded myself as being of help to the family, summonsed in their hour of need. But no, according to Trudy I was simply a meddler.

Miss Drake's typewriter clack-clacked from behind her closed door, a whiff of perfume suggested that Wolfe had recently passed this way and there was a murmur of male voices in Daniel's room so I couldn't knock and tell him what had happened. I ran downstairs to my basement which smelt, as usual, of must and ink, and stood at the window, waiting.

Sure enough, a few moments later, the street door opened and closed. I heard his steps on the stairs, gathering pace, then he knocked and came in. His eyes brimmed with anticipation.

'I couldn't keep away. I wanted to check all was well between us.'

My back was to the light so my face must have been in darkness, but I stumbled forward into his arms.

# Chapter Twenty-One

We knew we could have no secrets from Wolfe and Miss Drake, so once our engagement was decided I had no time to draw breath. On Wednesday there was to be a staff meeting to discuss the strike and we agreed to tell them then. It was as if I was on some precipitous path and dared not look to left or right. Above all I wanted clarity, and if our news was out in the open we could move forward and make plans.

At nine o'clock that morning Miss Drake came downstairs to summon me to the telephone and I knew, as I followed her trim figure, that soon she would dislike me more than ever. Daniel feared that Miss Drake might even resign but for now she was civil and stepped outside the office so that I might speak in private.

Annabel Petit was on the line. 'Mummy wants to see you today. She's coming up to town on purpose. I can't stop her. She doesn't want me to go to court at all. She wants me to agree to divorce Timmo and come home to Surrey. Please, Miss Gifford, tell her we're going ahead and that she's got to come to court and say that Annice is definitely Timmo's daughter.'

'It would be much more helpful if you and I could see her together,' I said. 'Then she would understand how you feel.'

'I'm busy this morning,' she said, too quickly. 'Please Miss Gifford, just tell her I won't back down.' The line went dead.

Breen had been right, of course. I shouldn't have touched the Petit case if it meant I was to be treated like a skivvy every time Annabel Petit needed me. But then there was Annice with her dark cap of hair and her small limbs and composed features. For all her family's wealth, she was no different, in her innocence and vulnerability, to Edmund or the Wright children who, like her, had seemed too compliant as they sat under their father's eye making paper dolls.

At eleven o'clock Miss Drake ushered Mrs Shawcross into the unpleasant upstairs meeting room which was furnished with a round table covered by a green baize cloth and an incongruous Victorian sideboard sporting a copy of *The London Illustrated News* dated June 1922. Annabel's mother, who had finely plucked brows, thin, painted lips and straight hair caught in a grip at the side, was many dress sizes larger than her daughter and wore a long eau-de-nil jacket over a matching gown. Once Miss Drake had left, she took command of the tea tray, stirring the pot so vigorously that the feathers on her hat waved.

'First,' she said, offering me milk and sugar, 'I want you to promise that what you and I say here today will be kept in absolute confidence between us.'

'Except for your daughter, of course.'

'Oh, Annabel knows perfectly well what I'm going to say. The point is we – that is, my husband and I – want the case to be dropped. My husband would have come himself but unfortunately he has pressing business due to the likelihood of a strike.' I detected a note of disapproval and thought that Mr and Mrs Shawcross might well have had words about his decision to put work above his daughter.

'It's up to Annabel whether or not she withdraws from the case,' I said.

'She's being very obstinate, as always, so I told her I would come and see you in person.' Her critical gaze took in first me then the drab net curtains and her smile came and went, as if she were posing for the cover of a knitting pattern. 'Perhaps you don't quite realise what will happen if Annabel is dragged through the courts. I think you are in the best position to work on her, don't you? She keeps telling me how much she admires you.'

'I have obviously given her my best advice, and will continue to do so.' I spoke coolly, braced for argument. Mrs Shawcross, I judged, would be used to getting her own way, at least in domestic matters.

'Miss Gifford, if you were married you'd know that there are certain situations between a man and his wife that cannot be repaired. I would not want Annabel to remain married to that man now, after all that has passed. No mother would.'

'But how is your daughter to prove that her husband is the father, if not in court? If Annabel accepts that Annice is not her husband's daughter, the little girl will have a very difficult life, as I'm sure you're aware.' Again I thought of Edmund, whisked away to France in part because his mother couldn't put up with the narrow-mindedness of London.

'Have you no concern for Annabel's well-being?' Mrs Shawcross was a little too forceful; it was obviously her custom to override uncomfortable arguments rather than listen to them. 'Could your conscience stand the knowledge that you had destroyed her? All the sordid details of their marriage would be splashed across the daily newspapers.'

'I presume, then, that you believe Annice is not Sir Timothy's daughter? Whereas Annabel is unequivocal in saying that she could not be anybody else's.'

'It doesn't matter what I believe,' she said petulantly. 'Either way, Annabel cannot win, I'm sure of that. And what if she did? What kind of a marriage would it be, when the husband has tried and failed to disown both wife and child?'

'Do you not think that, as a grown woman, your daughter should make her own choices?'

Mrs Shawcross drew such a long breath that the crêpe fabric of her dress strained against her bosom. 'My daughter is in no condition to understand what she wants. I can see I shall have to be very blunt. Annabel is a neurasthenic, Miss Gifford. When things don't go her way, or if she's under any kind of pressure, she is afflicted by frightening swings of mood. I'm afraid that if this case goes to court she will collapse entirely.'

'But she's a businesswoman,' I could not help saying, 'she runs a gallery.'

'That gallery is a playground for her. We've always had to provide diversions for Annabel. For instance, we were forced to take her out of school and have her educated at home. She's no doubt spun you some yarn about running her father's factory during the war. The truth is we put her there to keep her out of harm's way. She thought she had responsibility for one or two of the production lines, checking the girls in and out and such, but one could never expect too much of Annabel. She used to fraternise with the women so they ran rings around her. However, the work certainly did prove to be a distraction from those hysterical episodes of hers; the drinking, the sudden periods of low spirits when she would lie in her room and not say a word.'

I got up and reached for the door handle. 'Mrs Shawcross, please, it's not appropriate for me to hear all this in Lady Petit's absence.'

But Mrs Shawcross was now in full flood. 'Her marriage, from the point of view of her health, has been a disaster. I never liked Timothy Petit and it was against my better judgement that the whole thing went ahead. My husband tolerated him because of his prospects and because they were in business together for a while, but I knew Annabel wasn't happy. She was brittle. She wouldn't listen to me. It was all wedding dresses and decorating a grand new house and dashing about with the wretched Porters.'

So we shared a mutual antipathy towards the disdainful Kit. I could not help asking, 'You don't like Mrs Porter?'

She pulled the chair beside her closer and patted the seat invitingly. 'Kit runs Annabel ragged. Always has done. They were friends at school and it was one of the reasons I was secretly rather glad when Annabel had to be brought home. I disliked Kit's influence. It was typical that she should find a husband like Porter – rich and weak. However, I will say for her that at least she's proved loyal to Annabel.'

'And of course Mrs Porter will be a very useful witness for us in court.'

'Have I not made myself clear? There is to be no hearing. My husband said I was to remind you that if you lose there'll be no money to pay your wages. You can be quite sure that Annabel has spent everything she ever had. And whose family name will be dragged through the mire by the gutter press? Who will have to dispose of the little bastard child when Petit proves that Annice is not his?'

There, it was out. Mrs Shawcross had laid her cards on the table and now she stared at me with her hard eyes as if to say: I'm not ashamed of what I've said.

'Perhaps we should not take it as a fait accompli that we will lose,' I said quietly.

As Mrs Shawcross gathered up her gloves her face was deathly white and she was breathing heavily. 'We are sure that Annabel would never have contested this lawsuit had she been properly advised. Any other lawyer would have dissuaded her at once. Well, I'm warning you now, if you don't persuade my daughter to withdraw from this case, I shall ensure that you are never allowed to practise law again.'

'Then I shall work fast,' I said, 'while I still have time. You called your granddaughter a bastard, Mrs Shawcross. I shall not forget that and I will put Annabel on her guard.' I actually preceded her down the stairs to where Miss Drake was hovering by the doorway, alerted by our raised voices.

'Perhaps you would show Mrs Shawcross out,' I told her as I retreated to my office. I heard the front door close abruptly.

I contrived to be a couple of minutes late for the afternoon meeting and found the atmosphere laden with expectation. Miss Drake was already present, notebook and pencil poised, while Breen, seated in his swivel chair behind the desk, cast me such a loving look that I sat down abruptly, fussed with my papers and wouldn't glance up again. Several minutes late, as usual, Wolfe lumbered in and helped himself to a biscuit from the tea tray. He was sporting a dogstooth waistcoat in yellow and brown and I might have assumed he was off for a long weekend in the country had it not been for his dislike of the outdoors.

The start of the meeting was unusually disorganised, with Breen filling and wiping his pen while urging Miss Drake to hurry up and pour the tea. 'And perhaps you will join us in a glass of something stronger,' he said in a rush. 'I want you both to know that Miss Gifford has agreed to become my wife.'

Miss Drake started to her feet with a little cry and her notebook and pencil tumbled to the floor. Wolfe, ever the gentleman, got up and shook our hands vigorously. A bottle was produced from behind the desk and Daniel would not hear of even Miss Drake refusing a drink. The four of us stood awkwardly as Wolfe proposed a toast.

I felt as if all this was happening to some other person, especially when the meeting moved on and we tried to behave as if nothing unusual had happened.

'There will definitely be a strike,' said Daniel, 'I've given up expecting anyone to solve the issues by discussion or arbitration. Nobody has the will. The more bullish forces in the government – Churchill, Joynson-Hicks (reactionary thug), Petit – are disposed to flex their muscles. The union leaders are floundering and the Labour Party, I'm sorry to say, has proved itself to be vacillating and indeed vacuous.'

Wolfe grinned and tilted back his chair. 'Certainly Miss Gifford and I saw few signs of organisation when we visited Richard Leremer.'

'The strike,' said Daniel, 'is bound to have all kinds of repercussions for some of our more troubled clients. And there is likely to be civil unrest, even riots. We've heard that special courts are to be set up, and I'm sure they'll be draconian in their sentencing. I have been meeting with other like-minded lawyers who are prepared to work pro bono on behalf of the strikers and we shall draw up a register for the police to call on, should there be arrests.'

'I have a raft of other work,' Wolfe said hastily. 'As you know, I'm following up various enquiries to see if Timmo Petit is engaged in any clandestine activity that might help our case. Petit, I suspect, will be in the headlines a good deal should there be a strike. It's up to me to keep an eye on him, I feel.'

'Miss Gifford?'

'I will be happy to work pro bono if need be.'

'Communication, of course, will be very difficult. Courts will run but the postal service probably won't. Telephones may work; they may not. We shall have to walk or cycle to appointments.'

'Taxicab,' said Wolfe firmly. 'Or I'll use my motor.'

'I doubt there'll be any cabs – the drivers may be called out. And I suspect it will be foolhardy to venture on to a London street in a private motor car because they will be choked with people driving in from the suburbs. Miss Drake, you have the longest journey to work.'

'Nonetheless I shall be here at eight every day.' She spoke in a small, hard voice and would not meet his eye.

'Now,' said Breen hurriedly, 'what *is* the state of the Petit case?'

'I had a difficult meeting this morning with Annabel's mother, Mrs Shawcross, who wanted me to persuade her daughter to drop out of proceedings. We had an argument – in fact, I was grateful to Miss Drake for showing her off the premises.' I smiled at Miss Drake but there was no winning her over.

'It would be very late in the proceedings to withdraw,' said Wolfe, 'given that the preliminary hearing is next week.'

'How did you answer Mrs Shawcross?' asked Breen.

'I said that I was acting for her daughter and would do as Annabel wished.'

'Quite right.' When Breen smiled at me he could not keep the fondness from his eyes.

'But it struck me that Mrs Shawcross was not quite at ease – that perhaps some pressure had been put on her to come. She doesn't like her son-in-law, that's for sure.'

'Who is putting pressure on her?'

'Her husband perhaps, or even Petit himself.'

'Interesting,' said Wolfe. 'I'll look into it. I've found out a couple of things about our Timmo that might come in handy. I had a very good dinner at Brown's the other night with an old pal who used to be at school with him. Says, on the question of paternity, that to his knowledge Petit hasn't fathered any child other than Annice but that there are no rumours to suggest he's incapable – far from it. He's thought to have conducted a number of affairs immediately pre and possibly post the marriage, though he's a clever man and unlikely to get caught out. Even more helpfully, my pal said that when Annice was born Petit was aglow with pride and invited all his political cohorts to her christening.'

'That is indeed very useful,' said Breen, 'given that, as we all know, it is a presumption of law that a child born in wedlock is the child of the husband. I would have thought that if Petit accepted Annice as his when she was first born, it's going to be tough for him to rely on the non-consummation argument.'

'Nevertheless,' added Wolfe, 'the fact is that it's well known in the Petits' circle that Annabel and Leremer were running round together the minute she was back from honeymoon.'

'They're both adamant that they were not lovers,' I said, and received a furious glance from Miss Drake.

'But they *would* say that,' Wolfe replied rather curtly. 'The fact is, people *believe* Leremer and Annabel Petit were lovers at that time, so the damage is done. Petit will have plenty of witnesses up his sleeve. Incidentally, I've learned something else about Leremer which might be of significance.' He paused, pursing his lips. 'He has a Jewish mother.'

Breen reversed the rotation of his thumbs. 'Your point?'

'It's apparent, wouldn't you say, that the enmity between Sir Timothy Petit and Leremer goes somewhat deeper than their political differences.'

'Petit is an anti-Semite?'

'Bound to be, given that he works hand in glove with Joynson-Hicks. Annabel's parents were dismayed when they discovered that their daughter was having an affair with a penniless socialist from the North who also happened to be a Jew. So when Petit made a play for her, he received plenty of encouragement.'

'Made a play for her?'

'Petit seems to be the sort of chap for whom a woman is far more attractive if she happens to belong to someone else.' The ensuing pause weighed heavily in the room. 'What I was thinking is that we could perhaps persuade Leremer to give evidence, if he thought Petit was using the case to settle grievances beyond the purely domestic.'

'The whole thing is appallingly messy. I did warn you to steer clear, Miss Gifford ...' But Breen smiled at me with great sympathy, inviting me to share the joke.

Wolfe, who had hooked both arms over the back of his chair, continued as if in afterthought, 'There's one other bit of news. The other side has already appointed counsel. Nicholas Thorne. Family friend of the Petits, I gather.'

Miss Drake broke the tip of her pencil and had to search in her handbag for a fresh one.

'Oh yes, you told me he was back from South Africa.' Breen drew his papers together and tapped their edges sharply on the blotter until they were neatly in line. 'Thorne never used to specialise in family cases but who knows what he's been up to the past couple of years?' Fleetingly his eyes met mine and I could only smile and shrug.

A glance at his watch indicated that it was time for us to file out, except for Wolfe who had requested a private conference with him. I had a meeting with my group of women lawyers at four, so had no choice but to leave the building without speaking to Daniel again.

# Chapter Twenty-Two

So, Nicholas was well and truly back, not just in town, but at the dead centre of my working world. As the omnibus toiled past Holborn I raged against the Petits and all their acolytes, including Nicholas Thorne. Daniel, infuriatingly, had been right all along – these people were thoughtless and manipulative. And now Thorne was in the mix I felt overwhelmed by the forces pitched against me. If Wolfe had wanted to cast a cloud over Daniel and me following the announcement of our engagement he had certainly succeeded. Three times now I had been overthrown by the least sight or mention of Thorne, so I resolved to take action that would ensure it would never happen again.

At the Law Society, beneath the gilt-framed portraits of presidents past, with their leg-of-mutton whiskers and penetrating eyes, I felt a rush of relief to see my friends in their no-nonsense hats and blouses with plain, round collars, sharing tea from an institutional pot. This purposeful world, through which men came and went in their dark suits either ignoring us or, more rarely, favouring us with a friendly wave, felt like a refuge until I realised that even these professional women, noted for their high-mindedness, were in fact far less interested in the General Strike than in the likely fate of Annabel Petit.

As I settled in one of the leather chairs and poured myself a cup of rather stewed tea, three pairs of eyes turned towards me. 'Are you able to tell us anything about the Petit case, Evelyn? Everyone's wondering how Sir Timothy can possibly win, given that disproving paternity is such a high bar for him to cross.'

'I've been thinking about the case,' said Carrie, without giving me time to reply, 'and I think the real question is, surely, what has Petit to gain by going to court? Why not simply put up with the status quo, at least for the time being, however much he hates his wife? For a minister, especially one whose career is teetering on the brink of stardom – if he has a good strike, that is – to instigate these sorts of proceedings is an enormous risk. Either he must truly loathe his wife, or it's something else.'

'Such as?'

'Another reason for wanting a divorce,' she said darkly. '*Cherchez la femme*, that's what I say.'

'For what it's worth, I agree,' said Maud, 'although not necessarily that there's another woman. In my experience there's always more to these cases than meets the eye. What I've heard is that Lady Petit has become a political liability. She's unhinged, isn't she, Evie?'

'Unhinged? What a dreadful word. She's nervy and wayward, perhaps, but not unhinged. Whoever told you that?'

'Gracious, there's no need to be quite so defensive. What's the matter? You should be feeling absolutely on top of the world to have been instructed in such a prominent case.'

'It's because her flatmate, Meredith, has gone away,' said Carrie. 'Poor old Evie.'

As the tea party broke up and we shook hands and adjusted our hats, Carrie lingered beside me. 'You must really feel sad without your nephew. Are you catching a bus? I'll walk with you to the bus stop.'

'I have work to do in the library. I need to look up the Russell Case – do you remember, that other paternity trial?'

'Well,' she said, buttoning her coat. 'I enjoyed the farewell party in your flat, I really did. In fact I wished we could have stayed longer. As we were leaving we passed Daniel Breen on the stairs, by the way. Ambrose was most impressed. He said he'd never known Breen attend a purely social event before.'

'It was very kind of him to come.'

She was watching me closely. '*Kind* is one way of describing it.'

Tell her, I told myself. Why not? Because the ordeal of the office meeting was so fresh in my mind that I couldn't stand more congratulations and questions. I watched Carrie walk away, twitching up the collar of her coat, before I turned back inside and took a seat in the library. It was true that an understanding of the Russell

Case of 1923 was relevant to the Petit trial but I was conscious, as I read, of a wholly different motive for lingering.

Nineteen twenty-three had been an inauspicious year for me, spent writing letters of application to dozens of law firms or lurking at the back of magistrates' courts accumulating knowledge; forcing myself to accost liberal-seeming lawyers and beg them to consider giving me a clerkship. Better days came when I was rostered to help out at Toynbee Hall, the settlement in Spitalfields where lawyers were invited to offer advice pro bono to families threatened with eviction or to women crushed by violence.

But, even in an environment as wholesome as Toynbee, the Russell Case, reported at length in *The Times* as well as in less highbrow papers, had provoked much gossip. When the jury at the initial trial found in favour of the mother, the father instructed a big-hitting barrister, Marshall Hall, to contest paternity again on the grounds that the marriage had not been consummated and that the wife had instead committed adultery with an unknown lover. This time, the father won. The Lords, however, had found that the husband's assertion of his wife's infidelity was inadmissible because the law stated that neither party was allowed to give negative evidence about what had happened – or not – in the marriage bed in order to declare a child illegitimate.

'Quite right,' according to Breen, 'or the courts would be cluttered up with cases where the only evidence produced was that of aggrieved husbands and wives washing their dirty linen in public.'

The Russell Case was obviously helpful to Lady Petit's cause and I made copious notes, but after an hour I packed my briefcase and headed for the door. What I would do next was an idea that had been incubating for days, ever since I bumped into Nicholas Thorne at the Criterion, and Wolfe's intervention at the office meeting had increased my resolve. Here, in Chancery Lane, I was within minutes of Nicholas's chambers. I would not put up with the dread of seeing him again at next week's hearing. I would hold a proper conversation with him, as old acquaintances should, and re-establish our relationship on an entirely professional footing.

Within five minutes I had navigated the rush hour traffic on the Strand and entered the lanes of the Inns of Court where, though it was almost six thirty, many windows were still illuminated. The door to Nicholas's chambers was ajar and in the clerks' office I was greeted by the familiar fug of such rooms: tobacco, hot male bodies and freshly mixed ink.

'My name is Evelyn Gifford. I'm a solicitor. I was wondering if I might speak to Mr Nicholas Thorne.'

With finger and thumb the clerk gave his eye a brutal rub. 'He ain't here. Gone to Worcester. Back next week. I'll tell him you was asking for him. Write down your name for me, would you?'

Head high, I retreated into the April evening where the twilight sky was translucent between ancient, smoking chimney pots. My heart was beating violently and I stumbled on the uneven cobbles in my haste to get away. At least I had taken a step and had not waited feebly for our next encounter. But then, as the mood of reckless energy ebbed a little, it occurred to me that actually, by leaving my name, I had handed all control over to Nicholas and that it was up to him now to decide whether or not to get in touch.

# Chapter Twenty-Three

The General Strike approached like a tidal wave. Daniel told me that when he had first decided to get married during the war it had been like trying to hoist a small sail in the teeth of a hurricane. Now here we were, starting our new engagement on the eve of a general strike that everyone could see coming but nobody could stop. If there had been a tipping point, it was long past. It was as if we were all being shaken up in a gas bottle that was bound to explode.

Private affairs had to take second place. For the rest of that week Daniel was attending meetings during which Battersea, like every other borough, struggled to prepare itself for the coming conflict. In our snatched conversations on staircases and in doorways he told me of arguments that had gone on far into the night between councillors who were at once sympathetic to the strike but who also felt responsible for the elderly, the sick and the very young who would suffer if hospital power supplies were cut off and the roads blocked. The unions had been careful to call out only those workers not involved in essential services but still there was a danger that the vulnerable would suffer for want of adequate electricity or clean water. Daniel was haggard from dealing with men who were used to disputing the location of a street lamp or the day on which rubbish should be collected rather than issues of life and death. We certainly had no time to discuss Thorne, and the closest we came to a lover's tryst was to agree to meet up at the May Day rally in Hyde Park. Daniel would be marching there from Battersea with trade unions and socialists; I would make my own way less gloriously from Pimlico.

Even had I not arranged to meet him, historical imperative would have lured me to Hyde Park, not to mention the memory of my late grandmother who, in the days of her independence, would undoubtedly have teamed up with fellow thespians to march under a banner of fairness for all. And a thick envelope with a French postmark had arrived that morning which drove me out of the flat faster than any call to arms, because it reminded me so brutally of what I was missing.

Edmund had painted me a picture of a blue sea dotted with fishing boats while stout figures with naked arms and legs paddled at the shore. It smelt of the watercolour paints I had helped him pack; the black, flat tin that used to be his father's, with space for four or five brushes and a flap on which the colours could be mixed. I knew exactly how he would have knelt on the seat of a chair with his ankles crossed, propped up on his left elbow, tongue protruding as he dipped the brush.

In her accompanying note, Meredith wrote that she and Edmund had worn out the soles of their shoes walking about and looking at things, because even though the days were still quite cool at times, the air and the light were so bright and clear in Sanary-sur-Mer.

*My French has come in handy for the first time since the war and I am already accepted as one of the locals, or believe myself to be. Disappointingly, there are almost no other English people here, or painters. I think Angus might have got it wrong in that respect but they will come later in the summer, I hope. Angus has undertaken to teach Edmund arithmetic and art, and I shall give him French lessons, so you see he will be far better educated than if we'd stayed in London.*

*A's aunt, with whom we're staying, is not pleased to see us, I fear, and I shall shortly be looking for new accommodation. It's not that she disapproves of me but of her nephew, who seems to have given her very little notice that he was coming, let alone that he would bring me and E with him. She lives with a Frenchwoman called Mlle Veronique Leclos and they have rooms to let, empty at this time of year, so there is plenty of space until the summer visitors arrive. But she is very angry about the whole thing, and who can blame her, since this is their holiday time and they'd rather be without lodgers, particularly the kind who can't afford to pay a proper rent. However, they are very kind to Edmund and feed him too much cake when they think I'm not looking.*

*The truth is that all this has made me pretty homesick and I keep thinking, oh my gosh, if only Evie were here to watch the morning catch being brought in or to see the mimosa packed into boxes ready for shipping first thing in the morning – there is this yellow cloud of perfume – or to try out the way they bake eggs with cream. I'd love to see you unbending in the sun the way you do when you're happy, when your hat comes off and your hair is down. I'd like you not to be wearing those English woollen skirts but some airy dress and I'd like you to be drinking wine with me and squinting into the sunset.*

*What's going on back home? Do write and tell me about the strike, if it happens, and about your Mr Breen. I keep thinking about what you said, and praying that you won't sneak off and marry him while I'm not there. For God's sake don't rush into anything, dearest girl. Give it time. Come out here first and try a different life.*

Having read that letter and taken Edmund's picture to the window to study every last detail, I was out of the Pimlico flat as soon as I had clapped on my utilitarian, un-French hat. Only after twenty minutes or so of brisk walking did I feel more composed as gradually I became absorbed into an ever-swelling crowd that included children and the elderly, the wheelchair-bound, the one-armed and the limpers, all heading the same way. Some marched under banners: railway workers, manufacturers, welders, dockers and plumbers. Some wore fancy dress and I saw a charabanc of women wearing red caps and sashes as a reminder of the French Revolution. Hoards of policemen stood by but did not intervene. Very wise, given that the grass in the park was all but invisible under the mass of humanity.

I manoeuvred myself until I was on the edge of the crowd, near the green-tinged Serpentine where a pair of ducks proudly towed a family of eight. For me, Hyde Park was always associated with a touch of sleaze because Breen & Balcombe had represented a succession of girls who had been snatched from the bushes by assiduous policewomen for plying their trade in a public place. I was remembering a particular young woman who had worked with Carole at Lyons, and who had come to a very sad end indeed, when a young man seized my arm.

'Miss Gifford, I've been looking for you. I thought I'd see you here.' Robbie Wright was wearing too short trousers, highly polished shoes and a tweed tie. As usual he looked exhausted and the coal dust clung to his neck.

'How is your mother?' I asked at once.

'Getting better all the time. If only they'd keep him inside for a while, she would see how she might have a good life without him. She might get stronger. That's what I keep telling her.'

'Has he stayed away from her?'

'He has. But he does write and she does read his letters.'

All this was muttered as people around us struggled to hear the almost inaudible words of the speaker. Robbie said, 'Got to go now, Miss Gifford. I'm up next.'

'Are you going to be making a speech then? Aren't you nervous, Robbie?'

'I won't be, not with you watching.' His grin, though deferential, was just a touch flirtatious. 'Help us make sure she goes to court, Miss Gifford.'

I worked my way forward in time to hear him announce himself as, 'Robbie Wright, Coal Haulage Association.' Although he spoke much too fast and jabbed too emphatically with his index finger, his youthfulness and passion were compelling. I was standing beside a group of veterans, one of whom, missing an eye and ear, hushed the crowd.

'I make my money directly from coal. Day after day, I carry sacks of coal from the cart to the backyards of poor women like my mother who eke it out because it costs them dear. And I tip it into the cellars and coal sheds of great houses knowing full well that the owners never give a thought to what it costs nor where it comes from. But how cold their lives would be without it and how quickly they'd go hungry! Every day our brothers in the mines risk their lives in the dark and the dirt, and every day they are expected to work longer hours and earn less. Why? To maintain profits. And where do those profits go? Into the pockets of the wealthy few.

'The miners have been accused of holding the country to ransom but I say that it is the mine owners and the government who are at fault. They have called our bluff because they think we are too afraid of losing our jobs or going hungry to stand up for ourselves. How wrong could they be?'

The crowd cheered. Whereas the father would have used his forceful blue gaze to intimidate, Robbie charmed by his fervour. Behind us the police were gathering and I was hemmed in as the crowd surged forward again. Cigarettes were crushed underfoot and a veteran, leaning heavily on crutches because one trouser leg was gathered tight beneath his knee, muttered, 'Saklatvala. He's up next. Now we shall have some fun.'

Robbie had given way on the podium to a slight man – the notorious MP for Battersea.

'He will talk sense,' someone said, 'but all he really cares about is his own kind. India for the Indians. I don't see that matters much to the miners.'

Saklatvala's voice was so soft that the crowd craned their necks. Whenever I caught a glimpse of him I saw that he had expressive dark eyes but a slight frame. He was calling upon the army boys to, 'Revolt now and refuse to fight and then they will be the real saviours of their homes and the workers . . . young men in the Forces, whether Joynson-Hicks likes it or not . . . we have a duty towards those men to say to them they must lay down their arms.'

'Seditious talk. I predict we have at least one candidate here for the temporary courts.' Daniel was wearing his oversized raincoat and his hat was pushed to the back of his head. He gripped my hand and kissed my cheek. 'I've found you at last. I wasn't sure you'd come. There were about a thousand of us as we marched here from Battersea. I couldn't believe the numbers. I think we really are on the brink of something.'

'Saklatvala is saying they'll call out the troops.'

'Britain is not Russia. The British government would never order the army to turn its guns on its own people. The very idea is unthinkable.'

But there was a scuffle behind us and shouts of rage because the police were forging a pathway to the front of the crowd so that they could erect barricades around the podium. Apparently there were to be no more speeches. My hand was tucked under Daniel's arm as we walked away through a blast of warm sunshine.

'I have to be back in Battersea by four,' he told me. 'How about we go and find somewhere peaceful in the meantime?'

We exited the park by the Albert Gate and turned up the Brompton Road where the dispersing crowd queued at bus stops and children were being fed jam sandwiches to sustain them on the way home.

'I've been wanting to speak to you about Nicholas Thorne,' I said, matching my stride to his. As usual his pace left me slightly breathless.

'Ah, Thorne.'

'You know it makes not one bit of difference that he's back, but after the meeting on Wednesday I tried to see him at his chambers. I wanted to tell him about you and me but he wasn't there. As you know, he and I . . . we have a history, so I did want to clear the air before we meet again at the Petit case.'

He allowed me to stumble through this explanation then patted my hand. 'We are making too much of this. It's because you and I have had so little time together. Let's not waste any more talking about someone else.'

The tea room near South Kensington Station had a floor patterned with green, brown and cream tiles and we sat at a table looking out on to the thronging pavements. Daniel produced from his pocket a leather box with a tiny hasp. 'I bought you this. I just plunged into a shop because I thought you must have a ring. When the strike is over we'll go shopping together and buy you something decent but for now . . .'

The box sat in my palm and we were suddenly caught in a bubble of silence. Though he was smiling there was perhaps a hint of challenge in his eye. The ring was set with a topaz surrounded by marcasites. 'My mother has something similar,' he added and we laughed because the comment was so gauche.

He watched anxiously as I fitted the ring on the middle finger of my left hand – it was too big for the third – and the waitress hovered by my shoulder to admire it. When she'd gone, he tentatively kissed the ring and the finger beneath it. 'If only we had more time we could have had it made smaller,' he said, glancing at his watch. 'The thing is, I've been elected to a special committee called the Council of Action – makes a change from most committees which seem completely inactive. Our job is essentially to plan how to manage the strike in the borough. It seemed imperative that I accept – there was no one else suitable.'

'Congratulations,' I said.

'It means I'll be tied up almost every evening. Perhaps I should have asked you first?'

'You know what my answer would have been.'

'You see, I'm just not used to being accountable to another human being.' He again kissed my hand. 'But thank you. As soon as the strike is over, we'll have more time, I promise you.'

'You should be grateful for small mercies,' I said. 'At least until then you'll be spared tea with my mother. She's desperate to meet you.'

We ate hastily and I accompanied him as far as the entrance to the station where he kissed my cheek and both my hands. These small gallantries twisted my heart because he was so obviously unused to lovemaking. 'I've a two-day trial starting on Monday. If I don't see you in the meantime, I've bought tickets for the Wigmore Hall on Thursday at seven thirty in the hope you'll come with me. Think about it.' He looked happy and purposeful as he ran down the stairs. When I'd lost sight of him I set off along the underground passage to the Natural History Museum. It was strange to be without Edmund tugging on my hand but at least the small, unaccustomed weight of my new ring was there to distract me and in my bag was Meredith's letter inviting me to the South of France.

In the museum I stood before Edmund's favourite exhibit, a reconstruction of the dodo, and leaned my forehead on the glass.

'Why do you so like this great ugly bird?' I had asked him.

'Because I'm looking at something that's not there any more, Aunty Evelyn. Don't you think that's weird?'

'No stranger than a photograph or a painting of someone or something that used to exist but now doesn't.'

'Most things are replaced though, aren't they? There will always be more people but there will never be more dodos.'

His words echoed in the booming galleries of the museum. There was something in Edmund that was forever reaching out for the unreachable.

# Chapter Twenty-Four

Next day I arrived at Clivedon Hall Gardens for Sunday lunch, taking with me Meredith's letter, Edmund's picture and, protected by a brown envelope, Patrick Rusbridger's note to Grandmother. My omnibus was delayed by a convoy of delivery trucks parked along the side of Hyde Park where swarms of men were erecting marquees – so much for the government being prepared to negotiate up to the wire. The planning of this operation, which involved trestles, groundsheets, hoardings and piles of collapsible chairs, must have been going on for weeks.

The pavements in Maida Vale were wet from a recent shower and my feet were smeared with fallen blossom. From the outside my family home looked much as it ever did in that the stucco was peeling above the porch and the windows needed a good wash. However, it was Rose who answered the door; an unusual event as she generally confined herself to the basement. Because it was Sunday she was dressed to go out in her overcoat and a green hat, but she had been crying and seemed incapable of speech. Having indicated with her thumb that Mother was in the drawing room, she limped to the top of the basement stairs and disappeared. As I passed the dining room I noticed that the table had been spread with cold meats including Prudence's favourite – tongue – and slices of beetroot arranged in a cut-glass dish.

In the drawing room Miss Perry, the lodger, sat idle as usual and Mother was at the writing desk in Prudence's old place, studying an atlas. 'Prudence and Miss Lord will have reached Bombay by now. I'm surprised Prudence has not thought to write,' she said. As I kissed her I smelt her usual Yardley talcum powder and noticed that the well-thumbed programme of *Hay Fever* was also prominent.

Miss Perry wore a pilled cream jersey in sailor style with a V-neck which revealed too much of her crinkled chest. 'Your maids have given in their notice,' she said with relish. 'Your mother's very upset.'

'Yes, but we won't talk about that now,' said Mother. 'First we'll have lunch.'

My mind buzzed with the implications of this momentous news as I endured half an hour of munching cold meat and salad followed by a vanilla mould. Miss Perry had the most infuriating habit of grinding her teeth as she bit into the non-resistant jelly.

'Of course I shan't stay in London through this dreadful strike,' she announced.

Mother threw her a half-frightened, half-hostile glance. 'Where will you go?'

'I have a sister in Hitchin,' said Miss Perry, mystifying us – we'd always assumed she was alone in the world.

'I doubt the strike will have much impact on Maida Vale,' I said.

'Miss Perry says we should board up the windows,' said Mother, 'and in church they were wondering how to protect the stained glass.'

'It's a strike, not a revolution,' I exclaimed, exasperated. 'Nobody will try to smash the windows of a church.'

'These things can turn very nasty,' said Miss Perry. 'If you'd been a teacher for as long as I have, you would know how the animal nature in the lower classes can emerge just like that.'

'I think it will be fascinating to be in London during the strike,' I said provocatively. 'I wish *I* was in a union so that I could stop work and show my sympathy for the miners.'

'Whereas I,' said Miss Perry, 'am convinced that this is down to sheer greed. It would be a sorry day if our country's fate were to be decided by a horde of coal miners.'

'You'd be happy to see the greedy mine owners grow fatter still, would you, while the miners and their families starve?'

'Nobody's starving, as far as I know,' said Mother. 'You do exaggerate so, Evelyn. However, our new vicar has suggested that the ladies of the parish should organise a soup kitchen for the poor mothers and babies whose men are out on strike.'

'Will you put your name down?'

'I doubt it will be safe for a woman to walk the streets on her own, so I expect I shall be confined to the house.'

'They say the strike will start at midnight tomorrow,' said Miss Perry. 'I only hope I haven't left it too late to use public transport.'

While she went up to pack, Mother retreated to the drawing room to stoke the fire and I carried the tray of used dishes down to the kitchen. The basement was tidy but cold and the door to the maids' little sitting room shut tight. As there was no hot water I boiled a kettle for the washing-up. Outside, pots of daffodils, long overblown, were ranked on the steps, illuminated at pavement level by a strip of sunlight.

Upstairs I poured tea into our second-best cups. 'I have a great deal to tell you,' said Mother, 'and it must all be said before *she* – an upward nod of the head to indicate the lodger – 'comes down. The fact is, it's true. Min and Rose gave in their notice this morning just before you arrived.'

'This is very unexpected, I agree. Where will they go?'

'They tell me that they have decided to retire to *Seaford*, of all places, because it's where they've spent every holiday for the last forty years. Apparently they've been saving up, and they say they must do this before they're too old to make the change. I can't help thinking it's a touch disloyal of them not to have said a word before now, but then Rose will be sixty-eight next birthday. I hadn't realised . . .' She made a vague, aristocratic gesture with her hand.

'Well it sounds like it's the right decision for them. They couldn't go on living here for ever.'

'So that's settled it,' she said, replacing her cup and saucer on the tray. 'Of course I'm delighted that you're engaged, Evie, but I'm well aware that you modern girls don't want a mother dragging you down, whereas I obviously felt I had no choice but to take your grandmother in when she fell ill and went blind. And there can be no more talk of lodgers. I cannot possibly run the house without the girls. Nobody would expect me to.' Her bottom lip quivered as she lifted her chin to prevent tears from falling. 'So I've decided to buy a cottage in Ruislip.'

'*Ruislip.*'

'It's as good a place as any. Remember, I spent the first six years of my life there. My grandparents were all from Ruislip.'

'Which grandparents?'

'All of them. It was where my parents met, don't you remember? My father was the local schoolmaster.' There was not a hint of self-consciousness in this allusion to the schoolteacher as she showed me a page of *The Mercury* on which was featured a neat, semi-detached cottage with a gabled roof, Tudor-style lattice windows and a rustic front door.

'But you don't know anyone in Ruislip now, Mother,' I protested, trying to imagine how she would manage with all her stalwart companions gone, Prudence, Min and Rose, even Mrs Gillespie and the other church ladies. Her friends, like her furniture, seemed simply to have followed her ageing process – I'd never known her introduce anyone new to her circle.

'I'm not incapable of making friends,' she said, perhaps a little too firmly. 'I'd rather be lonely in a cottage than in this great, echoing house. What you said about living among memories may apply to me too, you know. I shall join the church choir for a start and I could learn bridge. I'm hoping that you'll come with me, perhaps next weekend, to view one of these properties?'

'Of course I'll come.' I hardly dared hope that she was really going to carry through such a daring and intriguing plan. Part of me was convinced that it was just her way of setting an impossible goal so that when it fell through she could blame me.

I showed her my ring, which I'd returned to its box for safe-keeping. She held it up admiringly to the light and declared it very pretty, though I could tell she was making comparisons with her own much grander diamond. Next, leaving Rusbridger's letter for the time being in the bottom of my bag, I gave her Meredith's to read as I poured more tea and pretended to study the houses advertised in *The Mercury*. How long before the Ruislip plan was defeated by the complications of house buying and selling?

'Poor Meredith,' Mother said, 'it appears that things have not turned out as she hoped. And she's expecting you to rush out and join her, but where does she think the money is going to come from when you've got a wedding to think about?'

'It would just be for a brief holiday.' In truth I'd not given any thought to a trip to France and couldn't really imagine taking time off work, booking a ticket, packing a bag. To plan a holiday abroad was out of the question when the country was in crisis. Mother turned the letter over and began reading it again. 'While you finish your tea,' I said, a little impatiently, 'shall I go up and begin sorting out Grandmother's books?'

She gave a *tsk* of irritation because on the rare occasions that I turned up at Clivedon Hall Gardens I was supposed to follow her own leisurely timetable.

Upstairs, Grandmother's room lay in semi-darkness with only the faintest hint of her cologne. When I swept aside the curtains dust motes clouded the air and fell on the tidied surfaces, the ornaments and the photographs, including that of my purported grandfather whose eyes still twinkled from behind his owlish spectacles. The trunk of theatrical souvenirs was kept at the end of the bed – fans, shawls, scarves, letters, flyers and programmes all tumbled together. I set about arranging everything in piles on the floor with some vague expectation that enlightenment lay at the bottom of the trunk.

Sure enough, lining the base was a layer of playscripts with pencilled underlinings and notes in the margin to show Grandmother's part. Inside *London Assurance* was a printed cast list headed with Patrick Rusbridger's name and, much further down, 'Miss Clara Fielding as Grace Harkaway'. Each member of the cast had signed their names. Rusbridger's signature was a thick-nibbed flourish, much showier than on the love letter he had sent Grandmother months later, but indubitably the same man's, and it made my heart beat faster.

I heard Mother leave the drawing room and take her customary slow, delicate steps up the stairs. Perhaps I should wait a while longer before confronting her with the question of who her father was. Why rush it? But I was aware of being overtaken by forces stronger than myself. Grandmother's death had thrust change upon us and I thought I might as well clear the air between Mother and me, especially while I was still in favour.

'What a mess you've made,' Mother said, perching on the bed, hands thrust into the drooping pockets of her long green cardigan. 'What are you looking for?'

'I'm just wondering which of these programmes to keep. I'd say anything that Grandmother was actually in, wouldn't you?'

'Oh, I've decided we should burn the lot. This is all ancient history as far as I'm concerned.' She ventured a little closer and must have seen the script of *London Assurance* on the floor by my knee.

'But the playscripts are of such historic – and family – interest.'

'Has it occurred to you that I might not wish to be reminded of those difficult times? We lived in great poverty, Mother and I, after my dear father died.' Having leafed through a couple of scripts she threw them aside. 'You haven't even started on the books,' she said, withdrawing a collected Ibsen from the shelf.

'Mother, there was something else I wanted to show you this afternoon – a letter that was hidden in Grandmother's writing box.'

She was reluctant to take the envelope and when she did merely peeked inside and then let it fall to her lap.

'You've seen it before?' I asked.

'Probably.'

'The letter is from a man who I presume to be Patrick Rusbridger, the actor.'

'I know who it's from.' The barriers were already up. Her mouth had tightened and her hands had gone limp.

The old irritation was rising in me and I willed her to be less feeble. 'Peggy Spencer, who was at Grandmother's funeral, seemed to suggest that Grandmother had an affair with this Rusbridger.'

Mother said nothing and I wondered again if I'd gone too far, too fast. Her sudden stillness was disturbing, and her lips were pursed, perhaps to suppress tears, though I could see little of her downturned face under the unruly grey hair.

'You see, as I'm getting married, Mother, it would be good to know the truth about our family,' I said more gently.

'What are you talking about?' She stood up, letting the envelope tumble to the floor. 'How dare you? What are you suggesting?'

'I just wanted to know if—'

'No! You want to dig about and discover all kinds of terrible things.' Her voice was low and emphatic and a flush flooded up her throat to her cheeks and forehead. 'I knew this would happen. You are so cold and unnatural, Evelyn. Not content with meddling in other people's lives, you have to meddle in mine. I've lost everything – my husband, my son, my mother – and now I am to be forced from my own home. And you, with your clever, bold face and your cool little voice and your suspicious mind, you are going to take away my past, too.'

'Mother, please. I'm only asking to be told who my grandfather was.'

'I know exactly what you think of me. Poor Mother, what a dull life she has compared to mine. How pointless. All she does is lose people and she doesn't even do that very well.'

'Whatever do you mean? Everyone grieves in different ways.'

'Oh yes, but yours is so superior. You think you can bring Jamie back by *becoming* him. Isn't that why you trained to be a lawyer? Whereas I just have an inconvenient tendency to mourn. And another difference between us is that I wish he could be restored to how he was, not how he might have been.'

I gave a little gasp as I registered how much she must have resented not only the work I did, but what she thought it symbolised, how she must have studied me and drawn her own conclusions about my feelings for Jamie.

'Don't look so shocked, Evelyn. I know it's true. You think I'm paltry and dull and fearful. Even when you were a child you couldn't hide your contempt from me. You tried to be a mother to Jamie because you thought I wasn't good enough.'

'No,' I cried, 'that's not true!'

But she was beyond listening. 'Well, I won't let you destroy my name and my childhood too. I loved my father. The years before he died were the best years of my life. I'm not letting anyone take that away.' She had worked herself into a frenzy. Scooping up the envelope she pulled out the letter, and before I realised what she was about to do, she tore it again and again, letting the pieces fall like confetti.

I knelt on the floor and scrabbled them into a pile, crying, 'You had no right to do that! It was *my* letter. Grandmother left it to me.'

'She probably didn't even know it was in the box.'

'Of course she knew it was there.'

'Then she was more of a troublemaker than I thought.'

Miss Perry had come creeping down and appeared in the

doorway, her face avid. 'Is everything all right, only I heard raised voices?'

'I'll come back another day to finish this,' I said, pushing past her. She winced as if I was about to strike her, then followed me along the landing and watched me run down the stairs.

'Is there anything I can do to help?' When I didn't reply she called after me, 'By the way, it slipped my mind earlier but the maids said someone was asking for you yesterday. A man. Did they tell you?'

'They didn't.' I stopped dead. Already I knew what was coming.

'They said he was a work colleague and he would probably see you sometime next week.'

'Didn't he leave his name?'

'If he did, I've forgotten it. He was a tall young man, apparently.'

I crossed the hall, took my coat from the stand, threw it over my arm and opened the front door but Miss Perry was at my side, gripping my arm with both hands. 'You really shouldn't leave with so much bad blood between you,' she said. 'Your mother has been terribly low. I'll be gone in the morning and I don't know how she'll manage on her own. I do hope you know what you're doing.'

# Chapter Twenty-Five

Robbie had asked me to encourage his mother to turn up in court so my first mission on Monday morning was to call at the Wrights' house in Wandsworth. Yesterday's row with Mother was fresh in my mind and it seemed to me that the whole world was in conflict. At a news stand near the bus stop I was confronted by a photograph of Sir Timothy Petit outside Number 10 Downing Street. Under the headline: BOLSHEVIK THREAT TO BRITISH WAY OF LIFE, the article claimed that Petit was investigating sources which had revealed that the prospective general strike was being funded by the Soviet Union in order to destabilise British democracy. In the meantime Petit, along with home secretary Joynson-Hicks, had undertaken to ensure that every British mother would be supplied with fresh milk during the strike and that vital institutions such as hospitals would operate as usual. Although the picture of Petit (caption: *Sir Timothy Petit sets forth to oversee last minute arrangements in Hyde Park*) was somewhat grainy, I could make out bony, purposeful features under a fashionably angled hat.

When Mrs Wright answered the door I was rewarded by a glimmer of a smile and invited into the kitchen.

'I can guess why you're here,' she said over her shoulder, 'Robbie said you might come.'

Both she and her house, on that fine May morning, were transformed. Her pinafore, in a paisley print, had been recently laundered, a scarf was knotted over her hair and the bruises on her face had faded. Worn floral curtains at the kitchen window were stirred by the sappy air blowing in through the open scullery door and she seemed to be in the midst of making a steamed pudding. There was no sign of Trudy.

'How are you feeling about the case tomorrow, Mrs Wright?'

'See, I knew you'd come to check up on me. Very nervous, is the answer.' The only child in sight was the youngest who was in a den under the kitchen table and had been equipped with spoon, bowl and cup so that she could play houses. A heap of washing was piled just inside the scullery. 'Are you sure it won't be called off, with the strike?'

'On the contrary, I think everyone will endeavour to maintain business as usual.'

'That's what Robbie says. He wants to be out on the picket lines but he says he'll come to court with me first.' She drew back a chair at the head of the table and urged me to sit down, then began to warm the teapot. It was as if she, too, was playing house, so precise and full of pride were her movements.

'Have you seen your husband since he was arrested?' I asked.

'Not once. He's kept away. Trude's gone to see him now. She says he's very sorry and wants to make amends. Poor girl, she's in a terrible state, trying to look after us both. I do wish she had a decent job just to get her out of the house. I've never seen her like it, crying and angry and sitting upstairs in her room. I hate to see her so unhappy in herself. Ned wants her to speak up for him in court and I tell her she must, if she feels she ought. I won't hold it against her if she says he's been a good dad – after all, it's me he goes for, not them. And he writes to me all the time.' She indicated letters stuffed behind the clock on the mantel, written on scraps of lined paper in a childish hand. 'He wants me to give him another chance. Says he's got hisself in with a winder cleaner who's training him up and will soon give him a round, so we'll all be right as rain.'

'Hasn't he promised you before that he will change his ways?' I tried to sound conversational rather than lawyer-like.

'Of course you're right. Shame, though. The children need a father and heck knows what we'd do if Robbie ever left home.'

'Never forget that your husband hit you so hard that you had to be taken to hospital.'

'You needn't have troubled yourself to come,' she said, settling at the table at last and stirring her tea vigorously. 'I'd have Robbie to answer to if I didn't show up in court and I'm almost as afraid of him as I am of my husband, would you believe? He's a lovely boy, but my goodness, the temper on him.'

'Did he tell you I heard him speak on Saturday to thousands of people? You must be very proud of him.' And then, perhaps because I wanted to even our relationship up a little and show that I had sorrows too, I said, 'He reminds me of my brother. He was about Robbie's age when he was killed. If Jamie set his heart on something, there was no stopping him. It was one of the things that I loved most about him.'

'I see the same quality in you, Miss Gifford.' Her great eyes were full of admiration over the rim of her cup.

'Oh, it's always very easy to see a clear path for other people. And sometimes, of course, it can lead to trouble.'

She looked at me with a flash of understanding. 'Listen, you mustn't think I'm so weak that I'm doing this just because others told me to. I know what has to happen. The trouble is, I get muddled about what's best for everyone and then sometimes, when I see him sitting there,' she indicated the empty chair by the range, 'I feel sorry for him, for being so foolish. He's his own worst enemy because he will never admit he's wrong. And so it all builds up in him. That's why it's not easy. But you need not worry. I know it has to stop.'

Thus it was she, in the end, who reassured me, rather than the other way round, as I drank up my tea, crouched down to give the child a couple of pennies to put in her saucepan and was led out through the frigid parlour.

# Chapter Twenty-Six

Meanwhile the final nail had been hammered into the coffin of any possible settlement by a leading article in the *Daily Mail* so critical of the unions that its own printers had walked out.

During the subsequent debate in the Commons on the legitimacy or otherwise of a general strike, the example of the *Mail*'s printers was used by Baldwin to show that 'the government found itself challenged with an alternative government . . . I do not think all the leaders, when they assented to ordering a general strike, fully realised that they were threatening the basis of ordered government and going nearer to proclaiming civil war than we have been for centuries past . . . it is not wages that are imperilled; it is the freedom of our very Constitution.'

So at dawn on Tuesday 4 May I woke to an uncanny silence because neither buses nor lorries were rattling by on Vauxhall Bridge Road. My first feeling was one of exhilaration and comradely zeal, even though I would have to walk the three or so miles to Lavender Hill Magistrates' Court where Edward Wright was to face trial on a charge of assault.

By seven thirty when I set out, every street was jammed and the air was clogged with fumes because those residents who could afford a motor car had driven themselves to work. Others had, even less helpfully, unearthed horse-drawn carts from crumbling stable blocks and we pedestrians were at risk from bicyclists who bumped up on to the pavement to dodge traffic. On Chelsea Bridge not a single car could move and there was a racket of horns as drivers wound down their windows to yell good-natured advice to each other.

It felt momentous, to be a moving speck in that great, disturbed city and I thought that Meredith should have stayed in London to share the thrill of it. I could have taken Edmund to school as usual; he would have loved it, swinging my hand, firing questions.

When I arrived at the court with just five minutes to spare for the ten o'clock hearing, the entrance hall was abnormally quiet and the usher told me that several defendants had failed to show up even though they lived within walking distance – 'any excuse' – but that there were sufficient magistrates to run three courts.

Wright had signed in early and was seated on a wooden bench, flanked by his sister and his daughter. He wore a suit and there was a nick on his clean-shaven jaw that, in my mistrust of him, I decided might have been self-inflicted, to reflect the fact that he felt hard done by. When he spotted me he gave his daughter a nudge and she turned away her face.

Of Mrs Wright and Robbie there was no sign.

The start of the trial was delayed by three-quarters of an hour because a backlog had accumulated due to late arrivals and a lack of police witnesses; the ushers called case after case, many of which had to be adjourned.

'By the end of the week you won't be able to move in here,' one of them predicted. 'We've been warned to expect long hours. They've booked a couple of stipes – stipendiary magistrates, you know – to run the strike courts. We've heard that there were dozens of arrests this morning, people interfering with vehicles suspected of carrying non-essential goods or workers. And a truck's been thrown into the river.'

'What about strike-breakers?' I said sharply. 'Has provision been made for them, should they be arrested for provocative behaviour?'

Again and again I went to the door and peered down the street, even ran to the corner, but there was no sign of Robbie or Mrs Wright. I tried to persuade an usher to have the case put back until after the coffee break but it was called anyway and I entered the public benches at the side of the courtroom where the single stipendiary magistrate, whose monstrous moustache compensated for thin white hairs trained to cover a bald patch, was drumming his fingers.

Wright stepped into the dock, took the oath with impeccable gravity, gave his personal details and reiterated his not guilty plea.

The police prosecutor rose to his feet. 'Your worship, I am forced to ask for an adjournment in this case. You'll be aware that police witnesses are in short supply today for obvious reasons. My witness, Sergeant Woodward, has sent a message to tell me he is required to assist his colleagues at Elephant and Castle.'

'Is the police evidence necessary to your case?'

'The officer in question was a witness to the injuries received but did not see the incident.'

'Well then.'

'But the victim in the case, the defendant's wife, has also not arrived. It could be that the lack of public transport . . .'

'How far does she live from this court?'

'I have not measured . . .'

'Half a mile,' put in Wright. 'At most.'

The magistrate raised a warning hand. 'Thank you, Mr Wright, you will be given an opportunity to speak in a minute,' but he softened the reprimand with a faint smile.

'Your worship,' said the police prosecutor, 'I know not why my chief witness is late but I cannot help but speculate. This is a case in which Mr Wright is accused of striking his wife so hard with the back of a chair that he fractured her jaw. The prosecution will say this was a deliberate, unprovoked attack.'

'I'm sure you will. But what assurances can you give me that Mrs Wright, who apparently cannot manage half a mile's journey without the assistance of an omnibus, will choose to appear in court next time.'

'I shall personally send . . .'

'Mr Wright, you are unrepresented. Stand up please. The chief witness for the prosecution, namely your wife, has failed to attend court. Can you explain her absence?'

Wright treated the magistrate to an injured, blue-eyed gaze. 'Certainly not. I ain't spoken to her. Been living with me sister these past days.'

'And what do you say to the suggestion that we should adjourn the case? Before you reply I should inform you, in the interests of fairness, that had you been represented your advocate would undoubtedly have leapt to his feet at this point and demanded that the trial go ahead. We've had no explanation of her absence from your wife and therefore cannot be sure that she will appear on a future occasion.'

Even though Wright stood in profile to me I sensed that he was trying to translate his seething resentment at finding himself in the dock into something more acceptable to the court.

'I can't settle to nothing with this case hanging over me,' he said pitifully. 'I never been in trouble with the courts before and I been offered a good job on the condition that I'm not found guilty and end up wiv a record. Anyway, she won't show. I know her,' he smiled fondly, 'she's always saying she'll do things and never keeps her word. If outsiders hadn't got theirselves involved we wouldn't be troubling the court.'

'You've pleaded not guilty to this offence. Have you brought witnesses?'

'I have indeed. My daughter and my sister are outside.'

'Did they actually see what happened?'

'Nothing happened. I keep saying. I picked up a chair to carry it across the room and she moves forward and gets her face in the way. She's clumsy like that, doesn't move fast on her feet.'

The magistrate smiled more warmly this time. 'Mr Wright, I have to consider the interests of justice in this court. When all's said and done, this is a case which appears to hang on two con-flicting stories – your own and your wife's. You are here, she is not. It seems to me that it would be quite unjust to put you through another hearing.'

The police prosecutor, who was yawning and adjusting his cuff-links, made no further intervention but I was so incensed that I leapt to my feet. 'Your worship, you must at least consider the pos-sibility that the witness, who is also the alleged victim, has been intimidated in this case.'

'And you are?'

'I'm Miss Gifford, a solicitor. I'm obviously not here in an official capacity, but I've spoken to Mrs Wright a number of times ...'

'This is highly irregular. What on earth do you mean, you're a solicitor?'

'I work for the firm of Breen & Balcombe. Here is my card. Since Mrs Wright is not here, I merely suggest that ...'

'You have absolutely no right to suggest anything. The matter is to go ahead today.'

'I can offer no evidence, your worship,' said the police prosecutor.

'Case dismissed.'

Not once had Wright looked directly at me but such was his loathing that I felt the force of it as he left the dock and walked to the door with his familiar stiff-backed gait. In order to avoid him I lingered a few minutes before leaving the courtroom but he was waiting for me in the lobby, where he said nothing but subjected me to a prolonged, unsmiling stare. Trudy chewed her lower lip and would not meet my eye at all.

# Chapter Twenty-Seven

My cheeks were burning as I walked away up York Road and by the time I reached Battersea Park I was exhausted and my spirits low. Having a case go the wrong way was always disappointing, even if a client ultimately deserved his fate, but I had been so convinced that Mrs Wright would give evidence that at first all I felt was the personal humiliation of having involved myself so fruitlessly in her affairs. Wright would undoubtedly use my ineffectual intervention in court to crow over her and therefore I'd only succeeded, as Trudy had suggested, in making things worse.

As I recovered, I grew more concerned for Mrs Wright's safety. She would be at home, presumably, braced for Wright to return with his battered suitcase and his triumph over the pernicious legal system. Whatever the reason for her change of mind she was bound to suffer dreadfully, poor soul. I only hoped that Wright would keep a few of the promises he had doubtless made her.

It would have been a comfort to confess to Daniel what had happened but he was in distant Toynbee Hall and even the security of my basement office was an hour's walk away. On the Thames private boats were speeding by, flags a-flutter, for once unimpeded by slow-moving barges and tugs. Next I faced a long haul up the King's Road where stalls and shops were open as usual, and traffic crawled towards the city. I thought I might as well take a look at Eccleston Square, nerve centre of the strike, but found the nearby streets completely jammed. The press of traffic, according to an obliging police officer, was due to the fact that the unions' head office was issuing special passes to the drivers of vans carrying essential supplies. The trouble was there was no proper system for issuing those passes and I had the impression that every Londoner who would normally have been at work had assembled there.

At the gates of Hyde Park a bespectacled woman whose hands were purple with cold and who had been equipped with a wobbly trestle table, ledger and pencil, was dealing with a queue of restless ladies wearing smart lace-up shoes and new-season hats.

'Are you here to volunteer?' a woman in the queue demanded officiously. 'Stand behind me if you are but I warn you, I've been waiting for hours.'

I put down my briefcase and thrust my hands into my pockets. 'What are you hoping to do?'

'We're all aiming to get into the police or bus driving, even to deliver milk. I'd do anything to show willing, wouldn't you?'

On the drive beyond the gates stretched a double row of idle buses and in the few minutes that I stood there, two milk lorries lumbered past, churns clanking. A posse of eager young men, a couple even sporting plus fours, immediately rushed forward to direct them further into the park. Their exuberant readiness to cooperate made me indescribably weary. Didn't they remember the war and how millions of young men had stepped up to the mark without question? The consequences of all this volunteering would surely be to strengthen the divide between the well-fed, well-housed rich and the labouring poor.

I picked up my briefcase, which had grown intolerably heavy, and trudged down Park Lane thinking how foolish I'd been not to have called at my flat and at least eaten something. Perhaps I should head for Regent Street, sit at my table in Lyons, order a poached egg and discuss the strike with Carole. But even as I considered that comforting prospect I heard a woman's voice ring out, 'Miss Gifford, Evelyn Gifford! Over here!'

Crawling along, among the little Fords and Austens and bi-cycles, was a stately charabanc crammed with passengers and emblazoned with the words *What Every Woman Knows* ... **To-night, at the Wyndhams.** Peggy Spencer, one of the actresses who had attended Grandmother's funeral, was on her feet, waving her hat vigorously and staggering as the vehicle swayed. When I ran alongside she leaned over and shook my hand.

'Isn't this an absolute hoot? How your grandmother would have loved it. We're in rep – came all the way from Chichester today with a stinker of a play – hush, don't tell anyone I said that – and we're on tonight so they had to send this vehicle instead of the train. We've broken down three times already. Set out about a year ago.'

'Five o'clock this morning actually,' said her nearest companion. 'Peggy always exaggerates.'

'At least you have transport,' I said.

'You *do* look tired. Where on earth have you been? Do you want a lift? Where are you heading?'

'To my office, near Euston.'

'Oh, come on up. I expect we'll be driving along Oxford Street. We'll drop you off somewhere convenient.' The driver was ordered to stop and I was hauled over the hubcap and into the vehicle, provoking a couple of wolf whistles from male pedestrians treated to a glimpse of my undergarments. Next moment I was crushed between the two actresses and my knees had been swathed in a red tartan rug.

'You're just in time for lunch,' said Peggy. 'We have mountains of supplies. Management is determined to keep us sweet because they want that curtain to go up tonight willy-nilly.'

Snuggled against Peggy's aged furs the world took on an entirely different aspect, especially as chicken sandwiches and ginger beer (laced with the odd tot of whisky) were passed around with reckless generosity.

'I'm so glad to see you, Miss Spencer,' I said. 'You left me in some turmoil after the funeral.'

'*Did* I dear?'

'You implied that there was a dark secret hanging over Grandmother's past. Mother and I have fallen out over it, actually.'

By now we were rumbling spasmodically along Oxford Street, halting every few yards as pedestrians spilled off the pavement. Selfridges was open but one of the windows had been obscured by scaffolding so that loudspeakers could be attached to the wall.

'Our friends in the BBC,' said Peggy, 'say that they will broadcast news bulletins even if there are no newspapers. Now let's see if we can guess whose side the BBC will be on.'

'Aren't they supposed to be impartial?'

'Ah, but who funds them?' She poked her elbow into my ribs. 'But you said you'd argued with your mother because of me. I hope not. I rather regretted what I said at the funeral, as a matter of fact.'

'There's rather more to it than that. Since Grandmother's death, Mother has been terribly lonely and sad but I'm afraid I don't have much patience with her. She's talking about moving to Ruislip.'

'Aha. Back to her roots, then.'

'She has fond memories of the place, apparently.'

'I remember visiting your grandmother – Clara – in Ruislip just before she was married.'

My grandmother's youth was thereby thrust tantalisingly within reach. 'You went to her house?'

'Oh yes. She was much too nice to say so, of course, but I can't have been very welcome.'

'Miss Spencer, please. Tell me. What was it like there? Do you remember what Clara said?'

'Of course. If I'm honest I was a little besotted with her and the romance of the whole thing. Anyway, I have an exceptionally good memory. We all have, in the profession. Trained. Aren't we, Gwenda?' she said, raising her voice and appealing to the woman on my left. 'There were rumours that Clara was unwell and that she had retired from the stage, so I just took the train one day and then a taxicab, horse-drawn, of course – cost me a week's wages – and arrived unannounced on her doorstep. It was rather a grand house. Her father had had some brief success as a theatrical entre-preneur and bought it on the proceeds. The money didn't last, of course, but as far as I recall they hung on to the property for quite some time. I remember her so well, in that garden. You know the way the grass grows more sparsely beneath a great tree – it was a cedar I expect – and how there is so much shadow? Her face was so pale it was almost violet and her hand was cold, because of the sickness. She and her mother had been looking at patterns for wedding clothes and there was such tension in the air that I'm surprised it didn't curdle the milk in my tea.'

'She was ill?'

'It was just before her marriage and I was too naive to realise she was sick because she was expecting. But later, when I heard that her baby was premature, I knew. During my visit, of course, she said nothing about it – only, when her mother was out of earshot, she whispered that she couldn't bear living at home again and was longing to be married.'

'The baby was definitely Rusbridger's?' How different it was, bowling along Oxford Street, my throat a-tingle from a swig of whisky, airing so freely the scandal of Mother's conception rather than speculating about it within the gloomy confines of Clivedon Hall Gardens. Out here in the charabanc it simply didn't matter whether Mother was legitimate or not – in fact, it was all rather to be relished.

'That's what we thought. Use your common sense, dear. You don't think a schoolteacher would forget himself so far as to be responsible for the conception of a child out of wedlock?'

As the charabanc rolled across the junction with New Bond Street a youth with a cheeky grin, acne and curly hair bobbed up above the side of the vehicle and demanded an autograph. 'Peggy Spencer! We're coming to see you on Wednesday . . .'

Having signed the slip of paper with a gracious smile she nestled back beside me. 'You see, I'd been there at the start of things. Rusbridger had cast us both in *Assurance*. He was twenty years older than she, with three children and a beautiful wife who had once been a singer and still had pearly skin and that abundant hair women seemed to manage in those days. She used to come to virtually every performance – she had to keep a weather eye on him, because he had a reputation for pursuing dewy young actresses.'

'So Clara wasn't the only one?'

'Good Lord no. But she was special. There was something electric between them – even on stage with Clara I used to think: I'm wasting my time playing to her at all. Her mind was filled only with him.'

'How did the wife allow it to happen?'

'She couldn't have stopped it. And in any case, I don't expect she noticed until it was too late. I remember Clara telling me that she couldn't *stand* Rusbridger as a director because he was so pompous and had no feeling for women's lines. Once, in an early rehearsal, he was exceptionally sharp with her, called her a little fool and would she please be *still*. We were all stunned but Clara raised her chin – actually, I noticed at the funeral that you have a similar trick – and for a while she kept her distance and he was like a great sorrowful bear, hating himself but not knowing how to put matters right.'

'He was a man who could never hide his feelings,' put in Gwenda, who had overheard much of this saga, despite Peggy's attempt at sotto voce, 'which is why he was such a splendid actor. I was taken to see his Lear when I was a very young girl. It was what made me decide to go on the stage – that purity of emotion, the concentration of the man.'

'He was so much taller than Clara, and heavily built about the shoulders,' said Peggy, a little riled by her friend's interruption. 'Beside him, Clara was elfin. He could have crushed her, but instead he enwrapped her with his talent and his desire. One night, before the dress rehearsal, I witnessed the most extraordinary thing, *the* moment, I think, when everything changed between them.'

First checking that she had my undivided attention, she drew herself up for the finale. 'Clara always arrived well before the half so she could walk the stage – get a feel for the theatre, as she said. I was in the stalls because I was worried about a sightline for one of my entrances and I remember her in a white dress, very plain except for three pale blue ruffles in the skirt and with her hair down her back because it had not yet been dressed, a whisper of a thing flitting from wing to wing, trying out all her entrances. And then I saw that he was in the auditorium and was just sitting there with his arms crossed.

'Eventually he stood up. The movement must have startled her because she walked to the edge of the stage and peered out.

'"Clara," he says, and he uses the rehearsal steps to run up on to the stage. "Clara." She's standing there above the footlights, at a loss, and he strides towards her and offers her his hand but she doesn't take it. Everything about her stops struggling as she looks up into his face, he puts the palm of his hand to her cheek and they just stand there, not moving. But my God, the very air between them is vibrating and I'm sure that when he takes his hand away there will be scorch marks on her cheek.

'But as I crept away I remember thinking: if only that could be me, blazing like that, utterly lost.'

The charabanc was moving more purposefully towards Regent Street. Peggy put her arm around me and her whisky-laced breath was warm on my cheek. 'At the time I was carried away by the sheer romance of it all. Now I know I was witnessing the first act of a tragedy because as soon as the run was over she disappeared to her family home in Ruislip and began preparations for her marriage to your grandfather.'

Still adjusting to this extraordinarily vivid evocation of Grandmother's love affair, I protested. 'It seems cruel of her to have married Grandfather when she didn't love him.'

'Ah, but that man would have known exactly what he was taking on. He was very persistent, as I've said, at the stage door night after night. He'd admired her from afar for years, and when I got to know him a little I realised that for all his helpless love for Clara, he was pretty astute. My guess is that they both went into that marriage with their eyes wide open.'

Yes, it all seemed so plausible, the passion and the pregnancy. Perhaps it was because Annabel Petit's case was so fresh in my mind that I thought to ask, 'And Rusbridger. Did he know about the child?'

'I doubt it,' said Peggy grandly. 'Clara would have been much too proud to tell him. He went to America with his family very soon afterwards, so one way or another his wife must have reeled him back in.'

For Mother's sake, I could not mention Rusbridger's letter and his last-ditch attempt to win Clara back, though I was a little sorry not to have supplied Peggy with some additional drama.

'Do you know what?' she said suddenly. 'You should go and see Rusbridger Junior – the grandson. There's more than a passing family resemblance. Then you'd have some idea of what your grandmother was up against. I have a feeling he's in a show somewhere, let me just ask Gwenda, she always knows what everyone's doing.'

'Isn't he in that Galsworthy in Birmingham?' said Gwenda.

We had now reached the corner of Tottenham Court Road where the charabanc rattled to a stop and I alighted into the crowd outside the Dominion, restored by food, a mouthful or two of whisky and, above all, such captivating information about my grandmother. Perhaps a dusting of stage glamour clung to me and it was as if my feet were clad in her tempestuous little boots as I reached the Euston Road at last and crossed to Arbery Street.

# Chapter Twenty-Eight

Although it was barely four o'clock the office door was locked – the first time that I'd ever known Miss Drake to leave early, but at least I had my own key. The deserted building drew breath when I entered, and exhaled just a hint of the family residence it had once been . . . a maid's footfall on the basement stairs, a tray resting on an aching hip. I lit the gas ring in the storeroom that served as a kitchen and put the kettle on to boil. Sometimes, if Wolfe had not found them, there were a few biscuits in the tin but today it was empty.

While I waited for the water to boil I took advantage of Miss Drake's unheard-of absence to creep about like an intruder and peek into each unoccupied room. First I visited her office where a stack of letters lay on the desk waiting to be posted, and three in-trays, two of oak, one of wire were labelled *Breen, Wolfe, Gifford,* each holding a sheaf of files. Propped on the covered typewriter was a note written in exquisite copperplate: *Since it took me more than two and a quarter hours to walk here this morning and I have completed the correspondence, such as there was, I have taken it upon myself to leave early.*

Next I looked into Daniel's office which was unnaturally tidy and therefore somewhat bleak, the desk cleared in readiness for strike business. I sat for a moment in my usual chair – upholstered in sage green leather with brass studs – and studied an extraordinary innovation. At the centre of a table previously employed to hold whisky glasses was a walnut-cased wireless, installed to keep us in touch with events. I was overtaken by a sense of unreality as I acknowledged the distance I had travelled since first entering this room to be interviewed.

It had seemed to me, having watched him many times in court, that Daniel Breen might be the one lawyer in London who would take on a woman clerk – mainly because he loved nothing better than to outwit his rivals by championing lost causes. My subsequent grilling in this same office had lasted barely twenty minutes during which Daniel had toyed with his pen and swung from side to side on his swivel chair, his bright eyes incredulous, as if I were a witness for the prosecution.

'Give me three good reasons, Miss Gifford, why I should take you on.'

'I have achieved excellent academic results and I work harder than most men.'

'That's two reasons and you can't prove the latter.'

'I have proved myself to be more determined to succeed than any man, given the hurdles I've already overcome. My third reason? Has it occurred to you, sir, that a woman might think and behave differently to a man and therefore add something fresh?'

'And what, precisely, is this fresh approach that you are going to bring?'

'I am an outsider. I don't necessarily want to be, but as a woman, I am. For instance, there is a certain clubby way in which lawyers talk to each other in court which excludes the defendant . . .'

'Was I *clubby*, as you put it, when you observed me in court?' He had leaned forward belligerently.

'There was a degree of collusion between you and the chair of the bench and it was very successful, a kind of shortcut to a mutual understanding. For me that will not be possible so I shall have to depend on other means.'

'Such as?'

'Such as seeing new approaches to an issue or by challenging the law.'

'So you're one of those young ladies who thinks she can reform every aspect of society.'

I had nearly said, 'But isn't that exactly what motivates you, Mr Breen?' Instead I was silent while he tapped his fingertips together. 'You won't find it easy either in or out of court,' he told me. 'The whole system is entrenched in outmoded traditions.'

'I do not seek an easy life, sir.'

He had smiled mischievously. 'I must admit I'm tempted, if

only to see you face down a couple of our more self-opinionated beaks.'

And now he and I were engaged to be married; I had stepped from one side of the looking glass to the other. In truth, I felt a pang for the old days when my relationship with him had been far less complicated – when I had simply been stimulated and on my mettle whenever I was in his company.

Conscious that I was trespassing, I sprang up and resumed my tour. On the first floor was the meeting room in which I'd done battle with Mrs Shawcross and at the back was Wolfe's locked office which I must have been invited to enter only half a dozen times over the last two years. He had a penchant for soft furnishings upholstered in gold velvet, a blazing fire and brass lampstands. The attic floor contained nothing but boxes of wills and deeds and ancient files, each representing some wronged, malicious, foolish or violent client, most of whom were long dead.

On the way down to the basement I collected the mail, which had reached my in-tray despite the lack of official post. The air in my office was stale and chilly but at least I was equipped with a cup of tea, could kick off my shoes, light the gas and wrap a blanket about my shoulders. The first hand-delivered letter was from the Harley Street obstetrician who had treated Annabel Petit.

*Lady Petit had a healthy pregnancy. The daughter, weighing six pounds and one ounce was born after a five-hour labour, free of any complication, on Friday, 23 March, 1923. I was present from the start and stayed until three hours after the child was born.*

*I served as Lady Petit's obstetrician throughout her pregnancy. My notes inform me that she first visited me on Thursday, 31 August, 1922. After examination I estimated her to be about eight weeks pregnant. She had been married less than four months and was a little disturbed to find herself pregnant so quickly – like many young brides she had thought the process would take longer. As I recall she questioned how I could be so sure of my diagnosis and explained that she didn't feel entirely ready for a child.*

*On the next appointment, a fortnight later, she told me that
the real cause of her surprise had been that no actual intercourse
had taken place between herself and her husband although they
had embraced intimately and slept in the same bed. Then how
was it possible, she asked, that she had conceived? I informed
her that I had encountered many patients in my time who had
found themselves in the same position as herself and that the
human sperm is very tenacious.*

Someone was hammering on the front door. Out of habit I waited
for Miss Drake to answer before I threw aside the blanket, crushed
my feet into my shoes and ran up the basement stairs. Through
the two strips of frosted glass, which allowed a glimmer of day-
light into the hall, I spied a tall figure wearing a hat.

His hand was raised in readiness to knock again as I opened the
door. Beyond was the familiar street of early nineteenth-century
houses, the scuffle of grit in the gutter and the cloudy sky across
which a lone black bird was flying. Nicholas wore a grey, belted
raincoat over a double-breasted suit and black tie. His face, minus
the moustache he used to wear, seemed considerably thinner and
older than when we'd met at the Criterion. I registered that his
eyes were somewhat sunken, as if with fatigue, and that his body
was full of tension.

'I appreciate this might be a bit of an intrusion,' he said in that
well-remembered, clipped voice of his. 'Tell me at once if you're in
the midst of something. It's just that I bumped into Daniel Breen
at Toynbee Hall and when I asked after you he said you might be
here so I hitched a lift as far as Holborn.'

'You've only just caught me.'

'What a stroke of luck.' Our eyes locked. I couldn't quite take in
the fact that he was actually here, alone, and my body was heavy
with the effort of not seizing hold of him and demanding: why
didn't you come back to me, all this time?

'Did you get the message that I'd called at your house on Saturday?' he was saying. 'By the way, are you still living at home? The
maid seemed to suggest that you were just a visitor.'

'I moved out a couple of years ago.'

'I see.' He nodded and was about to ask a further question but seemed to change his mind. 'Anyway, I was intrigued because my clerk told me you'd been looking for me at chambers.'

By now I had closed the door to the street and we were facing each other in the gloomy passage outside Daniel's office, so close that I could smell the faint perfume of Nicholas's soap, his familiar scent. 'Ah, yes,' I replied, 'I happened to be nearby because I'd been to tea at the Law Society. You see I felt rather awkward meeting up with you like that at the theatre and thought we ought to have a conversation, as I gather we're to be on opposite sides in the Petit case.'

Indifference was the card I had been determined to play but his gaze never left my face and there was an air of fragility about him, as if he had steeled himself for this moment.

'I was so pleased when my clerk gave me your name,' he said. 'I kept asking, "*Who* did you say? Are you *sure?*"' He'd taken off his hat and was sweeping a lock of hair from his forehead with long, scholarly fingers. 'It was such a shock seeing you at the theatre. I'd been thinking about you, inevitably, since I got back to London and I wanted to re-establish myself, get back on my feet before meeting you again but suddenly there you were. And looking so ...' He paused, and his eyes grew soft. 'I'd never seen you in evening dress. Whenever I thought about you, I always imagined you in the very sober clothes you were wearing when we first met.'

He had thought of me, then, and that *whenever* suggested often rather than seldom. Every word he spoke was a blow to my self-possession and I was struck again by the sheer beauty of the man.

'I'm afraid Mother and I were gatecrashers in the dress circle during the interval. We had much cheaper tickets,' I said.

'Yes, I looked for you afterwards but you must have left quickly.'

'Mother doesn't like to be too late home.'

His arms were folded as he studied me and it struck me that he might well feel some degree of self-justification or relief when he saw only a tired woman who deferred too much to the whims of her mother and who had ill-kempt hair, ink-stained fingers and half-undone shoes. But at least, I consoled myself, I looked as if I led a demanding life.

'How have you been, Evelyn, these past couple of years?' he asked with such concern that I felt my composure slip another notch.

'Very well. I'm fully qualified now, busy.'

'And you're representing Lady Petit. That's something of a plum. Congratulations.'

Better to be irritated, I thought, than witless with longing, so I seized the opportunity to say sharply, 'I'd rather be on her side than his.'

'It will be an interesting trial. I was pleased to be instructed because I was intrigued – until I heard you and I would be in opposition. That I found disturbing. It wasn't at all how I'd planned things. I had no idea what it would be like to see you again and I never imagined our first meeting would be in a theatre, or that I'd have to face you in a judge's chambers.'

He was becoming more vivid to me with every glance; the brilliance of his eye, how the fullness of his lips was revealed now that he was clean-shaven, the deeply tanned skin at his throat . . . I found myself remembering the tenderness of his first kiss and how my hat had fallen on to the dusty track. There was no doubt that he had dashed here from Toynbee in a spirit of eagerness and reconciliation. I'd always thought that when I met him again I would wonder: what on earth did I see in him? Instead layer upon layer of my defences were being peeled away.

'As I've said, the Petit case is the main reason why I called at your chambers,' I said. 'I thought it would be as well to meet and clear the air before the preliminary hearing.'

'Between you and me,' he lowered his voice, 'I think we'll settle. There'll be an offer on the table. I suspect they're both finding the whole thing pretty bloody.'

We went up to the meeting room where I sat as far from him as possible. The dirty window was behind me with its net curtains, stained by condensation, obscuring the view of other Victorian houses and their dark yards backing on to ours, smoke clouding the already occluded sky. Nicholas tossed his raincoat over the back of the chair though the room was chill, being unheated and unaired, and as he sat down he hitched up his trouser leg in exactly the old, familiar way.

'Actually I've known Petit for years which I guess is why I've been instructed,' he said. 'We served together behind the lines at one stage.'

'What was he like?'

'Very popular – a joy to be with, in fact. He was very funny, spirited and charming towards his men. Destined for a career in politics, I'd say, even then – so astute and eager to please. Shame that the war made us all grow old too fast. And that ambition gets its hooks into us.'

This was too much, I thought, coming from him. Ambition, after all, had been his undoing. We were silent a moment, perhaps both remembering the words I had flung at him when we parted, *How can I forgive you, when I have no idea whose side you're on?*

And his murmured reply, *Yours. I love you.*

'How long have you been back in the country?' I asked coolly.

'A couple of months. I have no idea why I stuck South Africa as long as I did. No, that's not true. Actually, I do.' In the ensuing pause, during which he watched me unwaveringly, I drew a long breath. 'Anyway, while I was there everything deteriorated. Have you heard of the pass laws? I wonder what has been reported about them in the newspapers here. Towards the end I thought being a lawyer was the worst possible job for a white man. I couldn't stand the thought of upholding the law in South Africa; I despised the whole system though there was plenty of money to be made if one buried one's scruples.'

'You must be disappointed to find England in such a state,' I replied.

'Not disappointed. A little puzzled as to why nobody's been able to prevent a strike. There will be so much hardship as a result. In fact, it was news of the strike that made up my mind to write to my old chambers – they were very decent about letting me have a room. Whatever happens here, it cannot be worse, at least I hope not, than the hell I was living through in South Africa.'

'You mentioned at *Hay Fever* that your friends had connections with the FBI. Is that who you're working for? Given your opposition to the strike that seems an odd choice. The Federation of British Industry is scarcely sympathetic to the unions.'

'The Hattons are old friends. And I believe I can do something useful – company law is an area of great interest to me.'

It made no difference to me, I told myself, what his relationship was with the Hattons, their daughter, or indeed anyone else, and it occurred to me then that Daniel had been at fault, sending Nicholas here and subjecting me to this.

'I wonder what you were doing at Toynbee, given your affiliation to the industrialists?' I said.

'Breen asked exactly the same question. The answer is that I had a moment or two to spare and thought I might find out what was going on there, for old times' sake.'

'You were spying on the opposition.'

'That's rather harsh. Actually, I don't regard the unions as opposition.' But he smiled and added, 'By the way, Breen says you are becoming an excellent lawyer. He says he's proud of you and that you have already gained quite a reputation.'

'Please note that he says that I am *becoming* a good lawyer. I'm obviously not there yet. But yes, he has been very kind to me. I owe him everything.'

'It seems that Breen feels the same way about you. He told me he was absolutely right to take you on. He said you had rejuvenated the whole firm.'

Nevertheless, Daniel had clearly made no mention of our engagement, so it was up to me. As I rose from my seat the words hovered on my lips. 'Did he tell you that he and I are to be married?'

There was a prolonged silence. When I glanced across Nicholas hadn't moved and his face looked stunned. For a treacherous moment I thought: what if I'd said nothing? Did he really hope, when he came here, that we might become lovers again?

'Breen said nothing to me,' he said, too lightly. 'Many congratulations.'

We went downstairs and I opened the front door for him. He was still pale as we shook hands and the light had entirely gone from his eye. 'So life is good,' he said softly.

He raised his hat. It was all over, I could breathe freely. But then, having walked a few paces, he turned as if puzzled about something. 'You never replied to my letter.'

I shook my head.

He came back and said very quickly, in a low voice, 'I wanted to know . . . I was in agony, wondering if the letter . . . You see I have thought about you every hour of every day since we parted. That's what I really came to say.' And he ran down the steps.

I closed the door and leaned against it. The hallway was dim and quiet and the tug of my work gave me no joy at all. God help me, I thought. Please, please help me. But it was all I could do not to throw open the door and rush out after him for one more word, one touch.

# Chapter Twenty-Nine

Daniel sent a message that he would not be attending the Petit hearing because he was needed in Battersea where Saklatvala was to be sentenced for incitement, specifically for using his May Day speech in Hyde Park to encourage the armed forces to rebel. To my consternation, we heard at the last minute that our counsel, Burton Wainwright, had also been detained in a convoluted fraud case at the Old Bailey. I was therefore left to handle the preliminary hearing on my own, apart from Wolfe, who had been sent along to back me up.

He and I arranged to meet at the Royal Courts of Justice an hour before the start of the case but he was thirty-five minutes late, dressed nattily as ever in a grey suit with a mauve stripe, nipped in at the waist, but mopping sweat from his brow because he'd been forced to leave his motor on the Embankment and walk the last half-mile. At least the ordeal seemed to have distracted him from the news that Daniel and I were now engaged.

'This strike nonsense is a complete waste of everybody's time,' he complained. 'Lord knows, I have little enough sympathy for the unions but you'd think they would at least try to make an impact. Shilly-shallying will get them nowhere. They're allowing through *essential* supplies? I ask you, how is the average picket to know whether a covered wagon is carrying "essential" supplies or something completely frivolous?'

Since the more liberal news-sheets could not be issued precisely because they sympathised with the unions, and specifically with the striking printers, we were dependent for information on *The British Gazette*, a special strike newspaper issued by the government and edited by none other than the chancellor of the exchequer, Winston Churchill.

'He's been given the job to keep him out of trouble,' said Wolfe, brandishing a crisp copy. 'Baldwin doesn't want him rampaging round the streets, haranguing the strikers. The unions have been caught on the back foot once again. If they don't publish their own newspaper fast, it will be Winston Churchill's version of the General Strike that goes down in history.'

According to the *Gazette*, the chaos envisaged by the more right-wing press in the weeks before the strike had been avoided thanks to the forethought of the government and the determination of a vast army of volunteers who were keeping the country going. Sir Timothy Petit, junior minister at the home office, was credited with exemplary planning and organisation. While the unions had been posturing in the weeks prior to the strike, he had discreetly got on with the business of ensuring that essential services would be maintained.

'Between you and me,' murmured Wolfe, 'this Petit is going to prove a slippery character. If he's able to outsmart the unions, what chance does his poor wife have against him?'

'As a matter of fact I met with Nicholas Thorne yesterday,' I told him, hoping that my casual tone would belie the extreme tension I was feeling, 'and he suggested they'd probably settle.'

A flicker of his right eyelid was the only sign of Wolfe's surprise. 'Are they going to withdraw?'

'That wasn't clear.'

'They'll want a divorce. I'm sure of that.'

'In which case we'll have to fight on.'

A young clerk was hovering at my shoulder. 'Miss Gifford, is it? Excuse me, madam, but Mr Pearman and counsel would very much like to have a word with you in private before the hearing.'

Wolfe and I were ushered into a side room that smelt of the coffee which had somehow materialised in a silver pot. Pearman in the flesh was almost exactly as his letter might have suggested, almost bald with narrow features, wire-rimmed spectacles and a tight collar. His fingernails were so highly polished that I suspected the use of nail powder. Nicholas stood with his back to the window and I registered with a sinking heart that what I'd been missing in the years since he left was the sense that every molecule in the room was charged because he was there, and that nobody else, not even Daniel, had such an effect on me.

'Miss Gifford, your reputation precedes you,' said Mr Pearman, 'one of our pioneering female solicitors.' I let the remark hang as I responded firmly to his tepid handshake. 'And this is our counsel, Mr Thorne.'

Nicholas's smile was impersonal and he gave no sign, even when we shook hands, that he remembered yesterday's conversation. I was wearing my most lawyer-like hat, dark grey with a curved brim trimmed with an intricate knot of black braid, and I felt suitably sober, compared to yesterday's untidiness. I retreated to a far chair, my back very straight and my papers neatly piled on the table before me.

'We have a somewhat delicate matter to put to you,' Pearman continued, addressing himself to Wolfe, 'so I'm delighted to take this opportunity for a private chat.'

Wolfe perched his coffee saucer on his chest above the second button of his waistcoat. 'I'm merely here in support,' he said. 'This is Miss Gifford's case.'

'The fact is,' said Nicholas crisply, 'that Sir Timothy is prepared to make his wife such a generous offer that we believe she will be hard-pressed to refuse. We're very much hoping that the matter can be concluded today.'

'I see.'

Pearman leaned forward, clasped his hands together and looked earnestly into my face though he would not meet my eye.

'Sir Timothy is willing to drop the entire case,' added Nicholas.

There had been a period in the past when I had been so in love with Nicholas that if a hair on his head had been out of place I would have noticed, just as I had registered each timbre of his voice and mulled over every word he said. We had walked together once to visit a crime scene on a rare summer day when the earth was baked hard and the grass panted for moisture. Afterwards, because of where they had led, I had re-examined every word and every gesture, as if they had been a trail of crumbs.

*I like your words*, he had said, *all of them.*

So because I knew him so well, I knew at once that what he was about to say was not to his liking and that there was something very much amiss.

'Excellent news,' I replied, 'but could this not have been put in writing to save both the judge and ourselves the inconvenience of coming to court today?'

'We thought it best to discuss such a delicate matter face to face, especially as the postal service is not to be trusted at the moment. The point is, there are one or two conditions attached. Sir Timothy is prepared to accept paternity of Annice provided that his wife grants him a divorce on the grounds of her adultery.'

I made a laborious note. 'And what is to happen to Annice, under this settlement?'

'Sir Timothy's offer is extremely generous. Annice will be fully accepted as his daughter, and indeed his heir, in the event of there being no future male child. He will further make a financial settlement upon his wife and ensure that she is able to see the child a number of times a year.' He paused to allow my pen time to catch up. 'The only other caveat is that Mr Richard Leremer should have no access to Annice.'

'I see.' I closed my notebook and put it away. 'I shall of course put this offer to Lady Petit but I believe her to be sure that she does not want a divorce and certainly not one that would entail separation from Annice.'

Nicholas's head was to one side as he nodded sympathetically. Presumably he knew as well as I did how closely we were being watched by Wolfe.

'I think you'll find that she has no choice in the matter,' he said. 'Sir Timothy believes the marriage to have broken down irretrievably and he has witnesses to his wife's infidelity with Leremer.'

'Witnesses to what infidelity, exactly?'

'To the fact that Mr Leremer and Lady Petit were conducting an affair immediately after her marriage. And his doctor will say under oath that Sir Timothy came to visit him in great distress shortly after the honeymoon because the marriage could not be consummated.'

Wolfe buttoned his jacket and I got up, forcing a scraping back of chairs as everyone stood.

'You will put this offer to Lady Petit?' said Pearman.

'I'm surprised that Sir Timothy has not put it to his wife himself since they are still living in the same house,' I said. 'I suspect the reason that he hasn't is that he knows his proposition to be grossly insulting. In fact, it is tantamount to blackmail. Do you think Lady Petit would be willing to give up her child, because that is what it would mean, especially on grounds which reflect so badly and untruthfully upon herself?'

'As I've said, in the circumstances—'

'Furthermore,' put in Wolfe at his most urbane, 'has Sir Timothy not somewhat jeopardised his own position by telling us that he is willing to accept Annice as his daughter after all, thereby suggesting that he is using the whole question of paternity as a means to punish his wife rather than because he believes himself not to be the father?'

'On the contrary. He knows that he is not the father and as a result wishes for a divorce. But he loves the child and seeks, I might say with astonishing generosity, by the means I have just suggested, to spare her a precarious future.'

'I will of course speak to Lady Petit and to our counsel, Mr Burton, but in the meantime we shall be late for our appointment in court.' I swept out, the pleat of my woollen skirt flicking against my upper calf and my head high though I was breathless with the knowledge that I had left them all fumbling to pick up their papers.

There was no time to recover before Wolfe caught up with me. 'Congratulations, Miss Gifford. You certainly put them in their place. I presume you're sure of what Lady Petit would want?'

'Lady Petit would never accept those terms. The very fact that they have put them to us so late in the day is sheer game playing.'

'I would be very interested to know what has provoked this change of heart. The most optimistic explanation is that they have taken advice from Thorne and begun to doubt their ability to win the paternity case.'

'That's what I hope. Certainly if they want to enrage Lady Petit they could not have chosen a more effective or a crueller way.'

We were now to meet Judge Poynter who, according to Wolfe, was an old buffer and bad news for Annabel Petit since he was a notorious chauvinist. Like many judges he looked a little odd without his wig; his wiry hair had been flattened into a sort of compressed halo following a recent appearance in court.

'Now the first issue,' he said, 'is time. I see we have been allocated three days. Are you sure that this gives us sufficient time? And of course if the strike is still proceeding on those dates we can hardly expect Sir Timothy to attend. He will have his hands full with matters of national import.'

'With all due respect,' I stood up from sheet force of habit, 'the date of the hearing has been known for weeks, as has the likelihood of a strike. Any prospective difficulties could have been raised long ago. It must be remembered that it is Sir Timothy who is pressing for these proceedings to go ahead as speedily as possible. It would be most unfortunate if the strike were to be used as an excuse for stalling now.'

'My dear young lady,' said Poynter, 'the strike is a national crisis. If Sir Timothy requests an adjournment, we shall certainly listen sympathetically.'

The issues, we all agreed, were the very narrow ones of whether or not the marriage had been consummated, and whether Leremer had become Annabel's lover again after her marriage. The couple's premarital relationships with other people were not at issue because Nicholas conceded that Petit had been involved in successful sexual relationships prior to meeting Annabel, though none had resulted in the conception of a child. Nicholas named the witnesses who would vouch for Lady Petit's infidelities with Leremer before and after her marriage, a professorial expert on conception and the doctor, Reginald Huskington, who would testify that the marriage had never been consummated.

On our side I tendered Lady Petit, her obstetrician, her friend Kit Porter and, with crossed fingers, Richard Leremer. Finally we argued about whether or not Annice should be produced.

'It's quite wrong to bring a three-year-old child to court,' I said, 'and have her scrutinised so publicly. She's far too young.'

'Mr Thorne,' said Poynter, 'Miss Gifford, as a lady, perhaps feels the delicacy of the situation rather more than we, as mere men do. What do you say?'

'We will say that Annice bears no resemblance to Sir Timothy Petit,' said Nicholas. 'If Miss Gifford is prepared to concede this point the little girl need not be brought to court.'

'On the contrary, Annice, though she looks most like her

mother, is undoubtedly a Petit,' I retorted. 'But of course it's well known that anything can be read into a child's unformed face. Have you met her, Mr Thorne? She is three years old, shy and devoted to her mother. Do you really insist that she should have a courtroom of strange men inspect her features?'

He hesitated, annoyed at being given such an invidious choice. 'We are not prepared to concede that she has none of Leremer's physical characteristics, if that's what you're asking.'

'Then the child must be brought to court,' said Poynter irritably. 'Good Lord, it need only take ten minutes.'

After the hearing Wolfe offered me a lift since there were no trains. There was fitful sunshine as we walked together down to the Embankment and somewhat to my surprise he suggested that we sit on a bench in the gardens by Temple Station and *take stock* as he put it.

Folding his arms he stretched his legs and crossed them at the ankle. 'You did well, Miss Gifford. You did not waver. And you caught them on the back foot. You're not what Pearman and Poynter expected, you see. They thought you were going to be a harridan or a bluestocking and of course you're neither.'

'Why thank you, Mr Wolfe.'

'Not at all.' He raised his hat with mock solemnity. 'Thorne, of course, already knew otherwise. The thing is, Miss Gifford, I am a rather useful commentator on your brilliant career because I'm one of the few men who won't loathe you for what you stand for, regard you as a tolerably interesting sideshow, or fall in love with you.'

Since he was not given to making personal remarks of any kind, let alone one which included a phrase as intimate as *fall in love*, I was too taken aback to give a response.

'You do realise that my loyalty to Daniel Breen is not merely professional?' he added. 'After the war I was floundering. Nobody else was interested in employing an asthmatic outsider who'd been too weak to serve. But our Daniel Breen, as you know, rather likes lost causes.'

'What are you saying to me, Mr Wolfe?'

'I tend not to get involved in these types of situations – when I gave you both my blessing I meant what I said, but I also feel that there are times when one must step out of one's corner, as it were, and speak one's mind.'

His new trilby, of some soft, expensive fabric adorned with a mauve ribbon the exact shade of the stripe in his suit, lay in his lap and he took it up and smoothed the dints on either side of the crown. 'I'm saying that perhaps you'll make him very happy, perhaps not. But you're both making a mistake if you think that the other will be the answer to your essential loneliness. You, him and me, we are three of a kind.'

'Essential loneliness?' His words were like chimes striking a kind of dread in my heart and I spoke rather too vehemently. 'You may feel that about yourself. I certainly don't.'

'Are you sure? I think of you sometimes, Miss Gifford, in that little basement room, head bent over your work or toiling from one magistrate's court to the next, taking endless buses, endless solitary meals in your flat – you're alone now, aren't you? – always battling on behalf of your clients, with the establishment, with us male lawyers – and I think, where does she get her strength? How does she do it, set aside a woman's usual cravings for love, and children and a home? Obstinacy is a lonely quality, it strikes me. Grit, nobility – all commendable, all lonely. Don't you want to lay down the burden you've taken upon yourself? Isn't that why you're marrying Breen? Because you're too tired of fighting your own nature as well as other people's?'

He got up and, with a rare touch of gallantry, held out his hand to help me to my feet. 'Forgive me. You seem a trifle shocked. At any rate I hope you have far too much sense – and respect for him – to expect him to change. The thing about Breen is that he is what he is. That's why everyone holds him in such high regard.'

'And I, too, hold him in high regard.'

'Of course you do.' He even patted my shoulder before offering his arm as if to say 'there now, the subject is closed', and we walked towards his automobile talking of Lady Petit and her likely response to her husband's offer. An urgent meeting with her was required, and with Mr Leremer, to see what he had to say to a clause that would cut him off altogether from the child who some insisted was his daughter.

Once we were on the road Wolfe was far too busy castigating other drivers to refer again to personal matters but I was still smarting from his words and knew that I had been warned not, under any circumstance, to let his beloved Daniel Breen down.

# Chapter Thirty

By the third day the carnival atmosphere of the strike was gone and my fellow pedestrians and I plodded wearily in our long over-coats and winter shoes because the weather was too changeable for summer wear. Congestion on the roads had been reduced by an army of volunteers drafted in to direct the traffic but less ob-vious disruption had begun to bite more deeply, and a day-long trial in which I was due to defend an assault on a police officer had been adjourned due to the unavailability of police witnesses.

When I arrived at work the ill-tuned wireless could be heard barking out information and on peeking into Breen's office I dis-covered that only Miss Drake was present, sitting bolt upright in her ivory-coloured blouse and grey knitted two-piece, as if the newscaster was actually in the room and would be disappointed if she slouched. At the sight of me she shrank deeper into herself. I hovered at the door and heard that the strike had taken a more aggressive turn. The doors and windows of a Newcastle news-paper office had been stoned in the night even though journalists had been attempting to produce a broadsheet sympathetic to the unions; trams had been attacked in Glasgow and their volunteer drivers subjected to verbal and physical abuse, and there had been street fighting in the East End of London.

The bulletin closed with a brief interview with Sir Timothy Petit. His radio voice was somewhat high-pitched and unmistak-ably upper class.

'His Majesty's government,' he informed us, 'is doing its utmost to ensure the safety of the nation, and that the well-being of the majority will not be jeopardised by the recklessness of the few.

'You have my word that I will not sleep while my country en-dures hardship inflicted by an undemocratic minority. If I have to bring milk to your doorsteps myself, then I shall do so. No British mother will see her child go thirsty under my watch.

'We are recruiting thousands more special police officers so that you may sleep easy in your beds at night, and to ensure that all our citizens behave in a civilised way in this largely civilised nation of ours.'

Having waited politely for the end of the bulletin, Miss Drake was pale when she switched off the radio. 'I shall leave at three today. It is clearly not safe for a woman to be alone on the streets when there are mobs of strikers on the loose. I shan't be missed. Mr Breen has telephoned to inform me that he won't be in today due to *strike* business.' She could not help, by the merest shift in intonation, revealing her distaste for her employer's radical inclinations.

'Miss Drake, I wonder if you could telephone Lady Petit and make an urgent appointment for me to see her. Likewise Mr Richard Leremer at his office in Eccleston Square.'

She could scarcely bring herself to acknowledge that I had spoken to her but returned to her own office, fetched a pad composed of scraps of blank paper cut from the bottom of old letters fastened with a bulldog clip and asked me to repeat, word for word, what I had said. Later, when I went back upstairs, there was a note in my tray . . .

*1. Lady Petit is not at home. The maid does not know when she will return.*

*2. Mr Leremer will see you at one o'clock for ten minutes.*

*3. Mr Breen has telephoned to remind you that the concert at the Wigmore Hall begins at 7.30 p.m. and that he will meet you there.*

At twelve I set out for Eccleston Square, which must still have been among the most congested areas of London. Drivers in shirtsleeves and flat caps had decanted themselves from the cabins of their vehicles and were clustered round the door of the union office. Occasionally a horn was sounded, somewhat forlornly, but it was clear that nobody would be able to escape the crush for some hours.

'Do you know what's going on?' I asked a woman who was leaning on the handle of a pram that contained a sleeping baby.

'Nothin's going on as far as I can tell. That's the trouble. The unions are supposed to be issuing permits for lorries carrying supplies, the unions still ain't organised and the permits still ain't ready so nobody can move.'

Raising my briefcase above my head I worked my way through the throng then plunged shoulder first into the crowd of lorry drivers in order to get through to the union headquarters. When I waved my card at a girl racing down the hall with her arms full of papers she stared at me, wild-eyed, and rushed on. Eventually I reached the bottom of the stairs and would have gone directly up to Leremer's office had I not been halted by a young man demanding to know what I wanted.

'Mr Leremer's called an urgent meeting of the Press and Publicity Committee,' he said, 'and won't be out for at least half an hour.'

'But he agreed to see me at one.'

'There's been an emergency.'

For want of anywhere else to sit I perched on the bottom step though people had to steer past me to get upstairs. I became absorbed in witnessing a bustle for which I mercifully bore no responsibility, though I could not help thinking that Miss Drake and other anxious listeners to Petit's statement on the radio that morning would have been much reassured to see the chaos that lay at the heart of the strike. Telephones were ringing, typewriters clattering, messengers appearing from every doorway so that the old floors creaked with the passing of so many feet. A desk had been set up in the hall to deal with a succession of disgruntled lorry drivers but it was evident that much of this activity was somewhat purposeless, and that what was required was a number of Miss Drakes to develop a system for dealing with all the requests.

'What about butter, is that classified as essential . . .?'

'Of course . . .'

'Cream?'

'Stepney Council is saying it's going to switch off the power station again tonight. Two hospitals will be affected. Can that be right?'

'Remind them they've got to keep essential services going.'

'They say that you can't cut off an area's power without affecting the hospitals, it just isn't possible.'

'For the Lord's sake, why didn't anyone think of this before we started?'

'Miss Gifford.' Leremer yelled down the stairs. It was now nearly two o'clock and I was stiff from my spell on the step so I limped up to his office, where the space had been reduced still further by mountains of newspapers.

'*The British Worker*,' said Leremer, thrusting one into my hand. 'We did it – got a newspaper out last night despite the best efforts of the government to stop us. You know they sent plain-clothes' officers along to search the building and confiscate the first few copies in case we were printing anything seditious.'

'And were you?'

'Of course not,' he said gloomily, 'our paper's much too bland for that, I'm afraid. We're so busy telling the world what we're not doing, i.e., staging a revolution, that we forget to say what we are fighting for.'

'It seems to me that the strike is holding very well.'

'Oh, it's holding so well that the main lesson I'm learning is that we could have been far more ambitious and called a mass strike rather than a general strike. But we're so terrified of upsetting anyone that we've told half the workforce to keep working, even though they're all champing at the bit to join us. Did you hear Petit on the radio this morning? It's driving us mad that the BBC isn't allowing us to riposte.'

He was so very alluring with his shirtsleeves rolled up, his hair dishevelled and his troubled brown eyes that for a reckless moment I wished he would simply admit to being Annice's father. She could and probably would do far worse.

'But what can I do for you?' he asked. 'I assume it must be urgent for you to brave coming here in the middle of all this.'

'We've had a conversation with Sir Timothy's lawyer – I can't say much about it because I haven't yet discussed it with Lady Petit – but it now seems that Sir Timothy has a particular vendetta against you. Could that be true?'

He shrugged. 'Vendetta is a strong word.'

'Lady Petit says she used you in the argument when she told him Annice wasn't his because she thought it was the name that would annoy him the most. We initially thought this was because of your politics; we now wonder if it's about religion.'

'You mean because I'm a Jew?'

'Petit associates with a number of vocal anti-Semites. We are thinking of using the argument that he's being vindictive because he can't stand the thought of his wife having had an affair with you.'

'Many people are anti-Semitic. I'm sure the jury would be very sympathetic to him.'

'Is there any other reason he might have for bearing you a grudge?'

Leremer pursed his lips and even flushed a little, and I had the impression that he was weighing something up. In the end he shook his head.

'If you think of something, perhaps you'd let us know,' I said. 'But the other reason for wanting to see you is to ask whether you've changed your mind about coming to court. Petit is not suggesting that there are other candidates who may have fathered Annice, so our success may therefore be guaranteed if you can find a way of verifying that Annice is not your child.'

'How many times must I tell you? She *isn't*. Bel and I have not been lovers since before she was married.'

'Sir Timothy seems to think he can produce witnesses who will say the opposite.'

'He may well be able to produce witnesses who saw Annabel and me together.' He ran the palm of his hand across his hair, opened a drawer at his knee and pulled out a couple of battered engagement diaries. 'I've even dug out a few dates when we met, once she was back from honeymoon, but we certainly did not make love. Not from want of opportunity – *he* didn't seem to care what she got up to – but she was too unhappy and too fragile at that time and I'd have been a brute to exploit that. And I . . .'

'Mr Leremer?'

'I was too *angry* with her. My God, that woman! First she ditches me for him, then she comes running back from Paris and tells me she doesn't love him. I do have some pride. Besides, as I've said, it soon became obvious that she was pregnant.'

'And you'd be prepared to say this under oath?'

'I suppose I would, yes.'

'Thank you, Mr Leremer, I won't keep you any longer.'

I was actually at the door when he called me back. It seemed to be a habit of his, perhaps learned from his time as a journalist, to hand out information in fits and starts. 'If I'm honest, part of my reluctance is that there's something I'm slightly ashamed of in all this. I'm being very open with you here, Miss Gifford, rather more than I'd intended.'

Softly I re-entered the room, closed the door and again sat down while he threw himself back in his chair and closed his eyes.

'You have to understand, Miss Gifford, that when Bel and I met in 1921 the Labour Party was in the ascendant and those of us in the thick of it were regarded as a novelty. We knew everyone and were invited to parties everywhere. Bel was part of all that intoxication. And it wasn't like today, when there's more of a divide between the parties. We were all in the same social mix – me and the likes of Petit, and Tom Mosley – even true-blue aristos seemed genuinely to welcome us, the great unwashed, into their world.'

He hesitated and I hoped that the racket from the floors above and beneath us wouldn't distract him.

'So I met Bel at a party. Very posh, it was. There was even a swimming pool surrounded by old brick walls. I wasn't quite myself; my head was definitely turned. And you must realise how very beautiful Bel was, always slightly out of reach, not least because she was never alone but always arm in arm with that blonde witch – the Porter woman.

'I couldn't believe it when Bel actually seemed to be falling for me. At first I thought she was teasing me. She'd watch me from a distance – I'd be aware of those enormous eyes of hers following me – and then she'd detach herself from her group and appear at my side in a cloud of perfume and cigarette smoke. "Good evening, Mr Leremer," she'd say, and her voice made me shiver.

'She was so unlike the other girls I'd known. So small. Even the polish on her fingernails fascinated me, and those eyes . . . I knew that she was a terrible flirt but I began to realise that she really was in quite a state over me and couldn't keep away. Then one night at the end of summer we were at yet another party, given by the Porters. You know, he was the automobile millionaire, quite a good man but very thin and unhealthy looking. Anyway, he had a house in Highgate with a garden running down to the Heath. Annabel was there, and Timothy Petit. She was a little drunk by the time I arrived.

'I stepped outside – sometimes it was all too much for me, those sophisticated people, and I was confused by Annabel. Sometimes I didn't really know who I was any more. Anyway Bel appeared at my elbow. She was wearing a pale blue dress that reached almost to her ankles and she was looking very fragile and shivering because the evening had turned cool. But it was she who said to me, "I've fallen in love with you, Richard Leremer. What will you do about it?"

'I wrapped her in my jacket and tucked her under my arm and sat with her in that garden, as if we were deep in the country, and I thought the world was at my feet. Bel and I became lovers that same night. You've probably realised that she never holds back, she has to do whatever she's doing with the whole of her being.

'And here's the bit I'm not so proud of. She wanted to get married. She knew her family would hate it if we did – I had no money, I was a Jew and a socialist, so she could hardly have chosen worse. But I hesitated. I was quite cynical and thought she'd chosen me simply to be perverse, but the truth was I lacked courage. Yet I did love her.

'And then I lost her. At first I thought I had a genuine rival – none other than Timothy Petit, who'd known her for years but never taken any interest in her. In fact Bel had always told me she was a little afraid of Timmo Petit and that he treated her as if she were a child, and she knew he was only being nice to her because of her father's money. But the minute she and I became lovers, he muscled in on her.

'Wherever we went, Petit appeared. I've seen him do what he did to her in a political context. When he wants to hammer home a point or win someone over he gathers himself up and just bears down on them. The stupid thing was, even while Bel was being seduced, I knew she really loved me. I think Petit knew that too – and so did her father. So on one front was her father, working away at his little Bel, feeding her who knows what poison about Jews and lefties and fortune hunters, and on the other was Petit, who, of course, is always fuelled by the idea of winning something that's hard to get. Then one night, at a Christmas party, he took her. Annabel was wearing this red dress and a crimson headband. She and I were very happy, not drinking, just dancing.

'Petit arrived late. He's the sort who's always invited to several places in one evening, so when he turns up everyone's supposed to be grateful he's there. He'd had a drink or two, and he just stood across the room and watched us. She knew what he was up to – you've seen Annabel, she's very self-conscious, she'd always know if someone was after her.

'We danced some more. Then one minute she was with me, the next he came up and said very casually, "Do you mind if I whisk her away, for just one dance?" She let go of my arm – I've always remembered the slight drag on my sleeve, as if she didn't want to do it. They danced and all the happiness went out of her face. He didn't look anywhere else in the room, just at her. He had her.

'By the end of the evening he'd proposed to her and she was stumbling about, drunk and haughty, hanging on to his hand. She looked at me just once, as if I were her lifebelt and she was drowning, but when I tried to speak to her, she ignored me. I've always known that I didn't fight hard enough either then or later. I could have won her back. The trouble was, there was just a little part of me that was relieved.'

The telephone rang and he picked up the receiver. 'One moment,' he covered the mouthpiece with his hand. 'I will come to court, Miss Gifford. I won't let that bastard win again. You can count on me.'

# Chapter Thirty-One

Bathing in Pimlico was an unpleasant affair. The shared bathroom was grubby and infested with mould and silverfish, and the geyser hardly spurted sufficient hot water to fill more than the base of the lime-stained bath. Consequently Meredith and I preferred head-to-toe washes in our kitchen. We used to shampoo our hair once a week, pouring jugfuls of clean water over each other's heads at the sink until the kettle and pans of hot water had run out and we were shrieking with the shock of the cold.

Since Meredith's departure I had learned to manage alone, soaping my swathe of hair over the bath and swishing it about in the basin until it was rinsed free of suds. An evening out at the Wigmore Hall was momentous enough to warrant silk stockings, my best, thin-soled shoes and a dress with a double-layered skirt and broderie-anglaise collar, bought last summer with Meredith in the sale at Peter Jones.

The evening was blustery but warm and due to the absence of street cleaners the pavements were full of litter. For once I carried only a dainty clutch bag, a cast-off of Meredith's, and felt frivolously disencumbered. Heads turned as I passed and I realised that adrenalin must have brightened my eyes and brought colour to my cheeks. Taxicab drivers had now joined the strike so Wigmore Street was filled with private cars depositing people in evening dress. There was no sign of Daniel and I decided grimly that the likelihood of him getting to the concert, amid so much turmoil, was small.

Although I was only twenty minutes early the foyer was relatively empty, save for a few shabby young men wearing creased trousers and with designedly tousled hair who lounged against the walls reading their programmes. The evening was devoted to the Czech composer Janáček, a unique opportunity, according to the notes, to listen to the work of a modern master. Tonight's performance was to be attended by the composer himself who was on a rare visit to London. An usher murmured that the strike would have put most people off, given the difficulty of travelling from the suburbs without private transport.

'And Janáček,' he said. 'It's not like it's Mozart.'

The five-minute warning bell rang and still Daniel hadn't arrived. I had no ticket but it was clear that others were in the same predicament and many would be late. The usher allowed me to sit near the back of the half-empty auditorium, the doors were closed, the conductor made his entrance and the concert began.

I thought the music cold, like the hall itself – a draught was catching on the weight of my still-damp hair. The piece called *Mladi* had been inspired by the composer's youth, especially his schooling and his parting from his mother. I was a little offended by its lack of rhythm and obvious melody, and felt more remote from Daniel by the minute for subjecting me to this. Better to be at home in my flat than here, with dissonance washing through my brain. So I extricated myself both from the music and from the shame of being here alone by looking angrily about at the audience and at the vibrant murals above the stage and in the cupola which would surely have provoked criticism from Meredith since they were decorated with 'droopy Pre-Raph' figures.

No wonder Annabel had named Leremer as the father of her child, I thought, as I tuned in to the music once more. It must have seemed like a perfect form of revenge given that Petit had snatched her from Leremer's arms. But how it had backfired on her. Petit was clearly not the sort of man with whom a woman could play games. One slip and you were finished, like a rat in a trap.

And now, ranged against her were Petit, Pearman and Thorne; the latter tanned, urbane and, to me, still devastating in his physical allure, but underneath as ruthless as the others.

The music nudged my thoughts towards his stumbled words when he came to the office. What were the questions he'd posed in the letter I'd burnt? His last statement at least had been unequivocal, '*You know, I have thought about you every hour of every day since we parted.*'

During the rather weak applause, a hand squeezed my shoulder and Daniel took the seat beside me. 'They wouldn't let me in until the piece was over. I'm so sorry I'm late. Fortunately I was offered a lift in a motorcycle sidecar.' He had found time to dress in a dark suit and dress shirt and his coat smelt of petrol fumes and the outdoors. *Feel* something, Evelyn, I commanded myself, but only anger remained because he'd left me to swim against the tide of such alien music by myself. It was now the interval and the composer, with his thick, silver-white hair, stood in the foyer amid a cluster of acolytes.

'Well?' Daniel asked me. 'What did you think?'

'Of the music? It wasn't so bad.'

He roared with laughter. 'At least you're not demanding to go home. Some people will sneak away, you'll see.'

'It's a shame so few have turned up.'

'Appropriate, don't you think, that Janáček's music should be performed during a general strike to such a small audience rather than to a concert hall packed with a rapt, culture-worn audience.' His eyes were full of love. 'It's so good to see you, Evelyn, I have missed you.'

But I wasn't ready for softness. 'You may as well know that I have been angry with you because you sent Nicholas Thorne to the office and he turned up without warning.'

His sideways glance seemed a little apologetic. 'He found you, did he? I wasn't sure you'd be there. Or that he would actually try to see you that same day.'

'He came at about four o'clock on Tuesday.'

'Then he left Toynbee and came straight to you. I had perhaps not taken account of how eager he was. Forgive me.'

Though we were returning to our seats I halted and the audience had to move around us. 'You *knew* he had been very significant to me at one time. The fact is ... perhaps you didn't realise ... he broke my heart.'

'Aaah,' a slow, sad exhalation. 'I'm sorry. I'd always supposed it was the other way round.'

He sounded so desolate that I wished for a moment I'd been

less forthright and I said more gently, 'Either way, I'd rather you hadn't sent him to me. I would have preferred to meet him again in my own good time.'

'You're right. As so often. I knew you'd tried to see him last week so I told myself I was doing you a favour. But perhaps I was protecting myself. I felt a certain jealousy, I'll admit. If they must be together, I thought, let it be sooner rather than later. For all our sakes.'

Leaning his elbow on the back of his chair he ran his finger-tip over my cheek, shaking his head as if to say: I can't find the words to tell you how much I love you. I seized his hand and held it fiercely because his honesty was jewel-bright as he struggled to comprehend this new landscape of ours. He laced his fingers through mine as the 'Kreutzer Sonata' began, with its scribble of violins and echoes of violence. At one point he adjusted the ring he had given me so that the stone was centrally placed on my finger.

Afterwards, arm in arm, he escorted me home through Mayfair where the streets were quiet enough except for a few cars and the occasional police patrol.

'What happened to Saklatvala?' I asked.

'Two months hard labour, as expected.'

'He's a brave man.'

'Indeed he is. And he was right about the government calling in the army. There are rumours that the blockade on the docks is going to be broken this weekend by the deployment of troops. In Battersea we are planning how to prevent the food lorries passing through the borough. Needless to say, we're going to have to be very vigilant that the pickets aren't infiltrated by troublemakers or it could get very bloody indeed.'

Victoria Station, in near darkness, was guarded by a number of pickets huddled round a brazier. Here the pavements had become more crowded and the night was full of the sound of running feet and angry shouts. Daniel and I walked swiftly, my shoes tip-tapping on the pavements. But a hundred or so yards into the Vauxhall Bridge Road a gang of half a dozen youths broke out of a side street and came tearing towards us. Their momentum was such that I thought they'd trample us, but they veered into a narrow turning to our left. In hot pursuit was a crowd of police officers and specials, coats flying open, batons raised. Daniel yanked me into a doorway but the sound of running feet suddenly came to a halt – the youths had run into a blind alley. Windows were being flung up and women were yelling obscenities down at the police who hurled themselves at the youths. Next minute a Crossley Vehicle screeched round the corner, obscuring our view, the youths were hauled out of the alley and driven away, and the windows went slamming down. The specials gathered in the main street, straightening their clothes and grinning at the assembled onlookers.

We walked on, pretending not to be shaken, talking about the heavy-handedness of the police and how we hoped the violence wouldn't escalate. When we reached my building Daniel stood behind me as I unlocked the front door and then followed me up the creaking staircase. As I fumbled with the key to my own door he waited by my shoulder. Inside, our feet compressed the ancient floorboards – to the right was the living room where a pale light shone from the street outside, to our left was the half-open door to my bedroom and the closed door to Edmund's room. The silence, at first, was profound.

He closed the door behind him, but not so firmly that the latch caught. We were pressed close, our mouths joined in a kind of half-kiss so that our lips touched then moved away, his hands on my wrists. I imagined drawing him into my bedroom, kicking the door shut, pulling the pins from my hat and lying with him on my bed. I imagined the unbuttoning of coat, jacket, waistcoat, shirt, and I knew, even as he pulled me closer, his breath quickened and I felt his tongue on my lip, that it would not happen because both of us had hesitated – he, because he could not be sure it was what I wanted, and I because I wasn't sure either.

So his kiss was sweet and sad and he said, 'You'll be all right now.'

I nodded and held him as he pressed his face to my neck. 'Listen, I've a meeting tomorrow at six in The Prince's Head, in Falcon Road. Why don't you come and meet me there for tea, say at five, if it's not too much of a trek? Otherwise I'll not see you all weekend – I'll be up to my eyes in strike business.'

'I'll do that.'

'I wish I didn't have to go.' I held on to him thinking, it isn't too late, he could stay, but he slipped away and I listened to his diminishing footfall on the stairs.

I again went to the window and saw him walk along the lamp-lit pavement. Yes, as I'd expected, he turned at the corner and waved up at me. I couldn't tell how much pain there was behind that smile.

# Chapter Thirty-Two

Next morning, as I walked to work, all seemed to be calm again. The spring was finally showing signs of establishing itself; the warmth in the air had a settled feel and Marylebone's more affluent streets were untouched by the woes of the miners. But when I arrived at Breen & Balcombe, Miss Drake was in the hall, actually wringing her hands, while a BBC newscaster's assertive voice barked out information from Breen's office.

'Where have you *been*, Miss Gifford?' she cried, more agitated than I'd ever seen her. 'The telephone has been ringing since I arrived. Poor Winston Churchill!'

'What about Churchill?'

'Surely you've heard that he's been *murdered*? Knocked down in the street and beaten to death with cudgels. His head was a pulp. I've had the wireless on but there's been no mention.'

'So how did you hear about it, Miss Drake?'

'On the way to work there were a couple of rough-looking men standing on a street corner and they told me. Neither took off his cap.'

'It's probably untrue,' I said with exaggerated calm as I remembered the hobnailed boots worn by the strikers the previous night. 'They were just trying to scare you. If it were true, it would certainly be on the news.'

'They wouldn't inform the nation of something like that straight away,' she hissed. 'That's what's so ominous. They'll be attempting to avert panic by managing the news.'

'But I've just bought today's newspaper and it makes absolutely no reference to an assassination.'

'That's the strikers' paper you have there. They're bound to tell lies. Anyway, there's certainly been a riot outside Clapham tram depot. Mr Breen telephoned and said you must go to Lavender Hill Police Station at once. Mr Wolfe has to go to Poplar but he's to drive you to Clapham first.'

'Who has been arrested?'

'Dozens of people.'

'Where is Mr Breen? Is he all right?'

She glared at me. 'Wandsworth, I believe, at the prison. According to the wireless there was a riot and someone was almost killed. You mark my words, we are on the brink of a civil war, but I expect you'll tell me I'm imagining that as well.' She flung this last remark over her shoulder with a shrill laugh.

'Miss Drake, I'm sorry to press you but I was wondering if there were any other telephone messages for me. Has Lady Petit returned our calls?'

She paused on her way back to her office. It was typical of her to withhold information unless specifically asked. 'Her father telephoned. Mr Shawcross. He says his daughter is too sick to speak to you herself but that she wants to withdraw from the case.'

'For goodness' sake. Did he say where he was calling from or leave a telephone number?'

'He did. Just before we were cut off. The lines are disrupted.'

'May I use the telephone to call him back?'

'You won't get through,' Miss Drake insisted. 'I've told you, the lines are jammed. They are destroying every part of our lives. They want to paralyse the nation.'

'Perhaps you would try Mr Shawcross again for me later. Tell him I must speak to Lady Petit in person.'

As I ran down my basement stairs I heard her mutter, 'I suppose this is how it will be from now on.'

Wolfe was also in a bad mood when he called down to say he was ready to leave. Miss Drake bustled out of her office to oversee our departure. 'I don't relish being employed by Breen as a taxicab,' he told us both. 'And for goodness' sake don't get into such a tizzy, Miss Drake. It's all nonsense about Churchill. I've heard many rumours this morning but none about him. There was mention of a cabinet minister being wounded – no one knows who or how badly.'

She ignored him and went to put the kettle on. If Breen was her favourite and I her sworn enemy, Wolfe she treated with a mixture of exasperation and caution, as if he were an apparently tame but potentially dangerous house pet.

His car reeked of cologne as we lurched off down Arbery Street. 'Before very long we'll have roadblocks,' he declared, tossing his hat on to the back seat, '*and* there'll be no fuel.'

'I thought fuel was an essential supply?'

'There'll be anarchy, you wait and see. Troops have been out in Bermondsey, firing over the heads of the strikers.'

'I don't believe it,' I said. 'The government wouldn't do anything so provocative.'

'You'd be surprised,' said Wolfe, tipping me out just before Battersea Bridge. 'It seems to me the government is being quite circumspect, but not for long.'

As I set forth on foot it occurred to me that what I needed was Grandmother's old bicycle which was stored in the shed in the back garden at Clivedon Hall Gardens. I'd borrowed it occasionally at weekends but had never used it for work because of the congested streets and the difficulty of storing it in the flat. During the strike, at least, the prospect of mobility and independence was very alluring.

Not that a bicycle would have been any use to me that morning. The mood on the streets south of the river was surly as a convoy of three armoured cars lumbered by, jeered by a crowd of strikers with their jackets buttoned tightly against the wind and their caps pulled low on their brows. The kerbs were guarded by uniformed police officers interspersed with young men and women wearing the armbands of the special police. They were tense, ready for action, straining at the leash.

Shop owners stood in their doorways, dressed in their overalls and feigning a casual interest in events as an omnibus driven by a young man in an ostentatious waistcoat came lumbering along Latchmere Road, thereby supplying exactly the provocation the crowd had been waiting for. Pressed up to the police they yelled, 'Scab! Blackleg! Traitor!'

A further brigade of police protected the bus, brandishing their batons as it wheezed along, dribbling fuel, carrying perhaps half a dozen uneasy passengers. Once it had passed, the crowd attempted to surge on to the road and there were tears and hysterical shouts from women onlookers as men jostled the police lines. 'Don't risk it, George, they'll take you in. Hold back.'

To make swifter progress, I turned into a side street where women, clustered on doorsteps, stopped talking to stare at the middle-class straightness of my spine and the quality of my lace-up shoes. If I attempted to meet their eyes they were wary and hostile. When at last I reached the police station it was surrounded by yet more strikers, some waving red flags and chanting, '*Let them go . . . Let them go . . .*' The noise came in waves and as soon as there was the slightest sign of movement at the door there'd be a jostling forward and ear-splitting shouts.

I retreated to the far side of the street to take stock. My blood was up and there was a part of me that was both curious and excited at the prospect of making a move. However, I did not want to confront the specials, whom I regarded as the opposition, so I leaned against a sunshiny wall and even closed my eyes to absorb the sudden blaze of heat and light.

When I opened them again, somewhat dazzled, I noticed two women standing on the steps of the police station and therefore raised above the crowd; one casually holding on to the railings, the other, much shorter, craning to see what was happening further along Lavender Hill. The latter I didn't recognise, the former I knew instantly because she was virtually the only person present who wasn't wearing a hat, so that the glossy opulence of her blonde hair was revealed. Her loose, dark coat contrived to emphasise the extraordinary slenderness of her wrists and throat. She touched the other woman's hand and offered her a cigarette (surely not permissible even to a voluntary officer on duty). Both wore the armbands of the special police and Kit Porter certainly seemed rather more bored than apprehensive, despite the state of near siege in which she found herself.

On raising the cigarette to her lips she noticed me and moved her head closer to her companion's to share a confidence. Kit then stepped down and asked the men in the crowd to let her through, which they did with surprising courtesy, perhaps because she simply raised her pale hands above her head and insinuated her body between them as if she were working her way through a packed ballroom.

'Good morning, Miss Gifford. What are you doing here?'

'I need to speak to a client in the police station.'

'Can't you get through? I'll escort you if you like. What fun. You look surprised to see me. Didn't I tell you I'd volunteered for the OMS?'

'OMS?'

'Oh, you know, the Organisation for the Maintenance of Supplies. We all saw the strike coming so we tried to do our bit, got together months ago. And now here I am, practically a policewoman. Who'd have thought it?' Her eyes followed every movement of my hands as I hastily straightened my hat and brushed specks of dust from my shoulders.

'You must have seen quite a bit of action today,' I said.

'Unfortunately nothing like the situations I've been training for all these weeks.' She gave the faintest of smiles. 'But then this is hardly the most radical part of Britain. You've presumably heard about the riots in Newcastle and Durham? The specials there really have had some fun, I should think. It's so tedious, simply standing around. There are far too many of us and we're forever in each other's way.' The critical gaze she cast along the street was akin to that of a headmistress supervising sports day.

She placed her hand on my arm and approached her face to mine. Up close, her irises were pale grey flecked with green and her skin was flawless. 'You've heard about poor Annabel, I suppose, being packed off to her parents' house in Kingston?'

'I gathered that she was away from home.'

'They left on Wednesday. She and Annice. There was one hell of a row.'

'I should think there was. Lady Petit seemed so keen to be in London during the strike.'

'That's just it. Timmo got wind of the fact that Bel was champing at the bit wanting to join me and the specials and he simply couldn't let that happen. Quite apart from the strain on her nerves, he thought it best that there should be no conflict of interest, you know, what with him managing essential supplies. She was beside herself with rage. He had to telephone me and ask me to help calm her down.' She took a long drag on her cigarette, withheld the smoke for a moment, then turned her head on its stem-like neck and exhaled softly. 'She had got hold of a sanitary towel, of all things, doused it in ink and was in her bedroom shrieking, "Tell your friends you've got a wife who's far better than them because she bleeds blue blood and sheds blue tears." Poor Timmo called in the doctor and I got her to lie with me on the bed until he came. It took an age. Fortunately, I'm used to Annabel.'

I did not like to think of Annabel cooped up in that great, intensely decorated house and the doctor arriving with his bagful of pills. 'Poor Timmo,' said Kit. 'When Bel had been dosed up, I said I'd escort her down to Kingston. In the automobile I had Annice asleep under one arm, Bel under the other.' This cosy picture did not quite accord with the Kit Porter I had witnessed thus far.

'Would it really have been so bad for her to have joined the volunteers?' I asked.

'Impossible, don't you think? Can you imagine how she'd behave in a situation like this? She's hopeless at hanging about. That's the thing with Bel – she's bound to get herself in the papers. Bad enough Churchill jumping up and down, threatening the Foot Guards and ball cartridges, without Lady Petit flinging herself into the mix.'

'The Foot Guards? I'd heard that Churchill was injured, or even dead.'

'Far from it. Fighting fit. Has to be kept in check by the rest of the Supply Committee.' She suddenly seemed a little discomposed. 'And then the paternity case is unsettling everyone, especially Bel and little Annice. The poor child isn't sleeping properly. Have there been any developments by the way?'

I suspected that Kit Porter knew full well that Annabel intended to withdraw. 'I'm glad of an opportunity to speak to you about that,' I said smoothly. 'I'm assuming you would still be prepared to attend court and speak up for Annabel?'

'Oh, I'll be there if it comes to it.' A faint flush bloomed on her ivory cheek. 'I'll say anything she wants me to. But you know what? Between ourselves, you really should prevent Bel attending court. She and I talked about nothing else on the way out of

London. Once she'd had a bit of a sleep she was quite calm. She knows the marriage is kaput, but if Bel gets herself into a hole she has no idea how to get out of it. So you'll just have to do it for her, Miss Gifford. Believe me it would be for the best.' She smelt of some cool, spicy perfume and nicotine, and had a way of tilting her head gently from one side to another as she spoke, as if her neck needed relief from the trial of holding up her head.

'Nevertheless, for the time being please assume that you'll definitely be needed in court, Miss Porter. Ah, it looks as if I might be able to get through to see my client now.'

'Come, then, follow me. I should have known you'd be in the thick of things, flying your little legal flag for justice.' Her fleeting smile was perhaps intended to soften this rather snide remark. 'I say, do excuse us,' she murmured, and once again the crowds parted, but at the top of the steps our way was barred by an officious young volunteer.

'May I know the lady's business?'

'Oh for God's sake, Monty,' said Kit, 'don't be an ass.'

Inside there was an unruly crowd of special officers queuing at the desk to make a record of their arrests. Their charges were ranged about the room on benches, either resigned or defiant. Kit whispered, 'I do wish you luck, Miss Gifford,' and to my relief she abandoned me as I battled my way to the desk where I brandished my Breen & Balcombe business card. Fortunately, the officer recognised me and offered me the list of that morning's detainees, among them one Robert Wright.

'What's he done?' I asked.

'You name it – criminal damage, assault, incitement. You must have heard about the omnibus being halted by nails in the street. That was our Robbie.'

'Any chance of bail?'

'None.'

'Can I see him?'

'Indeed you can. He named you as his legal representative, so ain't you the lucky one?'

After another half-hour or so Robbie was extracted from a cell and brought to an airless interview room that stank of dirty bodies. His face was white and his eyes full of rage, but the instant he saw me the fight went out of him. He sank down and buried his head in his arms.

'Robbie.'

'Now I've done it,' came his muffled voice.

'Tell me what happened.'

'I was guilty of throwing them nails.'

'Why nails, Robbie?'

He turned his head on his arm so he could look me in the eye. 'They was blacklegs. We'll never win if the buses start getting through.'

'Is there anything we could say in mitigation? For instance, was there anyone egging you on?'

'I got the idea off another bloke who done something similar but it was all me.'

'And you've never been in trouble with the law before?'

He raised his head. 'I've come close. They gave me a warning.'

'Does your family know where you are?'

'No.' He went whiter still and gnawed at the cuticle on his index finger.

'Would you like me to tell them?' My heart sank at the prospect of going back to the Wright house now that the father was living there again.

'S'pose so.'

'The police won't grant you bail and the case won't be heard until Monday so you'll be in over the weekend.' He shrugged again but was close to tears. 'Here's a tip for you, Robbie,' I lightened my voice, 'never commit a crime on a Friday, it always takes longer.'

Finally his bravado crumbled and he ground his palms into his eye sockets. 'I'm so worried about my mother.'

'Has something else happened to her? Why didn't she give evidence in court?'

'Why do you think?' My heart ached for him. His tone was resigned rather than insolent and he seemed very young in that moment. 'Miss Gifford, he wrote to her every day. I told her not to read those letters but she did. He made all manner of promises and he sent my aunt round and she cried and said how sorry Dad was and how he would die if he were sent to prison. Trude was no help, neither. My mother kept asking her: what shall I do, Trudy?

And she would just shrug and tell her she must make up her own mind. Trudy's not as clear as me, she's always been closer to Dad and she feels sorry for him so she tries to keep them both happy.'

'Is Trudy working?'

'She's got a bit of a job down the local pub but it's only evenings and Saturday lunchtime. The pay's terrible and I don't know who will keep them all if I go inside. In any case, we were told we'd not be taken back if we went on strike. Coal is supposed to be an essential supply but I don't see it like that. If people don't suffer there ain't no point in us striking. And now I've got myself arrested the boss ain't going to like it one bit. The only chance I got is that he's always said I'm a good worker but how will I keep my job now?' He was hot-eyed and rebellious as he cried, 'I can't look after her all the time. I have to get on with my own life. I wanted to be part of all this and now he'll blame her for what I've done. He'll say she's too soft on me. And there'll be no money coming in.'

'How have things been since your father came home?'

'He hasn't struck her, if that's what you mean, but when she tries to go out he says she's not fit, what with her face and her clothes. Trude does all the errands while he just sits and watches her. She's terrible low. And now this. How long will I be inside?'

'I don't know. I'd say up to three months – the penalty will be harsher because of the strike. They'll want to make an example of you.'

'No.' He sprang to his feet, knocking the chair on to its back. 'That's too long. I can't leave her in the house with him. You've got to get me off, Miss Gifford, get me home.'

'I'll do my best but we have to be realistic. Don't raise your hopes.'

He again snatched up my hand and kissed it, his eyes beseeching. 'The thing is, Miss Gifford, it all feels right when I see you. I don't know what I'd do without you.'

As I walked away I was close to tears and I didn't notice whether Kit Porter was still lounging on the steps. Robbie was too unguarded – joy had flared in his eyes when he saw me, his lips had been hot on my hand yet I knew that in these circumstances I, his only lifeline, was almost as helpless as he.

This time the front door to the Wrights' house was opened by the smallest child, who could barely reach the handle. Her hair was a tangled mop with a frayed ribbon hanging over one ear and the sty was more virulent than on my last visit. She stared at me for a few seconds then ran into the house shouting, 'It's that lady!'

Wright occupied his usual chair by the range and a cold wind blew into the room because the scullery door was open. He had been reading a two-day-old copy of *The British Gazette* and when he saw me he muttered 'Jesus Christ,' under his breath then flung down the paper and linked his hands behind his head.

'Is your wife in?' I asked. 'I need to speak to you both.'

There was a long silence while he drew back his head and fixed his piercing blue eyes on me.

'She's out the back,' the child piped up and ran outside.

'What do you want wiv her?' demanded Wright.

I waited until Mrs Wright came in, wearing the same paisley overall, tied tightly about her waist. She cast a nervous glance at her husband. 'It's about Robbie, I'm sure,' she said. She seemed to have shrunk since I last saw her and her shoulders were stooped.

'It is. He asked me to come and tell you that he was arrested this morning.'

Wright swore and planted his feet wide apart. The child put her head on the table and wailed while the mother stroked her hair.

'I fuckin' told you what would happen,' snarled Wright. 'You fuckin' wouldn't listen.'

'I told him to do what he thought right.'

'You said to him that you agreed wiv the strike.' He swivelled so that his entire body turned in my direction. 'You still here? I do wish you'd get yourself off my premises, Miss. Every time you come near us there's trouble.'

'Robbie asked me . . .'

'So you've told us. Ain't you a one for fetchin' up in the middle of my family's little dramas? The trouble wiv my boy is he makes the mistake of thinking he matters. He don't realise he's nothink. And that's down to her. She's always treated him like a bloody prince.'

His wife stood with one hand in her child's hair, looking away, so thin that I could see every bone in her free hand.

'Is there anything I can do for you?' I asked her and the look she gave me in return was at once proud and desperate. I couldn't think of anything I might say that wouldn't worsen her situation. 'May I speak to you for a moment in private?' I asked.

She shook her head emphatically and looked nervously at her husband.

'I best carry on with what I was doing,' she said, her eyes imploring me to leave.

'I'll go now,' I said. 'I'll discuss your son's case with our senior partner but I'll be back on Monday.'

Neither of the adults moved. An older child, who must have been in the backyard, crept in.

'Can I go see Robbie?' asked his mother.

'You can try. They might let you in when things have died down.'

She nodded and went on caressing her daughter's head. I hated to leave her like that, under his eye, but knew I'd only make things worse by lingering so I made my own way through the unused parlour to the front door.

# Chapter Thirty-Three

It was gone six by the time I reached The Prince's Head for my rendezvous with Daniel and when I opened the pub door I saw him sitting by the window, deep in conversation with a group of men wearing tired jackets with pint glasses before them. The air was grubby with smoke and Daniel gave no sign that he was expecting me. As the seconds ticked by I saw him throw back his head and laugh at some quip or other, then mark out a plan or design with the tip of his index finger on the sticky tabletop. Occasionally one of his companions glanced at me, puzzled or even hostile, but Daniel didn't look in my direction at all. I had seen him like this before, perfectly in the moment, animated and inspired, and knew that he was rarely distracted.

Eventually I walked away, crushing firmly a sense of rejection. No wonder he'd forgotten about me. After all, it was precisely his passionate commitment to justice that had first encouraged me to apply to him for a clerkship; hardly any other lawyer in London would have risked being seen among union men, communists and strikers.

'Miss Gifford.' A police vehicle had slowed and Michael Craig, Carole's fiancé, poked his head out of the driver's window. 'I thought it was you. Where are you off to? Care for a lift?'

I had been heading towards Pimlico but hesitated at the prospect of the unswept staircase, the silent flat; of waking tomorrow to yet another empty weekend. So instead, on impulse, I requested he drop me off in Maida Vale. I travelled sideways in the back of the vehicle, balancing on a bench usually reserved for felons.

It was well after eight when I arrived somewhat queasily in Clivedon Hall Gardens and I couldn't help hoping that Mother would answer the door herself so that I could show off my bizarre method of transport. Instead, Min peeked out, leaving the chain on in case I was a striker on the rampage.

'She's not in,' was the astonishing news. 'She's at a meeting down at St Mark's.'

'The truth is I'm worn out, Min. Is there any chance of something to eat and a bath?'

There was nothing Min enjoyed more than to bustle about solving a domestic crisis, no matter how minor. I was urged downstairs to the kitchen where Jamie and I used to sit at the table taking noisy slurps of cocoa during the evenings when our parents were out, and Rose was winkled from the snug basement sitting room with its cast-off Victorian sideboard and wallpaper patterned with pink birds and flowers. A boiled egg (the solution to most ills at Clivedon Hall Gardens) was required for Miss Evelyn while Min went up to thump the bathroom geyser into life.

They shared a pot of tea with me, Rose all the while knitting a pale green square for a patchwork blanket.

'Well, this is a treat,' said Min.

'We're running out of butter and there's none to be had so I hope the strike ends soon,' observed Rose.

'And of course our plans to move are on hold,' said Min, 'until we know whether the country has a future.'

'You will be sorely missed,' I told them.

'Yet it's time to go,' said Rose, her needles clicking and her weary face set stern. As cook, she'd always been more detached from the family than her sister.

'And there'll be the sea,' said Min, with rare animation. 'Imagine living by it.'

I remembered how Min had so relished the times when she'd collected us from school or taken us on trips to the country. They were buying a very small house, they informed me, in a street one block back from the sea. 'We'll hear it every night,' said Min, 'before we go to sleep, and Rose will only have two or three potatoes to peel each day.'

Trekking up three flights of stairs to the bathroom, I wondered if that was all we meant to Rose now – more potatoes. It was strange how Grandmother, the least demanding of us all, had been the unwitting glue that held Clivedon Hall Gardens together. Now she was gone, we were all fleeing in search of the wider horizons she'd always yearned for.

The bathroom at Clivedon Hall Gardens had been modernised just before the war when a capacious plunger bath had been installed and the walls tiled in swirling blue ivy leaves, the intricacies of which I knew by heart. Sinking into water liberally sprinkled by Min with Mother's attar of roses bath salts, I abandoned myself to steam and heat. The high ceiling sweated condensation along its many cracks and Min had drawn up a cork-topped stool on which she'd piled the guest flannel, embroidered with a sprig of honeysuckle, and the guest hand and bath towels.

When I closed my eyes my mind roamed in fits and starts, from the Wright child with her infected eyelid, to the delicate bones in the back of Robbie's neck as he bowed to kiss my hand, Kit Porter's gaze sliding down to my feet assessing my hemline, and Daniel in the pub, so happy, so absorbed.

To retreat from all the chaos, I had holed myself up in Clivedon Hall Gardens, the very place from which I'd striven to escape since girlhood. Nobody treats me as an intelligent human being, I used to rage, lying in the claw-footed bath among the stern black and white tiles of the bathroom's previous incarnation. Father had infuriated me the most, indulging what he thought of as my whims because he was convinced I was harmless. 'What a funny little girl,' he used to say whenever I insisted on buying books or being sent to a decent school. Mother at least, seeing my potential, had the wit to be afraid of it.

A timid knock on the bathroom door signalled her return. 'Evelyn, are you all right? The girls said you had come home.'

'Just for the night if you don't mind.'

I waited for recriminations – after all, we'd not spoken since the dramatic tearing up of Grandmother's letter – Your bed's not aired . . . You should have let us know . . . What a foolish thing to do, taking it for granted that someone would be in. Instead she said, 'Well, how lovely. I've asked them to light a fire in the living room. We'll have a glass of sherry, shall we?'

'I've no dressing gown,' I called. She crept away and there was a further rustling outside the door.

'I've found Mother's in the top of a trunk. I'll leave it here.'

233

Grandmother's dressing gown, of imitation silk in a lilac and cream floral design, barely reached my knees but at least concealed the fact that my nightgown, unearthed from a drawer in my old bedroom, was so worn it was nearly transparent. Mother was seated by the fire wearing her best navy-blue two-piece and a mosaic brooch. The crystal sherry glasses had been extracted from the corner cupboard in the dining room and there were little biscuits with scrapings of precious butter, each topped with a sliver of cheddar cheese. Mother glanced at me nervously, perhaps expecting me to reproach her over Rusbridger's torn-up letter, but those best glasses and the crocheted doily under the cheese biscuits touched me so that I plumped down, leaned my head on her shoulder and flung my arm about her neck.

'I've been all over the place today, Mother. I was so worn out I didn't know what to do so I came home.'

At first her body was rigid but then she patted my shoulder and her head touched mine. 'That's what we're here for,' she said.

We sipped sherry. 'What have you been up to this evening?' I asked.

'Oh, I've been out and about every day since the strike. Do you know, I think I will miss the excitement when it's all over. I told you last week we'd set up a soup kitchen and most of us are there from ten in the morning until two-ish and again in the evening so we can do some preparation for the following day. Tonight we were planning how to manage the weekend and what to do when the supplies run out and the markets are empty.'

'I admire you, Mother, because I know you don't agree with the strike.'

'I don't agree with people starving either. My hands are ruined from peeling carrots. We've all rallied round. It reminds me of the war, when I used to go down to the church hall and we rolled bandages before James ...'

The sherry was heating my blood. I held out my empty glass and as she filled it up she caught sight of my ring. 'Oh, Evelyn, it seems so odd that you're engaged when I haven't even met your fiancé yet.'

'He's completely caught up in the strike – he's a local councillor as well as a lawyer.'

'I don't see that I can mention him to anyone until I've met him, do you see?'

'I do understand, yes. But at the moment it's impossible.' I spoke rather sharply because I knew she was right. She ought to have met Daniel by now; no strike should have prevented that. But my heart sank when I imagined inviting him to Clivedon Hall Gardens, the eagerness of everyone to please, how I would thereafter be locked even more firmly into the future.

'But you were right,' she said suddenly. 'If you're getting married you should know about Mother. I regret tearing up her letter; it was very foolish of me. I was so hoping that we might have gone to Ruislip this weekend but with the strike that's impossible. I wanted to show you the house I might buy, and what it was like when I was a child, so you'd understand.'

'Shall we talk about it now?'

'Not now. Not yet. Not when we're both so tired.'

'You're right. I *am* tired. And I'm having all kinds of difficulties at work.'

The ensuing silence was so intense that I realised she'd been holding her breath and it occurred to me as I sat before the unseasonal fire drinking my third glass of sherry that I had never, in all the years since I began my training as a lawyer, asked her opinion or advice. So I recounted the events of the day, one by one, omitting only my visit to The Prince's Head. All the while her fingertips timidly worked my hair in the same way that Mrs Wright had comforted her child.

'It's Mrs Wright I fear for the most,' I said. 'I might have done real damage there. I can't help thinking she would have been better off if I hadn't told her to report her husband.'

'It sounds to me,' she said, in a Prudence-like burst, 'that when her husband was arrested and brought to court and you were prepared to stand by her, Mrs Wright had an opportunity to save herself which she failed to take. One can only do so much for these people.'

# Chapter Thirty-Four

At lunchtime on Saturday I set off, minus my engagement ring since I'd been threatened with washing-up duty, to visit Mother's soup kitchen. Our church hall, the backdrop to a variety of unendurably long concerts and lectures such as 'Eugenics, A System for Good or Evil?', which I'd occasionally been coerced into attending, had been transformed into a bustling canteen that smelt strongly of over-boiled cabbage. Mother, not to be outdone by the other ladies of the parish, stood behind a trestle table, a strand of hair clinging to her cheek as she ladled soup and winked at a small, ragged child who'd helped himself to a disproportionately large hunk of bread. It was the wink that made me smile the most. Since when had my mother turned a blind eye to faults in others, let alone tolerated them?

Most of the adult beneficiaries had the somewhat surly air of those who would have preferred to be at home, eating hardearned food at their own tables, while the ladies who attended them made cheery jokes about it being such fun to be *useful*, for once, and to please forgive the watery soup but potatoes were in short supply.

The new vicar, though a hard-pressed father of four, had a pink complexion, a round stomach and a hearty smile, his good nature apparently a match for the stream of ladies who approached to engage him in sotto voce conversations. They were outraged because, of all things, this hall was to be requisitioned on Monday by an organisation called the Civil Constabulary Reserve – 'It *sounds* legitimate,' said Mrs Gillespie – who were to swell their ranks by recruiting from the territorial army and the officer training corps. Once enlisted and trained, the Reserves would bolster the numbers in the regular army.

Mother, who seemed to be engaged in a power struggle with Mrs Gillespie, brandished a copy of the *Gazette*.

'Your friend,' she told me, referring of course to Timothy Petit, 'is beginning to throw his weight about. He's demanding that food lorries be escorted by armoured cars.'

'Mr Joynson-Hicks is requesting that fifty thousand more special constables should enlist by Monday. And the Royal Tank Corps will henceforth be in attendance on the food convoys. Also, the army is occupying Victoria Park in Bethnal Green. I do wonder if this isn't an overreaction.' Mrs Gillespie, a lifelong supporter of the Conservative Party, was nevertheless indignant that her reign over the soup kitchen was to end. 'Vicar, you must protest. We cannot have the army marching about on this parquet floor.'

'I shall indeed. My sermon tomorrow will be in support of a collection for the strikers,' said the vicar courageously. 'I cannot help thinking what Christ would have—'

'Ah, but few members of this church wish to encourage the strikers,' said Mrs Gillespie. 'We simply believe that women and children should not starve. Besides, the church should not meddle in politics.'

'The trouble is, politicians are meddling with the church,' said the vicar. 'Our Archbishop intended to make a very reasonable appeal on the wireless for the strike to end and for the miners' subsidy to be restored while an agreement is reached but he has not been allowed to broadcast.'

'Quite right,' said Mrs Gillespie. 'I'm amazed that he should take so radical a stand.'

'Don't you think, Mrs Gillespie,' I ventured, 'that the BBC ought to allow both sides of the argument, not just the government's? After all, we live in a democracy.'

'A democracy? Exactly. Which is why the workers should not hold to ransom a properly elected government.'

'It's complicated,' said the vicar. 'Cardinal Bourne has not hesitated to make your point, Mrs Gillespie, on behalf of the Roman Catholic community. He says the strikers are sinners because they are challenging a lawfully constituted human authority.'

Mrs Gillespie was actually dumbstruck and bustled away to

clear a table. Eventually she came back and said, 'That's exactly my point. It's typical of the Roman Catholics to take up an extreme and contentious view. The churches should simply keep quiet except on matters of doctrine.'

'Such an interesting debate,' said the vicar. 'I fully intend to cover all this in my lecture series, *Prophets of Democracy . . .*'

As I rolled up my sleeves to help wash soup bowls and spoons in greasy, tepid water I thought that I'd never spent such a fascinating hour at St Mark's.

'Evelyn has been seriously inconvenienced by the strike,' said Mother. 'I've never seen her look so thin, have you? Those apron strings go twice about her waist. It's because there are no buses and she's having to walk everywhere.'

'Hasn't she got a bicycle?' demanded Mrs Gillespie.

'Unfortunately she lives in a very cramped flat so there's no room for a bicycle and the roads are so busy I should worry about her all the time.'

Mrs Gillespie, whose own two daughters were safely married – though one was a war widow – and installed in handsome semi-detached villas, had stated to Mother often and vociferously that she did not approve of my career. Her need to supply the answer to any problem prevailed, however. 'But it's foolish not to have a bicycle, especially in these difficult times. Our girls have left theirs with us until the children are older. You're welcome to borrow one.'

'What do you think, Mother?' I said. 'We could ride out to Ruislip tomorrow if we took Mrs Gillespie up on her kind offer. How would that be?'

The next morning, waved off by an anxious Min, Mother and I wobbled away on our bicycles, hers borrowed from the Gillespies, mine Grandmother's boneshaker. Our skirts were tucked up under our knees and our hats clamped down hard. After half an hour I was tired of the hat, which threatened to blow off every time I picked up speed, so I stuffed it into the basket and enjoyed the wind fanning my forehead and tugging at my hair. As we headed out of town along the Harrow Road, I actually laughed with exhilaration. Mother, who rode straight-spined as if on horseback, proved to be an excellent bicyclist, though to my knowledge she'd not ridden for a decade or more.

Our first destination was the new-built house she wanted to look at off the Ickenham Road. We pressed our foreheads to the casement window and saw a compact, low-ceilinged room with an oak floor.

'I shall have to start from scratch,' she said firmly. 'None of the furniture from Maida Vale will fit in here. I'll need everything new.'

'Are you sure about this, Mother? The garden will need a lot of work to get it into any kind of shape. And what about Mrs Gillespie and your other friends at church? You won't know a soul here.'

'I'm surprised at you, Evelyn. You do nothing but tell me I have to move on and then, when I do, you throw obstacles in my way.'

By the duck pond in the High Street we sat on a bench to eat Min's picnic lunch and take swigs from the bottles of ginger beer I'd been permitted to purchase from the pub.

'It's still as I remember it,' said Mother who had taken off her cardigan and even rolled back the cuffs of her blouse. 'I was so happy here as a child, so very happy.' Her normally sallow complexion was flushed with exertion and her eyes bright with the sheer novelty of being outside. Occasionally she'd cast me a jubilant glance as if to say: I bet you thought I could never do this. Almost for the first time in my life I saw Grandmother in her.

'I never realised until now that you had such fond memories of the place.'

'Obviously those were the best years, before Father died. I was only six.'

She took me to the little school where her father used to teach and pointed out the schoolhouse across the yard. 'The rooms in the front were rather dark because of the oak tree. I remember Mother complaining that in our shady garden the washing would never dry properly.'

'Was she happy here, do you think?'

'Of course, why wouldn't she have been? We were a *family*. And my father was such a dear. I don't remember much about his funeral except that the church was full of children. They loved him, you see. He died very suddenly of some kind of brain fever. One week he was healthy, the next he was gone. Mother always said he must have caught it from one of his pupils.'

As we wheeled our bicycles towards the churchyard to seek out his grave she said, 'We didn't need a carriage – the coffin was carried across the road to the church by men from the village.' Eventually, in a far corner, close to the wall, we found a stone inscribed:

*Philip James Croft*
*1838 – 1878*
*Beloved*

'Why did you never bring us here before?' I whispered. 'You even named James after him.'

'Yes, but it was so long ago and it always made me sad to think of those early years. But since Mother died and after what happened last week, you know, with that letter, it has all come back to me. I remember the smell of pipe tobacco on Father's clothes. He had a tweed jacket which was very rough on my cheek. I was an infant in the same school of course, and I was aware of this swarm of older children in Father's classroom next door. I was very proud that although he was everybody else's during the day he was ours when school ended. In the summer evenings he worked in the garden sometimes, although there was always a heap of marking. He used to let me climb on his knee and he'd show me how he'd marked spelling mistakes by underlining the word and putting a cross in the margin. He made a list of the most common errors – *Conscious. Exaggerated. There or their.* I've always had excellent spelling as a result. When I was older, he said, I could enter the marks in his ledger, but he died too soon. Mother didn't cry much in front of me but she was very quiet for a long time.

'I remember once disturbing them in the garden. They were standing with their arms around each other. Her head was resting against his shoulder and when she saw me she held out her hand and gave me a smile I have never forgotten. *Happy.* We couldn't stay in the cottage of course, once he died. In a matter of weeks we'd upped sticks and moved to that flat in London you used to visit when you were small. My mother had to work because there was hardly any pension.'

'What about your grandparents, were they no help?'

'My father's parents lived in a cottage off the High Street. They were not kind people and I have since realised they didn't approve of their son marrying an actress. And you see, Mother's family, the Fieldings, had a reputation in Ruislip for being somewhat outlandish,' she lowered her voice, 'because of the stage and the drink.'

'Peggy Spencer told me that the Fieldings used to live in a lovely house out here.'

'They did, yes, on Sharps Lane. I could show you if you like. And then we could have tea at The Poplars if it's still open.'

It amazed me that she seemed impervious to the significance of these leafy Middlesex lanes. Patrick Rusbridger's words in his letter to Clara Fielding haunted me. Why couldn't Mother hear their plangent beat? The image of her parents standing together in the garden was somewhat sepia toned compared to his insistent words of love. But she showed no sign of tension as we bicycled between deep hedgerows until we came to a red brick house nestled within a walled garden complete with a silver birch brushing at a corner window and the door almost buried in Virginia creeper.

'Oh, it's all very grand,' said Mother, noting my surprise, 'but it meant nothing because it was mortgaged to the hilt.'

'Did you ever visit your grandparents here? Do you remember the house?'

'Vaguely. But whenever we came I felt uneasy because there were always people sprawled on the furniture who smelt peculiar.'

Here was the corner where Rusbridger must have waited after delivering his letter at the white-painted door. *Draw aside the curtain, darling . . . All you've told me about this schoolteacher of yours is that you find his attentions touching. Don't marry touching.*

'I want to see inside,' I said suddenly.

'But we don't know them. Goodness knows who is living here now.'

'Do you mind if I go in?'

'Oh, you'll do exactly as you please,' she said, 'you always have,' but she was smiling a little nervously as she retreated up the lane.

She was right; I couldn't have turned back. I suppose I wanted to see how it had been, when Peggy Spencer made her unannounced call on the pregnant Clara, like the Virgin Mary visiting her cousin Elizabeth. Already, since the tearing up of the letter, Mother was less guarded, so how would it be if she stopped hiding from the truth altogether? And as for me, I had a lawyer-like desire simply to set things straight. And perhaps there was more to it than that. Engaged to Daniel Breen but forever wrenching my thoughts away from Nicholas Thorne, I thought there might be some resonance in Grandmother's choice that would put things right for me. Though thwarted in her latter years by blindness, she had always seemed like a woman without regrets.

Thrusting my bicycle against the hedge I marched up to the front door, my heart beating absurdly fast. As I rang the bell it occurred to me that I must look a fright with my damp blouse and creased skirt.

'Is your mistress in?' I asked the maid.

The authority in my voice provoked an automatic bob of the knee. 'The family is out for the day. I'll fetch the housekeeper.'

She left the door ajar and I stood in the quarry-tiled porch, listening to the jubilant birdsong of May.

The housekeeper, a stolid woman who'd probably been disturbed in the midst of her Sunday nap, nevertheless had a gleam in her eye. Yes, she'd heard that the family before last had been actors, name of Fielding.

'So your grandfather was the Ruislip schoolteacher,' she said wonderingly. 'I expect he taught my mother.'

The house was resonant of money well spent, with clean-lined modern furniture and soft furnishings in mellow floral prints. We stood in the main drawing room overlooking the garden where roses still in tight bud basked against an old brick wall.

'When she was a young woman, my grandmother had a bedroom in the corner of the house.' I told her. 'It's mentioned in a letter.'

She nodded and escorted me up a red-carpeted staircase with polished brass rods on to a crooked landing from which doors opened to left and right.

'I'm very fond of this house,' she said, 'though there's not a straight line to be had. You can tell why them actors might have liked it.'

The bedroom was full of shifting shadows because the birch tree outside filtered the light. From the window I could see the corner of the lane where Rusbridger's purported daughter now looked anxiously to left and right as if expecting to be arrested for loitering.

As Clara stood in this room clutching his letter to her breast, his words would have snagged in her heart. Perhaps she had thrown open the window and shouted at him to leave. Or run down and kissed him a passionate goodbye. Or she had unlocked the writing box, tucked the letter away and lain on the bed like a sacrificial lamb, straining to hear the receding hoofbeats that would tell her Rusbridger had finally gone away. Next morning, she'd have placed her hand on her father's unreliable arm and walked with him the few hundred yards to the church. I imagined her hesitating at the church door. I saw my schoolteacher grandfather, steady and loving, as he drew her to his side.

'If I'd known it was going to make you cry ...' said the housekeeper.

'She had rather a sad life,' I wiped my eyes with the back of my hand. 'She went nearly blind whereas when she lived here she was so young and ardent, and could see. That's what makes me sad. But I shouldn't be because she was never sorry for herself.'

'Well now, she must have been very proud to have a granddaughter such as you. I would like to think my own might have as much regard for family one day, but I doubt it.'

We shook hands. At the gate I paused, and it seemed to me that there was a hint of Rusbridger there, a theatrical sigh in the nodding stalks of nettle and cow parsley. Along the lane, Mother beckoned impatiently and off we set for The Poplars tea rooms, where deckchairs and little metal tables were set out under trees and a bored waitress said we could leave our bicycles wherever we liked as far as she was concerned. The day had been deathly quiet because of the strike.

'We used to come here when I was a little girl,' Mother told me. 'It was a great treat. Birthdays and such.' She looked at the tables dotted about and the open door to the house and I realised that

I had been brought here so that she could show me more of her version of the past.

'Mother always preferred to sit in the shade. See the oak tree on the slope over there? That was her favourite place. She was vain about her complexion. Father could juggle teaspoons, two at a time. He had this trick of flicking them up so that they twirled over and over and then he would catch them in one hand.'

'Poor Grandmother. After playing Ophelia, sitting in the shade while her husband juggled with teaspoons must have seemed a trifle dull.'

She regarded me gravely. 'Not dull. You refuse to believe that she was happy and that she had the life she wanted. She counted her blessings every day because she knew how close she'd come to ruin.'

I couldn't help laughing. 'Oh come, Mother. Ruin is such an old-fashioned word. Do you think Meredith is ruined?'

There was a long pause. 'Her life is difficult, yes. But she does love Edmund, I can see that, as Mother loved me.' Her voice broke and her lip trembled.

'Listen,' I said gently. 'When the strike's over and the trains are running I'm going to Birmingham. One of Rusbridger's grandchildren is in a play. What do you think? Will you come with me?'

Mother was following the progress of a bold sparrow that pecked a crumb from her plate. 'Perhaps.'

I was to remember that quiet hour in the week that followed; the flock of sparrows darting from the dense cover of a pyracantha, and Mother lying back in her chair, dabbling her foot in a patch of sunlight.

# Chapter Thirty-Five

Robbie's case was to be heard at eleven on Monday by a stipendiary justice, Mr Sandbach, in the specially convened Strikers' Court. In the cells Robbie looked grubby and feverish; already he smelt of enclosure and unwashed bodies and he'd obviously not received a change of clothes.

'Have you seen my mother? Is she all right?'

'She said she would come and visit you.'

'She never came. Nobody came. I've got to get home. You've got to get me out of here.'

'I'll visit her this evening and find out how she is, but Robbie, you must be prepared for the worst today. There's been a hardening of attitudes, even over the weekend. The best you can do to keep your time inside as short as possible is to behave well in court and apologise. Don't argue with the judge.'

'No, no. That's not good enough, Miss Gifford. I've told you before; you've got to persuade them to set me free.'

'Robbie. Hush.' I put my finger to my mouth. 'The courts are using cases like yours as a deterrent – to warn others that if they make trouble they'll be punished.'

'It's not fair. I won't be quiet if he sends me down. I'll have to shout out.'

It was unbearable to see him like that, on the cusp of manhood, eager, trammelled, intent on destroying himself.

There had been numerous arrests since Friday and the foyer was crammed with hostile or nervous relatives. Ushers dashed about self-importantly and I realised with a sinking heart that cases were being dealt with much too quickly. Sandbach was red-faced with a head of curling dark hair which he frequently crimped with his fingers. His court was running late and for nearly an hour I

245

watched him sentence offenders for obstructing police business or throwing stones in the course of violent disorder. Reporters scribbled in their notebooks and the public benches were crowded with union men and wives and mothers who wept and shouted out when their boys were taken down.

Penalties ranged from a fine to several weeks' hard labour. One defendant was threatened with the birch ... 'If only our criminal justice system would allow it in a man of your age.' Defendants were given little opportunity to speak for themselves, especially as the morning progressed and we heard the same facts time after time. I became ever more pessimistic about Robbie's chance of a fair hearing and, for once, I wished I could have handed the case over to Wolfe or Breen; being represented by a woman in Sandbach's court would do Robbie no favours at all.

Robbie, when called to the dock, was trembling like a greyhound as he glanced hopefully at the public benches. There was no sign of his mother, only Trudy, who slipped in at the very last minute, avoiding my eye. Touchingly, Robbie straightened his shoulders when he saw me but hung his head to show remorse.

The charge was read. 'That Robert Wright had offended under the law of sedition by being present in a public place with intent to create a violent disturbance and further, armed with a hundred or so nails, had thrown them with intent to cause injury or death.'

'Your worship,' I cried, leaping to my feet, 'this is double counting. Mr Wright should only be charged with one or other of these offences.'

'The police prosecutor clearly has a different view.'

'Indeed I do,' said the prosecutor, 'I'd say they were quite different offences since one concerns Wright's presence during a riot, the other the fact that he used ammunition.'

'It was hardly a riot and the second offence covers all contingencies,' I protested.

'I think not. Sedition and assault are two very different ...'

'Not assault, your worship. Mr Wright assaulted no one. He merely made a misguided attempt to slow down an omnibus.'

'He was reckless. Imagine if a nail had bounced from the road and blinded someone ...'

Sandbach raised a hand. 'Miss Gifford, I have half a dozen or so more cases this morning and I cannot afford to spend hours squabbling over each charge.'

The facts were read, including Robbie's previous history of causing a public disturbance. Rolling his eyes, the magistrate invited me to say a *very* few words on behalf of my client.

'As someone who had risked his job in order to join a strike of hundreds of thousands of people who feel passionately that they must have a voice . . .' I began.

'Thank you, Miss Gifford. I don't require a lecture on the purpose or extent of the General Strike.'

'. . . Mr Wright was frustrated by the fact that certain public vehicles were breaking through the pickets. His was a political gesture, not a violent one, and was certainly not premeditated.'

'It seems to me, Miss Gifford, that to buy a bag of nails from Jackson's hardware store on Philip Street is unquestionably an act of premeditation.'

'Any man may carry a bag of nails in his pocket for perfectly innocent reasons, but the point is this, Mr Wright made a brave gesture of solidarity despite his own desperate situation. His sister is here in court and will vouch for the fact that he is the household's chief breadwinner. His father has not worked for nearly a decade and there are three younger siblings. The strike has put this family under pressure, like so many others. We all want a speedy end to the conflict and Robbie Wright is no exception. This was not a crime but an act of anger and frustration.' Sandbach was already reaching for the next file. 'Sir, if you will let him speak, Robbie Wright wishes to apologise to the court.'

'Fortunately that won't be necessary,' said Sandbach, 'as I have a punishment in mind that will give him ample opportunity to make reparation for the harm he has done, and deter others from committing a similar offence in future.'

'But it would be quite unjust, and in fact an act of political prejudice, for the court to punish him more severely just to make an example of him.'

'On the contrary,' said Sandbach, 'that is precisely my intention. You have hit the nail on the head, Miss Gifford, if you will excuse the pun. What is the country coming to that excuses should be made for a man who has used such reckless means to stop an omnibus? There are plenty of opportunities for lawful demonstration through the unions and such. Stand, Mr Wright. For each of these offences you will serve three months' imprisonment with hard labour, to run concurrently. Be grateful for the latter concession. Take him down.'

Robbie gripped the brass rail of the dock with both hands. 'No. No.'

'Take him down.'

'Miss Gifford . . .'

'If you're not careful, you'll be charged with contempt, Mr Wright. Please go with the officer.'

He looked at me with anguish and my heart ached because despite my warnings he had believed I could save him from prison. As he was bundled away I saw Trudy dart out from the public benches and head towards the door. 'Miss Wright,' I called, 'I could arrange for you to have a word with Robbie if you wish.'

She stood sullenly while I asked a kindly usher to arrange an escort.

'Robbie was hoping to see your mother over the weekend,' I said at last. 'She didn't come. Is she all right?'

Without raising or turning her head she muttered, 'How could she have come? How could any of us? He just sent me today to find out what would happen.' And then the words forced themselves from her, as if torn from her throat, 'It's torture at home. The only time I can breathe is when I'm out of the house, working at the pub.'

I drew her into a witness room and tried to make her sit down on one of the hard wooden chairs but she twisted away from me. 'Trudy, why didn't your mother come to court last week?' I asked. 'What happened?'

'Don't blame me,' she retorted, her cheeks mottled, 'don't you dare do that.'

'Trudy . . .'

'No, you just try this. You try to imagine what it's like in that house. Oh Robbie's escaped now all right, but for the rest of us it's hell. Why didn't she come to court? You may well ask. Because can you imagine how it would have been if she'd spoken up against him and he'd still been set free?'

'They would have found him guilty if she'd told the magistrate what he did to her.'

'You don't know that. She couldn't have found the right words with him looking at her the way he does. She'd have been too scared. She'd have said she couldn't rightly remember. It was me who told her to keep away. You think I'm a fool but I worked it all out, what would happen, because he'd be there in the courtroom, just like he's there at home, watching everything she does.'

'Then what hope is there, if we don't at least try to get him to court?'

'There ain't any hope.' She looked at me with dull eyes. 'He won't change. He hates her and he hates himself. He treats her worse and worse, just to see what will happen. He won't do it if one of us kids is in the room but we can't be keeping watch for ever. She won't leave him because she's trying to save us kids, and it's her home, and it's all she's got.'

The usher knocked on the door. He'd spoken to a gaoler who'd arranged for Gertrude to be allowed a few minutes with her brother.

'Miss Wright, please understand, I am on your side,' I told her as she walked away, but she threw up her hand to warn me off, and disappeared through the door leading to the cells.

# Chapter Thirty-Six

The only advance we'd been able to make in the Petit case was an undertaking from Annabel's father that he would be at work on Monday afternoon around four, if Miss Gifford felt she had to see him in person. As I mounted Grandmother's bicycle it struck me that Shawcross had been singularly thoughtless, inviting me out to Greenford in the midst of a strike. Strategically situated on the London to Fishguard Trunk Road, Shawcross & Sons was a gleaming white building with massive, green-painted windows and lawns fronting the road behind high iron railings. However, as I drew closer I realised that the factory was actually under siege because a mass of pickets had assembled in front of the high metal gates, which were padlocked and being patrolled on the inside by a couple of security guards.

Everyone seemed calm apart from a handful of strikers who periodically rattled the gates and yelled, 'Don't be a bloody black-leg. Come off it,' at the guards. 'Get out here, Tony. You're on the wrong side, mate.' Otherwise they just stood about smoking and chatting.

Half a dozen policemen were on hand, with truncheons thrust into their belts, but their relaxed manner implied that they were not expecting real trouble. Three or four strikers clustered round a brazier fuelled with what looked suspiciously like fencing, others had set up folding chairs behind a trestle table and were selling news-sheets, and the pavements were littered with scraps of paper and cigarette ends. A few pickets had even brought their wives and young children who were playing fives together on a kerb. A couple of slightly older boys of perhaps nine or ten, one wearing a man's red shirt so big it fell to his knees, were kicking an ancient football.

I wheeled my bicycle over to a heavy-set police officer who was regarding the proceedings with folded arms, as if he were at a sporting event. 'I have a meeting inside with the owner, Mr Shawcross,' I told him.

'I think you'll find you don't, Miss.'

'My name is Miss Gifford. I'm a lawyer.'

'I don't care who you are or what your name is, you're not going in.'

'It's a family rather than a work matter. Could you at least confirm that Mr Shawcross is here? I've come quite a long way to see him and it's very urgent.'

He jerked his head towards the gates, beyond which a gravel drive ran up to a dry fountain modelled on the clean lines of a classical sculpture. Beyond was the colonnaded entrance to the factory adorned with gold lettering and a royal crest, and parked in front were several automobiles, one a midnight-blue Rolls-Royce.

'Don't you think the pickets would let me through if I explained to them?' I asked.

'They'll more likely laugh at you, Miss. Now why don't you take yourself off and visit our Mr Shawcross at a more convenient time, preferably at his home if it's a family matter.'

I had indeed already attracted unwelcome attention from the strikers who were jostling closer to overhear our conversation. Almost to a man they were grey-faced, surly and far too thin. While I worked out my next move, I pedalled away and performed a circuit of the entire factory, which perhaps extended for a third of a mile along the trunk road. All the service gates were locked and guarded and there was a picket at the entrance to the delivery yard.

Back at the main gate I approached the cluster of older men seated behind the trestle table, one of whom had wild white hair partially covered by a bowler hat. His eyes were rheumy as he smiled at me kindly.

'I need to speak to Mr Shawcross.' I showed him my card and a letter headed Breen & Balcombe. 'It's concerning his daughter. Private business. Nothing to do with work. Would you please ask your men to let me through?'

'They won't like it, Miss. They're not in the mood for doing any favours for Shawcross.' He laid his hand upon a crumpled sheet of paper on the table. 'This was pinned to the gate this morning. It's an ultimatum. If we don't return to work by Wednesday, we'll lose our jobs.'

'So you think you'll have to go back?'

'We've called all the men here to a rally later today. But this isn't the only factory where this sort of notice has been given. We think the unions will retaliate nationally by pulling out more men. The likes of Shawcross are losing thousands of pounds a day because of the strike. They need this to be settled as much as we do.'

'Have you worked long for Mr Shawcross?'

'Since he built the factory. More than twenty-five years.'

'Is he a good employer?'

'He's an employer. Profits first.'

'Do you remember his daughter? She used to work here during the war.'

'Oh, I've known Annabel since she was a little girl. She's quite a favourite of mine. Cheered us all up with those bright eyes of hers. Cheeky.' He eyed me with considerable shrewdness. 'All right. I know when my arm's being twisted. But I warn you, even if they let you in, there'll be no guarantee you'll get out again.'

'I'm prepared to take that risk.'

'Then follow me. You and your old boneshaker.'

I had made a good choice of champion because a quiet word from my new friend resulted in the men allowing us to pass until we came to the gates, where words were exchanged with the un-happy – and somewhat puny – security guard, Tony. Eventually he unlocked a side gate, held it open a foot or so and allowed me through. Once on the drive I remounted my bicycle with as much dignity as I could muster and, still under scrutiny from the pickets, I rode round the fountain, then leaned Grandmother's bicycle against the steps and hammered on the massive double doors. A stout receptionist answered, so startled at receiving a visitor that she had failed to put down her copy of *Good Housekeeping*.

The lofty entrance hall was more like the lobby to an audi-torium than a factory, and from behind closed doors came the murmur of male voices and, even further away, the faint thump of machinery. My escort first showed me to the very grand ladies' lavatory where I adjusted my respectable little cloche hat above my flattened hair. Next I was shown up the wide, curving staircase to an upper hallway panelled in strips of light oak where Shaw-cross himself awaited me, hand outstretched, subtly perfumed and dressed in a grey suit belted at his trim waist – not quite leisure wear but not business garb either. Presumably his status as factory owner ensured that he could dress as he pleased.

I had anticipated, following my meeting with his wife and especially since hearing of his threats to his workers, that he would be stocky, self-satisfied and brash. Instead he was open-faced with well-cut silver hair and Annabel's translucent grey eyes. In Yorkshire-tinged vowels, he thanked me profusely for agreeing to travel so far by bicycle.

'It was thoughtless of me not to have called at your office when I heard you wanted to see me but somehow I thought you'd have a driver. Because of this strike I don't like to leave the building.'

One side of his office overlooked the drive and it was disconcerting to realise that he had undoubtedly witnessed the scene outside the gates and my ungainly progress round the fountain on Grandmother's bicycle. A further wall, entirely of glass, enabled him to oversee the factory floor, each row of machinery with its massive cogs and wheels and levers at a standstill, and row upon row of disembodied machine parts in various states of construction, resting in their allotted grooves or bins. Instead of what must have been the usual cacophony there was a distant whirr as the sleeping lines ticked over in readiness for the strike's end, and that rhythmic, subterranean thumping I had heard earlier. Light poured through the immense windows and was split by the arching metal pillars supporting the roof so that the factory seemed, in its stillness, almost ecclesiastical.

'You must be exhausted, Miss Gifford. But then my wife tells me that you are an extraordinary woman so perhaps you're not.'

'I hadn't expected to meet with opposition at the gate.'

'Did my men give you a hard time?' He laid a concerned hand on my wrist. 'You see, we've received instructions from on high to make them all redundant if they don't return to work on

Wednesday. Since we pinned the notices on the gate this morning the protest has been growing.'

'Surely you, as the owner of the factory, didn't need to obey the instruction? Where did it come from?'

'You're right, I can do what I like, but we factory owners must stand together on this. You'll perhaps be aware that the unions have called out another wave of workers on Wednesday and we can't allow a further show of strength. So, on the advice of our lawyers, we issued an ultimatum.'

'By *we*, do you mean the FBI? Nicholas Thorne, I believe, would be the barrister in question.'

'You *have* been doing your homework. Ah, but then I remember, wasn't there some kind of connection between you once?' He quirked an eyebrow and I felt a stirring of unease. 'You'd be surprised what we hear on the grapevine,' he added. 'I'm fortunate to have a wife and daughter who love to gossip. Thorne's view is that everyone will drift back to their posts sooner rather than later so it's best to get the misery over with before too much trade is lost. There are many men who would love to be at work but who cannot get through. That's hardly democracy. And there are communists out there. I don't like that. Didn't you notice they were selling copies of the *Workers' Bulletin*? Well I won't have it. We have good relations in this factory, by and large, and I am losing hundreds of thousands of pounds every day. I need those men back at work.'

'If you need them so badly, couldn't you be a little more accommodating to their point of view?'

'Ha. A cosy, dare I say a womanly proposition, Miss Gifford. I'd like to show some understanding but I can't do anything that might be construed as weakness. The bottom line is the unions cannot win because they don't have leaders who have the courage of their convictions – and that, it seems to me, has always been the key to success. Wouldn't you agree?'

His manner throughout this conversation had been warm and his darkly lashed eyes made a somewhat disturbing contrast to his shock of silver hair. I realised that his frankness was calculated to disarm, and that he was engaged in a well-practised game of flirtation – probably, I thought, because he knew of no other way to treat a woman other than to dominate or seduce. When the receptionist brought in a tea tray Shawcross ushered me to a deep leather armchair.

'You must build yourself up for the journey home,' he said, handing me a cup and saucer decorated with sunrays and orange clouds so assertively modern that it must have been supplied by his daughter. 'My wife told me about your conversation with her, Miss Gifford. I admire you, truth be told, for standing up to her and I'm glad that Annabel has chosen to be represented by a lawyer with spirit. This is the thing about her; she has flashes of surprising astuteness interspersed with behaviour that can only be described as crazy.'

'From what I have seen so far, I would hardly describe her as crazy.'

'Would you not? I think you must allow me to understand my own daughter a little better than you do. Now I know exactly why you're here; we've told you Annabel's going to withdraw and you don't like it. You'll say that, as Annabel's lawyer, you can't take instruction from a third party, even her father. Well, I had a feeling we might run into just such a difficulty, so I sat me down with Annabel at the weekend and together we composed this letter. I was going to have it delivered to you, but here you are.'

On notepaper headed *The Maltings, Kingston-upon-Thames* was a scrawled note from Annabel stating that she would agree to the terms of her husband's latest offer. The swirling signature certainly looked authentic.

'I'm afraid this is insufficient,' I said. 'I must have a meeting with Annabel.'

'Not possible, I'm afraid. She's too ill.'

'Then I shall have to get the case adjourned. I'm sure you understand, Mr Shawcross, that I have to be one hundred per cent convinced that this is Annabel's wish, not just at the time when the letter was written, but after full consideration. She is effectively signing away not only her marriage but her right to bring up her own daughter.'

Shawcross ran his finger round his hard, starched collar and leaned towards me. 'Do you mind my saying that from the instant you rode up my drive, Miss Gifford, I have been struggling to retain a grip on what I had intended to say to you? I'll be totally honest; my wife was hardly complimentary about you but now I've seen you in the flesh I entirely understand my daughter's faith in you. Instead of the she-devil I had expected I discover a young woman who insinuates her way through the pickets by means of sporting a most fetching, unlawyer-like hat. No wonder you've rattled Petit's team.'

I placed my cup and saucer on the arm of my chair, determined to keep my head in the face of such unashamed flattery. 'This letterhead is presumably the address where Annabel is staying at present. I'll visit her as soon as possible.'

'Come, Miss Gifford. See sense. There's nothing to be gained by further delay. All I want is for my little girl to get better. I'm suggesting to her mother that the pair of them go away to Switzerland or somewhere else warm and pretty. Annabel's marriage was a dreadful mistake, and I hold up my hands and say that it was I who persuaded her.'

'Indeed.'

'Not that she took much persuasion, but yes, it's easy to get swept along by Petit. During the war, we had to pull together to churn out enough guns for our troops. I found him charming, as did everyone else; he was the blue-eyed boy of the war office. Oh yes, I'll admit to acting out of self-interest when I encouraged the match. I'm a businessman, what do you expect? But I also thought Petit might just be the perfect solution for Bel, moving her into circles where she could be a political wife at the heart of things.'

'Even if she really had no interest in politics?'

'I didn't see it like that. I knew that clever, modern women like you and Annabel would not have an easy time after the war so I decided marriage to Petit would be an opportunity for her to find a purpose.'

That warm, rueful regard was very calculated and his gaze drifted from my eyes to my mouth, breasts and lap so that I was reminded, sickeningly, of Wright watching me from his armchair in the kitchen.

I got up and stood at the glass wall. Annabel Shawcross, poor little puppet – let's take her out of school ... find her a place in

Daddy's factory . . . marry her to Timmo Petit. I had been about to mention Leremer but Petit got there first.

'You've doubtless heard,' he said, 'that Annabel has got back at us all by naming Richard Leremer as the father. That was another thing; she would keep running around with the wrong set.'

'What do you make of the clause in Sir Timothy's offer to your daughter that Annice must have no contact at all with Mr Leremer? If you believe that he's the father, doesn't that seem very cruel?'

'I'm beyond knowing or caring what's true. I only know that I don't want a granddaughter of mine mixing with Leremer.'

'Because he's a Jew or a socialist or because he's poor?'

Shawcross stood beside me and pressed the flat of his hand to the glass panel above my head. We were practically touching and I wondered how best to show my distaste; by holding my ground or ducking away.

'Now then, Miss Gifford, what Timothy – *Sir* Timothy – plans for Annice is an excellent education, preferably boarding, which is exactly what we would wish for the little girl. She's a bright child. We want her to be whole and healthy and in the company of lots of other children. We don't want her to remain stuck in that great house in London while her mother either repines in some asylum or—'

'*Asylum?*'

He covered his eyes. 'If we don't put a stop to this, that's where it's bound to end. Annabel is driving herself mad. She spends her time either drugged into a coma or banging about in a rage. I can't bear to see her like this.'

'Mr Shawcross, I don't understand you. On the one hand you show appreciation of your daughter's intelligence, on the other you talk about managing her life to the point of agreeing to her being separated from Annice.'

'All right, I'll be blunt. I see it as the only way out for Annabel. She can't win – *you* can't win, however much you want to flex your legal muscles on my daughter's case. If I'm absolutely honest I'll say that I wish I'd never clapped eyes on Petit. He will destroy my daughter.'

'Yet you still seem keen to stay on the right side of him by dissuading Annabel from appearing in court. Is Petit putting you under pressure to persuade Annabel to divorce him?'

'By God, you're a demon, Miss Gifford. I should have listened to my wife after all.' Approaching his mouth so close that his breath fanned my ear, he added, 'She said she wouldn't trust you within half a mile of any man she knew and now I've met you I think, yes, this is the kind of woman who could utterly undo a man.' He leaned on his elbow so that his mouth was inches from mine. 'My wife would not have meant what she said as a compliment whereas I do. I hope your beautiful integrity is never compromised, Miss Gifford, it is a precious thing. What about the men in your life, what do they think of all your gadding about on a bicycle? They must find it exceptionally hard to keep a grip on you.'

I took a step back but held his gaze, leaving him, I hoped, in no doubt about what I thought of him. 'I'll visit Annabel in person later this week. Because the date of the paternity trial is so imminent, if I'm not able to meet her in the next couple of days I shall ask for an adjournment. I'd be grateful if you could tell her that you and I have met.'

With a flourish he opened the door and bowed me out, still with that infuriating smile, but as we reached the top of the stairs a young clerk came racing towards us. 'Mr Shawcross, there's trouble. The men are trying to break through the gates.'

Shawcross's step faltered only briefly and he drew a long breath. 'Are they indeed? Well, now we shall have some fun, eh, Miss Gifford?'

In the entrance, a dozen or so other clerks had gathered with a handful of women, including the receptionist. From this distance and behind those heavy doors nothing exceptional could be heard, but once they were opened there was a distant roar and we could see that the relatively small crowd at the gate had become a swarm. Beyond the strikers I could just make out a number of vehicles which must have arrived in the last hour or so; Crossleys, a couple of armoured cars and a black van.

'So now we shall see up close what happens when these communists show their true colours. Isn't that so, Miss Gifford?'

'There are so many police. Your men will be trapped against the gates.'

'Oh, there'll be a few bruises at worst. Come, Miss Gifford, where's your bottle? I'll have a word with them and tell them to go home peacefully. If they report for work on Wednesday as usual we'll see that most of them keep their jobs.'

My bicycle was propped against the steps. Half a dozen of Shawcross's minions, uneasy in their suits and stiff-collared shirts, followed him round the fountain towards the gates. I thrust my briefcase into the basket and wheeled my bicycle a short distance behind, thinking that though I needed to disassociate myself from Shawcross my position might seem cowardly or equivocal if I held back too long. There was now an immense roaring and chanting from the crowd, though as Shawcross approached a restless hush gradually came over them.

'Come,' he began, projecting his voice so that even those at the very back must have heard, 'you and I have always been friends and worked together. We cannot let national politics destroy all that.'

'Then don't,' called the elderly trade unionist who had helped me gain entrance. 'Withdraw your ultimatum.'

'Come back to work and then we'll talk,' Shawcross called.

'We cannot give that much ground. You've made us no promises.'

'All we need—' continued Shawcross.

'—is a revolution,' roared a man wearing a green knitted scarf and peaked cap.

A policeman shouted back, 'That's it. Let them have it,' and with raised baton he hurtled towards the man in the green scarf who dived into the crowd.

A war cry arose from inside the black van and men in plain clothes, some bearing the armbands and batons of the special police, surged out and began laying into the strikers. At first I couldn't comprehend what was happening; the taste of Shawcross's tea was still on my tongue and I was holding the handlebars of Grandmother's old bicycle – surely those details could not be harbingers of a riot – but then I saw a man go down and a booted foot kick out at his groin and thighs.

'Stop this,' I shouted at Shawcross. 'Call off the police.' But he stood back, arms folded.

More and more men clambered out of the vans and soon the

strikers, pinned against the perimeter fence, were defending them-selves from a barrage of blows. I saw their leader's cheek pressed to a railing as he protected his bare white head with his hands. Some were handcuffed and led away, arching their backs and thrashing out, to the police vehicles, while others wandered about, stunned and bleeding. A youngish man was gripping the fence with one hand and I saw him fumble at his belt and draw out a knife even as a baton cracked against his head and he fell back.

'Let me out,' I yelled at a security guard. 'Let me out, I'm a lawyer.'

He was too busy gawping at the chaos beyond the gates to hear me so I turned to Shawcross. 'Let me out,' I begged him.

'You'll be lynched,' he said calmly. 'I can't let that happen.'

'Let me out or I shall make sure every newspaper in the country hears of this.'

'You'll have to sit it out with the rest of us, I'm afraid, Miss Gifford.'

'My God, if you keep me here I shall have you prosecuted for unlawful detention.'

He grinned. The battle beyond the fence was a churning, bleed-ing, unstoppable force and yet I refused to be penned in with Shawcross and his cronies. Still clutching my bicycle I rushed up to the security guard and seized him by the shoulder. 'Let me out of these gates. *Now*.'

Shawcross was behind me. 'Don't say I didn't warn you.' He must have nodded at the guard who released the padlock to the side gate and next moment my bicycle and I were on the far side of the fence, the gate had clanged shut behind me and I was being forced backwards as a man took a sudden plunge, clawing at the shoulders of a policeman who was lashing out at a striker. Some men resisted arrest by kicking and tearing at clothes and hair but the specials simply beat them until they were so cowed they could be carted away. I had somehow thought that if I stood among them in my sturdy skirt and with my briefcase stuffed into the bicycle basket, sense would prevail. Instead, I was ignored, so I gripped my handlebars and tried to work my way out of the melee.

After a few steps I was turned back by the pressure of the crowd and decided to skirt round it along the fence but my route was again obstructed, this time by a fair-haired youth brandishing a raised baton. At first I couldn't see his quarry, then, over his shoulder, I saw that backing away from him, still with the football clutched to his chest, was the boy in the red shirt.

'Nobody speaks to me like that and gets away with it,' the youth intoned, very quietly. 'Animal. Scum.'

The child was trapped against the fence and instinctively I rammed my bicycle up against the youth so that the wheel cracked into his calf and he turned on me, his eyes enraged. His baton dropped to waist level and, in the moment of distraction, the little boy ducked away and made a dash for it, charging along the side of the fence. The youth yelped and set off in hot pursuit, followed by a couple of other young men wielding batons.

Flinging down my bicycle I ran after them, somewhat hampered by the narrowness of my skirt. The child had turned the corner of the perimeter fence and was now racing along an alley between the fence on one side and a high brick wall marking the backyards of a row of terraced houses. The noise of the riot receded as I ran, my low heels catching on the uneven ground. There was a clang of metal on stone followed by a further shiver of noise, as if a pan lid had been dropped on a flagged kitchen floor.

When I reached a narrow gap in the wall to the right, I was confronted by a scene eerie for its stillness. The youths had kicked aside a couple of overflowing dustbins, while the child, cornered at the far end of the blind alley, was ashen-faced, the ball still clutched to his chest. The youths were panting and even as I thought, they won't hurt him, they wouldn't, he's too small, too unprotected, the first of them, the one who had been insulted by the child, raised his baton.

My mouth opened as in a nightmare but no sound would come. The little boy was shaking now, the fight gone out of him; I saw a flash of premonition in his eyes as he brought up his arms to ward off the blow and the ball bounced once, twice and rolled away.

'Don't touch him,' I screamed at last and hurled myself forward but the baton had already cracked a blow on the side of the child's head. He crumpled and fell, doll-like.

'Get *away* from him. I'm a lawyer. Your behaviour is criminal.'

'Now I really am afraid.' The blond youth waved his baton and pranced from side to side like a boxer, taunting me. One of his mates must have worked his way round behind me because he glanced over my shoulder as a blow felled me and pain ricocheted across my back. I could no longer hear the distant crowd or remember where I was; only that I was utterly alone with these madmen.

None of them is wearing an armband, I thought indignantly as hands seized my arms, my head was pulled back and I was silenced by a hard palm crushed to my mouth. The blond-headed one was hanging over the child, prodding him with the toe of his boot. I bit down on to hard flesh, and when the grip slackened for a moment, twisted away and managed to pitch forward and tear weakly at his collar and jacket.

'Bitch, bitch,' they shouted and sharp stones hit my knees as they shoved me down.

'Bitch, we'll have you.' The grey sky rushed by overhead, framed by high brick walls, and I was aware of the stench of cabbage stalks before everything was blanked out by the blond youth's face, his features a clenched mask. He clutched the front of my jacket and raised me several inches from the ground but his attention had wavered. Released, I rolled on to my knees. Pain toppled me again as I tried to use my injured arm for support and by the time I'd recovered all three youths had formed a semicircle to confront a new arrival. I saw his shapely black shoes first; then something about the length of his legs, the quality of his stillness made me jolt my head up: Nicholas.

# Chapter Thirty-Seven

It couldn't be him. Nicholas was always there in my head – it was just that the shock of my fall had shaken his image out on to the cobbles.

The youths shifted and drew closer to the phantom while I crawled backwards in the direction of the boy. Nicholas took a step forward and his arm flashed up so fast I lost sight of what happened, only saw the blond boy flying backwards and landing amid the filth from the bin. I gathered the child into my lap. There was another smack of fist on cheekbone, then the rush of retreating feet. Streams of blood were pouring down the child's forehead into his fair hair.

'Keep breathing, little boy. Please breathe,' I groped for a handkerchief to staunch the shocking flow of blood. The handkerchief had been initialled by Prudence, *EG,* in no-nonsense magenta chain stitch. Around me the alley was littered with crumpled news-sheets, peelings and broken glass and the child's football had rolled against the wall.

Nicholas was behind me, I knew he was there; I didn't need to look up or reach for him. The boy's cheek, cupped in my hand, was smooth and cold, and his eyelids were blueish. Nicholas's hand felt warm and real enough when he gave me another wad of linen to press to the terrible wound.

'Is he breathing?'

Needles of rain fell on my forehead and I saw him so clearly now. My world was reduced to this; a boy in my arms and the intentness of Nicholas's eyes as he crouched beside me and with his fingertips lifted a strand of wet hair from my cheek.

'Can you walk?' Taking off his coat he wrapped it round the

263

child and lifted him from me. 'Keep up the pressure on his head. Come with me.'

We stumbled forward. The rain fell more strongly still as I pressed Nicholas's handkerchief to the boy's head with the strength of my good arm. We reached the mouth of the alley and headed back towards the factory gates. A couple of vehicles went screeching off but the Crossley remained. A woman with an infant in her arms was coming towards us, her hand outstretched to ward off bad news.

She put a fingertip to the little boy's cheek. 'That's our Jack, my sister's boy. He'll have come down here with his pa.'

'My car is close by,' said Nicholas. 'I'll get him to the hospital.'

A crowd of women collected around us. Snatches of information reached me; the mother, it seemed, was sick, about to give birth, and couldn't keep a close enough watch on the boy. Jack Whickett was forever running wild. The father had been arrested and carried off at the very beginning of the skirmish. But what had Jack done, to get himself injured like this? The King Edward Memorial Hospital was nearest. That's where he should be taken. 'And who are you, Miss? We saw you go after them.' The sky had darkened and pain pulsed up my neck and into my skull.

A motor car was in a side turning, the very same black Ford, unless I was mistaken, as Nicholas had driven in the old days. The child's aunt had kept up with us.

'I'll get down the hospital as soon as I can. Trouble is, I've no one to leave in charge at home. I'll tell my sister what's happened. She's terrible sick, her legs all swelled up. I can't thank you enough ... Take care of him ...'

I sat on the narrow back seat and the child was placed on my lap, while somebody cranked the engine. My teeth were chattering and I couldn't speak. Nicholas was in his old place at the wheel and the car smelt the same as before, leathery, fumy. The child's complexion, whenever we drove under a light, was greyish. He had neat features except that the eye beneath the wound was now totally obscured by swelling. His neck, within the too-wide collar of the shirt, was very dirty. He needed a Prudence or a Min, I thought, to give him a good scrub. Bending my head to listen for his breathing I tried to summon him back from the darkness.

'Jack. Jack.'

He smelt of rain.

I saw Nicholas's left hand on the wheel, his tense shoulders and wet hair. Sometimes he glanced at me and I was stunned by what I saw in his eyes.

The emergency ward was full of men clasping makeshift bandages to their skulls while their wives, often accompanied by young children, demanded that they be attended to. Nurses bustled about in a whirl of starched cap and apron. Their fast-moving, polished shoes and black-clad ankles were mesmerising and I couldn't think how to attract their attention, but Nicholas etched a sharp line through the turmoil, demanding that as he was a young child with a head injury, Jack should be seen at once. It's his voice and height, I thought, nobody else stands a chance. His next ploy was to stand unmoving over a doctor in a white coat until all at once there was a flurry of activity and Jack was taken from his arms and wheeled into some other place. Nicholas pursued them, disappearing between a pair of doors, leaving me seated on a hard chair in a queue of casualties.

The man beside me had extended his leg so that his heel was to the floor and his toe pointed at the ceiling. Occasionally he winced. There was a round metal clock on the wall opposite. Surely I was misreading the time; it seemed to be nearly nine o'clock. Some disturbance nagged at the back of my mind but flitted away. The blow to my shoulder, the shocking impact of wood on muscle, pulsed through me once more.

The swing doors opened. Nicholas spoke to a nurse and then knelt before me. My bloodied hands were clasped in my lap. He unfurled my fingers and kissed my knuckle and the inside of my wrist, as if it was obvious that he should, then held the palm against his cheek as he spoke to me, so that I felt the slight movement of his jaw against my skin.

'They are going to X-ray his head,' he said, and the softness of his voice made me shiver. 'We will just have to wait.'

I stared at him. Nicholas.

'Can you tell me,' he said, 'where you are hurt? No, I'm being foolish, don't try to speak, you're too shocked by what has happened. We'll sit here and wait for them to look at you.'

I hadn't realised that I was weeping until he drew up a chair and enclosed me with his arm. My cheek was against his heart and I felt its steady beat.

'Hush, hush.' His lips were pressed to my hair. 'He will be all right, you'll see.'

Time passed. Daniel's ring was twisted round the wrong way on my finger until Nicholas straightened it. The hospital was a distant hive of activity, but he and I floated above it all. I grew warmer. I could smell the damp cloth of his waistcoat, the remembered tang of his sweat, and I noticed that the knuckles on his right hand were bruised. The struggle, the appalling tangle of our lives was undone.

At eleven I was ushered into a curtained cubicle that smelt of methylated spirit. 'Sorry to keep you waiting, dear. I've never known a night like it. Your hubby says you may have a broken shoulder.' The nurse was weary and disinterested. 'Is that right?'

At last I found my voice. 'I hope not.'

'I hope not too.'

She summoned a junior with large brown eyes and nervous fingers and they removed my jacket and blouse and exclaimed over the bruising to my shoulder and back. 'There's nothing broken, just a wrench.' In half an hour my shoulder was strapped and my arm firmly riveted to my chest by a tight sling. They picked grit from my knees and declared my stockings ruined. 'We can't mend them, I'm afraid.' The nurse smiled faintly as she filled out a form.

In the waiting room Nicholas was talking to a police officer. His arms were folded and he seemed as calm as in a courtroom except his hair was dishevelled and he was in need of a shave. For a moment he was unaware of me and then he glanced up and his expression changed.

The police officer was officious, ponderous, very slow at taking down my statement. He told us that he'd not been present at the riot outside the Shawcross factory but that there had been seventeen arrests for offences ranging from sedition and unlawful assembly, to assaulting a police officer in the course of his duty.

'Mr Thorne here tells us you were a witness to an assault during the riot, Miss.'

I had recovered my wits at last. 'It wasn't a riot. It was a peaceful demonstration invaded by thugs.'

'That's not what I've heard.'

I described the young man with the floppy fair hair. No, I didn't know his name. No, I hadn't seen whether he'd come by van or had simply arrived on the scene on foot. No, he hadn't been a member of the specials.

'That'll make him very difficult to trace,' said the officer. 'We've had a fair bit of this over the last couple of days. You get all sorts of opportunistic offending in these circumstances. That's what makes the whole strike so dangerous. Now you say there had been some provocation.'

'I have no idea what the little boy – Jack – said to provoke the attack but this was an armed assault on a small child.'

'An assault, or was his alleged attacker defending himself?'

As I signed my statement I suspected that nobody would be arrested for the outrage at the Shawcross factory except the strikers, although when the three of us were summoned to Jack's bedside the officer flinched at the sight of the child's ashen face and heavily bandaged head.

'His skull is fractured,' said the nurse. 'In these cases, it's very difficult to say what the outcome will be.'

The officer, with rather more dedication than he'd shown hitherto, wrote down the child's name and injury and departed. I said I wouldn't leave until a relative came. At least Jack's hand was warm, and he was breathing deeply. A good sign, said the nurse.

The emergency room was quieter now, no more admissions, the casualties dispatched to the wards or sent home. The clock's hands ticked noisily past three o'clock. 'Do you think they'll catch the youth who did it?' I whispered.

Nicholas shook his head. 'I doubt it. Nobody will know who he was. Those types melt in and out of a brawl. They turn up everywhere, fascists, anarchists . . .'

He'd undone his tie, rolled up his bloodstained raincoat and pushed it under his chair. Questions bubbled beneath the surface of my mind but I couldn't catch them yet. In any case I did not want to disturb the peace of the ward, which had a dreamy sense of being underwater. Nor would I for the world have moved a muscle as we sat side by side, our fingers locked tight.

It was dawn before the aunt arrived, dressed in what looked like her best coat and hat. There had been mayhem at home, what with the men arrested and the children running amok, and Jack's mother had been beside herself with worry over her husband and son. In the end the entire tribe had been carted round to the grandmother's house but still the aunt's own baby wouldn't settle.

At the sound of her voice Jack opened an eye and gave her a long, bleary look before falling asleep again.

Eventually the nurse sent us away. Now Jack was showing signs of consciousness he could be wheeled up to the children's ward and the aunt was welcome to return later, at visiting time. The aunt sat in the front of Nicholas's car and I in the back while he drove her home to a street about a quarter of a mile from the factory. We watched her push her key into the lock of a neat mid-terrace, complete with a pot of geraniums on the step, before he helped me into the front seat. We then drove to the factory where the light from gas lamps was fading and all was peaceful; the picket had gone and the street had been swept. The immense factory buildings were in darkness except for security lights burning in a few of the windows, and there were no vehicles parked outside. Nicholas left the engine running while he spoke to the guard at the gate. When he came back he said that the guard, who'd been on duty only since ten o'clock the previous night, had not seen my hat, briefcase or bicycle.

'All my keys were in that case,' I said. 'If you wouldn't mind dropping me in Arbery Street I can wait for Miss Drake to come and open up the office.' I couldn't bear the thought of returning to Mother's house in Maida Vale, or the lonely stillness of Pimlico.

As we drove to Arbery Street, time and the city were closing us down; the morning was upon us. 'It's barely six,' he said after parking the car. 'I know a place where we can have breakfast.'

Nicholas always knew a place, of course, but this was a surprising choice for one as elegant as he; a greasy spoon alongside Euston Station with steamed-up windows, and empty save for the woman behind the counter. The red gingham tablecloth was dirty, the glass cruet set smeared with grease and the metal lid of the salt cellar corroded. My hair had worked itself out of its pins so I attempted to tidy it with my fingers. Tea came in a thick mug and the toast was smeared with margarine.

'We should make the most of this,' I said. 'Soon there'll be no flour.'

'It won't come to that.' Nicholas leaned forward and reached for my hand. 'Evelyn, why did you never reply to my letter?'

'I burnt your letter.'

'But did you read it?'

'I couldn't read it. I changed my mind – but it was too late.'

Beyond the misted windows the street was no longer empty.

'Perhaps it's just as well. It wasn't a very coherent letter. As I recall, I wrote that I held up my hands and admitted that my behaviour, at least when we first met – until I knew you better – had been far from transparent. Self-seeking, in fact. It was a plea for forgiveness.' He stared at Daniel's ring. 'And of course it was a love letter.'

Of course it was a love letter. I felt a stab of grief for the moment when the flames had taken it, unread. I remembered opening the front door at Clivedon Hall Gardens, spotting the letter on the hall stand and testing its weight in my hand. I had taken it upstairs, locked my bedroom door and gripped the mantel with one hand, the letter in the other. In a burst of anger and self-righteousness, before I could change my mind, I had tossed it into the fire, watching the flames lick first the sealed flap, then the stamp. When they had started to consume my name and the address I had knelt, seized the tongs, lifted it out and tried to save a few scraps – I still bore the scar on my right thumb. Finally, fuelled by pain and the fact that most of his words were already lost, I had thrust it all into the flames again and watched it disappear.

'A love letter?'

He was stroking the back of my hand with his thumb. 'Oh yes. I might have mentioned that I hadn't slept for more than a few hours in weeks. How I was riveted, whenever I was with you, by details such as this translucency in the back of your wrist, or the way you raise your chin when you're about to disagree with me, and how I didn't think I could live any kind of meaningful life knowing I would never make love to you again. Oh God, Evelyn, or find out what it was like to grow old with you. I was an exile in South Africa but in the end I told myself I needn't punish myself for ever.' The urn had stopped its hissing and the spasmodic roar of traffic on the street outside had stilled. 'I came home because I couldn't bear to be away any longer, and after two years I thought you might just give me another chance.'

'But I saw you in Fitzroy Street,' I whispered, 'and then at the theatre, with that young woman.'

'Catherine Hatton is just the daughter of an associate at the FBI. When I'm her escort it's a business matter, that's all. I have never given her cause to hope for anything else.'

'Why did you come to the factory yesterday?'

'I needed to speak to Shawcross. He had asked me to look into the legal position with regard to the men returning to work. I was getting out of the car when I thought I glimpsed you. I couldn't think how it could possibly be you.'

'Annabel – I wanted to talk to her father about Annabel.'

'I couldn't get through the crowd in time. I saw you more clearly than I've ever seen anything in my life. It was as if there was nobody else there. I can't lie to you. I can't pretend.'

'Nicholas.'

'I spent the last two years trying to forget you. I travelled thousands of miles and took on more and more work, went to parties, made long journeys and all the time, without wanting to, I was measuring everything up against you.'

'Please. I can't bear it . . .'

The light of a summer morning lifted the gloom of the unlit cafe. I knew his face so well, the texture of his skin, the slight, perfect hollows in the side of his face above his cheekbones, the arch of his brows, his beautiful mouth.

'I won't do anything that makes you sad, but one last throw of the dice is all I have, Evelyn, I know that. Let me explain. This is how it started. I saw you first in court, very defiant, shoulders braced, extraordinary with your flashing eyes and that strange, no-nonsense hat. Then I caught sight of you in Toynbee – yes, I went there deliberately to see you, purely for business reasons, or so I told myself, though actually I couldn't get you out of my mind. You were listening to music, your eyes were closed, your face so sad. And then you walked beside me on the street and your eyes were first shy and then sparking with anger. We sat in that little tea shop and I thought, even then, my God, I have never met a woman like this. I already had a kind of premonition that my peace of mind was gone. And how right I was. When I set foot in England again, when I came to London, I kept thinking: I'll see her soon, I'm bound to see her and I must expect nothing. But when I did, it was like a door flung open. Yes, it's the same, I thought, nothing's changed. I love her. I *love* her.'

I allowed myself to touch his face; brow, cheekbone, lip and I kissed the palm of his hand. My chin was propped on my fist, our foreheads almost touched. The minutes ticked away.

'But I'm engaged to marry Daniel,' I said finally. 'I promised him.'

'It's not too late, if you love me.'

But it was too late. My affair with Nicholas had brought me such joy and such suffering. And now he was back, tearing me to shreds again, surging in and out of my life, demanding so much. Could yet one more terrible wrong lead to right?

He must have seen the torment in my face because he said, 'No, I see. I can't ask that of you. I am in love with all that you are, and it would break you, I think, to go back on your word.'

We sat a few minutes longer until it was he who had courage to push back his chair, walk to the counter and pay the bill. We had the attention of the woman behind the counter now, certainly we did.

We didn't speak again but as we neared the office we saw that the door had been thrown wide open and that Miss Drake was on the steps.

She was holding a slip of paper and her voice was thin and high, 'Miss Gifford, I have just received a telephone call from the police at Lavender Hill. It seems that there has been a fatality, name of Wright.'

'What can you mean?'

'Murder. There's been a murder.'

# Chapter Thirty-Eight

Nicholas offered me a lift and I sat beside him again, in those ever-dwindling moments when I could be this close to him, alone, and I had a sense of keeping catastrophe at bay for just a while longer.

Vauxhall Bridge Road was unnaturally quiet but as we crossed the river our wheels ran over the words STAY SOLID chalked in giant letters across the road and we became caught up in a slow-moving queue of vans and cars. I told him about the Wright family, the aborted domestic assault case and Robbie's appearance in court yesterday.

'I promised Robbie I'd go and see her yesterday evening. We knew there'd be trouble at home. The truth is I forgot all about it.'

'You were otherwise occupied, as I recall.'

There was the usual crowd outside the police station, including a couple of photographers, but they were motivated this time by curiosity about the murder rather than protest.

'I'll wait,' Nicholas said.

Inside I had to elbow my way through a gaggle of reporters but as soon as he spotted me the duty officer lifted the flap and let me through. 'You've taken your time. Now perhaps we can get things moving and persuade this lot to go elsewhere. Ain't they interested in the strike no more?'

'I don't really know why I'm here,' I told him. 'Wright hates me and I'm not prepared to represent him if that's what he wants.'

'She's been goin' on about you all morning. She said you was bound to stand up for her. She says you'll know all about why she done it.'

'*She*? Who do you mean? I thought Mrs Wright was dead. My secretary . . .'

'It's not Mrs Wright what's dead. It's her husband. She killed him.'

'So *she's* all right?'

'For now she is, but you'll have to put up a pretty good fight to keep her from swinging. She stabbed him with a kitchen knife. *Three* times.'

He passed me over to the gaoler who plucked a key from the ring at his waist and unlocked the door of an interview room where Mrs Wright was seated on a bench wearing the same hat, an unforgiving shade of orange, in which she'd met me for tea at Lyons. The little I could see of her face was deathly pale.

'Ah,' she said, and a shudder ran the length of her body.

The door was left open, the officer retreated and I sank down, put my arm about her thin shoulders and held her. She neither resisted nor responded except to subside against me as if I'd toppled her off balance. Her black overcoat sagged open over a faded floral dressing gown and her feet were clad in a pair of ancient tartan slippers, the right toe of which was ominously stained a dark, reddishbrown. Her bitten fingernails were black beneath the nails.

'Have they not allowed you to wash?' I asked, turning over her clammy right hand and studying the palm which was also ingrained with a rust-coloured stain.

Her teeth were chattering and it was a while before she could speak. 'Not yet. Different people keep coming in to look at me. They want to know why I done it. I think they'll want to ask questions now you're here.'

'Let me see your face.'

Gripping the brim much too tightly she lifted off her hat. Under her crushed hair her forehead was disfigured by a massive bruise, so raw that in places the skin was broken and beaded with blood. But it was a defiant face for all its pummelling; the one fully open eye was bright, almost feverish. Before yesterday I might have been more shocked by her wound; now violence seemed to have become the order of the day.

'Did the police take a photograph of this bruise?' I asked.

'I haven't taken my hat off since I been here.'

'Have you any other injuries from last night?'

'I told the policeman I wouldn't show him where he hurt me.

273

They said a doctor would come and make me take my clothes off. I don't want that.'

'I'm assuming that you got that head injury last night?'

'Oh yes.'

'Mrs Wright, Harriet, isn't it . . .?'

'Hetty. They call me Het.'

'I must see the other wounds before they fade and so must the police. We need to prove to everyone that you had to save yourself by stabbing your husband. I'll stay with you all the time but we must get someone to make a record of what he did to you.'

At last she loosened the dressing gown under the coat and un-buttoned the nightgown beneath. I noticed further spots of blood on the yoke – the police had been very lax to let her go on wearing it. There was a livid diagonal mark across her thin belly from rib to hip and another on her left breast above the nipple. After further persuasion she showed me a new bruise on her buttock and then, with reluctant hand, raised the hem of her nightdress up and up until I saw the savage imprint of fingermarks at the top of her thighs.

'He come home more drunk than usual,' she told me in a whis-per. 'It were because of Robbie being put inside that he were in a rage. He blamed me for winding up the lad about the strike. I tried to keep him off, but it's difficult with the children asleep in the room next door. I've found over the years that it's best to be quiet and let him do his business but it does hurt, you know, be-cause he's very big and when I'm frightened it's . . .' She gave me a shy, apologetic look as if this was all too rude to mention. 'Oh it does hurt, Miss Gifford. It tears me. Sometimes he drops off straight after but last night he weren't satisfied and dragged me downstairs. I banged me head on the wall at the bottom.'

'Let me be clear,' I said, barely able to control my voice. 'Your husband raped you last night.'

'Rape? Oh no. He's my husband.'

Of the two of us, she was the more matter-of-fact. Her injur-ies and all that she had endured while I was at the hospital with Nicholas were so terrible that I could hardly bear to go on ques-tioning her.

'All right. So afterwards he made you go downstairs. Why?'

'He always takes me downstairs so that he can do it without the children hearing.'

'What weapon did he use?'

'A leg off his own chair. It's loose. Comes off easy. He done it before – turned the chair upside down and wrenched the leg out of its socket.' She bit her lower lip and shuddered again. 'I seen it coming, but I couldn't stop it.'

I gave her a few moments. 'So he beat you with the chair leg. What happened then?'

Pause. 'It's hard to remember exactly. I keep the sharp knife on the mantel because the little ones always have their fingers in the kitchen drawer. I got hold of it and jabbed him.' She stared at me in horror. 'It were in the throat. The blood, it were everywhere.'

'Can you say why you stabbed him in the throat?'

Another long silence. 'I don't know. It was where I could reach. I weren't thinking about it.'

'What did you do next?'

'I done it again. Twice more. Even though I'd jabbed him so hard, and the blood was pumping, I thought he would keep coming back at me.' There was a kind of lurid relish in the way she described this, as if she were reliving the horror from a safe distance.

'So you admit to stabbing him three times?'

'That's it. Three times. After that I didn't know what to do so I sat tight.' She fiddled with a tie of her dressing gown while we both perhaps reflected on how still the Wright kitchen must have been in that moment, with the children asleep upstairs, the fire out and the dead man on the floor. 'Then Trudy come in. She were very late home, all dressed up. She come in through the back door as usual and found me with the knife in me lap. She were very shocked. She shouted at me, "What happened? What were you thinking of, Mother?" Then I told her she should get them kids out the front and into the neighbours so they wouldn't see nothing and then go to the police.'

'Did she do all that?'

'She did. Except they say she didn't go herself but sent the boy next door for the police. She were in too much of a state. I couldn't get any sense out of her. I didn't see her again.'

There was a tread of heavy boots in the corridor, the rumble of male voices.

'The police are coming to interview you now,' I said. 'We must insist on having your injuries photographed as soon as possible. There's one other really important question they're bound to ask. Why did you stab your husband last night when he'd been beating you for years? What was different this time?'

She put her bloodstained hand on mine, suddenly much more sure of herself. 'I been wondering about that. What I think is, it was when I had tea with you, dear. You give me the courage.'

I stared at her. 'But you didn't come to court when they arrested him.'

'Court was no good, like Trudy said. I knew that even if they put him inside for mebbe a few weeks he'd come out raging all the more.'

'Listen, you don't need to say anything in the interview if you don't want to. You can keep quiet for the time being.'

'Oh, I'll say I done it and I'll say why. I don't mind.' Her manner was utterly changed, her thin face flushed and determined. 'The one I do worry about is Robbie. I'll write him a letter, when they let me, but would you go see him first? It would be best if he heard it from you.' She looked at me with the old dogged devotion, and added, 'You look in a right old state, dear. What you been doing to yourself?'

When a police officer came, heavy-bellied and grim-faced, she stood up and faced him, eager to do right like a dutiful schoolgirl.

A couple of hours later I emerged from the police station to find the sun had come out. Nicholas was leaning on the bonnet of his car, apparently immersed in a copy of *The British Worker* which he tossed aside immediately to open the door for me. Once inside, the warmth of the interior enclosed me and it all came flooding back – how we had sat in the greasy spoon and he'd told me he loved me.

I looked away from him, out of the window. 'It was *she* – Mrs Wright – who'd asked to see me. She killed him. She stabbed him three times.'

'So I gather. I've been talking to reporters.'

'It took ages because I insisted the doctor make a list of her injuries. I suppose the best hope is to try to get them to accept a plea of manslaughter.'

'Three stab-wounds in the throat?' Had I been less preoccupied and worn out I might have reacted to the way he so quickly assumed an interrogatory stance. 'Very tricky. Have you thought about justifiable homicide? I was wondering if she could plead not guilty to murder, if she was in fear of her life, though it's a very difficult one to argue ... and *three* stab wounds ...'

'I asked the officer if I could go to the house and see what happened for myself.'

He turned the key in the ignition. My hands felt cold despite the heat of the car.

'She took off her clothes, Nicholas, to show the doctor. Hardly an inch of her body was unmarked, either with old bruising or fresh wounds. And the police doctor was so harsh. He started with her feet and dictated a list.'

Worst of all had been the dispassionate way in which he'd taken a tape measure to the stripes across Mrs Wright's buttocks and had made her lie on the bench and spread her legs so that he could examine the inflammation of her genitals and upper thighs while she clenched her jaw and averted her gaze.

At the Wrights' house a crowd was being kept at bay by a couple of uniformed police officers. Once I'd shown my card and a chit from the detective constable at Lavender Hill I was allowed through, Nicholas following. The front door was on the latch and we walked down the hall to the kitchen, which was crowded with two further officers who were taking measurements and examining the furniture for fingerprints. I might have saved them the trouble by telling them we were not going to dispute Hetty Wright's involvement in the killing. The only chair with arms, Wright's, was askew because the fourth leg, about three inches in diameter, had been wrenched out of its socket. The hearth, as I'd noticed before, was of painted metal, the old-fashioned type with a range and a mantel at shoulder height. Certainly, if that's where the knife had been stored, along with the clutter of teapot, empty vase, decorative plates and a blue jug with a white glazed interior, the younger children couldn't have reached it, at least without climbing on to a chair. A drawer containing cutlery was half open under the table.

Nicholas and I stood side by side and I remembered how, as we waited in the hospital, we had been so close that I had felt the slow beat of his heart against my cheek. The room was more sharply defined because he was there. Although the body had been removed, there were other gruesome reminders of the killing – a pool of blood had seeped into the bare floorboards, chairs were overturned and a knife with a chipped bone handle, presumably the murder weapon, lay on a cloth on the table beside the missing chair leg. The argument in court would come down to this: the bloodstained blade of a cheap kitchen knife versus a chunk of wood.

'Where are the children?' I asked.

'They've been taken next door.'

'And the oldest girl, the witness?'

'She's also with the neighbour. She's very shocked.'

'May I speak to her?'

'She's not fit.'

We glanced into the Wrights' scullery, which consisted only of a sink, a high window, a draining board and a couple of shelves containing an assortment of bowls, washing materials and a pottery jug for utensils including a wooden spoon, ladle and a vegetable knife. The door to the backyard was shut.

'May we look upstairs?' asked Nicholas.

The staircase was steep and uncarpeted with faded paint on each side of the treads. There were three rooms on the first floor, the front, occupied by the parents' double bed, a middle room in which were crammed two unmade beds, one with a pillow at either end, and a third with a single pillow which I presumed to be Robbie's, and beyond that a box room occupied by Trudy, judging by the hairbrush and lidless lipstick on the little chest of drawers. On the shiny pink bedspread was a heap of clothes – stockings, a black dress with fringing on the skirt, a creased slip and on the floor a pair of flimsy evening shoes with satin bows.

As Nicholas lifted the clothes one by one, the cheap fabric hung in his long fingers. The dress had a stain on the bodice, dried so that the material had gone hard and the slip, hanging from his fingers by a narrow strap, was forlorn and stained with blood near the hem. We both stared at it for some moments. It exuded a faint perfume. Next he picked up the stockings and we saw other dark splashes on the lower legs. Finally he replaced everything much as it had been before and when he turned to me I saw in his eyes the consciousness of what had been endured here, in this house.

The marital bedroom was furnished with a wardrobe and dressing table in cheap veneer and a couple of chairs upon which were heaped an assortment of children's clothes. The quilt on the bed had been pulled to one side and the sheet, worn so thin that the stripe of the mattress could be seen beneath it, had been half torn from the bed. Tucked under the pillow was a book with a pale blue cloth cover. The police officer nodded when I asked if I might pick it up. It was by Thomas à Kempis, *The Imitation of Christ*, and fell open on a page which began:

*Blissful is he whom truth herself teacheth not by figures or voices but as it is.*

# Chapter Thirty-Nine

On the way back to Arbery Street Nicholas and I spoke only of what we had seen in the house.

'Walter Rickard is the best young criminal barrister I know,' said Nicholas. 'You'll need someone very sharp.'

'The blood on Trudy's stockings and dress . . .' I said. 'She must have knelt over the body, poor thing. She was very loyal to her father, even though she recognised what he was like. There must have been so much blood.'

'Do you know how long there was between each stab wound?'

'Mrs Wright said one straight after the other. She said he kept coming at her, he wouldn't stop.'

'Straight after the other. Are you sure?'

But I wasn't paying attention. We had arrived outside the office with shocking speed and sat side by side, not looking at each other. I didn't know how I would force myself out of the car but I found that I'd opened the door and was standing on the pavement. Leaning forward I saw that the long night had taken its toll on him too – I had never seen him so unshaven, red-eyed, unkempt. I knocked my palm once on the car roof and closed the door. By the time I'd reached the top step he had driven away.

My bicycle was parked in the hallway and Miss Drake emerged from her office.

'Really, Miss Gifford, I hope you're not intending to leave that vehicle there. It constitutes a considerable hazard. A couple of urchins delivered it half an hour ago. And these.' She held up my briefcase as if it were emitting a bad smell, and my hat, very crushed.

I gave her Annabel's address in Kingston and told her to let them know that I intended to visit on Thursday morning, then I manoeuvred Grandmother's bicycle, which was sound save for a bent mudguard but suddenly seemed to weigh half a ton, out of the door, released my arm from its sling so that I could balance and set off for Pentonville.

Fortunately I was known by the officer at the gate but it was half an hour before Robbie could be brought from his cell. Meanwhile the prison rattled and slammed about me and I sat in a daze of exhaustion and pain, listening for Robbie's steps in the corridor. Clutching my damaged arm to my breast I drifted again through the suffering and joy of the past day and night.

Footsteps, a jangle of keys, a clang as the door was thrown back and there stood Robbie in his prison clothes, very slight, with the pallor induced by the prison about him and the sheen of coal dust faded from his skin. Already, like so many other prisoners I'd visited, he looked as if something vital had been taken away. Expectation flared in his eyes when he saw me. He seemed as nervous as a colt.

'Why have you come?' he asked. 'Are they letting me go?'

'I wanted to tell you myself . . . I'm afraid I have very shocking news. Your father's dead, Robbie.'

His eyes darted to the gaoler as if he might deny or confirm my words but he fiddled impassively with the keys at his waist.

'What do you mean?' he said.

'There was a terrible scene. Your mother killed him, with a knife.'

'No. No! You're mad to say so.'

'She had to defend herself from him.'

He was unflinching. 'She never could. She wouldn't. Stab someone? What knife?'

'Robbie.' I touched his hand but he jolted away, electric with disbelief.

'Tell me again.'

I told him one more time, quietly, while he fixed me with his hounded eyes and shook his head. 'No,' he said. 'She wouldn't.'

'She was sitting with the knife on her lap when Trudy found her.'

'Found her?'

'Trudy was out. She came in too late.'

'But Trudy's usually home by eleven. Oh, this is all my fault. How was Mother when you went to see her yesterday? What did she say when you told her I'd been be sent to prison?'

I had known the question would come; I had felt it surging towards me. 'Trudy told them about it. I couldn't go, Robbie. There was a riot at a factory and I was involved. I had to take a child to hospital. I was injured too.'

His eyes flicked to the sling. He nodded twice. 'I don't know what I feel. Where is Mother now? Is she all right?'

With heavy heart I realised that he had not registered the implications of what had happened. 'They've arrested her.'

'Why?'

'You know why.'

He leaned towards me. 'Tell me. *Tell* me.'

'She's accused of murder. She will have to stand trial.'

He sank into a chair and his head went down. He groped for my hand, clenching it so hard I thought the joints would crack.

'Save her, Miss Gifford. Please save her.'

# Chapter Forty

Mrs Wright was adamant that she did not wish me even to try for bail. She said there was no one she knew who could pay the surety, and she seemed to think that, in the end, she would be set free because it was self-defence. The crowds, crammed into public and press benches and fired up by the prospect of glimpsing a murderess, were therefore doomed to an anticlimactic five-minute hearing on Wednesday morning.

When the prisoner was brought up to the dock she wore her habitual oversized hat, which unfortunately concealed her injuries. Although her supporters called in low voices, 'Eh, Het, over here. You keep your chin up, love . . .' she paid them no attention but concentrated all her energy on what was being said to her.

'Your name,' intoned the clerk.

'Harriet Wright.'

'What was your maiden name, Mrs Wright?'

'McNamara.'

'Date of birth?'

'Eleventh October 1886.'

'Mrs Wright, you are charged that on the night of Monday, 10 May or very early in the morning of Tuesday, 11, that is between the hours of eleven o'clock, when your husband was seen returning to the house, and two in the morning when your daughter Gertrude came home, you did unlawfully kill your husband, Edward Wright, with malice aforethought, by stabbing him three times in the throat with a kitchen knife kept ready for that purpose and concealed on the mantelpiece. How do you plead?'

Her eyes glinted as she responded to my mouthed instruction. 'Not guilty, Your Honour.'

There was a collective intake of breath and the magistrate raised a quizzical eyebrow. The case was listed for committal and Mrs Wright was taken down. When she'd gone, there was a buzz of excited conversation and I sensed that although many of those present had been sympathetic to the defendant, who had looked very small and harmless in her heavy coat, few believed that she could possibly be found innocent of murder.

In the cells afterwards she behaved with composure, though up close I could see she was trembling. 'How's my boy?' was her first question. 'Does he blame me?'

'Of course he doesn't blame you. He knows what his father was like. But he's worried about you.'

She nodded. 'He's a good boy. I hate to make him anxious.'

She was being treated pretty well in Holloway, she said, and would rather I didn't arrange for Trudy to visit her – she was looking after the children, and already had too much on her plate. 'And I don't want you going over there to see her neither,' she insisted. 'That Trudy ain't fond of you any more Miss Gifford. Best leave her alone.'

'She'll be called as a witness so I will need to speak to her.'

'Don't have her as a witness.' She gripped my hand with her work-worn fingers. 'I don't want to put her through that. She didn't see nothing. Only the blood afterwards and him dead on the floor.'

'We'll need her to talk about the state you were in when she found you. You see when I visited the house I noticed bloodstains on Trudy's clothes. I was just wondering how they got there.'

'There was blood everywhere. What do you expect? I couldn't believe the blood when I done it. Oh please, Miss Gifford, don't let that poor girl have to relive it all!' She put her hand to her mouth and her eyes filled with horror. When I asked another question she shook her head and went on shaking it from side to side as if she had simply run out of words.

By the time I emerged people were running along the pavement, waving newspapers, and there was an excitable pinging of bells as other cyclists overtook me. Outside Euston Station I pulled up at a stall selling copies of *The British Worker* and read the headline:

'General Council Satisfied That Miners Will Now Get A Fair Deal'.

The strike, it seemed, was over.

Having padlocked the bicycle to the railings outside the office, I found that Daniel had re-materialised at last and was yelling, 'Is that you, Miss Gifford?' through his half-open door. He was rocking on his heels before a blazing fire, the radio had been pushed to one side and his desk was laden with documents. Even his sartorial neatness had been undone by the last few days; his suit needed a brush and his hair was not as trim as usual. The relief of actually being in his company – of registering how familiar he was, how *Breen-like*, was tempered by my memory of those hours with Thorne.

With both hands extended he kicked shut the door, drew me into the centre of the room and turned my face to the light. 'Miss Drake said you'd been hurt.'

'Just a clout on my shoulder. Outside the Shawcross factory.'

'Did you make a statement? Did they arrest anyone?'

'I made a statement but they weren't interested. I'm sure it won't be taken further.'

'We'll chase that up. I have missed you so.' He studied my face lovingly. 'This blasted strike. And after all this pain, all the sacrifices we've made, the unions have called it off.'

'Isn't that a good thing?'

The searchlight of his attention swung away from me; he dropped into his chair and glowered.

'It is a total fiasco. I spent the entire weekend trying to make them see sense. They'd got it into their heads that union leaders would be arrested for incitement or that union funds could be frozen. I told them that any such gestures would be illegal but they were running scared and wouldn't listen.'

'Is that why they called off the strike? Out of fear?'

'Oh, there are numerous reasons. The government has played a clever hand. In the end I think the unions were duped into believing concessions would be made whereas none have been. The miners are still on strike. There are no undertakings from the government that strikers won't be victimised by their employers. It's a mess.' He scrambled to his feet again, dashed across and kissed my hand. 'And all this while I have left you high and dry. You've had a terrible time of it – and now I hear that your Mrs Wright has got herself into very deep water.' Leading me to my customary chair he sat beside me, pressing my hand between his and occasionally raising it to his lips. 'How did it go this morning? Did they accept a plea to manslaughter?'

My feelings were as volatile as his – one minute I felt wracked with confusion and guilt, the next, cherished, happy.

'Justifiable homicide, is what we're going for.'

'What on earth do you mean?'

'I shall say that Mrs Wright had no choice but to kill her husband.'

'But she stabbed him three times with a kitchen knife, as I understand. There has to be entirely proportionate use of force to plead justifiable homicide and no premeditation. Even manslaughter would be a pretty long shot. Do you really think you can argue self-defence?'

'I shall try.' I was irritated now, that he seemed to be questioning my judgement.

'But if you fail she will hang for murder. Curse this strike. I should have been there to support you. Well, it's not too late to get the charge changed. I shall be at the next hearing.' He spoke with infinite tenderness, 'Are you sure you want to continue with this case? I'd understand if you felt it was all too much.'

'No, no. She's relying on me.'

'Then you and I must arrange a meeting with the prosecutor and get the charge altered. I obviously need you to fill me in on all the facts but in a domestic situation, when the likes of Mrs Wright has had years and years to respond to her husband's brutality, and suddenly chooses a night when a kitchen knife happens to be to hand . . . No, it must be manslaughter at best.'

'I will obviously give what you've said a great deal of thought but at the moment I'll stick with justifiable homicide.'

His tone was gentler yet and quite unlike the usual scepticism he employed when faced with a ludicrous argument. 'You said you felt guilty about Mrs Wright, Evelyn, that you felt responsible.

You're not responsible, but you certainly mustn't let your feelings get in the way of your judgement.'

I was seething now. 'This has nothing to do with my feelings. It's to do with what's right. I don't understand you. It was kill or be killed with Mrs Wright.'

He was silent a moment, then asked, 'Is this what Thorne advised? I gather he was here when you heard the news about the murder.'

'He was able to drive me to visit Mrs Wright in the cells and he thinks pleading not guilty is the only way to proceed.'

'Oh well then, if Thorne says so, it must be right.'

'Whatever else I think of him, I know he has a good instinct for winning a case.'

'He knows nothing about crime. He deals almost exclusively with business. Have you thought about that?'

On the surface, this spat was no different to others we'd had over the years. Wolfe managed our Daniel Breen by skimming along on his own quiet trajectory, ignoring any injunctions or instructions he didn't like but never overtly contradicting them. I, being less slippery, had frequently come up hard against Breen's somewhat adversarial style and emerged from his office battered only to find that all had been forgotten by the next day, and that he'd come round to a different point of view. Indeed, usually I had enjoyed our little fights. This time he was silent, then looked me in the eye.

'I will support any decision you make, of course I will. You have some difficult times ahead and I've been neglecting you. Whenever I can, I will be there in future to back you up.'

But as I left the office I still felt angry and somewhat vertiginous. I'd always relied on Daniel's guidance – even at times when I'd fundamentally disagreed with him I had trusted his judgement. But twice recently, in the case of Lady Petit and in this weightier matter of Mrs Wright's murder trial, he had backed down. We both seemed to be floundering because of love.

# Chapter Forty-One

The Shawcross family home backed on to a golf course and was a sprawling, newly built house in red brick within much older, mossy walls, which must have marked the boundary to the original maltings. Judging by the neat maid who answered the door and the sight of a gardener's stooped back hanging over a border on the far side of the front drive, this household paid its minions well enough to be unaffected by the servant crisis. In the morning room sunshine poured through modern latticed windows, the garden was bright with spring blooms and beyond the striped lawn a couple of golfers were deep in conversation on the green, one sporting a daffodil-yellow jersey.

Mrs Shawcross received me warily but, perhaps, with less hostility than she had shown before. I was very formal and said my journey, by taxicab, had been uneventful, and no, my arm, still in its sling, was not painful. We then stood in silence while the maid went upstairs to check whether Annabel was awake.

'How is your granddaughter?' I asked at last.

'Oh, she's a sweet girl.' Suddenly dropping her veneer she added, much more warmly, 'I will say this for you, Miss Gifford, you are being very thorough as my daughter's representative. My husband told me that you visited his factory by bicycle,' she glanced a little nervously at my sling, 'and your journey here today can't have been easy.' I wondered what account of events at the factory Shawcross had given her but she continued, 'If you happened to be on my side, that's a quality I would certainly applaud.'

Eventually I was shown up a flight of plushly carpeted stairs by a maid whose neat rear was clothed in a morning uniform of soft grey cotton. No wonder poor Annabel had been so keen to escape into marriage, however ill-fated. Life in this house was overheated and muffled and there was no sign at all that three-year-old Annice was staying here. The bedroom was full of flesh-coloured lilies, so pungent they made me sneeze, and on the kidney-shaped dressing table was a marble statuette of a naked girl bearing an urn. The dog nuzzled in to one side of its mistress, its snout resting on her arm. On the other, propped against pillows with her legs stuck out before her, Annice was turning the pages of a book. Lady Petit wore a cream satin negligee with an intricate lace trim and had managed to apply eye make-up, though the rest of her face was ashen. An attendant nurse sat on a chair by the window holding a small, circular embroidery frame up to the light.

I refused coffee. The lilies, I knew, would soon make my head ache and the bedroom, with its overwhelming scents and wash of diffused light, was far too warm. The maid drew me up a chair and I took out my notebook. The dog resumed its sleep but mother and child gazed at me from near-identical greenish eyes. Their hair had clearly been coiffed by the same hand, though the mother's was much finer and lay smooth whereas Annice's was wavy.

When I smiled at Annice she did not smile back.

'They told me you were coming,' Annabel said in a small, exhausted voice, 'but I said there was absolutely no point since I've made up my mind to back down and do what Timmo wants. Good Lord, what have you done to your arm?'

'Just a sprain. I'll tell you about it later. May I look at what you're reading?' I asked Annice.

Obediently she pushed the book towards me; an ancient volume with cardboard covers and the unpromising title of *Bunny Fluffkin*.

'Which is your favourite picture?' I asked.

The little girl's bobbed hair fell forward as she turned the pages.

'She doesn't just like the pictures, she likes words,' said Annabel, caressing her daughter's cheek.

'Is this your wedding?' I picked up a silver-framed photograph of Annabel and her husband in their wedding outfits, pictured outside St George's Hanover Square. It was the clearest image I'd seen yet of Petit; his eyes were a little too wide set and his cheeks were sunken as if he did not eat enough. His mouth was distinctive, being full-lipped and rather too large and his top hat was set back rakishly on his fair hair.

'He *is* stunningly handsome,' said Lady Petit. 'You can see why I fell for him.'

Lady Petit's bridal gown had a tulip-shaped skirt falling to a foot or so above her ankles. Her little face reached no higher than her husband's upper arm and was framed by a half-halo of stiff lace and a long veil. The couple flashed smiles into the camera like film stars. I looked first at the photograph, then again at Annice.

'She's very like her father,' I said. The resemblance lay in the wide mouth and the slightly protuberant forehead.

'Do you think so? Everyone always used to say she takes after me, but just lately, as her face has thinned down, she has more the look of him.'

'Could you spare me just a few minutes alone?'

'Listen, darling Annice, Mummy has to talk to this nice lady now, so you run along.' The pair exchanged kisses so fervent that the dog was disturbed and had to resettle itself, the nursemaid held out her hand and the little girl reluctantly scrambled off the bed.

When she had gone and we were alone I drew my chair closer as Annabel had subsided into the pillows with the back of her hand over her eyes.

'Lady Petit, you do realise that if you agree to your husband's terms you'll lose Annice?'

'Oh, don't be so harsh. They've all explained to me again and again that I won't really be losing her and I'll be allowed to see her often.' She thrust her head further back so that blue veins were exposed in her white throat and her voice became even more gravelly than usual. 'I didn't want you to come here because I knew you'd argue with me. Daddy is so clear that we should do as Timmo says, and Kit is too.'

'When did you last see Kit?'

'She drove down at the weekend because she wanted to tell me all about the strike. She said I wasn't really missing much but she was lying, and now I hear it's over so I'll never get another chance to be in the police. She said the most important thing is for me to be well. Settle this once and for all, she said, it won't be as bad as you think. She brought me those flowers and this compact. Look, so pretty. It's by Lacloche Frères, would you believe? She always brings the right thing. She just lay beside me on the bed and was so lovely and made me think clearly about it all.'

'What else did she say?'

'She said Annice would have to go to court to be looked at and did I really want that? She said that I was gambling with my own life and Annice's and that if Timmo wins in court I will lose everything.'

She plucked at the sheet and looked nervously at the door, as if Kit might appear at any minute with further reproofs. The more time I spent with her the more I realised how very dosed up she was on some concoction of drugs or other, and that I was by no means equipped to tell whether she was in her right mind.

'You must be sure you've made the best decision, Lady Petit,' I said.

'I'm beyond making decisions.'

'Don't say that. Remember how strong you've been in the past. What about when you worked at the factory? When I talked to some of the men there, they said how much they liked you and how you were great fun.'

She rolled on to her side so that her body was cupped round the greyhound, one thin hand supporting her chin and the other stroking its back. 'You went to the factory?'

'As a matter of fact I got involved in a bit of a brawl – that's how I hurt my arm.'

As I'd hoped, her peculiar glassy eyes showed more of a spark.

'Lucky you! Oh, I wish I'd been there. The men were all such darlings to me. Those were my best days, apart from when I was with Richie.'

'Quite a lot has happened over the past couple of weeks, Lady Petit. Mr Leremer says he will now appear as a witness to testify that Annice is not his daughter. And, as you know, your husband, for some reason, has said he will accept paternity under certain conditions – we think this has weakened his cause. What I'm saying is that you would have a strong case in court.'

She received my words as if they were little smacks that pained her too much to be borne.

'Don't go on at me. What's the use? I've made up my mind. I told you that in the note Daddy and I wrote. I don't want to go to court. I want it settled.'

'So you wish me to tell Pearman, your husband's solicitor, that you agree to his terms after all? That Annice will live with your husband and you will see her several times a year?'

'Then everyone will be happy. Kit and Timmo and Annice and Mummy and Daddy.'

'Are you sure about Annice? She obviously loves you very much. How would she feel if you lived apart from her?'

'I'm no good to her. That's what they say. It's all wrong for her to see me like this.' With an immense sigh she seemed to fall asleep.

The lilies had done their damage and a headache hovered on my brow so I went to the casement window and flung it open. The sun was out for once and the shadow of a cloud chased across the manicured lawn. Beyond enthusiastic birdsong I heard the faintest thwack of a golf iron on a ball. There were other photographs of Annabel besides her wedding picture, including one of herself, brilliant-eyed, leaning winsomely towards the camera and holding the infant Annice whose billowing christening robes poured over her mother's feet.

I didn't want to leave her. I imagined how it would feel to be her, weak and nauseous, lying in the bed listening to my retreating footsteps, to the closing of the front door, and then only birdsong again. Reach for the bromide, Annabel, I thought, they have you now. But I had no reason to stay.

After I'd closed the window and actually tiptoed to the door she said, with great effort, as if her mouth were full of treacle, 'Thank you, Miss Gifford, you have been very kind.'

'I have just tried to do my job, Lady Petit.'

'Do you think I could have won?'

'I don't know.' I paused. 'The barrister who would have represented your husband is a very powerful advocate: Nicholas Thorne.'

She opened her eyes. 'I know him slightly. He's a nice man. Oh yes, isn't he the one who ... Kit told me you'd had a love affair with him. Is that right?'

'It is. I didn't know until recently that he had been instructed by your husband's solicitor but of course I would have discussed it with you had the case gone ahead – you might have felt there was a conflict of interest.'

For the first time she was fully awake. 'Lady Curren and Kit, they both said that if the rumours were true he must have lost his senses when he fell in love with you. It was one of the reasons I was so curious to meet you. But you were the one who ditched him in the end, isn't that right? Why?'

'There were complicated reasons.'

'Did you love him?'

Those huge eyes were remorseless as mirrors. 'Yes ... I loved him. Very much.' I paused. Finally I had got her to engage with me. 'But I don't ... I didn't trust him.'

She raised herself on an elbow. 'Why on earth not? He was engaged to marry Sylvia Hardynge. She's stunningly beautiful and worth a fortune and yet he gave her up for you.'

Her eyes were so mesmerising and the fact that I was building a bridge, coupled with my desire to confide in someone, made me rash.

'It was complicated, he was so ambitious. You see when we first met he pretended it was by chance. He even researched my dead brother's war record in order to win my trust.'

'But he gave up everything for you. Wasn't that enough to convince you he was in earnest? It would be for most women. Perhaps you didn't love him as much as you thought.' She flopped back on to the pillows.

'Oh, I *did* love him, so much,' I protested. 'But he let me down very badly. Either way, I'm engaged to marry someone else now.'

In the overheated room the lilies gaped at me with their crude pink petals. Annabel had closed her eyes again.

'Well, as long as you know what you're doing. Don't, for heaven sake, make the same mistake as me. I was very much in love with Richie – he's the only man I've ever truly loved. When I was with him I just felt so *right*. And excited, and happy. Myself, in fact. I wanted to be with him all the time. Then Timmo came on the scene and everyone was so pleased that I'd chosen him.'Tears were spilling between her closed lids. 'When I got back from honeymoon and I needed Richie, he did come, and he did look after me, but he wouldn't make love to me because he said I was married and he didn't want to make me unhappier than I already was. That proves he loves me, doesn't it? Otherwise he would have just taken what he could get.' There was another long silence. 'What would you do if you were me, Miss Gifford?'

I sat down on the bed and grasped her thin shoulder.

'I can't tell you what I would do, Lady Petit. Especially since you're quite right, I can't always see clearly for myself. But I do know one thing. I might have given up a lover, but I could never give up my own child. Perhaps I would say to myself: they've got me in a corner. If I go along with what my husband wants then I shall have no Annice and no marriage. If I put up a fight there's a strong possibility that my husband will win his case but even if he did, I would not lose my child.'

'So you would fight it.'

'Yes, I would fight.'

She rolled on to her back and flung an arm behind her head, smiling, transformed.

'Go on then, let's do it!'

# Chapter Forty-Two

In the aftermath of the strike, mail arrived in fits and starts but at last a packet plunked into the dingy Pimlico hallway, postmarked Sanary-sur-Mer and dated 1 May. Meredith had included a picture by Edmund, on lined paper torn from an exercise book, of a row of narrow houses crayoned orange and yellow. In the foreground was a dark blue sea, complete with sailing boat. She had also, at what must have been crippling expense, included a postcard-size portrait of a woman in a brown dress and quaint cap, shawl and apron, seated on a low stool, trimming green beans. Meredith's style of painting had become even more impressionistic than before, but the overwhelming mood of her picture was one of tranquil light, soft brown shade and slow, considered activity. The same woman might have sat in the shadow of that same porch for five hundred years.

Though her tone was cheerful, overall I sensed disappointment that the art world had not yet turned up in Sanary.

*Most people seem to be just passing through, although there are several Italian newcomers who can't stand being in Italy where they feel they are in danger from Mussolini and the fascists. People, they say, have a habit of disappearing in Italy at present, especially if they have a reputation for being remotely socialist. I don't like the sound of that, do you?*

*Angus has gone drifting off to Cannes; it didn't work out for him here so Edmund and I have found a little apartment tucked just back from the sea. We work on the beach if it is warm enough, or in our front room where I also sleep or, at the end of the week, when money is not so tight, in a café. I support us by teaching English to three Italian families. A new generation, therefore, will grow up with Canadian vowels.*

*But Evelyn, Evelyn, what are you up to? How is your life? Whatever you're doing or planning please come and see us first. Edmund currently has his feet buried in the sand, he's wearing the cotton sailor cap you bought him (yes, we already have a touch of warm sunshine here, and he and I are cosily ensconced on the little town beach), and he keeps saying, 'Have you written it yet? Have you told her she must come?'*

*He misses you dreadfully and has cried for you at night. Yet we are in paradise, Evelyn. A warm wind blows through the masts in the harbour and they chat away, and the awnings on the cafés rattle and the scent of fish and flowers wafts past. When the sun is out, and soon it will be out for ever, the sea is an achy blue I can never quite manage on my palette and the sky is clear and lovely. You have to come, Evelyn, just to see that there is a world other than your grey London. You can catch a train to Marseille or Toulon, either would do, and then the local train. There is not much room in our little apartment but there is a couch, and in the morning you would be able to get up and push aside the shutters and let the sun in. Beneath us, in our square, which is more of a triangle, a fountain plays and there is a shop selling all kinds of things you think people would never buy more than once in their lives, such as doorknobs and soap holders. The proprietor and Edmund have become very good friends and they sit outside together with their arms crossed, keeping an eye on things. Your nephew's French will have a Marseillaise twang, but he is nearly fluent.*

*Let me know when you are coming and he and I will start crossing off the days. We will be on the platform at dawn waiting for you on the day you arrive.*

Then her tone grew wistful again, as she admitted to being homesick, even for our Pimlico flat.

*Sometimes I look forward to washing the salt wind out of my hair once and for all. I don't seem to be able to make plans and I feel restless and useless without you and I think of you with your brows drawn together as you read one of your unintelligible tomes and you work your fingers through your hair until it stands up in a frizz and I do miss you, Evelyn. I know exactly what's got to me. Here I am among so many strangers – Germans, Italians, French from the North – who don't really know who they are either, or where they are going. And then there are the people who really live here, the fishermen and their wives, and the baker and the priest and the schoolteacher and they are all so busy. That's how I want to be. Maybe I am a shifter like these others but if I am, it frightens me. For Edmund's sake I want to become someone who has roots.*

*We both send paintings. If you think we are trying to tempt you, you'd be d----d right. That woman I have painted will spend half an hour on those beans and then serve them with a little poached rockfish for supper.*

*Come. Come. Come. Come.*

# Chapter Forty-Three

At the start of the Petit trial Daniel and I took our seats behind Burton Wainwright, who was to represent Annabel. I was spared any kind of encounter with Nicholas who was already in his place to my right at the front, so that I could see only the side of his face and the back of his wig. When he glanced round and nodded to Daniel I averted my gaze. Pearman was of course present, very sleek in his wide-lapelled suit and with a pile of neatly tagged papers.

After the jury had been sworn in and the parties called, Lady Petit entered the courtroom on her mother's arm. There was no sign of Shawcross who, we were informed, was managing the disruption from the strike at his factory. His wife wore a dismal shade of dark blue while her daughter peeked about fearfully and offered one of the two lady members of the jury the glimmer of a smile. Annabel's costume was of dove grey trimmed with lace along the hem and cuffs, and the brim of her matching hat was caught back by a silver pin wrought in the shape of a shamrock. Occasionally she stole a pleading glance at her husband, with eyes made huge by the merest hint of kohl and dark shadows formed by drugs or insomnia, but he simply ignored her.

Above medium height, lean and with silvery-blond hair, Petit had the air of one who had taken time out from other vital business and was hoping that these proceedings wouldn't go on very long. Although, in my opinion, his good looks were marred by those wide-set eyes, I did acknowledge a kind of vibrancy that drew energy from the rest of the room, evident from the way his gaze roved the court, taking us all in, the grip of his hands on the rail of the witness box and the briskness with which he responded to questions. And yes, there did seem to be more than a hint of Annice in his features.

The judge, Poynter, began in fine fettle, excited by the prospect of a high-profile trial peppered with salacious titbits. He insisted that the issue was the very narrow one of whether Petit could prove that he was not the father of Annice. If the jury found in his favour, it would follow that his wife had engaged in an adulterous liaison. We had all agreed that the press should be barred and the judge said emphatically that neither party, nor indeed the jury should think of selling the story afterwards. Furthermore, he cited the Russell Case of two years ago, and forbade the introduction of detrimental evidence from either husband or wife derived solely from marital intimacy.

Nicholas rose to his feet while Daniel leaned back in his seat beside me. I took the lid off my pen and made copious unnecessary notes.

'The Petits might be said to have been the golden couple of London,' Nicholas began quietly, 'but tragically, for reasons that will shortly be made clear to you, the marriage was never consummated. Nevertheless, when Lady Petit announced her pregnancy, Sir Timothy's disbelief was suspended by two factors. First, he was immensely excited about the prospect of becoming a father. Second, he went along with his wife's argument that Annice had actually been conceived on the journey home when they shared a first-class cabin, though we will argue that both parties had drunk so much that neither was capable of performing a sexual act, let alone remembering whether or not they had done so.'

It registered with me that this trial would be little short of torture. It wasn't just that I would be seated next to Daniel while before me, every minute, would be Nicholas Thorne, remote in wig and robe but more present to me, if possible, because he was unreachable. It was that the words he used all seemed to touch on the time we had spent together, and my desire. Did he too think of that first-class cabin on the train journey from Paris, think that if it had been us, alone on that train, what a time might we have had together? I was used to being wholly focused while in court; now I was so awash with emotion and memory that I could scarcely take in the fact that Nicholas wasn't speaking solely to me.

'Even when it became apparent that Lady Petit had no intention of giving up her extramarital activities, Sir Timothy was prepared to stand by her and the unborn child who is, incidentally, just three years old. It was only when his wife actually supplied the name of the true father that Sir Timothy's resolve finally broke down. Even then, he was prepared to accept Annice as his daughter for the little girl's sake, provided his wife would divorce him. This offer was refused. Hence these proceedings.'

The courtroom was painfully quiet; Annabel's little feet were pressed tightly together and her eyes were closed. Wainwright took a while shutting his file, drawing together the edges of his gown so that they almost met across his belly and adjusting his wig. Then he glanced at the jury as if surprised to see them, and addressed himself to the panelling above their heads.

'Members of the jury, let us be clear. Lady Petit is not going to pretend that her character before marriage was without blemish or that, in a fit of rage, under severe provocation, she did not name another man as the father of her daughter. She will, however, prove that her husband did indeed father their child on the last night of their honeymoon.

'The tragedy for Lady Petit is that she is emotionally frail and Sir Timothy has decided that such a wife does not suit an ambitious politician. The fact is, he will do anything to get a divorce, provided he emerges as the injured party – hence his recent offer to accept the child as his after all. His decision to contest paternity has nothing to do with the truth, and everything to do with the desire to rid himself of his wife.'

Nicholas protested, 'This is an outrageous slur, Your Honour.'

'You will withdraw the latter remarks, Mr Wainwright,' said Poynter.

Sir Timothy, when called, rose from his seat with some difficulty due to a pronounced limp in his left leg which reminded the jury that he had been wounded at the second battle of Ypres and was subsequently decorated. After taking the oath he rubbed the back of his hand across his eyes, perhaps to indicate that he had also recently vanquished, at considerable personal cost, the dark forces of the General Strike.

His account of the courtship accorded with Annabel's.

'I admired her because I'd already noticed, during the war, that she had a wonderful way of bringing the very best out of the female workers in her father's factory and she was so vivacious. Also, she has marvellous taste in art and I am an amateur collector so we took to visiting galleries together. And of course I found her very beautiful.'

Thorne said, 'You must forgive me if this seems a somewhat indelicate question, Sir Timothy, but did you and your wife enjoy full sexual relations before marriage?'

'No, we did not. Not for want of opportunity, but because I saw marriage as sacred. I had grown up a little, you see, and had learned that abstinence can have its own rewards.'

'What was your future wife's view of this?'

'She thought it rather odd of me.'

Thorne glanced quizzically at the jury while Annabel tilted back her head and compressed her lips to hold back tears.

'So all was well until the honeymoon?' said Thorne.

'All was well *during* the honeymoon. We had the happiest of times dashing about Paris. It was early summer and half of London had nipped across the Channel. Except . . .'

'Except?' prompted Thorne softly, as if he were addressing an innocent child.

'Except . . .' Down went Petit's head. 'Quite simply I wasn't able to . . . to love my wife as a husband should.' The jury was treated to an apologetic look. 'It might have been the drink, but really I think it was the war. Oh, there was nothing overtly physical wrong with me, although my wound was to the upper thigh, a close shave, one might say.' An appreciative smile was exchanged between Thorne and the jury. 'It was more of a mental thing. I was shot while we were raiding a wood and for years afterwards I couldn't rid myself of the image of me lying there, helpless, with all kinds of horror happening about me. Even at the most inopportune moments . . . even when making love . . .'

The jury now brimmed with compassion for this courageous, haunted man.

'My head, you see, was full of the noise and my body reverted to its old self, as if I were back in the trenches again.'

'This will be the incident for which, I believe, you received a

Distinguished Conduct Medal. Had this condition manifested itself when you were with other women, before marriage?' asked Thorne.

'No. Or at least at times it had, but I'd been inclined to ignore it or put it down to particular circumstances. But with Annabel it was no go at all, so as soon as we were back I consulted a doctor who declared that the emotional burden of the wedding and possibly the fact that we had visited France, of all places, had re-awoken the pain and rendered me . . .'

'Yes?'

'Impotent.'

'So there was no way that a child could have been conceived while you were on honeymoon.'

'No, although my wife tried to convince me otherwise. On the journey home we had again drunk far too much.'

'How much would you say you drank on that journey?'

'A couple of bottles of champagne between us as we left Paris. The Channel crossing was very rough and it was nightmarish being confined to the hot berth.'

'What were you wearing?'

'Nightclothes, of course. Pyjamas. Annabel claims that's when conception took place but I think one would know whether one had had intercourse with one's wife, especially when the whole business had become such an intolerable burden.'

'And yet you were willing to believe your wife's story about Annice's conception.'

'I confess to a degree of ignorance about women and their amazing bodies.' Petit lifted his blond head and scanned the courtroom benches as if in search of something. Eventually his gaze, with just a gleam of interest, alighted on me. 'Until finally, earlier this year, my wife told me the name of the child's real father – Richard Leremer.'

'Who is known to you as a political opponent, I believe.'

'It makes no difference who he is, surely? They'd been lovers before we were married and I suspected that their affair had resumed soon afterwards. When Annabel told me, I looked afresh at Annice and knew beyond the shadow of a doubt that she was indeed Leremer's.'

'And yet, a few weeks ago, you offered to accept the child as your own.'

'It was a foolish gesture, I admit, but I love Annice and I'm convinced that she would not have a secure childhood with Leremer and my wife. We were in the midst of a general strike, remember? Perhaps my judgement was swayed by the fact that the task I'd undertaken on behalf of the nation was to create order out of chaos, so it seemed only right to settle my private affairs in a similarly adult fashion.'

Daniel and I exchanged the swiftest of glances – the audacity of the man – while Petit added, 'Besides, Leremer has shown no sign whatever of wanting a permanent relationship with Annabel.'

Thorne lowered his voice. 'But if you love Annice so much, wouldn't the kindest thing be to drop the entire case and remain married to her mother?'

'It would not be a kindness to any of us. I have been so wounded by what has passed between us that I simply cannot go on.' His voice faltered and he seemed about to break down as he gripped the edge of the witness box. 'I was devoted to my wife and child. You see, all my life I have striven to do the right thing, to be a person who keeps his promises, who never compromises. And now I have been forced . . .'

Following this further display of emotion, Poynter felt the need to call a break and the case was adjourned for lunch.

In a more run-of-the-mill trial, the courtroom in the afternoon might have been slumberous as the sun beat through the dirty windows and on to the dusty crevices of the jury box. Wainwright's meaty fingers fumbled with his papers.

'You've told us that you first met your wife through your business relationship with her father. Could you describe the exact nature of that relationship?'

Petit looked puzzled and adjusted his stance. 'Indeed. During the war Mr Shawcross's – Annabel's father's – factory was one of the many ordered to suspend normal business in favour of manufacturing weapons. It was part of my job at the war office to draw up contracts and ensure supply kept up with demand.'

'Thank you,' said Wainwright, at his most avuncular. 'And what was your relationship with Annabel at that time?'

'Oh, I simply knew her. It was several years later that I began to fall in love with her.'

'Now, you've already told us that you had a number of love affairs prior to your engagement to Annabel Shawcross in 1922. For the benefit of the jury, perhaps you'd tell us whether at least some of these relationships were sexual, in the fullest sense of the word.'

'They were.'

'Who was Lady Petit courting – if you'll forgive the old-fashioned phrase – immediately before you proposed to her?'

'She was always surrounded by young men, but there was Richard Leremer of course.'

'So why did you propose to Annabel Shawcross?'

A broad and incredulous grin. 'Why does anyone propose to a beautiful young woman? Because I was in love with her.'

'Just asking,' said Wainwright mildly. 'What did you think of Richard Leremer?'

'I didn't think of him at all except as my political opponent – he was a backbencher with the Labour Party for a brief spell.'

'Do you know his cultural background?'

'What on earth do you mean?'

'Oh, come now, Sir Timothy. We are talking about someone upon whom this case partially rests, a man whom you specifically asked to be excluded from your daughter's life, should you continue as her father.'

Petit's expression was non-committal. 'Well, he's a Jew, of course, if that's what you mean.'

'It is indeed. I'm amazed it has taken us this long. At any rate you became engaged to marry Annabel Shawcross, snatching her, as it were, from the arms of your political rival—'

'Really, Mr Wainwright,' said Poynter.

'Forgive me. And you've told us that you refrained from indulging in sexual relations until the honeymoon. Very commendable, if I may say so, especially given that abstinence was obviously not your normal practice when in a relationship with a young woman.'

Thorne, without getting up, observed, 'I wasn't aware that anybody's moral attitude to sexual matters was on trial today.'

'Very well,' said Wainwright. 'My client accepts that intercourse did not occur during the early stages of your honeymoon, although she will say she was puzzled and upset by your apparent lack of interest. But perhaps you'd explain once more what happened on the journey home.'

'We lay together and held each other. That was all.'

'You've told us you were both wearing pyjamas. Did you touch each other intimately?'

'Of course we touched. We were sharing a narrow berth.'

'Exactly where did you touch your wife?'

'Really, I can't . . .'

'Sir Timothy, you will appreciate that this is absolutely pivotal to the case.'

'As I say, I was very drunk. I remember Bel making a very crude attempt to force herself on me . . . to stimulate me. She even taunted me. But I was exhausted. Nothing happened.'

'You see, your wife will say that she did arouse you and you did ejaculate, albeit outside her body. What would you say to that?'

'I think one would know, wouldn't one?' Petit said irritably.

'When you returned from honeymoon, relations did not resume and you embarked on your busy political life. Is that not right? But what about other aspects of your marriage? Would you describe yourself as being close to your wife?'

'Very.'

'How many parties and gatherings would you say that you and she attended together after Annice was conceived?'

'I couldn't possibly say. One or two . . .'

'Why so few?'

'She has a nervous condition.'

'Perhaps you would give the jury an example of your wife's *nervous condition*.'

'Must I?' For the first time he looked at his wife and his eyes filled with compassion. 'Very well. Last autumn we were at a cocktail party attended by many influential people. Annabel was rather drunk and towards the end of the evening, in full view of everyone, she tore off her shoes and stockings and splashed about in a fountain, shouting, "Bored, bored, bored!" She's not been invited to a function since. She's simply not been well enough. If only I had known when I married her.'

'Had known what?' demanded Wainwright.

Petit smiled regretfully. 'That she was fragile. I loved her, nothing would have dissuaded me from marrying her, but I might have had a much better understanding of how best to look after her. As it is, she has received the most expensive treatments but to no avail.'

Having taken Sir Timothy through the events leading up to Annabel's assertion that Leremer was Annice's father, Wainwright said, 'Sir Timothy, the question that everyone in this courtroom must be asking themselves is: why, if there was no way Annice could have been fathered by you, and your wife had become a political liability, did you wait until she'd named Leremer as the father before asking for a divorce?'

'Because when she did so, on that unspeakable night,' he covered his eyes with his hand, 'she was confirming what I knew in my heart to be true.'

'Is it not the case that you were perfectly willing to accept that Annice was your daughter until your wife rashly named Richard Leremer, a pacifist, a socialist and, more to the point, a Jew, as the father, choosing that name because she knew it would cause maximum irritation?'

To my right, Annabel was leaning forward and nodding passionately.

'I said before, I had my doubts . . .'

Wainwright ploughed on. 'Let's talk about one of your political sponsors, our eminent home secretary, Mr Joynson-Hicks. Perhaps you'd tell us, in open court, what are his views on foreigners and especially Jews?'

'What on earth . . .?' cried Thorne.

'Since becoming home secretary, has he not warned his critics that Jews are *the alien refuse of the world*? You are not one of his critics, are you, Sir Timothy? Would you be so kind as to read to the jury this extract from one of your own speeches of 1925?'

'This is a *paternity* case,' cried Thorne. 'I really must object.'

'But Mr Thorne,' said Wainwright, apparently astonished by the interruption, 'Sir Timothy is attempting to disinherit his own child and I'm merely striving to find out why. Here I have a speech in which he describes Jews as a threat to the purity and vitality of the British nation. Ladies and gentlemen of the jury, this case has nothing whatever to do with the paternity of Annice, but it has everything to do with a man who is both malicious and cruel to his enemies. And one of his enemies is now his wife.'

Poynter smacked the bench with his gavel. 'Mr Wainwright, I have allowed you every possible leeway but you have managed to turn a simple paternity trial into what amounts to a character assassination of one of our most respected politicians. You will not say another word unless it impinges directly on the case in hand.'

As he rose to his feet, Thorne adopted the air of pained clergyman. 'Sir Timothy, might I ask why you instigated these proceedings?'

'Because my wife admitted that I was not the father of our beloved child.'

'Did it make a difference to you when she said the actual father was Richard Leremer?'

'It made no difference. It was my wife's betrayal that broke me. And the fact that I felt such a fool for having allowed myself to be deluded into thinking I could possibly have fathered that little girl. My offer to adopt Annice as my own was foolhardy, I know, but it was done with the best of intentions, and because I am devoted to her, whoever she happens to be.'

During the latter part of the afternoon the court heard from Professor Lamming, an expert on human fertility, who stated that in his opinion, cases where a child had allegedly been conceived, as it were, without penetration, were generally normal conceptions where lovemaking had been less than satisfactory to the female party.

'Less than satisfactory?' queried Nicholas.

'The lady may scarcely be aware that anything has happened while the gentleman, I suggest, would be conscious that he had ... e-jac-u-lated.'

In other circumstances Lamming's ponderous pronunciation of each syllable would have been laughable.

'I accept that it might be unlikely, but perhaps you could tell the

307

court,' Wainwright suggested, 'whether it is *possible* for a woman to conceive even though penetration has not taken place.'

Lamming was pleased to deliver a lecture on the life expectancy of the human spermatozoa outside the human body, his conclusion being that it could only last for a few seconds.

Sir Reginald Huskington, who succeeded him, was the consultant whom Petit had visited on his return from honeymoon.

'My client,' said the bearded and emollient Huskington, 'had found, to his dismay, that he was unable to consummate his marriage.'

'For the benefit of the court,' said Nicholas smoothly, 'could you define what you mean?'

'By consummation? Isn't it obvious? He entirely lacked the capacity to make love to his wife because he was temporarily impotent. It seemed to me that he was suffering from the after-effects of his war experiences, reignited by an unfortunate choice of honeymoon destination. He and his wife had booked a holiday in Paris with no thought to the fact that this was the first time Sir Timothy had returned to France in nearly seven years. He described looking out of the train window at the fields of northern France and being wrenched back to those days when so many of his fellow officers had been killed.'

'He never said that to me,' I heard Annabel whisper to her mother.

'Such was your diagnosis,' said Wainwright. 'What was your suggested remedy?'

'My advice was that Sir Timothy should give the matter time,' said Huskington . . .

It was at this point that an usher loomed up at my elbow, bearing a folded note.

*Urgent message for Miss Gifford. Pentonville Prison. Robert Wright.*

The usher stooped down and whispered in my ear, 'Apparently the prisoner's had a bit of a turn, Miss. They telephoned your office and then here so they must be worried.'

# Chapter Forty-Four

This time I was collected from reception by a prison officer with the eyes of a patient labrador who told me that Wright had been upset by a visit from the police earlier in the day. Apparently they had been asking for clarification on a few matters regarding the death of his father. When he returned to his cell, Robbie had hurled himself about and banged his head against the wall until he'd been carried off for his own safety. The only coherent words that the guards could get out of him were that he needed to see Miss Gifford.

Inevitably he'd been locked in a padded cell and was curled on his side facing the wall. The enclosed space stank of urine and stale sweat. The officer stood in the doorway and murmured Robbie's name, holding me back with a protective arm. When there was no response I ducked round him and crouched beside Robbie.

'Robbie. They said you'd been asking for me.'

His head whipped round, revealing bloodshot eyes, deathly white skin and a bruised forehead. 'You,' he said. 'You won't look at me like that when you've heard what I done.'

'Tell me.'

It took a while for him to be coaxed off the floor and over to the bed but at last he confessed.

'They asked lots of questions about my father and how he'd treated her over the years. And then they wanted to know about the kitchen knife. They said where did she keep it? I said in a pot in the scullery. They asked was I sure, and I said of course, it was always there, on the windowsill. And when I asked why they wanted to know, they said it was a minor detail but that Mother had said she'd got it off the mantel. But it wasn't a minor detail, was it?'

I couldn't lie to him. 'It wasn't a minor detail, no.'

'So what will happen now?'

'Your mother says the knife was on the mantel, you say it was in the scullery. The point is, we don't want it to look as if your mother is lying or that she planned to kill your father by moving the knife in readiness. We are going to argue that everything happened in a second, on the spur of the moment, out of desperation. But remember your mother won't be relying solely on your evidence – there's Gertrude too. As far as I know she will say that the knife was on the mantel, and after all your sister must know the domestic routines of the house much better than you do.'

'All I ever wanted was to save her from him and now she's going to die.'

I held him. He was just a boy, thin-shouldered and tense, and after a while he began to sob, his shoulders heaving and his hot tears soaking into my jacket. I cursed the strike which had led him to this dead end. At that moment I felt as if we were both hemmed in by the unyielding machinery of the criminal justice system. A few miles away, the Petit case would have wound up for the day. So many words to uncover such a small truth; agile minds tugging the jury this way and that, and all to decide whether Annice should be allowed her father's name. Meanwhile here was this lovely boy, cornered.

Of course what Robbie had said was true. His mother, who'd had very little chance of being found not guilty before, would have virtually none at all now that her own son had contradicted her evidence. His hair, when I stroked it, was dense and matted.

The gaoler was pointing to his watch – time to go. I hated to leave Robbie in that muffled, lightless place. I remembered him in Hyde Park, lively, ardent, at the start of everything.

'What shall I say in court?' he asked.

'You must tell the truth. Always tell the truth. In the end, it's the only way.'

'And if she dies?'

I made him look at me.

'If she dies, it will be nobody's fault but your father's. She killed him because she had no choice. *We* know that, and whoever defends your mother – we're appointing someone called Mr Rickard who's very experienced in this sort of case – will seek to persuade the jury to think the same way.'

'But if it's true what you say, that she had no choice, why would she die? Why won't the jury see? We can tell them how she suffered. We can describe her bruises. You saw her in the hospital, so did a policeman. What else do they need?'

'Sometimes the law seems too rigid because it always wants proof. Perhaps a case is won by the wrong person because they had the best argument or because there's something missing from the evidence and that can seem unfair. But how else can we get near the truth? I'd rather these harsh rules, Robbie, than a law that anyone can bend. If nobody asked difficult questions, imagine what people would get away with. We know your mother isn't a murderer, but we have to prove that to a jury. We have to convince them.'

'And if we don't?'

'Then we don't. But Robbie, we won't give in easily, I promise you that.'

# Chapter Forty-Five

The next morning Daniel, who had to be at Great Marlborough Street at ten for the start of a two-day trial, informed me that after the doctor had given his evidence a couple of high-ranking witnesses had vouched for Petit's integrity. They had been shocked to realise that Leremer and Annabel had been seeing each other so soon after the latter's return from honeymoon. One even swore that once, when he'd delivered Timmo home in the small hours, he'd actually seen Leremer leave the house.

'At the moment I'd say we have a fifty-fifty chance,' Daniel murmured, 'provided Lady P. and Leremer are consistent in saying they've not been lovers since her marriage. But the jury is full of sympathy for Petit. We've not really found a chink.' We sat on one of the marble benches in the vast, mock-Gothic great hall where lawyers and clerks strode across the patterned marble floor like players on an elaborate board game.

'I must admit we could do without Thorne,' Daniel added with a droll smile. 'He's got a knack, that chap, of hitting the perfect spot – right tone, right question, right intervention.'

It disturbed me that for once I couldn't read Daniel and had no idea whether he was being ironic.

'Wrong side, though,' I said lightly.

I was off to Birmingham at the weekend with Mother and wouldn't see him until Monday, so he pressed my hand and wished me luck. I watched him pause to chat with one of the clerks at reception before waving to me – since that first time, at the station, it had become something of a ritual for him to walk away and then look back. As he turned he almost collided with Nicholas who had entered the building with his arms full of files and his gown flying. They each recovered swiftly, exchanged greetings and moved on, Nicholas scarcely acknowledging me as he swept past.

For her spell in the witness box Annabel chose blush pink, a colour that suggested both fragility and loss of innocence. Her bottom lip was raw from being gnawed between her teeth and whenever the courtroom door opened she jumped. Wainwright, huge in his rusty black robes, looked as if he could have snuffed her out. As she raised her hand to place it on the Bible her sleeve fell away to reveal a slender, trembling wrist. Afterwards she scanned the courtroom and cast her husband an imploring glance. In response he looked studiously at the floor so that her voice broke piteously as she confirmed her name.

Wainwright began by asking about her premarital relationship with Richard Leremer.

'Were you and he lovers, Lady Petit?'

'Of course we were. We loved each other so much. Why shouldn't we be?'

'So why, if you loved Mr Leremer, did you become engaged to Sir Timothy Petit?'

'I just couldn't resist him and it was so easy, you know. It was what everyone wanted.'

'And did your sexual relations with Mr Leremer end with your engagement?'

'Of course.' She quivered, biting her lip as her eyes filled with tears. 'He was terribly upset and angry with me.'

'And have you made love to Mr Leremer since that time?'

'Oh no. He wouldn't.'

'But you would have liked to.'

'I would, yes. You see, it soon became obvious that Timmo wasn't going to love me in that way, hardly at all.'

'*Wasn't going to love me* ...' Wainwright rolled the words sorrowfully on his tongue. 'What do you mean by that, Lady Petit?'

She peeked out from under her long lashes. 'Do I have to explain to everybody here? It's so personal ...' And she shot her husband another pleading, tender glance.

'Which is precisely why this case is being held in private – away

313

from the prying eyes of the press. Please speak as freely as you are able, Lady Petit.'

'Why then, what I mean is that my husband couldn't bring himself . . . He was always too drunk or found some other reason, like it was too late or we had to get up and make a start . . . so we never actually, you know . . .'

'And yet you're claiming that he's the father of Annice.'

'When I came back from honeymoon I was pregnant. I felt different. You ask my friend Kit.'

'I'm asking you, Lady Petit.'

'Well there was no one else on honeymoon with us so it had to be my husband.'

'And if, as you say, your husband was unable to perform the sexual act, how did this conception take place?'

Lady Petit took a handkerchief from her little embroidered bag.

'It's hard to explain and it is true that we were both drunk but the thing is, on the boat train we were rather excited to be going home – though we'd had a grand time in Paris and he'd bought me so many lovely things. My favourite of all was a Baldessari lamp. When he gave it to me he said its wonderful clean lines reminded him of me, so you see I can't have been wholly unattractive to him. And there's this necklace.' She showed us a beaded tassel falling from a long crystal necklace.

'Thank you, Lady Petit, I believe we all now understand that your husband was lavish in his gifts . . .'

'I was so grateful to him and I really wanted to make a go of our marriage, so I thought, well, let's give it one more try as we were sharing a berth, and you know how the train rocks and he really did get quite excited so that he was lying on top of me and we were nearly naked and though he never . . .'

'Nearly naked? But your husband says you were both wearing pyjamas.'

'Yes, but you know, pyjamas are made to allow . . . things to develop.' Someone in the jury tittered but Annabel retained her wide-eyed earnestness. 'He did not manage the full sexual act but, well, he was moaning and something certainly happened. He seemed pretty satisfied too and fell fast asleep. And when we got home and I discovered that I was pregnant, Timmo was just delighted.'

'Conception according to you was 24 June, but your obstetrician, who will later give evidence, will say that Annice could have been conceived at any time between 26 June and 4 July. Roughly.'

'That's what he said, *roughly*. And I said, "Oh well it can't be any of those dates because it must have happened on the train night," and he said, "Well, I expect it was, because these things are notoriously unreliable."'

'What about Richard Leremer? When did you take up with him again?'

'I didn't. That is, of course I telephoned him when I was lonely but he and I have not made love since my marriage.'

'But you told your husband that Annice was Leremer's.'

'Because I wanted to hurt him. And I succeeded.' Her head drooped within the exquisite bell of her hat. 'But in the end I knew it was wrong, because it wasn't true.'

Now it was Thorne's turn to question the witness. He was very gentle in his manner, but every question he put was like unpeeling a layer of skin. I tried to view him dispassionately. Those were a lawyer's hands, the fingertips of his left lightly pressed to his notebook, and there was his lawyer's voice, deceptively kind.

'Lady Petit, did your husband, during the night you spent on the train home from Paris, at any time penetrate your body?'

'No, not exactly.'

'Then how do you know that he achieved orgasm?'

'I felt him, you know, shudder against my thigh. And, afterwards, I had to wash.'

'You had to wash.' The way Nicholas repeated her words was both mesmeric – that reflective voice, like a soft echo – and profoundly disturbing. The atmosphere in court was thick with the rocking of the Petit carriage, sweaty nightclothes, Annabel's struggle to connect with her husband. 'And is this your only evidence that conception took place?' he asked.

'The evidence is Annice.'

'Yet when you returned from honeymoon you took up with Leremer again.'

'We saw each other a few times.'

'Were you still in love with him?'

315

'Don't ask me that! I only know I needed him because Timmo was so mean. So Richie took me to dances and parties and sometimes he came to my house. He would talk to me and comfort me.'

'What form did this comfort take?'

'We drank together. Sometimes he would have a maid put me to bed and then he'd sit with me until I slept.'

As Thorne's questions rolled on and on, Annabel's piteous eyes fixed on his face.

'He sat beside your bed. Why?'

'Because I needed him!' she cried. 'I told you. I was so lonely. I wanted him badly, I wanted him to love me like he used to . . . I was so in love with him. Yes, I was.'

Someone in the jury gasped. Thorne, like everyone else, went very still, listening to the reverberations of Annabel's admission. Only Annabel seemed oblivious until he shot the words back at her. 'You were *so in love with him.*'

'But he wouldn't make love to me,' she said forlornly. 'And anyway, I found out I was pregnant with Annice.'

Wainwright, in re-examination, got her to reiterate that Leremer had been beside the bed, not in it, but Annabel's answers sounded wistful and uncertain and she left the witness box clutching her little bag to her breast with one hand.

We next heard briefly from her obstetrician who was required back at his clinic at two, but was happy to confirm that, in his opinion, the child could have been conceived in the way described by his client and that although 24 June would have made Annice's arrival rather late, these things were notoriously difficult to predict and certainly the baby had been full term. Poynter then said we should take an early lunch because it was clear that Lady Petit was struggling; her eyes were red-rimmed and her head hung down. Her mother carried her off to a nearby hotel, muttering that they might not be back, it was inhumane to put her child through this. Though I asked Wainwright whether he wished to discuss anything with me, he shrugged and disappeared to his chambers and I could tell he thought it was all over.

When Leremer was called the tension in the courtroom was heightened still further. Exuding energy with his ruddy complexion and powerful body, he confirmed that he and Annabel had fallen in love, but that she had suddenly married Timothy Petit. He had brought the diary – crammed with bits of paper, memos and invitations secured with a rubber band – in which he'd noted his engagements for 1922, after her return from honeymoon. There was only one reference to Annabel.

'But that's not to say I didn't meet her more often. I certainly did. I was one of her favourites and she was in a terrible state when she got back from her honeymoon.'

'Mr Leremer, the critical dates are the end of June to the beginning of July that year, 1922. Do you have any references to meeting her then?'

'Oh, we definitely met from time to time. Here's one night I did mark, July 16, when we went to The Gargoyle Club in Soho. It's actually in the diary: *The Gargoyle with BS*. That stands for Bel Shawcross because I still wasn't used to her married name. The Gargoyle was a favourite and she'd begged me to go with her since her husband was at some political bash. No doubt we drank a fair bit – no one could stay sober for long at The Gargoyle. I expect we went back to her place afterwards and I saw her to bed and waited beside her until she fell asleep. That's usually what happened.'

'You waited beside the bed,' said Wainwright. 'Is that all?'

'Sometimes I held her.'

'Were you still in love with her?'

Leremer glanced sadly at Annabel whose eyes were again brimming. 'I'm afraid she'd hurt me far too much.'

'So you were *hurt* by Annabel's marriage,' said Thorne when he stood up to cross-examine. 'You were his political opponent. Is *hurt* how you would describe your feelings when she first became engaged to him?'

'And sad, and bitterly disappointed and anxious for Bel. I thought, and still do, that Timothy Petit was the worst possible choice for her. She's always been said to be fragile, but with the right kind of encouragement I believe she could thrive. Instead, she chose someone guaranteed to make her unhappy. Her own fault because, as I've told her many a time – sorry, Bel – she has a snobbish, ambitious side that wanted Petit, and besides, her family were all against her marrying me. I was in the wrong political party and she told me quite frankly that neither she nor her family liked the fact that I'm Jewish.'

'So you effectively gave up on Annabel?'

Leremer leaned on the witness box and regarded Nicholas distastefully. For once I thought Nicholas, who appeared lean and scholarly beside the stocky, handsome Leremer, might have met his match.

'I did *not* give up on Annabel Petit. She gave up on me. But yes, perhaps people like me, of my class and type of background, lack confidence when it comes to squaring up to the likes of Petit.'

'And yet you did not hesitate to insinuate your way back into her life once she had returned from honeymoon.'

'I don't recognise that word, *insinuate*, Mr Thorne. It's not how I behave, either in my political or my private life.'

'I do apologise. Perhaps you'd supply a better word.'

'Bel *invited* me back into her life, and out of compassion, because we had once been lovers, I tried to help her. Obviously I misjudged the situation because here we are in court, but I was simply trying to do the right thing.'

'Please wait where you are, Mr Leremer.'

Annice was now brought in, her legs and arms locked about her nurse and her face buried in the navy-blue clothed shoulder. After much whispering and coaxing she was persuaded to raise her head and Wainwright instructed the nurse to clear her hair from her ears so that the court could study them. He said that their shape was always a telltale sign, according to experts in physiognomy, and that in this case the child's were an exact replica of the father's.

When she did venture a terrified glance at the court it was Annice's eyes that were her most striking feature. In my view there could be no doubt that she was her father's daughter; she bore not the slightest resemblance to Leremer and her features definitely resembled Petit's. But any support her face might have offered was immediately obscured because when she saw Poynter in his wig, and the curious faces of the jury, Annice began to wail and stretched out her arms towards her mother. Her mouth was now simply that of a frightened child and her features were distorted by terror. Her father failed even to smile at her, only leaned forward, resting both hands on his knees and shaking his head as if to say, 'if only she were mine'. Leremer looked away, embarrassed, but Annabel rose from her seat then rushed across and seized her daughter who clung like a monkey round her neck.

'I don't care, I don't care whose you think she is,' Annabel cried. 'She's mine at least. I would *never* deny my own child. Oh Timmo, how could you do this to us?'

The judge ordered that the screaming child be removed and the case adjourned until the next day, but for a while after Poynter had left we stood in silence, collectively ashamed that a three-year-old child had been subjected to such an ordeal. Finally the courtroom emptied and I left the building. But even the late spring afternoon didn't cheer me. I felt soiled.

# Chapter Forty-Six

The final witness for Lady Petit, her friend Mrs Kit Porter, wore a loose coat over a dress of dark grey with a fashionably full bodice and dropped waist that emphasised her blondness but obscured the clean lines of her body. She kept us waiting a few minutes because she was late arriving in the building, but words of reproach faded on Poynter's lips as she stood before him in all her aloof loveliness. His were the only eyes she would deign to meet, though Annabel waited, spaniel-like, for a crumb of her attention.

Kit answered Wainwright's questions in her usual flat tones. Yes, she was a close friend of both the Petits. Annabel in particular she'd known for donkey's years. And yes, she was a very proud godmother to Annice. 'I couldn't possibly comment upon whether or not the child is Sir Timothy's but I've always assumed so.'

Wainwright was exasperated. 'Oh come, Mrs Porter, you can be more helpful than that. You and Lady Petit are intimate friends. What did she tell you when she returned from honeymoon?'

The courtroom was so dark that the electric lights had been switched on and all the windows were shut to stop the latches rattling in a sudden fierce wind. Annabel was back in her seat, every nerve aquiver. The strain of witnessing her distress had begun to tell on the jury who were fidgety and distracted. Petit, on the other hand, looked entirely relaxed.

'Annabel said they'd had a marvellous time in Paris,' Kit was saying.

'And with regard to physical relations?'

'As I recall, she told me very little about that.'

Kit was undoubtedly very beautiful, especially to those with a penchant for greyhounds, being so sleek and androgynous and disdainful. In fact, I could not really understand why she had maintained a friendship with Annabel Petit all these years. The woman with whom she'd shared a cigarette on the steps of Lavender Hill Police Station had seemed much more her type. How coldly they'd both scrutinised me.

I remembered every word of my conversation that morning because Kit had put me down in so many ways, not least with her superior knowledge of current affairs. 'Bad enough Churchill jumping up and down threatening Foot Guards and ball cartridges without Lady Petit flinging herself in front of a picket,' she'd said.

'Foot Guards? I'd heard that Churchill was injured or even dead.'

'Far from it. He has to be kept in check by the rest of the Supply Committee.'

She'd hesitated afterwards, as if she had given too much away and at last, so suddenly that I almost cried out, it occurred to me to wonder how she could possibly have known about what was said and done by the Supply Committee when her source, Annabel, had been closeted away in Kingston by then. Was it possible that Kit knew others on the Committee or that she'd simply had a conversation with Petit himself? They were friends, after all. There he sat, relaxed on a side bench, with his head down and his arms folded.

No. Actually, he was like a coiled spring; a muscle was ticking in his jaw and his heel lightly tapped the floor.

I studied Kit Porter again. Surely not? After all the arguments and accusations, could it really boil down to so humdrum and brash a betrayal? Kit Porter, Timmo Petit; running with the same crowd, ambitious, competitive and edgy. Where had he been on the night when he returned so late that Annabel, in a fit of frustration and rage, had declared that Leremer was Annice's father? Talking into the small hours about the prospect of a strike, he'd said. With whom? Could it be the case that all this time, when poor, bewildered Annabel had been clamouring to be believed about the conception of her child, all she'd achieved was to make us look in precisely the wrong direction?

I scribbled a note to Wainwright. After studying it for a few moments he apologised for the irregularity but asked for an adjournment.

*

Having held a tense discussion with a sceptical Wainwright and furnished him with a list of additional questions, I went in search of Annabel who was tucked away in a witness room with her mother.

'What's going on?' demanded Mrs Shawcross. 'Why did it all stop again?'

I pulled up a chair. 'Lady Petit, I might be wrong – and forgive me if I am – but I believe that we've all been missing the point.'

'What point?'

I drew breath. 'That your husband and Kit are having an affair.'

The mother gasped while Annabel retained such a vague, sightless look in her eye that I wondered whether she'd heard me at all. I'd expected outrage; instead she whispered, 'What are you talking about? How could you say such a thing?'

'I think she may even be pregnant. Look closely at the clothes she's wearing. You see, I've realised that she knows things she shouldn't and she could only have learned them from him.'

In her shock Annabel seemed to be dredging up every word from some swamp deep in her memory.

'I've told you. We move in the same circles. They've known each other for years. Of course he tells her things.'

'It would explain so much, not least the desperate rush he's been in, if she's carrying his child.'

'It's not true. You don't understand. Timmo sometimes hates Kit. He says she's very bad for me. He says she should cut her hair. He says she was cruel to her husband.'

'He might have been—'

'Kit loves me! She *loves* me.'

'Will you allow us to ask the question, at least?'

'Ask, ask. I know exactly what the answer will be. It's an utter lie. I should have listened to Mother. You're a wicked woman. You're poisonous. Ask Kit, she'll tell the truth.'

Meanwhile Mrs Shawcross had been staring at the window. As I left she cast me a long, furious glance, daring me to be right.

Once the court had reconvened, Wainwright said cosily, 'Mrs Porter, I wonder if we could just review your relationship with the Petits one last time?'

'Of course. I've known Annabel since school and my husband was a friend of Timmo's. We went around as a foursome.'

'Your husband's business was to make parts for automobiles, wasn't it?'

'That's right.'

'And since his death you have retained shares in his factory, which I believe is now manufacturing motors for aeroplanes as well?'

'Indeed.'

'How soon after the Petits' marriage did your husband die?'

'About a week after their wedding. He'd never fully recovered from a bout of influenza after the war. He was so ill that I could not attend Bel's wedding – I was to have been her matron of honour.'

Wainwright half turned towards me, seeking affirmation. I noticed that Thorne had cupped his chin in his hand and was listening intently.

'Had your husband died a few weeks earlier, I suspect that would have been more convenient for you.'

'What on earth do you mean?'

'What is the current status of your relationship with Timothy Petit, Mrs Porter?'

An infinitesimal pause, just enough to steady my heartbeat.

'He's my friend, as is Annabel.'

'Perhaps you have a rather loose definition of friendship, Mrs Porter.'

Thorne said coolly, 'Your Honour, perhaps my friend should be reminded that his job is not to pose riddles but to ask questions.'

'Actually, since even direct questions don't seem to be helping, I'll put my cards on the table. I'm suggesting that you and he are lovers, Mrs Porter,' said Wainwright imperturbably, 'and I'm wondering if by any chance you are pregnant. Say three or four months? I'm suggesting that the child is Petit's, conceived soon after that fortuitous argument with his wife.'

I would have thought it impossible for her complexion to be whiter or for the courtroom to be so quiet. She threw back her head and looked at him contemptuously.

'What difference would any of this make? The point is that

Annice is still the daughter of the J— Richard Leremer.'

The court collapsed and the jury broke into excited chatter. In the time it took Poynter to restore order Pearman had begged leave to speak to Sir Timothy. A hurried conversation ensued while Thorne calmly jotted down the odd note. Pearman whispered a few words in his ear, he nodded, rose to his feet and smiled amiably at Poynter.

'Your Honour, as I'm sure everyone in this court understands, Sir Timothy Petit's love affairs are his own concern. They are not relevant to this case but I will humour my friend by making a few enquiries of Mrs Porter.' He looked Kit in the eye. 'Are you having an affair with Timothy Petit and if so, when did it begin?'

'At the end of March.'

He paused a moment, calculating, then came his next question. 'And are you lovers, in the fullest sense of the word?'

'Of course.'

'And are you expecting his child?'

She smiled faintly, nodded, and inclined her lovely head to one side. 'Poor Timmo was a wreck, do you see? We'd loved each other for years but I wouldn't leave my husband whose timing, poor dear, was always a little awry. So Timmo married Annabel, put up with all her crazy moods and even tried to believe that Annice was his daughter but when Bel told him about Leremer, of all people' – an unguarded look of pure venom passed across her face – 'it was the last straw. We'd been holding back all that time. So yes, we became lovers.'

Thorne again pondered awhile. 'Mrs Porter, you'll be aware that Sir Timothy's case is that he could not have fathered his daughter because sexual relations never took place between him and his wife – in other words, that he was incapable. How, therefore, do you explain the fact that you have conceived by him?'

For the first time since I'd met her I saw Kit Porter give an open-lipped smile, revealing her perfect teeth. 'Of course he was incapable with Bel. He'd found out during his honeymoon that my poor husband had died. He told me afterwards that he couldn't bring himself to make love to her when he might have had me.' She glanced across at her friend who was wide-eyed with shock, and gave a rueful little shrug. 'Sorry, Bel.'

'And perhaps you have a view on why Sir Timothy very recently made an offer to his wife to adopt the child.'

Another disdainful glance. 'We wanted to speed things up when we realised that I was with child, and above all avoid this sordid little hearing.'

Wainwright lumbered to an upright position. 'Your Honour, given that she has admitted to having an intimate relationship with Timothy Petit, much of what Mrs Porter says in evidence must be compromised.'

'And yet, since we allowed Mr Leremer's evidence,' said Thorne smoothly, 'we must surely be even-handed. Nevertheless, I have finished questioning Mrs Porter.'

The lunch break allowed Thorne and Wainwright time to regroup and prepare their final statements. Had Daniel been there he might have calmed me. As it was, I sat in an agony of self-doubt, wondering if I'd done the right thing in exposing Petit's affair with Kit. Undoubtedly it must cast a shadow on his integrity but had it fundamentally changed anything? Even now, Nicholas would doubtless be concocting some spellbinding web in which to enmesh the jury.

When he stood up he composed himself by twitching his gown and putting his hand to his wig.

'Really,' he began, 'this case turns on a very small point. Did Timothy Petit have intercourse with his wife? She says he did, he says he did not. Out of desperation my learned friend has produced a completely spurious, eleventh-hour argument on behalf of his client, which boils down to the fact that, once his marriage had irretrievably broken down, Sir Timothy was unfaithful to his wife.

'I would ask you to remember that this entire case was brought only because Lady Petit told her husband that he was not the father of her daughter. What she said that night did not, sadly, come as a surprise to him. It was what he had known all along but had kept hidden even from himself out of love for the child. Who could blame him, under those circumstances, for embarking on an affair with a woman who had remained loyal to him throughout? He had always loved Mrs Porter and now his wife had struck him the cruellest blow imaginable.

'In some ways there is a terrible symmetry to this case. Mr Leremer and Annabel Shawcross were lovers. Sir Timothy Petit won her and married her at the very moment when Kit Porter's husband died. No wonder he was stricken with confusion and probably grief. Perhaps there are those in this courtroom who know what it is to love a woman who is permanently out of reach, ever present, if not in the flesh, in one's inner eye; whose face, voice and movements, whose very being torments and distracts. Such, perhaps, were Timothy Petit's feelings for Kit Porter. Yet, he remained faithful to his wife until she finally broke his heart, first by letting him think the infant Annice was his, then by telling him she wasn't.

'Members of the jury, you must ask yourself, could such a man who, in public life, has served our nation with utter commitment to the common good, and in private has revealed an almost superhuman ability to remain faithful, lightly give up his own child?'

Wainwright, showing a degree of sprightliness quite out of character, expressed incredulity at the way his opponent had so adroitly turned Petit's reprehensible behaviour into a virtue.

'We have the evidence of the child who, as we all could see, resembles Sir Timothy. We have the evidence a man of great integrity, Richard Leremer – I challenge any member of the jury to tell me that they doubted his word. But above all we have seen how Annabel Petit has been ill-treated, manipulated and betrayed, not only by her husband but by her best friend. While Lady Petit has been struggling to hold herself steady in readiness for this trial, while she remained true to the best interests of her beloved daughter, the two people nearest to her were carrying on a love affair – which, incidentally, has proved beyond a shadow of a doubt that Sir Timothy is not impotent.

'In my view, Sir Timothy has revealed a degree of arrogance and disdain for the judicial process that is quite breathtaking. You cannot possibly believe his word or that of his mistress against his wife's. The truth is that Lady Petit made the one, fatal mistake, when she was at her lowest ebb, of goading her husband with the name of another man and for that she is being asked to pay a wretched price.'

*

The jury retired. While others left I remained in my place, pretending to work on a file. What was this knack Nicholas Thorne had of conjuring an argument out of the air? He had trumped my momentous revelation about Kit by reiterating the facts of the situation and twisting them on his tongue so that they emerged as an entirely different reality.

And his closing remarks to the jury haunted me. Hadn't he once told me in a letter: *I have thought of you every single waking moment . . . I want you to be shaken . . . You deserve to be, since you have utterly shattered my peace of mind . . .* He must surely remember his own words, the sense of frustration and incredulity that anyone could have affected him so. And how beautiful he'd looked, how infinitely alluring when he gave the jury a heart-wrenching smile as if to say, I speak from the heart.

Ominously, the jury came back after only an hour. I thought the foreman looked sheepish and deliberately avoided Annabel's gaze. At any rate, when asked to stand he said confidently, 'We find that Sir Timothy Petit is not the father of the child Annice.'

In a white haze I listened to the judge dismiss the case and award costs against Lady Petit. Though Petit and Kit Porter were seated far apart a crackle of triumph passed between them. Annabel was like a statue beside her mother and couldn't be raised to her feet when the judge retired. I tried to speak to her but she neither roused herself nor appeared to recognise me. Wainwright said he would flag down a taxicab.

'I told you this would happen, Miss Gifford,' hissed the mother above Annabel's head. 'I hope you're satisfied.'

When Wainwright returned, Annabel stood before us like a puppet, allowing her coat to be buttoned. Wainwright waited by to offer a fatherly arm and escort them to the door. Once Annabel was inside the taxicab the gloomy interior swallowed her up and her face turned back to me, a pale smear.

I felt utterly numb. Returning to court to collect my papers I came upon them all clustered together: Nicholas, Pearman and Kit Porter, who was now arm in arm with Timmo Petit as he talked in a low voice about handling the press. My head went up and I skirted round them but Kit's slender hand darted out and arrested me.

'The extraordinary Miss Gifford,' she said.

Petit fell silent; the eyes of the group were upon me as I paused and looked directly into Kit's face until at length her hand fell away and I walked on. Nobody made any attempt to follow.

# Chapter Forty-Seven

Surely Nicholas would come after me. He must realise that Annice was actually Petit's child. Did he have no care at all for Annabel? I felt this defeat to my core because by the end of the case I'd known beyond a shadow of a doubt that she was telling me the truth. The very same quick-wittedness which had saved little Jack Whickett had annihilated Annabel and I felt personally stricken. As he'd stood in that poisonous little victory group Nicholas had stood slightly apart, and though I had the distinct impression he was attempting to catch my eye, I wouldn't look at him. It wasn't too late, however, for him to follow me. But there was no hand on my shoulder; nobody called my name. In the end I walked down to the river and stood with my chest pressed to the Embankment wall, watching a scuff of grey water lap against a slow-moving tug. Nicholas was far too clever, could make words do anything. And once again he had used his talent on behalf of the rich and corrupt. Well, thank God I need have nothing more to do with him. That night at the hospital had been pure fantasy – we had both been tired and overemotional. Enough. It was over. I was going to marry Daniel. Generous Daniel, full of integrity, who never let me down.

When I met Mother at Euston Station next day I was somewhat too bright and brittle in my mood. She and I planned to view the three o'clock matinee of Galsworthy's *The Skin Game* at The Rep in Birmingham and still be home by midnight, although we each took a portmanteau of night things in case of an emergency. Though the strike had been over for ten days the newspapers warned that public transport was still subject to cancellation or long delays. Rolling stock had ended up in the wrong place and demoralised staff had been allowed back on less favourable terms as punishment for taking industrial action. Others were determined to show solidarity with the miners who were still on strike.

On the forecourt men were hanging about as if unsure whether they were to picket or not. An official, dressed in a frayed jacket, patched at the elbows, was yawning across the top of a placard that read: *RCA MEMBERS SUPPORT THE MINERS*. The fact that he was wearing scholarly wire-rimmed spectacles encouraged me to approach, whereupon he straightened up and removed his cap.

'Could you tell me please,' I asked, 'first, whether you think it's likely that trains will be running on time today and, second, whether you consider that it's appropriate for me to travel, since I'm on the side of the miners?'

He laughed ironically. 'Ah, Miss, what you do is up to you. The strike is over so you may take a train to wherever you want provided you can find one.'

'Do you mind me asking, why are you still here?'

'Fact is, we hardly know ourselves what's going on. A month ago I was a senior clerk. Then I went on strike although my union, the Railway Clerks Association, tended not to hold as firm as the rest. Now they tell me that I can only be employed on a temporary basis at about two-thirds the wages I was on before. And this after fifteen years in the railways.'

'I'm not surprised you're angry.'

'Angry isn't the word. We paid our union rates, we did what the union leaders asked us to do by standing together in the strike, but then we're told we must return to work with nothing gained and that every union must make its own arrangements with its bosses. Don't they see the weakness in that? If we are alone, we are nothing.'

I stood beside him for a moment longer with a vague sense that in so doing I was defying Petit, then shook his hand and went with Mother to the booking hall. The official who sold us tickets was gloomy about our chances of reaching Birmingham but thought there might be a train later in the morning.

'Then we'll miss the matinee,' I said. 'Are you sure you want to go ahead, Mother?'

'There's always the evening performance,' she said recklessly. During the next hour we ate our picnic lunch on a draughty bench and read *The Times*. The Petit paternity case had been afforded a small paragraph on the third page. In a brief statement a friend of Petit's said how devastated Sir Timothy had been to learn that Annice was not in fact his child, but he would, of course, take a lively and affectionate interest in her future. Mother read it gleefully, convinced that in fact this was some kind of triumph for me, just because one of my cases had reached the national press.

And behold, a train to Birmingham did at last rumble in, hissing and grinding as if in protest at being restored to duty. Our LADIES ONLY compartment was crowded with women bemoaning the abysmal service. Mother and I exchanged letters – I gave her Meredith's and she showed me the one that had at last arrived from Prudence.

*20 April, 1926,* SS Rawalpindi
*As I begin this, we are still on the voyage out and how extraordinary it is to think we have been travelling for weeks and still not arrived, when the furthest I have been before is to the Isle of Wight (and then I was seasick). I have become obsessed with the idea that I somehow left myself behind in London and will be quite a different person when I arrive. The question I ask myself is, who shall I be?*

*Miss Lord, though in many respects an ideal companion because she makes a point of never complaining, does not read books of any kind. Furthermore, she would rather not make friends because she says they may become an encumbrance in such an enclosed space, whereas I have found several kindred spirits on board, including a seventeen-year-old girl called Esmé – her mother is French – on her way out to join her parents. She has a chaperone about twice my age who has scarcely been seen above deck since we left the dock. Then there are two very elderly ladies who are on holiday like us, but obviously have much more money and are not averse to a couple of whiskies at night. There is also a smart girl, Daphne, who is on her way to take up a position as a lady's maid, recruited in England and sent out by a dowager to care for a precious daughter, newly married in India.*

*Some people have far more money than sense. Daphne is not*
*alone in getting involved in all kinds of activities on this ship to*
*which one is forced to turn a blind eye, but her vivacity reminds*
*me just a touch of Meredith and I like to think she would confide*
*in me if necessary.*

*We have heard about the General Strike and if I am honest*
*I am a little sorry to have missed it. I am reading, Miss Lord*
*permitting, the E.M. Forster novel so kindly provided by*
*Evelyn, though Mr Forster has some rather disturbing ideas*
*about human nature, and particularly about the behaviour of*
*English people in India.* The kindest thing one can do to a
native is let him die, *says one character, a Mrs Callendar. I*
*cannot help wondering how we are to be received in India if*
*such attitudes prevail but on the other hand perhaps Miss Lord*
*and I will be able to redress the balance and show the Indians*
*that not all British people behave like barbarians.*

*They say that travel broadens the mind. Well, so it seems.*
*Now I understand why our dear Meredith is so different to us. I*
*remember visiting art galleries with her, listening to her words*
*of information and appreciation, and wondering how she knew*
*so much and had such a fresh and original mind . . .*

'And shall you go to France,' said Mother, having finished
Meredith's letter, 'now that you're engaged to be married?'

'I'm not sure. I do need a holiday,' I said a little pitifully.

'Would Daniel go with you?'

'We couldn't easily be away at the same time.'

She looked at me severely but said nothing more. By the time
we arrived it was four in the afternoon and we had no choice
but to agree to book an evening performance and splash out on
boarding house lodgings where we would share an undersized
double bed in a dingy room overlooking a backyard. The prospect
of being pressed close to Mother for an entire night, especially
when I was so restless and agitated, filled me with dread but she
was in a very strange mood as she dashed about, switching on
the light and arranging her comb and face cream on the dressing
table. She then sat before the spotted mirror, removed her hat and
snipped off the stitches holding the veil in place. Head to one side,

neck elongated, she admired herself in the dress of green and blue paisley silk which she wore beneath her long black coat.

'Are you excited at the thought of seeing Rusbridger's grand-child?' I asked provocatively.

She watched me steadily in the glass, hands raised to re-pin her hat. 'Evelyn, there's really no need to make such a drama of everything.'

'This is important, Mother. Don't you see, I've spent the past week trying to prove who a little girl really is?' But in truth I felt the hollowness of my own words. No good had come of Annabel's attempt to make Petit acknowledge paternity of his daughter, so why stir up a hornet's nest with my own mother?

But she seemed unperturbed. 'The trouble is, since you went into the law, you've been paid to complicate matters. Most people have all kinds of difficulties in their lives that they manage pri-vately, without having someone stand up in court to create a song and dance about them.'

'Things come to court,' I protested, 'because people will not tell each other the truth. Can't you see? No wonder you are so difficult with Meredith and Edmund when you were in exactly the same position yourself.'

'My father was married to my mother. Never forget that. His name was on my birth certificate.' She was dressed for the outside as she again faced my reflection in the mirror, her eyes sparking with anger. 'Don't judge me, Evelyn, just because I choose to keep sacred my father's memory.'

'But it's about the *truth*, Mother. Think about what it will do to the child Annice. Because we lost, Annice Petit – or Shawcross, or whatever they'll call her now – will grow up never being sure of her identity.'

'Has the child a mother? Does she love her? Well then, for heaven's sake, as I've said before, what's so precious about the truth? Isn't that little girl far better off without a father who doesn't want her?'

Thus we set off, at odds with each other, to buy tickets. The city was bedraggled in the aftermath of the strike, an unseasonal wind blowing the litter through the streets. Shops were closing and the theatre, between matinee and evening performance, seemed almost tawdry, like a dancer in her imitation silks and velvets exposed to the light. While I paid at the box office Mother browsed the photographs of the cast displayed in the foyer. Rusbridger's was tucked away in an alcove and I could see no family resemblance at all behind the extravagant moustache and piercing eyes.

For the next half-hour we plodded through the damp and windy city to view the art gallery (closed), the museum (closed) and finally to retreat to a café for egg and cress sandwiches and a pot of stewed tea. We still had more than an hour before we could decently turn up again at the theatre.

'Do you know what we should do?' said Mother, leaning towards me and lowering her voice. 'Go to a public house. I shall treat you to a glass of wine. What do you think of that idea?'

As we left the café she took my arm. I didn't resist – I couldn't. I understood that some mighty barrier that had always stood between us was beginning to fall apart.

The theatre, even on the last night, was barely a third full so they closed the balcony and gave us seats in the stalls in what was essentially a rectangular box with none of the fusty glamour of old London theatres except for the red and cream panelling. Mother, examining the programme, pronounced that *The Skin Game – A tragic-comedy* – was unattractively named. 'You'd think a writer of Galsworthy's experience could have come up with something better.'

The curtain rose to reveal an English country house with French doors opening on to a garden and a father and daughter engaged in an asinine conversation about their lower-class but upwardly mobile neighbours. I felt I was looking at a portrait of the Shawcross family, with poor Annabel cooped up in her Surrey home, fretting to be out and about in the big bad world while the daffodil-yellow golfer strolled past the end of the garden.

The plot thickened. Prudence appeared on stage in the form of Mrs Gilchrist, protesting about modern people who believed in nothing but *money and push*. Prudence must be in Calcutta by now, I thought; the new Prudence who had waved goodbye to her old self on the dockside. Enter Charlie at last, callow son of the up-and-thrusting neighbour, Hornblower. Charlie was another young person with no obvious profession although this Charlie – Patrick Rusbridger, unless I was mistaken – was hardly young, being actually nearer forty than twenty-eight. Behold the man with whom I shared a grandfather. At first any family resemblance eluded me but then the actor Rusbridger took his bluff old father by the arm and said, 'Come along, Father. Deeds not words . . .' and at that moment Mother and I leaned forward, transfixed.

The character Charlie was weak, little more than his father's skivvy, possessive about his young wife and snobbishly hostile to his neighbours. As for Rusbridger, even I who knew little about acting could tell that his timing was poor and that his voice lacked timbre. And yet moving through him, dressed not in spats and a flash waistcoat but a soft-collared shirt and grey flannels, was another young man with just that same high forehead and thicker hair of exactly the same light brown. Now I recognised that the set of the shoulders, the profile, the way in which Rusbridger had looped his hand through his father's arm, were all my brother James. I saw him again as he used to sprawl on the drawing-room couch with his feet dangling over the arm, as he bounded down the stairs and snatched his hat from the stand, as he stowed the socks Min had rolled so lovingly in his kitbag on that last day of packing.

Neither of us moved during the interval but allowed others to clamber past. Nor did we speak as we waited to see him again. And what a wait, watching the extravagant gathers of the curtain, huddled together in entirely unanticipated grief.

At the curtain call the actors bowed to tepid applause. After carnations had been presented to the leading ladies the curtain did not rise again. We waited at the stage door alongside a couple of other women who clutched their programmes with the air of professional autograph seekers as the cast came dashing out into the chilly night. Rusbridger emerged a little later than the rest, turned up his collar and pretended that he wasn't hoping that someone would ask for his signature.

'Mr Rusbridger,' I called and he halted with a practised smile, dipping into an inside pocket for a pen. Even if this Rusbridger was a pale shadow of his grandfather, I understood the allure. His cheekbones were chiselled, while his eager uncapping of the pen and the winsome smile he gave us as he signed were contrived to captivate. Perhaps, as he returned the programme, his gaze lingered on my face at first with a practiced flash of admiration, then with a touch of uncertainty and he definitely gave Mother a wary glance but it might have been, we agreed afterwards, because he was embarrassed about the play and couldn't understand why we wanted an autograph from a minor character. By tacit agreement, for better or worse, we watched him walk away into the night without a further word.

Afterwards we linked arms and returned to our room where we undressed with considerable difficulty, contorting our limbs to avoid exposing our naked flesh to each other and then lying side by side on our backs, not touching. The curtains were very thin but the proximity of the surrounding walls ensured almost complete darkness and the floorboards above us protested as another resident climbed into bed.

Mother whispered, 'How odd for me to be sharing a bed. Six years, it is, since your father . . .'

'Do you miss him?'

'Yes. At times,' she said obscurely. 'Modern young women seem to be so different, don't you think?'

'I suspect they are just more demanding.'

'*Demanding*,' came the reply after a pause. 'I rather like that word. I suspect my poor mother was rather demanding, in her way.'

So, the subject was to be broached after all.

'Rusbridger visited our flat in Clapham,' came the whisper at last, 'and afterwards Mother told me who he was and his relationship with me. When I was much older she asked me if I wanted to read that letter.'

'You *met* him. Why didn't you tell me?'

'Because I have spent all my life trying to forget. It was just once, a few months after Father had died and we'd moved out of the schoolhouse into the London flat. We had a great many visitors there, sometimes late into the evening, because Mother gave classes to adults as well as children and I was used to sleeping through the doorbell. But one night there was such a persistent ringing that I woke up altogether. I heard Mother walk to the door and then after she'd opened it nothing happened for a very long time until a male voice said, "Let me in, Clara." And then more forcefully, like a command, "Let me in."

'The door closed and Mother and the visitor went into the room where we spent our daytimes. I expect you remember it from when you were a child. It was where she taught. I was frightened because the man had spoken strangely so I crept out of bed and went to the door.

'"You've not answered a single one of my notes, Clara," he was saying. "You're being very cruel."

'Mother was much too quiet and I was about to rush in when I heard him say, "I've told you, all I want is to see the little girl. You can't blame me for that. I could help you, Clara, you must be very lonely."

'Still Mother said nothing. "Is it my child?" he asked. "In America I had no news of you but since I've been back I've heard all kinds of rumours."

'And then Mother said, so low that I could hardly hear, "I've told you before. Leave us alone, Patrick."

'"You need not be afraid," he said. "I've no intention of making a nuisance of myself. I just want to know where I stand."

"You have nothing to do with me. I don't want you here." Then there was a long silence and she said, "Don't you dare touch me!"

'"But I still love you, my little Clara, I've never stopped loving you, ah, don't pull away . . ."'

'I don't know what would have happened next had I not thrown open the door. Mother was wearing a long, soft red skirt I used to like very much and a white blouse with a fall of lace at the front. She picked me up and held me tight. Rusbridger seemed to me a very large person and he smelt funny, of being a man, I suppose, because in those days we had very few male visitors. He put his finger under my chin and stared into my face until his eyes, which frightened me because they were so large and sorrowful, watered. "This is my child, Clara," he said. "Anyone could see that."

'She just held me and I felt the tension in her neck and arms.

'And his voice, smooth as silk, said over the top of my head, "I'll do whatever you want, Clara. Because I have never stopped being in love with you. I still want you, so much."

'"Leave," my mother said.

'He shook his head very slowly. "You don't mean it," he said. "You'll want me back. At the very least you'll want my money."

'And then Mother said in a voice I didn't recognise at all, "If you come near me again I swear it will be the end of you. Do you understand?"

'He laughed. Still carrying me, Mother went towards him and edged him out into the little hallway and he looked at us one more time before she shut the door. She put me to bed and stroked my hair and kissed me and sang to me like she used to before Father died. Next morning she told me that when I was a grown-up I would understand better the part Rusbridger had played in my life but that I was her girl, and my dead father's, and Rusbridger would never take me away. Even so, night after night I lay awake dreading that he might come and look at me again with those eyes which had terrified me because somehow they didn't seem quite real. He never did. Fortunately he died soon afterwards. And that was that. Except . . .'

'Mother?'

'Except, you know, I never forgave her and – this is the worst thing – I was always more than a little ashamed of her. Isn't that wicked of me?'

'Not wicked, Mother. Just sad. Very sad.' I lay in silence then asked, 'Why do you think she left me the writing box with the letter from Rusbridger? It was not like her to play such games.'

'You don't think it was a mistake after all?' she asked tentatively. 'She might not even have remembered it was there.'

'I got it all wrong. And so did Peggy Spencer. I thought Grandmother was heartbroken over Rusbridger.'

'Well, perhaps she was at first. But feelings can change you know Evie.' There was a long pause. 'You'll still go ahead and marry your Daniel, I presume.'

'Why ever wouldn't I?'

'You can't blame me for asking. After all, it seems very odd that I've still not met him. I've heard his voice once, I think, when he came to the house, but I've never seen his face.'

'It was the General Strike; he's just been so busy.'

'Yes, of course. You and I are very different, I accept that, but I

338

married above all because I wanted to be safe. Oh, I don't regret marrying your father but what a fool I was to think that a grand house and servants could protect me from everything. Nothing saved my son, did it Evie? And you're much more resourceful and independent than me, I know that. I've come to hope that you would marry someone who knew you inside and out and would satisfy you. You're so hungry, Evelyn, so desperate to save everyone. You don't need security; in some ways you need the opposite, someone who will make you young again and stop you getting bowed down by the responsibilities you take on.

'The thing is, Evelyn, you're supposed to have a trained mind so I hesitate to give you any advice, but I should be sorry if too much thinking led you to believe that you had to go ahead and marry a man because you'd promised him you would, rather than because you couldn't live without him.'

# Chapter Forty-Eight

Daniel, the defence barrister Walter Rickard, and I held a meeting with Mrs Wright on the morning of her committal. Rickard, as recommended by Nicholas, was an expert on domestic assaults including murder, but had an unpromising hangdog expression, compounded by eyes which turned down at the outer corners.

Mrs Wright, though pale and shaky, might even have put on a little weight thanks to a couple of weeks on remand in Holloway. The swelling on her face had subsided but one eye was still blood-shot and her jaw was crooked. I could tell from the way he studied her that Rickard was thinking it unfortunate that her wounds would be barely apparent by the date of her trial.

Casting her disfigured gaze over Rickard's black coat and crisp tie Mrs Wright whispered, 'I can't afford him.'

'This is a murder charge, Mrs Wright. Your defence will be paid for out of public funds.'

'Why's that then?'

'Because it's considered such a serious offence.'

Though she nodded I rather thought that she had still not fully taken in what the consequence would be if we failed. After some persuasion she sat down at the table with us, folded her hands and waited.

'I suggest you keep your hat off when you stand in the dock,' Rickard told her. 'The magistrate needs to see that you have been injured. He won't be insulted. You can put it on again afterwards.'

'Shall I tell him why I've taken it off?'

Rickard had a kindly way of leaning his head on his hand so that his eyes were on a level with hers.

'Mrs Wright, today you'll only need to give your name and date of birth. But even at your trial it would be best, under the

340

circumstances, if you said as little as possible. What I'll be arguing is that there was a very long history of you being attacked and beaten by your husband. We're hoping that some of your neighbours will bear witness, not today but at the trial, and we'll have your son Robbie produced from prison.'

She nodded. 'I'd like that.'

'And I shall say something about the knife to reinforce our case that the reason it was on the mantel was not because you planned to kill your husband, but so that the younger children couldn't reach it.'

'That's right.'

'Unfortunately, your son Robbie has said something different, but we're hoping that your daughter Gertrude will corroborate what you've said – tell the court it's true. Will she say the knife was always kept on the mantel?'

Mrs Wright's jaw was clenched. 'She wouldn't know.'

'Did she not help with the preparation of food in your house? Surely she knew where the knife was kept.'

'Yes, she did help. 'Course she did. But the knife were moved this way and that – in the scullery, on the mantel. Always out of harm's way. So she wouldn't be able to say for sure where I'd put it that night.'

Rickard made a brief note. 'And then the other question they'll dwell on, I'm afraid, is the three stab wounds. It would be helpful if you could tell me, in the privacy of this room, why you felt constrained to stab your husband three times rather than once.'

'*Constrained?*'

I said, 'Mrs Wright, the prosecution will say that you used unnecessary force because you stabbed your husband again and again. What's your answer to that?'

'He were still going for me. It were dark. I didn't know what I was doing.'

'That's three answers, Mrs Wright,' said Rickard gently. 'We'd be best off with one.'

'What if they're all true?'

'You see, this is crucial. In order for us to use the defence of justifiable homicide – self-defence – you must have been in absolute fear of your life so that to stab your husband was the only possible course of action. The jury might think, all right, we understand why she stabbed him once – but *three* times? If what you really wanted to do when you stabbed him was to stop him hurting you again, and by mistake it all went too far, we'd be better off pleading to manslaughter.'

She took a long breath as if making up her mind. 'What's the punishment for manslaughter, then?'

'It varies – usually some form of longish prison sentence. But for it to be manslaughter, you mustn't have intended to kill him.'

'Tell them I had no choice but to kill him,' she said. 'What will they give me for that?'

Rickard slotted the lid back on to his pen and gathered up his papers.

'Mrs Wright,' I said, 'provided we can prove you had no choice, you will not be punished at all. Do you understand? But it won't be easy. You must trust Mr Rickard and do everything he says.'

'I trust *you*, Miss Gifford. I know that you will make it all come right.'

After the committal, during which Mrs Wright again pleaded not guilty to murder, Rickard ushered Daniel and me into a side room and turned on us.

'Forgive me but I cannot win this case. By no means can three stab wounds and that business with the knife lead a jury to a finding of innocence. That woman was much too hesitant when I spoke to her this morning. She's undoubtedly hiding something. I'm obviously not here to judge her, but it seems to me she'd planned to kill him all right. This was malice aforethought, no question.'

'She's not capable of such a thing,' I said. 'If you'd met her husband you would know exactly why she did it.'

'But that's exactly the point. She's alive and he's dead, which gives him a distinct advantage when it comes to winning the jury's sympathy.'

'Then what would you suggest we do, Mr Rickard?' said Breen, placing a restraining hand on my arm.

'Go back to the prosecutor, cap in hand, and plead to have the charge changed to manslaughter.'

My face was stiff with nerves. 'But will they accept that now?

Won't the same argument be in their minds about the three stab wounds?'

'Well, you tell me, Miss Gifford, hand on heart. What do you think really happened?

'I think she killed him because she thought she had to. She thought it was kill or be killed – if not then, later.'

'Then perhaps we should plead guilty and pray for mitigation – she might get life imprisonment.'

'She would rather die.'

He was actually backing away as if he wanted nothing more to do with us. 'Let me know as soon as possible if you change your minds about her plea. As things stand, I defy anyone to get her off.'

By the time we got back to Arbery Street Miss Drake had gone home and there was no sign of Wolfe. In Daniel's office I dropped into my usual chair and buried my face in my hands.

'What have I done?'

'Evelyn, this is not your fault.'

'But if she dies . . .'

'Very little time has been lost so far. In any case, I doubt they would have accepted a plea of manslaughter even if you'd made the argument on the first day. Perhaps now our best hope is to do as Rickard says. Plead guilty. We might have a merciful judge.'

'But if he's not merciful . . .'

Breen prodded at his blotter with the nib of his pen.

'Tell me again why you went for justifiable homicide in the first place.'

'It was Nicholas Thorne's suggestion. After all, he'd been in the house with me.'

'Well now, he's no fool. I wonder why he suggested that?'

'Perhaps he was swayed by what he saw. It was all so pathetic, so terrible; blood on the floor, blood on the daughter's clothes. The house had an air of utter hopelessness. It felt as if there had never been any children there, ever, nothing joyful. Wright's brutal spirit remained. I think it was obvious to us both that Mrs Wright must have known she had to do it.'

'If Thorne saw a way out – and he must have done – why don't

343

you ask *him* to represent Mrs Wright? Tell him what Rickard has said and see if he'll take the case on instead.' He was smiling at my stunned face, rolling the pen on his blotter. As so often these days, I simply didn't understand him. Did he really imagine that I was so indifferent to Thorne that it would be safe to thrust me his way? 'Don't look at me like that, Evelyn, it is the obvious thing to do, surely. What's stopping you? Thorne won Petit's case against all the odds. You've seen him at work.'

'But this is Rickard's case.'

'He doesn't want it.'

'Nicholas – Thorne doesn't specialise in crime.'

'I wasn't aware that he specialised in paternity cases, either. What we want, surely, is for him to use his miraculous powers of persuasion to work on behalf of your Mrs Wright.'

'I can't ask him. You don't understand.'

'Why are you reluctant, Evelyn? What are you afraid of?' He regarded me with unflinching candour. 'And is your fear really going to prevent you from doing the one thing that might save Mrs Wright?'

# Chapter Forty-Nine

The boy Jack's aunt had written a formal letter thanking me for my trouble and informing me that Jack had made a full – *almost too full* – recovery and should I ever be in the vicinity of West Ealing I would be very welcome. Having given them a couple of days' notice I bicycled first to the Shawcross factory where I allowed myself to stay for a few minutes on the opposite side of the road and watch the massive building with its gates wide open, the fountain playing and machinery thrumming behind its hundreds of windows. It was hard to imagine the furious crowds, the violence and anger. What if Nicholas had not caught sight of me that afternoon?

I rode swiftly on to seek out a narrow street of flat-fronted houses from whence came the racket of children released from school. As I dismounted, a football bounced up to my feet and I found myself face to face with Jack himself, his hair cropped so close that his ears protruded disproportionately and with a livid scar blazing on his forehead. He and all the other children were silent when they saw me.

'Hello, Jack,' I said.

Another boy crept up behind him. 'That's her. The one from the factory. With the bicycle.'

Jack hung his head and went crimson.

'I came to see how you are,' I said. 'Are you well again now?'

He nodded, tongue-tied, while the other children clustered about and steered me towards a house in the middle of the terrace. While one of them took my bicycle, the others guided me through an open door and along the passageway to the back room where Jack's aunt was buttering bread at the table. A younger woman, nursing a baby in a cane chair by the door, hastily covered up an exposed breast.

'It's my lady,' said Jack.

The aunt tore off her apron and shook my hand.

'Jack, have you thanked Miss Gifford for all she did?'

Jack's mother, who had an open, harassed face propped the baby on her knee, supported its minute chin and rubbed its back.

'You should have shown the lady into the parlour, Jack.'

'No, I'd rather be here,' I told her.

The kitchen was a balm, being of similar proportion to the Wrights' but filled with activity and kindness. A couple of little girls still clung to my skirts as I edged forward to take a closer look at the baby.

'Do you want to hold her?' the mother asked shyly.

She surrendered her seat and I found myself enthroned with the infant on my lap, a dense, warm weight. The baby gazed with rather more confidence into my face than I into hers. The children were permitted to drift away and preparations for tea continued.

'We've had ever such a lot of visitors after what happened,' said the mother. 'Police, all sorts. We can't thank you enough for what you did. But you know, we think at least some good will come of it. Perhaps Shawcross was ashamed because all our men were taken back to the factory and hardly anyone got prosecuted. My husband Charlie come home the next day. And then this great big basket comes, crammed with ham and pickles and all sorts. For Jack, from Mrs Shawcross.'

'And Jack, is he fully recovered?'

'He is, except for bad dreams. It were dreadful to see him like that, all silent in the hospital. Now I sometimes wish he'd be struck dumb more often. He's a wild boy. We asked him what he said to the young man, you know, the one who went for him, and he won't tell us. He's got a mouth on him, that's for sure.'

The baby was lifted away and I missed her soft bulk and lambent stare. We took tea in the chilly parlour, the aunt, the mother and I. They'd gone to a touching amount of trouble, with the best china brought down from the dresser and doilies under the bread and butter.

Afterwards a number of men in their overalls and smelling of oil and metal paraded through to greet me. I felt far too Prudence-like for comfort as I received their thanks and I was glad when the baby, who had been thrust into a crib in the back room, drew their attention by wailing.

When I emerged into the street, Jack was yelling at a friend with ear-splitting candour about his failure to guard the ball. The experience of being lauded in his mother's kitchen must have gone to my head because I felt a degree of proprietorial pride at seeing him so healthy. This, at least, was one child I *had* managed to save. Others in whose lives I'd recently intervened –Annice and the Wright children – were faced with a far less happy outcome.

'Hey Miss, catch!'

The ball thudded against my chest.

'Goodness me, what's happened here?' I asked. 'Where's that old ball you were playing with outside the factory?' This football was brand new, with oiled leather and fresh laces.

Jack took it from me. 'He brung me a new one,' he said. 'Didn't you know? Your young man.'

'The one with the Ford,' said his friend. 'He come here, didn't he, Jack, and he saw you in the street and he threw you the ball and said, "Just checking you were on your feet, Jack." Then he drove away.'

As I rode off, I could still hear the thump of the ball against a wall and their boyish yells. I was smiling a little, and somewhat discomposed that Nicholas, in the midst of the Petit case, had made such a kind gesture towards Jack, when he had seemed so indifferent to the well-being of Annice. Well, let's see, I thought, how far his altruism goes, and I determined to do as Breen had suggested – set aside my pride, and the desire to protect both myself and Daniel, and ask Nicholas to represent Mrs Wright.

# Chapter Fifty

Miss Drake scheduled an urgent appointment with Nicholas Thorne at his chambers and, after court the next day, I took an omnibus as far as the Royal Courts of Justice and walked across the Strand and down Middle Temple Lane towards the river. For half an hour I prowled the narrow gardens by Temple Station and peered over the Embankment wall. A low tide had exposed shingle slick with oil and weeds and the weather was foul, with vicious gusts of wind driving flurries of rain into my face. In such conditions my umbrella was useless.

This time, when I entered the clerks' office at Nicholas's chambers and presented my card, I was directed up three flights of narrow stairs to the second room on the left of a confined landing. The door was ajar and I was told abruptly to enter. His face was impassive as he rose to his feet.

'Congratulations on the Petit case,' I said.

He nodded. His wig had been flung down on to a heap of papers and his hair was ruffled.

'I really thought, when I realised what Petit and Kit Porter had been up to, that we would win,' I added.

'You did well to make the connection between them. I had not done so. I must admit I was very angry with them both. It was a near thing.'

Hardly aware of my actions I unbuttoned my coat, propped my umbrella against the wall and sat down, so keyed up that I had only a vague impression of the low-ceilinged room, its uneven floor and shelves overflowing with books.

'I want to talk to you about the Wright case.'

He reached for a box and packed his wig away. I was aware of a draining of tension, a kind of wretchedness in his movements.

'At the moment we've instructed Mr Rickard as you suggested,' I said.

He nodded. 'Walter Rickard. Good choice.'

I should not have come. I could not sustain this; I so wanted to be having quite a different conversation. The fact that I was here at all – let alone that I should be about to ask an impossible favour – now seemed cruelly audacious, so I continued at a gabble, 'But he's bound to lose, because he agrees with the prosecution that the three stab wounds make it seem like a deliberate and malicious murder. Also, Robbie has overturned his mother's evidence about where she left the knife. It's going to look as if she put it on the mantel in readiness. Everything points to premeditation.' His face was expressionless. 'As a matter of fact, I'm beginning to think she really did plan it, Nicholas, that she did mean to kill him.'

'Is that so?'

'So I have come here to ask you to take on the case. You were there in her house. You know how things were.'

'What are you talking about? Apart from anything else, you've just told me the case is in the hands of another barrister.'

'Rickard has virtually washed his hands of it because he knows he'll lose. I believe that you, on the other hand, could win. You see, we even know that the knife had been recently sharpened; the knife grinder will give evidence, although we will say it was just a regular call. But it won't make any difference – Mrs Wright is bound to hang. The cards are all stacked against her – but you could get her off, Nicholas. I believe you could do that.'

He glanced at the raincoat on his coat stand. 'I'm sorry, but I have another appointment.'

'*Please*, Nicholas.'

He stared at me in disbelief, pushed back his chair, picked up his hat and lifted the coat from the hook. 'I can't do this. Excuse me, I'm late.'

He took the stairs three at a time but I ran after him, down flight after twisty flight and outside into the rain. Through Middle Temple he dashed and into the gardens. I caught up with him as he strode down the wet gravel path towards the fountain.

'For Christ's sake,' he said, turning on me so that we faced each other while the rain drove against our shoulders.

I was beside myself, beyond thought and certainly beyond retreat. 'Persuade the jury to find Mrs Wright innocent.'

'How?'

'I don't know. But when we first saw the house, you thought she
stood a chance. You did. You told me to go for self-defence, for
justifiable homicide.'

'I've no idea what I said. I wasn't in my right mind.'

'She claims she wanted to be sure he wouldn't get up and hurt
her again. That's why she stabbed him three times.'

'But that's not what happened! Can't you see?' He looked at
me incredulously. 'Good God, Evelyn, you really don't get it, do
you?'

I couldn't look away. Overwrought, pleading, here in the gardens, I loved him. I'd rather be standing in the rain with him than
be anywhere else.

'Why should Mrs Wright hang? He was bound to kill her one
day and she was so desperate. Once she fought back she had to
make sure he was dead or imagine how he'd have punished her
later. What choice did she have? And yet she will be found guilty.'

'It's the law,' he cried. 'That's how it works. The jury will decide
on the facts that are put before them. You, of all people, know that
the innocent sometimes fall foul of the law.'

'No one can be sure of the truth. You know that. You simply
have to guide the jury to see things differently. It's what you do
so well.'

Again he stared at me as if about to say something, then
changed his mind and strode away. But when I went after him
again he halted.

'I thought you would be the last person on earth to expect
anyone to manipulate the truth.'

'I think you can win. Please, Nicholas. If Mrs Wright was your
client you wouldn't hesitate to sow just a little seed of doubt in the
jury's mind.'

'Rickard can do that.'

'I don't trust him to succeed. I trust you.'

We were walking again, out of the gardens between beds of
regimented flowers which had been crushed by the wind and rain.
'Listen,' he said. 'You're going to marry Breen. Good. I'm glad you

are if that's what you want. But that means there can be nothing between us. Don't keep dragging me back.'

'I'm not dragging you back. I'm asking you to do this for Mrs Wright's sake. Please, Nicholas. The Wright family has suffered too much already.'

Thus far, despite the weather, his coat had remained open. Now he put down his briefcase, did up each button and buckled the belt.

'Does Breen know that you're meeting me?'

'Of course. He encouraged me to ask you. It was his idea.'

'Then why didn't he come himself? For Christ's sake, what are you doing to me?'

We were now on the Victoria Embankment. Irritated pedestrians jostled us and the filthy, homeward-bound traffic roared by. My heart was swollen with grief and a desperate certainty that I had burnt all my boats. He was about to walk away, indeed he took a few steps, but then he turned and said, 'Tell me again why you want me to do this.'

'For Mrs Wright's sake, because otherwise she will die.'

'Not good enough.' And he strode off.

I was after him again, barging into a furious woman who stank of mothballs.

'For me, then, do it for me. I beg you.'

He slowed; he halted. 'You know damned well I would do anything for you.'

# Chapter Fifty-One

When I telephoned Lady Petit's home to enquire about her health and whether she was up to signing a number of forms, the maid just said she would pass on the message. But a few days later I received an invitation to visit Annabel, not at the house, but at the gallery. In my gloomy office I was deep in preparation for the forthcoming Wright murder trial so the brief bicycle ride, with the sun warm on my neck, provided some welcome respite.

My first surprise on entering the gallery was to find the assistant, Claire, actually working, or at least taking down the details of a customer who was buying a decanter and four glasses as a wedding present for her niece. Nor was this the only client; at least six ladies were browsing the exhibits and Annabel was holding court in a far corner, wearing a pale green frock with a fringed skirt. On the flat of her dainty hand she displayed a paperweight so that it caught the light.

'The designer is Goupy of Maison Rouard. Do look at the shoes the little enamelled figure is wearing – the detail of the toes, curled over like a harlequin's.' When she noticed me she didn't break off but indicated that I should go through to her office.

In the back room were Annice, who was kneeling on a chair and drawing a picture, tongue caught between her teeth in concentration, the nursemaid and the dog that I now learnt was called Willow. The desk had been cleared to allow space for Annice's crayons and the window was open.

'I'm so glad you called,' cried Annabel, flitting in and shaking my hand vigorously. 'I've been so wanting to catch up with you since the trial.'

Although she was still painfully thin her eyes were clear and her cheeks a little flushed. Seizing a holder from a low table she lit a cigarette and flapped her hand to keep the smoke away from her daughter's head.

'I tell you what, nurse, would you mind taking Annice for just the tiniest of walks while I talk to Miss Gifford?'

Without a murmur Annice slid from her chair and waited with her customary obedience while a sun bonnet was tied on and the dog attached to its lead.

'It's very good to see you, Miss Gifford,' Annabel said when we were alone, closing the door with a flick of her toe. 'You are so sweet to have called the house. It's a relief to see someone different to the usual crowd.' She tilted her head towards the gallery. 'They are all agog because of course word has got out about Timmo and Kit. Marvellous for business.' Her voice faltered and she bit her lip. 'I miss her more than him, actually. Rather telling, don't you think?'

'I'm so sorry—'

'Oh don't be sorry. You've done me a *huge* favour. Imagine the humiliation of finding out about it later. As I told Mummy, we might have lost but at least I'm free. And I do feel better. I know where I am, you see. And to be honest, I rather think Annice will be better off without her father's name, don't you?' There was a hint of humour in her eyes, although I sensed she was also struggling to convince herself. 'I have a present for you, Miss Gifford.'

'Oh, I can't accept—'

'You can. And you must. Just a little something, because I know I gave you a very hard time.' She withdrew from a drawer a flat tissue-wrapped parcel which I hadn't the heart to refuse. Inside was a pair of bright red leather gloves. 'You ride a bicycle, don't you? Daddy said so. Well, you have to be seen by other road users, Miss Gifford, we don't want to lose you.' We laughed as I pulled the soft gloves on to my fingers. 'I bought large. Look at the size of your hands compared to mine! I've made all sorts of discoveries about what went on at the factory when you visited Father. You got yourself hurt, and all because of me. And then there was that little boy . . .'

'Jack. Yes, but at least he's quite all right now. I visited him.'

'Of course you visited him. You follow up everything and I applaud that. And actually, Mother sent a hamper of food to the family; she's also good at that sort of thing. It's not something I excel at but I'm vowing to do better. Daddy told me Jack had made a good recovery – he's been very sweet, not at all like him, but even he has a conscience somewhere and of course he's furious with Timmo. I don't think Richie will have me back, ever,' she added, with one of her lightning changes of mood, 'but I won't give up hope. And I know that we would have won had it not been for your wretched Nicholas Thorne. He was just too smart for everyone, even you. Goodness me, you've gone all pink. I can't blame you. How intriguing to have had a love affair with someone like him.'

I gathered my things. 'At any rate, you are surviving, Lady Petit.'

'I am. And that's a miracle in itself, Mummy says. It just shows you how bad Timmo was for me. What a fool I have been. That's what makes me weep, when I think I nearly married someone so much better in every way. But at least I have Annice.'

We parted company at the door to the gallery where she stood on tiptoe to kiss my cheek. The nurse was walking along the pavement holding Annice by the hand but the little girl pulled away when she saw her mother, her solemn face transfigured by a smile of pure joy, and she started running, her legs pumping as she flew towards us across the paving stones.

On my way home that evening I took a detour to Thomas Cook's travel agency in Berkeley Street. Perhaps I'd intended simply to check the opening hours but the window display featuring photographs of joyous tourists with triumphant grins, standing before a temple in India or a forest in Kenya, were so enticing that finally I stepped inside. In an instant, I was lured to a desk by a keen young clerk with a thumb and two fingers missing on his right hand, who looked as if he'd never been on a holiday in his life. Having pulled out one dog-eared volume of railway timetables after another he plotted me a route from London to Sanary-sur-Mer.

'Le Train Bleu,' he said excitedly, 'is first-class tickets only. I'm told it's the only way to travel through France. Shall I find you a price?' But closer inspection of my briefcase and rugged shoes must have convinced him that I was no first-class passenger. 'Actually, much the cheapest way is to take the train to Dover, then the ferry, then a train to the Gare du Nord and make your way independently across Paris to the Gare de Lyon and on to Marseille where you can get a local train along the coast.'

Half an hour later, with a page of closely written itineraries stuffed into my briefcase and a timetable earmarked for a couple of days after the end of the Wright murder trial, I made my way back to the flat. It appeared to be the case, I thought, as I plodded up the unloved communal staircase, that I actually would soon be heading south to Meredith and Edmund. The clerk had made it all possible, and I pictured myself as a tiny figure in a railway carriage, disappearing into the blue yonder.

# Chapter Fifty-Two

In a dark little room beneath courtroom five of the Old Bailey, Nicholas and I met Mrs Wright an hour before the start of her trial, which had been allocated two days. He arrived slightly later than I, and our greetings were entirely businesslike, our bodies tense within the uniform of the law – I in my black jacket and calf-length skirt, he in wing collar and pinstripes, robe and bands but not as yet his wig, which he placed on the table. Mrs Wright was wearing an oversized dress in an unbecoming shade of ginger and her hair was drawn into a loose bun from which fluffy, newly washed strands had escaped. Although her wounds had healed, a vicious scar sliced through her brow and her jaw was still swollen where it had been broken.

She had lost any vestiges of bravado and her soft brown eyes were filled with terror.

'The other women say I'm sure to hang,' she said.

Nicholas, seated beside her at the table, extended his legs as if he were in a gentleman's club and had all the time in the world. The slow, reassuring smile he gave her was the same that had en-snared me the first time I met him. Every cell in my being is attending to you, it said. Trust me.

'It's a tricky situation, Mrs Wright, but believe me, I wouldn't have taken on the case if I thought we would lose. There are just a couple of things I wanted to discuss with you and the first might surprise you. I believe you are a Roman Catholic? We found your copy of Thomas à Kempis – not a book generally read by Protestants.'

'My husband couldn't abide me being a Catholic, so I don't go to church but my family was Irish. I kept that book hid. It was my mother's.'

'In court I'm going to ask you about your faith and especially Thomas à Kempis. It will enable me to show the jury what you're really like.' His manner was soothing and conversational. 'Now, let's hear exactly what you are going to say when I ask you to describe how your husband died.'

She told him about the sequence of events that had led her to snatch the knife from the mantel.

'Which is, of course, rather high,' he said, 'level with my shoulder, as I recall, and I'm considerably taller than you, Mrs Wright. Could you remind me how you reached it?'

She looked at him nervously. 'Well, I knew it were there so I found it when I reached upwards.'

He smiled. 'There we are. Between us we shall do very well, you'll see. I would advise you to answer all questions as briefly as possible. Don't say more than you need to – that's what I tell everyone when they go into court.'

As we left the interview room he stood back for me at the door and put his wig on as I went ahead up the narrow stairs. He was so formidably withdrawn that I didn't even dare ask him if he'd read the file I'd sent, documenting the details of my relationship with the family and every argument I could muster on Mrs Wright's behalf.

Unlike Lady Petit, Mrs Wright didn't have the advantage of privacy, so the courtroom was packed with reporters and members of the public, many of them women who muttered sympathetically when the defendant was brought into the dock.

The prosecutor, Greenacre, was as tall as Nicholas but bulkier, with a deceptively light, high-pitched delivery and a warm smile for the judge and jury. As he outlined the facts, however, any sign of affability drained from his face and his voice deepened portentously.

'You will have to decide whether Mrs Wright acted in self-defence and with proportionate force, or whether this was cold-blooded, premeditated murder. There was a sharpened knife at the ready and Harriet Wright admits that she stabbed her husband in the throat not just once but a second and third time. We say that she must have known after the first time she struck him that he was dying. With that knife to hand, Wright could have defended herself in any number of different ways. Instead, she quite literally slaughtered her husband, who furthermore was drunk at the time and therefore unable to defend himself.'

A grey mist hung over the courtroom because the windows were open and dust and fumes from the street had blown in. The first witness was the knife grinder, a good-humoured soul who used to sharpen Mrs Wright's kitchen knives regularly though not so often of late because she'd been short of money.

'Once I've done my business, them knives are sharp enough to cut through the toughest bit of gristle as if it were butter. I sharpened Mrs Wright's about the middle of May – that would have been about six months since the last time. She come out special on to the street to call me in – said her daughter had a little job at the pub so there was a bit of cash.'

When Nicholas cross-questioned him it was established that the Wrights' house was on a well-trodden route for the grinder and that he passed that way every fortnight.

The prosecutor next called neighbours who bore witness to the volatile nature of the Wright marriage, the noise echoing through the thin walls of pans and furniture being hurled about, and the number of times the little Wright children had popped round for a bit of cocoa and comfort while their mother was laid up.

'He were a brute,' said one, a Mrs Carr, folding her arms and letting rip. 'A layabout. And when he were drunk he were twice as bad. She bore the brunt, week after week.'

'Why do you suppose Mrs Wright never left her husband?'

'Ain't it obvious? She wouldn't abandon them children and if she took them wiv her, where would she have gone?'

'And on the night when Mr Wright was killed, how were you involved?'

'My husband were on nights. The first I heard there was a knock on the door 'bout three in the morning, and there's poor Trude and a clutch of them kids, all shivering in their night things. She said, "Something dreadful has happened, Mrs Carr. Your boy Geoffrey will need to go for the police." So they all come in and I built up the fire in the range and we huddled up. Trude were in a heap, holding on to her poor little sisters. By the time I'd got them settled, the police was next door and they wouldn't let me in to see poor Het.'

Nicholas spoke to her with great courtesy. 'You obviously can't comment on what actually happened on the night Mr Wright was killed, but you are a friend of Mrs Wright's, I believe.'

'She were a very private woman. She only come to me when she were desperate, when Trude wasn't there and she couldn't hardly stand for the clouting he'd given her.'

'Would you say the attacks on Mrs Wright were always the same? In other words, did they vary in how brutal they were?'

'*Brutal* is a very loaded word, Mr Thorne,' observed the judge, Mr Justice Thurgood, who at first had seemed elderly and distracted but in fact was proving to be highly attentive.

'It varied,' said Mrs Carr, 'a black eye one week, swollen fingers the next. But she'd only landed up in hospital that one time, just recently. Bit of a turning point, I'd say.'

'In what way, a turning point?'

'He used to care what we all thought and didn't like to hit her too often or too hard where it would show. That night he wasn't bothered one way or another.'

Trudy Wright was called after lunch. Her old brown coat drooped disconsolately, her face had broken out in a rash of spots and she wouldn't look at her mother. When questioned about her parents' relationship she mumbled that her mother had been beaten up regularly by her father.

'Why was that, do you think, Miss Wright?'

'I dunno. The drink made him worse. And when there was no money. And when they argued about politics or the kids.'

'Did your mother try to avoid those arguments?'

Gertrude looked at Greenacre as if he were mad. 'Of course she did. But sometimes she couldn't keep quiet. Often it was about Robbie, or money.'

When it came to describing events on what Greenacre termed the *fateful* night, Trudy became almost sullen. 'What time did you arrive home, Miss Wright?'

'About two.'

'I believe you work in a public house. Two o'clock in the morning seems very late for you to be getting home on a weekday.'

'I took my time.' She flushed beneath the brim of her felt hat. 'I was wiv a fella.'

'Have you given this *fella*'s name to the police?'

Silence.

'Miss Wright.'

'I don't know his name. Except it were Tom. That's it.'

'All right, we'll leave the matter for now. So what happened when you did arrive home?'

'The kitchen were dark except for a bit of a red glow from the stove and one oil lamp. At first I couldn't tell what had gone on. Then I seen my mum's face and I knew he'd beaten her up again.'

'And what was she doing?'

'Just sitting there.'

'And your father?'

Her head went down so that her face was concealed.

'Answer the question, Miss Wright.'

'I didn't see him at first,' she mumbled so low that the court had to strain to hear. 'Then ma pointed at him. She were holdin' a knife and she pointed to where he was lying on the floor.'

'So what did you do?'

'I started crying to see my dad all bloody and still like that. He weren't perfect, my dad, but he was my dad.' She sobbed into a grubby handkerchief. 'Then I just stood there, I didn't know what to do but ma said I needed to get the kids out the house before they seen what had happened so I ran upstairs and stripped off my clothes – there was so much blood – and then I took them next door.'

'How exactly did the blood get on your clothes, Miss Wright, if, as you say, you *just stood there*?'

For the first time she glanced at her mother. 'I think it must have splashed up a table leg and I brushed against it.'

'So there was blood everywhere. Was it on your mother's clothes too?'

'On her nightdress and the knife and her slippers and the floor by her feet. He were laying in a pool of it.'

'We are not disputing the amount of blood,' observed Nicholas, 'there is really no need to distress Miss Wright by pursuing this line of questioning.'

Greenacre smiled, presumably satisfied that the jury would retain the gory picture painted by Trudy who was shaking so much that she could hardly hold herself upright.

Nicholas gave her a reassuring smile. 'Miss Wright, you told my friend Mr Greenacre that sometimes your mother couldn't help arguing with your father.'

'Because she were stubborn, you see. Above all she stuck up for us, especially Robbie, like when he went on strike. Or told him there was no money. And then he would beat her.'

'So sometimes there was a reason – at least in your father's mind – for him to get angry with her. But what if your mother said nothing and tiptoed round your father every day? What if she was kind to him and let him have the money he asked for?'

'Then he'd go out and get drunk.'

'And when he came home? What happened then?'

'Sometimes he'd give her a clout, like if he fell over a shoe that had been left on the stairs or such.'

'So there was usually something that would upset him, even on good days.'

She nodded. 'Could be anything.'

As Nicholas quirked a brow at the jury to ensure they'd understood the point, I was struck, as so often before, by how the chaos of human lives was tidied up in court, discussed and sorted by elegant, bewigged men in gowns.

'Let's talk about something else, Miss Wright,' continued Nicholas. 'Please don't look so worried. I'm not going to ask you to dwell on what happened to your father. I'd prefer to talk about other things.' But why stop there? I thought. Surely he should tackle her about the knife? He needed to establish that it was on the mantel, not in the kitchen, and that it was regularly sharpened, whenever there was sufficient cash. 'You left school at thirteen, I believe,' he was saying, 'and went into service with a Mrs Jane Derbyshire whose household you stayed in for five years, working as a general servant, before you were dismissed.'

She looked mutinously at me. 'Yes.'

'Tell me, Miss Wright, do you think you were treated fairly by Mrs Derbyshire? For instance, were you well paid?'

'She were just normal. She didn't pay me much because I was very young. And when I broke things I had to give her the price of them, and sometimes she would make me work on my half-day holiday if I'd been sulky or clumsy or such.'

'Did she ever lay hands on you?'

'Not hands . . . But sometimes she'd hit out with her hairbrush or take a ladle off the hook in the kitchen and beat me about the shoulders.'

'And so you applied for another job?'

'My Lord, I do wonder where this line of questioning is taking us,' commented Greenacre.

'What happened when you applied for that new job, Miss Wright?' asked Thorne.

'Miss Gifford knows perfectly well what happened,' shouted Trudy. 'She shouldn't have told you! I got the job all right, but in the end I couldn't bear to let Mrs Derbyshire know I were leaving.'

'Why?'

'I was too scared of what she'd do to me, so when the letter come asking for references I burnt it.'

'You ended up in court, on a charge of theft, I believe.'

'Yes.' Her cheeks were livid.

Nicholas smiled apologetically. 'You are wondering why I'm asking you these questions. Well, if it's any consolation, I'm sure the jury is too. The point is this. My friend the prosecutor has suggested that in some ways your mother was asking for trouble when she argued with your father but I'm saying that there are some people, like your father and Mrs Derbyshire, who are always ready to find fault. Time and again you ran into trouble with Mrs Derbyshire, however hard you tried, and in the end you were so browbeaten and terrified that you behaved recklessly enough to end up in a criminal court.'

'Forgive me,' said Greenacre, 'but are we comparing the burning of a letter to murder?'

Nicholas's manner had changed entirely. With Gertrude he had been gentle and even avuncular. Now he was uncompromising, and apparently several inches taller, as he addressed the jury directly.

'We are looking at the effects on mother and daughter of systematic physical and mental abuse. We are talking about women who become so intimidated and confused that they are sometimes incapable of behaving in a rational way.'

'I think we have stretched this point to its absolute limit,' said Thurgood reprovingly. 'Can we move on?'

Nicholas had no further questions for Miss Wright, who was by now sobbing so copiously that she had to be escorted from the court.

The police witnesses could only give evidence about the scene that greeted them when they arrived in the Wrights' kitchen at about three thirty in the morning. Next came the obligatory army friend who could vouch for Wright's bravery and comradeship during the war.

'Yeah, he liked a drink or two but he were a great bloke. I'd trust him with me life. Shame that his back got so bad he couldn't work. He were a proud man and wanted to do his best by his family. No wonder he were fond of a beer.'

'Was he violent at all, during the time you knew him in the army?'

'No more than anyone else. We had the odd moment. He liked a bevy. But he were a good skin.'

The most damning evidence was given by the police doctor who had examined Wright's body both at the scene of the crime and later in the morgue. The same doctor had made an inventory of the bruises on Mrs Wright's body and his dark eyes glanced beadily from her to me as he gave his evidence.

'Yes,' he said, 'there was no question that when I saw Mrs Wright that morning in Lavender Hill Police Station, in the presence of her lawyer, she had been badly beaten very recently.'

'Could the injuries have been self-inflicted?'

'Unlikely. It's possible she could have fallen down the stairs, improbable that she would have beaten herself about the body with a chair leg, and impossible, in my experience, for her to have inflicted upon herself the kinds of bruises I've seen on victims of rape.'

'Would you say that Mrs Wright's injuries were life-threatening?'

'Sexual intercourse with her husband and then a beating with a chair leg? The answer is before us all in court. There stands Mrs Wright in the dock, alive.'

The clerk paused in his note taking while the judge coughed and glanced with distaste at the doctor then rather more sympathetically at Mrs Wright.

'As for Edward Wright's body,' continued the doctor, 'there were three jagged stab wounds to the throat, the second and third completely unnecessary if you'll forgive the rather odd turn of phrase. What I mean is this, that in order to disable her husband, and indeed to kill him, the first stab, which cut deep into a vein, would have been more than enough. But in no way could even this be described as a display of necessary force. A simple slash across the cheek or hand would have done the trick and deterred him, surely. As it was, Mrs Wright must have stabbed him with considerable and calculated force in the one place that even the most ignorant of us knows to be fatal – the jugular.'

'I'm surprised at the witness for presenting such speculative evidence.' Thorne observed. 'As a medical man he might be an expert on the causes of death but I challenge him to define what constitutes necessary or unnecessary force in the mind of a defendant. A woman who has just been raped and beaten by her husband might not be quite as clear-headed as the good doctor.'

'Raped?' queried the judge. 'I'm surprised at you, Mr Thorne. We are talking about a husband and wife, are we not?'

'And after being stabbed in the jugular vein, what would have happened to the victim?' continued Greenacre suavely.

'There would have been a quantity of blood. The victim would have fallen to the ground and continued to bleed copiously. Indeed, he had quite a large contusion on the back of his head. I would say he had fallen to the floor and was probably unconscious by the time she stabbed him again.'

Thorne shot to his feet. 'You are a police doctor and have been so for a dozen years. Where is your evidence for saying that he was unconscious after the first stabbing? My Lord, I beg you to intervene. We accept that Mrs Wright stabbed her husband in self-defence; we utterly refute the suggestion that she did so while he was unconscious.'

'I agree, Mr Thorne. I cannot allow such an allegation to be made at this late stage. I would ask the jury to erase from their minds any suggestion that Mrs Wright stabbed her husband while he was unconscious.'

'And just to be clear,' added Thorne, 'you tell us, doctor, that the first stab wound was calculated. Are you sure it was not simply chance that the knife fell where it did?'

'It's a remote possibility. But why strike again and again in the same place? It seems to me that Mrs Wright knew perfectly well that these blows were fatal.'

'Or she might, in her overwrought state, have been beyond knowing what she was doing.'

'Do forgive me,' said the doctor, emollient as ever. 'Was that a question? If it was, as you've pointed out, it's not my job to speculate.'

The prosecution case was thus concluded on a bad-tempered note and the courtroom waited in taut silence while the judge retired and Mrs Wright was returned to the cells. Before she was transported back to Holloway we were allowed a brief word and found her in an almost delirious state with a deep flush coming and going in her neck and cheeks.

'He's scrambled my mind with all that stuff about conscious and unconscious,' she said. 'I don't know how I'm to stand up to-morrow and say what happened.'

'Try to think about it quietly tonight,' Nicholas advised her. His manner, outside the courtroom, was so intimate and kind that he might have been her older brother. 'Tell them what happened in your own words, and all will be well.'

'What if I just don't know any more? What if I can't remember?'

'Then say that. Anyone would be confused about a terrible in-cident such as this.'

'It just gets worse and worse, don't it? Why does that doctor hate me so?'

'I don't think he hates you. I think he's a little puzzled about what happened, has taken a view and is trying, in his way, to get at the truth. That's what we're here for, to test his word against yours.'

'But I was there,' she cried, 'he wasn't.'

'That's just it, Mrs Wright. And that's why everyone will listen to you tomorrow.'

As Nicholas and I made our way out of the building together I was steeling myself for a conversation but he bade me a curt farewell and did not even discuss the prospect of the case ending the next day or what he thought of Mrs Wright's chances.

# Chapter Fifty-Three

When Mrs Wright entered the witness box the following day, she seemed an incongruous figure within the stately oak panelling of the courtroom, like a puppet finding itself by chance on the set of an opera. She took Nicholas's instruction to answer his questions as briefly as possible so literally that at first I wondered if she might lose any vestiges of sympathy. Actually, a rhythm was set up that perhaps helped to establish her credibility in the jury's minds.

'How many children do you have, Mrs Wright?'

'Five living, two dead.'

'We've heard that you were beaten by your husband time after time. Why didn't you leave him?'

'The children. Where would we have gone?'

'A few weeks ago you reported your husband to the police and then failed to turn up at his trial to bear witness to what he'd done to you. Why was that?'

'He kept writing me letters telling me he'd got a job. And in any case . . .'

'In any case?'

'I knew what he'd do if I turned up in court and then he were set free.'

'What was his behaviour like after he came home following the court hearing?'

'He were very angry. He just sat there. I knew he'd turn.'

'Did he take up the job offer?'

'There were no job.'

'Why was the knife kept on the mantelpiece?'

'Out of harm's way.'

In painstaking detail, Nicholas guided Mrs Wright through the events which had led up to the stabbing; the news of Robbie's arrest, the menacing atmosphere in the house, the brief, peaceful interlude while Wright was out at the pub, his lumbering return, forcing himself upon her and dragging her from the bed by the hair.

'We were on the landing. He give me a shove and I sort of tumbled down and down. I couldn't save myself. My head cracked against the wall at the bottom of the stairs.'

'We have heard evidence about the injuries sustained by you as a result of that fall, Mrs Wright. And you showed the police the mark on the wall.'

'I did. So then he lifts me up by the elbow – I have to keep quiet, you see, because of the kids being asleep – and he takes me into the back room and by now he's got hold of my throat and he picks up the chair and wrenches out the leg and gives me a clout across the stomach. That's when I reached back and got hold of the knife. I thought he was going to kill me. I'd never seen him so bad. So I jabbed him, in the neck.'

'Then what happened?'

'After a moment he let go of me and fell down. Then I stabbed him again, twice.'

'You say he fell down. How did he fall?'

'There was blood. A little bit then a gush. He give me a look, one of them staring looks of his. Like he hated me and was blaming me for what I'd brung him to. Then he fell.'

'The police doctor has told us he believes your husband was already on the ground when you stabbed him the second time.'

'That's true.'

'The doctor further said that you didn't need to stab your husband more than once because the first time would have been enough.'

She shrugged.

'So why did you?'

'Like I said. Imagine if he were still alive, what he would have done to me.'

'Mrs Wright, one of the questions that my learned friend the prosecutor will ask the jury to consider is why you killed your husband on that particular night when he had attacked you on so many others. He will say that it was because the knife was handy and that you'd even had it sharpened for that purpose.'

'That's right. I knew it were there and that it were sharp.'

'So you planned to kill him?'

'Of course not. I didn't want to kill him.'

'Then why did you?'

'Trudy was out. Robbie was in prison. He weren't going to stop with that chair leg. What could I do?'

'Are you a religious woman, Mrs Wright?'

'I suppose. But he wouldn't let me go to church.'

'You were christened a Roman Catholic, I think. What does your religion tell you about suffering?'

'That you have to put up with it because Jesus did.'

'I have a little book with me that was found under your pillow, by your lawyer, Miss Gifford, and myself when we visited the house after you'd been arrested. It's called *The Imitation of Christ* by Thomas à Kempis. Here it is. Perhaps you could tell the court what à Kempis says about suffering.'

'Can I find the page in the book?' The usher handed her the book which she held with great tenderness, and easily found the place she was looking for. '*If I send thee any heaviness or contrariness, have no indignation thereof, nor let thy heart fail . . .*'

'And yet you killed your husband, Mrs Wright, which shows rather a lot of indignation, I'd say. So why did you, a gentle, Christian woman, who had put up with all that her husband had done to her before, suddenly stab him with a kitchen knife?'

She stared at the little cloth-covered book in her hand. 'Because I didn't want to die. It seemed to me that the kids needed me more than they needed him.'

Greenacre, when he rose to question her, first looked at the jury as if to say: I ask you, do I need to take this case any further? Next he gave the defendant a long, pitying look from his weary eyes.

'You do realise, Mrs Wright, that all Mr Thorne has managed to find in your defence is that you are a religious woman who acted out of character when you stabbed your husband. Can you tell us again why you killed him on that particular night?'

'He were so mad about Robbie being arrested that he terrified me, and I knew Robbie wouldn't be back to protect me.'

'We've heard from the doctor who gave evidence about your injuries, Mrs Wright, that none of them was life-threatening. So why, if you weren't afraid for your life, did you kill him that night?'

'But I *was* afraid. I didn't know what I was doing.'

'But if you so were so afraid and so wounded, how on earth did you manage to reach for a knife and find the strength to jab it deep into your husband's throat?'

Nicholas protested, 'That is an impossible question for Mrs Wright to answer.'

'You said that he fell, after you stabbed him the first time,' said Greenacre. 'And then you stabbed him again, not once, but twice more. Why was that, Mrs Wright?'

'I said. I were afraid.'

'Afraid of a man lying in a pool of his own blood? Why didn't you just leave the room or go next door and get help?'

'I – I just didn't think of it.'

'But you did think to stab him twice more.'

Silence.

'Mrs Wright, when he fell to the floor, was he losing a lot of blood, was he even unconscious?'

'I don't know.'

'If he was, why did you need to stab him again?'

'I don't know. I don't know!' She covered her face with her hands while Greenacre shook his head sorrowfully at the jury.

Our next witness was Robbie who looked gaunt and weary in an oversized suit and tie. He was accompanied by a guard, who stood at a discreet distance. Although he managed to smile at his mother he studiously avoided looking at me. As he had been locked up on the night of the murder he could only talk about his father's violence on previous occasions and his fears for his mother's safety.

'I hated to be the cause of grief and yet she told me time after time that I must be sure to live as I would wish to, and not worry about her. She's the opposite to him. All he could think of was his own self, and who to blame for what he called his miserable life.'

'I'm sure the jury will wish to know why you are in prison, Mr Wright,' said Greenacre. 'Ah dear me, I see from my notes that you threw nails in front of a bus during the recent unrest. Perhaps it's a family trait, to be somewhat reckless with dangerous metal objects.'

'That remark is unworthy of my friend,' observed Nicholas, 'and should be struck out.'

'During your interview with the police, what did you tell them about your mother's kitchen knife and where it was stored?'

'I said it were kept in a pot in the scullery. Sometimes it was.'

'Perhaps you could clarify the word *sometimes*,' put in Thorne.

'Not always, that's what I meant.'

Finally we called the coal merchant Martin Withers, whose face and hands were ingrained with soot and who spoke sympathetically of the Wright family's predicament.

'I took the boy Robbie on because I knew his father of old, and that he was a drunkard and no good. I thought I could help the boy.'

'But now he's in prison.'

'He's a good boy, though wilful. Not at all like his dad. I'll give him that. The father was bone idle from the start. When Miss Gifford come to see me and asked if I would go to court I said I would, because I want to see the boy and his mother safe home. I know that family could come good if all the money weren't thrown away on booze.'

'Will there be a job for Robbie when he gets out of prison?'

'There will.'

Greenacre's eyebrows had shot up under his wig.

'I have never in my life heard a defence such as this. The jury is effectively being told that Mrs Wright cannot be found guilty because her son's employer is kind enough to keep a job open for him. Desperate measures indeed.'

Thurgood adjourned the case until two o'clock and the courtroom disintegrated into a hubbub of speculation. I rushed over to the nearest court official and asked if he would persuade the custody sergeant to let Robbie have a few minutes with his mother before he was returned to Pentonville. They must have decided Mrs Wright was doomed because they were painstakingly civil and told me they would bring him to her and that he could spend as long with her as he liked.

A half-eaten bowl of soup lay on the table before her. She had perhaps tucked into it quite heartily before she realised the significance of where she was and what was happening – I remembered the relish with which she'd tried to eat a teacake in Lyons'. But by the way she was now playing with the remaining soup I could tell she was at the very end of her tether. Robbie, when he was brought in, sat beside her, and for want of knowing what else to do, he picked up the spoon and prepared a mouthful for her.

'You should eat your soup, Mother.'

She smiled at him sadly. 'I will, Robbie, in a minute. Now listen, I'm glad Miss Gifford brought you here because I want you to know that I don't regret what I done. It was nobody's fault but my own that it turned out like this. And I want you to be strong and get out of that place and be free, my boy. What I want is for you and Trudy and all the others not to be afraid in this world. And if you're not, it will all be worth it, do you understand?'

He nodded and she took the spoon from him, as if satisfied.

'Will it all be over this afternoon, Miss Gifford?' was her next question.

'That will depend on the jury, how long they take, and of course we haven't heard what Mr Thorne intends to say.'

We were all talking much too brightly, as if holding on to a sliver of sanity. When the time came for Robbie to leave, he pressed his forehead into his mother's shoulder while she clasped the back of his head and kissed him as if he were a little boy. He turned his face into her neck and gave one long sobbing breath before he dashed from the room. I touched his arm as he passed, and then I sat at the table with Mrs Wright as she resumed the eating of her soup, applying herself as if it were a vital task that required her full attention.

# Chapter Fifty-Four

When the court reconvened and Nicholas began his summing up, I sat very tidily in my place behind him, pencil and notebook aligned on the ledge, hands folded. Daniel, who had arrived in the nick of time, had adopted his customary pose, leaning back in the seat beside me, legs extended. My whole being was concentrated on Mrs Wright whose head was now drooping with exhaustion, and on Nicholas.

Save her, I begged him silently.

'Mrs Wright is a good woman,' he began, 'who made the mistake of marrying a man who proved to be a drunkard and a wife-beater. Wright was a heavy man, over five foot ten inches in height, whereas she is a small, frail woman. The story of her marriage is all too familiar – a feckless husband, the struggle to bring up children decently, a constant battle to make ends meet. And on top of all that, she had to endure violence on an ever-increasing scale, such that a matter of weeks before her husband died she was taken to hospital with a broken jaw.

'As a result of this brutality, her life was reduced in every possible way. We've heard from her neighbours and her son how Wright belittled, confined and beat her. He refused to work, claiming a damaged back for which he sought neither medical help nor compensation, thus condemning his family to great poverty until his oldest children were of an age to earn properly. Despite all this, we have heard that Mrs Wright remained a religious woman and a loving mother who encouraged her son and daughter to think and act freely, even though she knew her husband would punish her for it.

'The question is: how is such a woman to defend herself? Her husband has trapped her in the house and diminished her confidence and physical strength; her only protectors are away from home for much of the time. In the end, she knows, he will either kill her or beat her so savagely that she will never recover. She prays and reads a religious book. She longs to do what is right.

'If someone is physically weak, they cannot retaliate in kind when a stronger person hits them. Wright had brute force on his side and even, as I'm sure he would have told us in no uncertain terms, what he believed to be the moral right to treat her as he wished because she was his wife. His behaviour knew no boundaries. So let us, for a moment, place ourselves in Mrs Wright's shoes. Imagine her terror at being dragged night after night from sleep to have sexual intercourse forced upon her, to be flung downstairs, to be beaten with the leg of a chair loosened specifically for that purpose. The prosecution argues that on the night she killed him, she took advantage of the fact that her son Robbie wouldn't be coming home – and indeed, I agree that we shouldn't ignore the wider context of this tragic event. The nation was in the grip of a general strike. The Wright household, like so many others, was divided in opinion about how the strike could and should proceed, and it was under even more stress than usual because Robbie would probably lose his job. It was as if history itself was leaning on this family, pushing it over the edge.

'Much has been made of the three stab wounds. But I say, one stab wound or three, what does it matter? If Mrs Wright had stabbed her husband only once, I'm quite sure my learned friend the prosecutor would have accused her of almost surgical accuracy. After all, no one in her right mind would stab again and again. But the most reasonable explanation for the three wounds is that Mrs Wright thought her husband was still alive after the first and was afraid of him.

'What I'm asking you to believe is that, in the end, everything Mrs Wright did was out of love for her children. Note the arguments over school shoes, over Robbie's participation in the strike, the silent endurance of so many beatings. All for the children. Imagine their plight if she had only wounded her husband and he had lived and was still lurking there in his armchair by the hearth, waiting for the next excuse to beat her? She made no attempt to cover her tracks but sat with the knife in her lap until the police came because she wanted them to see exactly what she'd done. Until that moment Mrs Wright had never, in all her years of married life, been safe in her own home. She was very clear. It was kill or be killed, if not on that night, then in the days, weeks, months or years to come. And if he killed her, what would become of her children?

'And which one of us, hand on heart, would not have done the same? Who has not performed some uncharacteristic action, great or small, because they were too frightened or confused, or because they were so full of love that they couldn't see any other way? Be in no doubt, of those three emotions – fear, confusion and love – it is the latter that drives the woman before you and her love is of the purest kind. For her there could be no contest in a choice between saving her own life and the future lives of her children.

'Members of the jury, this was certainly not a proportionate act. How does the seizing of a kitchen knife by a woman – already weakened by sexual violence followed by shameful blows to the head and body with a loosened chair leg – compare with more than two decades of intimidation and endless, shattering injuries? I'd say that, under the circumstances, this was rather a small act of defiance. Don't compound the tragedy of her marriage by finding Hetty Wright guilty of murder. Find that she is innocent because she had no choice. Let her go free and return to her children, thereby allowing some good to come of this desperately sad case.'

But the judge, in his directions to the jury, effectively overturned Nicholas's argument.

'Of course the Wright family would be better off with a mother. Having lost one parent, they are now perhaps to lose the other but you must not be swayed by pity. You must consider whether this was premeditated murder or the act of a desperate woman who feared for her life. The defence in this case is that Mrs Wright was using what we call proportionate means to defend herself. If you feel that a woman's use of a sharp knife is proportionate against a man's brandishing of a table leg, then you may find her innocent. But you will also need to take into account that she had been beaten many times before and had always survived. Was she really in fear of her life that night? This is what you will need to ask yourselves. Or was she simply at the end of her tether, in which case you should find her guilty.'

The jury retired. Mrs Wright was taken to the cells and an usher threw open another casement because the fitful sun was now blazing through the glass. Nicholas untied the pink ribbon from a new brief and set to work on it. Eventually Daniel and I left the building and walked round the block. The high buildings on all sides cut out the sun and I was shivering until he drew my hand through his arm to protect me from the gusty wind. When we'd performed a couple of circuits I waited on the steps while he went back inside to ask for news. In a few minutes he was back.

'The jury is on its way,' he said. 'They've only taken two hours. Not long enough, surely?'

'Perhaps they'll ask for more time.'

'Thurgood won't like that.'

'I don't think the judge was with us. He more or less directed them to find her guilty.'

'Sometimes that can work in the defendant's favour, if the jury feels he's being too harsh.'

We raced along the corridor and arrived just as Mrs Wright was brought back to the dock. Nicholas glanced round and gave Daniel a formal smile. The judge took a while settling himself and there was the customary flipping down of seats and shuffling of feet as at last the foreman rose.

'Did you reach a unanimous verdict?'

'We did.'

'What do you find?'

The foreman had a strong, fatherly face, and he glanced sideways at Mrs Wright before answering, 'We find Mrs Wright *not* guilty.' Then he smiled.

The court was in uproar as women in the public benches cheered and stamped. Mrs Wright swayed and was helped to sit down by her gaoler. It seemed to take many minutes for the formalities to be over and the judge to leave the courtroom but at last I stumbled to the dock.

'You're free, Hetty. You're free!' She shook her head and wept and went on sitting there long after the gaoler had unlocked the

door and thrown it open. The women in the gallery were still clapping and cheering and shouting out to her. By the time I'd seen
her escorted away to collect her things, Nicholas had gathered up
his papers and was already leaving.

'Nicholas,' I cried.

The rush of joy and relief had not yet faded from his eyes.

'I'm amazed. I thought we'd had it. We really must have found
the right words, Evie.'

'Don't forget Thomas à Kempis. He helped.'

We were like lunatics, laughing and gazing at each other in
delight and disbelief.

Daniel came to my side. In response to his vigorous handshake Nicholas gave him a gratified smile but then the handshake
changed into something different – both men stood quite still as
the smile faded from Nicholas's eyes and was replaced by a puzzled withdrawal. Eventually I saw Daniel give a little nod, clap
Nicholas on the shoulder and move away. By the time Nicholas
and I shook hands he was reserved and received my repeated congratulations with bent head. The prosecutor wanted a word, Mrs
Wright must be spoken to again and arrangements made for her
to be taken home. I went to gather my papers and when I looked
up Nicholas was gone.

Daniel and I were to have an early supper in a restaurant near
Victoria so that I could go home and pack. After we'd studied the
menu he leaned back in his chair, folded his arms and regarded
me across the expanse of tablecloth.

'So you're going away for three weeks. How shall I manage
without you?'

'I daresay you'll all get along rather well. Miss Drake will be
especially solicitous.'

'Oh indeed, Miss Drake will have things all her own way again.'

We were silent as the waiter poured white wine. Daniel, who took
all such things seriously, swirled the contents of his glass, sniffed
and took an appraising sip. We talked about my journey, Paris,
trips he had taken to the Pyrenees. I had ordered fish but when
it came I found I couldn't eat. 'So what would you say swung it
today?' Daniel asked. 'Everyone thought we were done for.'

'Mrs Wright undoubtedly had the jury's sympathy, don't you think? She looked so vulnerable. And we have Thomas à Kempis to thank.'

'And an extraordinarily eloquent advocate.' When he offered his hand, palm up, I laid down my knife and fork and drew my chair closer into the table so that I could reach him. 'It seemed to me that there was rather more going on in that courtroom than the defence of a poor, abused woman.' I knew that smile of his so well now; a little shy, very tender. 'I would say, Evelyn, that what we were witnessing this afternoon was a man throwing his hat into quite a different ring than that of a murder trial. Not just his hat . . .'

It was early evening and the quiet restaurant was dim and monochrome except that each table was decorated with a little vase of two carnations, one yellow, one pink, and a sprig of gypsophila.

'We got engaged at the very worst time,' Daniel said, 'right at the start of the strike, with your flatmate leaving and everything changing. I know you would never go back on your word and you are aware that I have been stung once and you are thinking, I mustn't hurt him again. But Evelyn, if you don't love me enough, you shouldn't be marrying me. She – the woman in the war – was callous – you, perhaps, do not protect yourself enough. If we are to marry, it must be as equals, in every sense.'

'Sir . . . Daniel, I would never . . .'

He kissed my fingers. 'The devil of it is, Evelyn, that at one time I would have given everything I possessed, and I do mean everything, to see you look at me the way you looked at him at the end of that trial.' A waiter approached to remove my plate but thought better of it. 'I really thought I could win you. I thought everything was in place, love and work and our future. But I'd reckoned without something I'd not fully understood until today. Perhaps, after all, it would have terrified me if you had loved me that much. Perhaps I'm not designed to be loved on so grand a scale.'

My throat hurt. 'I didn't know, I didn't realise, when I accepted . . . I'm so sorry. To have hurt you . . .'

'I'm not apportioning blame – neither of us is at fault here. Perhaps love, like the law, has to be tested, knocked about a bit. Don't waste time regretting what's happened, Evelyn. I shan't.'

'But I so want to . . .'

'Go to Sanary-sur-Mer. Spend time with your nephew. Talk to Meredith. Have some fun. My dearest girl, I will survive, as I always have done – perhaps a little too well – on my own. And when you come home we can continue as we used to. Do you understand? I'm releasing you. I'm exonerating you.'

Afterwards he found me a cab and insisted on paying my fare home. He kissed my cheek and when he'd closed the door I looked back as usual, half-blinded by tears, but he'd put on his hat and was rapidly walking away. It was only as the cab pulled out from the kerb that I saw him falter; his head went down and he put his hand up to his face, then I lost sight of him.

## Chapter Fifty-Five

Mother came to Victoria to see me off. I felt as if I were sixteen as she peered into my compartment to check that my travelling companions were not too unsavoury and that I had not mislaid the parcel of sandwiches Rose had supplied for the journey. The residents of Clivedon Hall Gardens either thought that there was no food to be had in France or that the prices would be extortionate and the ingredients dangerous to the constitution.

As the train pulled away we waved at each other vigorously and I felt the snag of her habitual fearfulness as she edged through the crowds, handbag gripped on her arm, looking anxiously about for the entrance to the Underground station. But I was travelling away from Clivedon Hall Gardens and the lonely flat in Pimlico and the Petits and the Wrights. Goodbye, Miss Drake, and your knitted suits and your implacable frostiness; goodbye, Mr Wolfe, and goodbye my dear, unsettling, heartbreaking Daniel Breen. The train huffed and puffed through the Kent countryside, past all the paraphernalia of those thousands of lives that went on alongside mine: farmyards, allotments, chickens and rickety outhouses.

At one point – perhaps as I boarded the ferry at Dover – something inside me came loose and I felt light as air and truly alone. Meredith and Edmund were waiting for me in a distant place but in the meantime it was just Evelyn. In a kind of trance I plunged in and out of a novel by Dorothy L. Sayers and avoided thinking about what had happened in London after the Wright trial. I didn't even dwell on Jamie and his deadly wartime journeys through Calais. I let them go, let them go.

In Paris, I took a taxi to the Gare de Lyon, lapping up the strangeness of the Parisian streets, then booked my two suitcases into left luggage and set out armed with a map kindly supplied by my new friend in Thomas Cook's. I walked down to the Seine and along the river until I came to the Île de la Cité and Notre Dame. Next I ventured north-west into the fashionable Rue St-Honoré, peering at the windows displaying chic couture gowns, then at the smaller windows above them.

Here I am, Grandmother, and I imagined her on the other side of the glass on the first or second floor, in Rusbridger's arms. Did you know even then that he would break your heart? You must have done. He was a married man and you a very young girl. But you were rescued by your schoolteacher, was that it? And if Mother is right, you lived to count your blessings. I remembered how Mother had described her in the garden of the Ruislip schoolhouse, standing in her husband's arms, so happy. Life in her wake felt explosive and unpredictably fraught with danger and tragedy. But it seemed to me that everything she had done, even as a star-struck young actress, had been for love. Better to feel, even if afterwards I must suffer, than not feel at all.

Because Mrs Wright was alive, I too could breathe freely, and though pain and confusion frilled my veins, though they were clustered about me on the fringes of my consciousness, the dead and the wounded, the ones I loved and the ones I could not love enough, it was like being new born into a new light.

The Rue St-Honoré was choked with traffic; on the narrow pavement I stepped aside for an elderly woman swaddled in furs with delicate ankles and tiny, patent leather shoes who cast me a swift, bird-like glance. I smiled and suddenly so did she. Next I trekked down to the Place de la Bastille which I discovered to be unromantically flat and vast so that we pedestrians were insignificant as ants, then back to the station a prudent hour and a half early to retrieve my cases and find my seat. A local wag, watching me eat my picnic, told me that the British always complained that French food gave them stomach ache whereas in fact it was the festering sandwiches they brought with them that were to blame.

I hardly slept that night, propped upright on a hard seat and jolted awake time after time until I saw the milky dawn rise over foreign hills. The countryside was lush with early summer and we arrived at the clanging station in Marseille at eight in the morning. The remaining sandwiches went in a bin and I bought coffee and brioche thinking all the time, I love this.

At eleven the slow-moving coastal train set off through the scruffy suburbs and into stations with names that had seemed impossibly fictional when pointed out by the clerk at Thomas Cook – Aubagne, La Ciotat, Cassis and Bandol. To my left I glimpsed rocky hills, forests and farmland, to my right occasionally a blue sea speckled with boats.

At Bandol I glimpsed a proper French seaside with a cluster of painted houses tumbling towards the sea, but as we left, the track went inland until I saw the next town, Sanary, steam past and I thought I must somehow have missed the station altogether but we slowed down by a shabby colonnaded structure signed Ollioules Sanary. Toppling out into the searing sunshine, dragging my cases after me, I heard a high-pitched cry, 'She's there. Aunty Evelyn. Aunty Evelyn,' and a missile in the form of a small boy hurtled towards me, butting my stomach with his head and clutching my skirts as I reached down and hauled him into my arms.

Outside Meredith was waiting with a hired donkey cart. The heat shimmered and enrobed me and I sat in the cart with my arm around Edmund, smiling and smiling. Meredith wore a broad-brimmed sun hat and pink dress and teased me for my impossibly heavy English summer blouse and twill skirt. They talked about what they would show me, the preparations they had made and the meal that awaited us. The lugubrious driver hardly needed to manage his ancient charges as we wove through the little town which was just as Meredith had described it, with a warm wind blowing along the shadowy streets, apricot-painted stucco peeling from the walls and people pausing mid-conversation to stare as we passed.

We halted in the oddly shaped Place Albert Cavet where Meredith paid the driver and I followed her through a door beside a charcuterie and up to a tiny second-floor apartment reeking of oil paints, with a vase of brilliant pink flowers on the sill and canvases stacked against the walls. A feast had been set out upon the table and Welcome Aunty Evelyn was writ large on a banner on the wall.

By the end of the day Edmund had shown me every inch of the little town, taken me along the promenades, into the church with its luminous wall paintings in coral and blue and up to the oratory on the hill where we lit candles for Jamie and Grandmother. Honestly, Aunt Prudence, I thought, in this warm Roman Catholic place even you would have thrown caution to the wind and done the same. Late in the afternoon they had taken me to a favourite beach under a slanting cliff and for the first time I swam in transparent blue water.

In the mornings that followed Edmund was required to study with his mother but she decreed that I might have a few days off before I embarked on a course of English poetry with him, so I went out on my own. Opposite the little restaurant which Meredith had painted to lure me here, with the woman shelling beans under an awning, I had noticed a coiffeuse.

At first, the hairdresser was reluctant to cut my hair. My French was rusty but I understood that she had no idea how it would hang when short, given the curl. Gradually we both became mesmerised by the slicing of steel blades through thick, wavy locks and the fall of one tress after another on to the blue and yellow tiled floor. I watched Evelyn arise like a phoenix from piles of my own tresses, still pale but with skin touched by the sun and hair which sat in a cloud above my ears and in a curling fringe on my forehead so that I resembled Mother, in her pre-war glory days, and my grandmother in her misty greatness as Grace Harkaway in *London Assurance*.

That night I treated Meredith and Edmund to a meal at a table outside that same restaurant with its check cloths clipped in place to guard against a sudden residual gust of the mistral. Neither approved of what I'd done; Edmund because he hated change – 'You don't look like you any more,' he complained – and Meredith because she'd told me not to have my hair cut.

But I was wearing Grandmother's ornament in the shape of an edelweiss and I loved the way my hair swung over my ears and the night air breathed on my neck. We ate mussels and swordfish and finally, having been struck dumb for a couple of days by the enchantment of Sanary, I began to talk of everything that had happened over the previous months, the Petit case and the trial of Mrs Wright.

'It was all touch and go,' I told them. 'We had to prove that Mrs Wright had no choice but to kill her husband – in other words, that if she hadn't he would have killed her.'

Edmund's knife and fork hung suspended over his plate. 'What do you mean *prove*?'

'Make the jury sure. Which was very difficult, because we only had Mrs Wright's word about what had happened. Two things helped. The first was that we had instructed a fine barrister called Nicholas Thorne.'

'Gracious,' said Meredith sharply. 'Nicholas Thorne, of all people. Well, Evelyn.'

'The second was a fifteenth-century priest, Thomas à Kempis, who wrote a very eloquent and famous text called *The Imitation of Christ* about how to be a Christian. Mrs Wright kept a copy under her pillow. Thorne managed to persuade the jury that such a religious woman, who believed that faith could transcend all wrong, would never kill except if she was absolutely forced to.'

'*Make Lord every trial of tribulation to me amiable and for thy name desirable: for to suffer and be vexed for thee is full wholesome to my soul*', recited Meredith. 'I used to know that book by heart.'

'But there were all kinds of difficulties. For instance, Mrs Wright said the knife was usually kept on a very high mantelpiece, you know, so high that the children couldn't have reached it, whereas her son told the police it was usually kept in a pot in the kitchen. So it looked as if Mrs Wright had deliberately taken the knife out of the pot and left it somewhere she could reach in a fight.'

'And is that what she did?' demanded Edmund, so engrossed that Meredith had to jog his arm to remind him to eat.

'No, I think she was telling the truth about the knife. She'd left it on the mantel, so the children wouldn't find it.'

'So what happened?' asked Edmund, who had concealed the last of his green beans under his knife and was keeping a weather eye on his mother.

'Well, her husband had hold of her, and she must have been near the mantel and remembered the knife and reached up . . .'

'Reached up?' said Edmund. 'Why, is she very small?'

384

'No, the mantel was high, above her head. Goodness, Edmund, this is worse than being in court.'

Meredith laid down her knife and fork. 'It all sounds very strange to me. If the knife was on the mantel above her head, and he was attacking her with a chair leg, how could she have reached it?'

'I expect she hooked her arm over her head and just made a grab for it, you know.'

Her eyes were incredulous. 'But if he was strangling her with one hand and hitting her with the other, surely it would have been almost impossible for her to reach the knife. Look.' She got up, gripped her throat with her right hand and pretended to ward off an assailant with the other. 'So come on, Evie, what really happened?'

I put down my fork and touched the back of my head to test the new lightness of my shorn hair. 'Somehow she managed to get hold of the knife,' I said, with less conviction this time.

'Not in the way you described. The knife must have been on the table . . .'

'She would never have left it on the table. It was kept either in the scullery or on the mantel.'

'And of course she couldn't have collected it from the scullery while she was being strangled . . .'

'Dear God.' I leaned back in my chair and looked up at the stars, my thoughts forming themselves into a different picture altogether. 'Trudy, the daughter, came in late through the backyard and into the scullery. She wouldn't name the boy she'd been with, so there were no other witnesses to say where she'd been that evening or what time she'd come home. There was blood on her clothes she couldn't really explain.'

'What are you telling us? That she saw what was happening to her mother and she got the knife from the scullery?' said Meredith.

'And then what?' gasped Edmund.

'Well, I don't suppose she handed her mother the knife, do you?' I said. 'I rather think it was she who must have grabbed her father's shoulder and killed him.'

'And then,' said Meredith, 'the mother, of course, has to protect her child so she stabs him twice more for good measure and, lo and behold, *she* is the killer.'

385

I shook my head. 'It can't be true . . . It's not possible that all the police and the prosecution could have missed that. Nicholas . . .'

But of course Nicholas hadn't missed it, as I saw clearly now, sitting in that balmy French evening with the sigh of the sea close by. As I had chased him through the rain-blurred Temple gardens I had been blind to the enormity of what I was asking him to do. We had stood together in Trudy's bedroom, after all, and he had held up her bloodstained petticoat, the thin straps caught in his long fingers, the cheap fabric rumpled against his thigh. And I had not seen the truth because I had been so caught up with him rather than the evidence in his hand.

After Edmund had gone to bed, or rather was tucked away amid a heap of cushions in a far corner of the room, Meredith and I sat in the window with our feet on the sill, sharing a cigarette and drinking crème de menthe.

'Has it been all right here, Meredith?'

'It's been good and bad. Apart from feeling homesick, Edmund has been very happy. He is friends with everyone, he's lapping up French, as you've seen, and he never protests about his other lessons. I, on the other hand, have been lonely. I keep thinking hordes of fascinating people will arrive but they never do. Sanary turns out to be a bit of a backwater.'

'Aren't you pleased with your paintings? They're so striking. I've never seen you use colour in this way or capture the atmosphere of a place so completely.'

'Bless you, Evelyn, you try so hard to say the right thing but what I need is teachers. I was hoping for a community of artists and so far I've not found one. But I've discovered, I think, that I'm a Bohemian. I might not like it, being on the edge of things, but that's where I always end up. So I expect we'll come back to London soon and Edmund will go to school and we'll settle down for a while, then once again I'll be off.'

Taking a long, unaccustomed drag at the cigarette I watched a half-moon waver over the rooftops opposite and told her about the letter in the writing box and Grandmother's love affair.

'Typical of your mother to have kept something like that a secret – no wonder she hated me if she was nearly a bastard too.

Oh come on, Evelyn, that's what she was. And I suppose you feel vindicated.'

'Vindicated?'

'By Clara's choice. Isn't that why you're marrying your Daniel?'

'Grandmother made the right choice. She was happy.'

'Choice? What choice did she have? Rusbridger was a woman-iser and a brute. She was pregnant – she might have been saved by the schoolteacher, but she had no *choice*, whereas you do. So tell me, are you going to marry him?'

'As a matter of fact, no.'

'I see. And are you going to say why?'

I narrowed my eyes and said nothing. We sat far into the night as the town prepared itself for sleep; we heard the familiar clatter of pots being washed, a baby's cry and always the hush of the sea.

The days passed in a series of small adventures. We took a rattly old bus along the coast to Bandol and admired the pleasure boats moored on the quay, and Edmund and I climbed the ancient stone tower in Sanary which gave us a bird's eye view of the town and of Meredith, who disliked heights, waving nervously from a bench below. We walked along the cliff to our favourite beach and swam and lay in the warm sand while Meredith sat in the shade and painted. In one of her pictures I was a willowy figure in a blue dress, my face defined by the Rusbridger jaw, my short hair hay-wire in the sea breeze as I strode by the water's edge.

'It's for you,' she said. 'It's called *Evelyn under the sun*.'

'A rare sight.' But I loved the picture because I was intrigued by the woman in it, who was apparently so engrossed in the act of walking by the water, although in reality her thoughts were far away.

Despite her complaints, Meredith had made friends with the Italians who sat in the café reading day-old newspapers about Mussolini's latest crazed edicts as well as with a couple of German writers who had come to Sanary and stayed. Also there was an English woman who was accompanied by her little girl and a dashing Italian lover, and Angus's fierce aunt and her woman friend, with whom Meredith had lodged at first. We met these people in cafés or for impromptu suppers and I had never, in my

387

entire life, led such a formless existence or been so sure that I was about to take the biggest risk of my life.

I had been lying on the beach watching Edmund paddle in the shallows, feeling the heat of the sun in my blood, when I had reached my decision. That night I held a brief discussion with Meredith and afterwards I sat at the rickety white table by the window to write a note. *If you came, if you would make the journey, I would be more than happy to see you.*

I heard nothing for almost a week by which time there were only five days left of my holiday. And then, at last, his letter arrived. It took every ounce of courage I possessed to open the envelope and afterwards I stood, transfixed. Next day I caught the old and smelly station bus and stood in the shade of the ticket office, forty minutes early, watching the empty track, unable to look anywhere else.

The train, seventeen minutes late, appeared as a dirty plume in the distance. I didn't move as it pulled into the platform and ground slowly, slowly to a halt. Doors were flung open. A woman with a basket containing a squawking hen appeared, porters heaved boxes of fruit into the freight carriage, a grandmother greeted two little children.

I thought that he'd changed his mind, that I'd got the wrong day or the wrong time, but then a further door in the last carriage opened and I started along the platform, hesitant at first, then faster, faster, because Nicholas was alighting from the train.

We didn't touch or even smile but stood face to face while the doors slammed behind us and the train wheezed and huffed little gusts of smoke. He dropped his bag. The warm air fluttered against my skin. I stepped forward and, as I kissed him, I felt, through my dazzled eyelids, the pressure of sunshine and the staggering blue of the sky.

# Acknowledgements

With thanks to Sue Sleeman for her legal advice, and to my travelling companion, Charonne Boulton. Thanks also to Margaret Metcalf for her inspiration on the Actresses' Franchise League and to the writer Fiona Shaw for insight into the General Strike. And as always, thanks to Kirsty Dunseath, my editor, and Mark Lucas, my agent at LAW for their wonderful advice and support.

Of all the books I've read to research this novel, one of the most inspiring was Helena Kennedy: *Eve was Framed* (Vintage).

**blog and newsletter**

For literary discussion, author insight,
book news, exclusive content,
recipes and giveaways, visit the
Weidenfeld & Nicolson blog and
sign up for the newsletter at:

## www.wnblog.co.uk